The Hug

Book

The Conundrum of the Decapitated Detective

S.L. Kotar and J.E. Gessler

To Marilee,
Thank you for reading this!
S. Kotar

Ahead of the Press Publishing
St. Louis, Missouri

Library of Congress Cataloguing-in-Publication Data

The Conundrum of the Decapitated Detective
The Hugh Kerr Mystery Series Book I
/ S.L. Kotar and J.E. Gessler: Authors
Liesha Crawford: Editor

ISBN	EPUB	978-1-945594-06-9	(ebook)
ISBN	KINDLE Mobi	978-1-945594-07-6	(ebook)
ISBN	Paperback Book	978-1-945594-23-6	

© Copyright 2017 S.L. Kotar and J.E. Gessler. All rights reserved
No part of this book may be reproduced or transmitted in any form or by any means, electronic or mechanical, including photocopying or recording, or by any information storage and retrieval system, without permission in writing from the publisher.

This story is a work of fiction. The names, characters, places and incidents are products of the authors' imagination. Any resemblance to actual events, locals, or persons, living or dead is entirely coincidental.

ALL RIGHTS RESERVED

Ahead of The Press Publishing
St. Louis, Missouri

Table of Contents

DEDICATION	4
CHAPTER 1	5
CHAPTER 2	16
CHAPTER 3	31
CHAPTER 4	50
CHAPTER 5	65
CHAPTER 6	76
CHAPTER 7	93
CHAPTER 8	113
CHAPTER 9	126
CHAPTER 10	144
CHAPTER 11	159
CHAPTER 12	177
CHAPTER 13	190
CHAPTER 14	206
CHAPTER 15	222
CHAPTER 16	234
ALSO BY S.L. KOTAR AND J.E. GESSLER	253

Dedication

In an ironic twist of fate, the first edition of this book was published without a dedication. This second "reprint" now affords me the opportunity of dedicating Book I of the "Hugh Kerr Mystery Series" to my best friend, writing partner and spiritual shadow: Joan E. Gessler. Nothing I have ever done, am doing, or will creature in the future, is without your influence, Old Friend. I am what I am because of you, now and for forever.

I sign this, as always,

                        SLK   JEG

Chapter 1

The policeman standing just inside the double outer doors of the government institution stiffened to attention. He had detected a shadow and then the form of a woman, disguised by the warped bevel of industrial glass. He had been alerted to expect her, perhaps as recently as half an hour past. That he anticipated her would have been a lie. Dreaded her appearance would have been closer to the truth.

The young woman who slipped through one of the twin doors was dressed smartly in a winter-length coat. She wore white gloves and a small hat, which, had he known better, the youth would have identified as having been purchased with an eye toward economy. A haberdasher in one of the upscale department stores that catered to the film crowd would have immediately classified her as a working girl; a secretary to a mid-budget producer. Had he glimpsed her at just the right angle when the sun highlighted her profile and her eyes sparkled with intensity, or if caught unguarded with a bemused expression, the hatter might even have taken her for an actress. One of the up-and-coming ingénues starting her career in the developing medium of television; perhaps co-starring on a series for the new 1955-1956 schedule. With enough money to spend on a fashionable wardrobe but lacking the luxury of accessorizing it with a matching hat. The one she wore he would have dismissed as "all purpose." Despite her natural beauty, her value to him would have diminished considerably.

Her worth to the beat cop had nothing to do with looks or finances.

The object of his attention proved the better observer of either the officer or the imaginary salesman. With senses acutely attuned to detail, she immediately determined the man before her to be twenty-three or twenty-four years of age, recently discharged from the service. A corporal, perhaps: one grade up from private. In her estimation, his stiff back, jutting chin and serious attitude earned him that promotion. The sharp crease that ran down his shirt sleeves, the starched collar and studiously hand-polished boots indicated that he was new on the force and took his job seriously.

Without consciously detailing the man's history, she decided he had been in Korea and seen action. When he applied for his civilian job, the men interviewing him would have been impressed by his coolness under fire. That he exhibited an ill-covered nervousness under the present circumstance conveyed two more facts: he was unaccustomed to dealing with women and the task he was about to perform was decidedly disagreeable.

"Hello," she said, trying a smile to cover her own trepidation. "My name is Ellen Thorne. I was asked to come down to…" Words failed, requiring her to regroup before continuing. "To come down to the morgue and identify a body."

Although she had rehearsed the line more times than the haberdasher's actress, it sounded flat. And scared. She would have liked to re-enter and take it over but this was real life and there were no "Take two's" to protect her image.

"Yes, ma'am," the policeman agreed. Like her, he fumbled his line. "Mrs. Thorne, I mean."

"Miss Thorne," Ellen corrected, permitting a small smile to light her face. Some facts were easier to accept than others. They both understood its more subtle purpose was as a delaying tactic.

Embarrassed by his mistake, he flushed. "Miss Thorne. I beg your pardon, Miss." The army had done its work well. She appreciated a polite man. "You… I mean, Lieutenant Wade explained why you were asked to come down here? Over the telephone?" He did not want to go into details.

"Yes." Dull, this time. Chipped. Professional with a trace of hysteria.

He had seen death and knew fear. Hers did not steady his soldier's nerves.

"We called – I mean, Lieutenant Wade called another gentleman –"

"Hugh Kerr," she smiled. The words gave her strength.

"Yes, ma'am – Miss," he agreed. Too quickly. "But he's away." The words had the tone of disapprobation.

"He's a lawyer," she explained. "He's taking a deposition in San Francisco."

I should have gone with him, she thought. *He asked me to go. I was all packed and then the attorney up there called and said he had his own assistant to do the job. No need for Mr. Kerr to go to all the expense of bringing his secretary with him.*

After taking the sworn statement that may or not have been a self-serving lie, they had planned on dinner and dancing at some cozy restaurant along the wharf. She could still hear Hugh chuckle. "We'll write it off as a business expense, Ellen. Not even the tax man can argue against the fact a man and his secretary have to eat." He had winked at her in that sly way good attorneys developed when they were obfuscating the truth. "Instead of flying, why don't we rent a convertible and drive back on the Coast Highway with the top down? I'll get sunburned and your hair will be a mess. We'll be quite the pair to rush into court Monday morning looking like a couple of vagabonds. The district attorney will be afraid of us and concede the case on a technicality." He had smacked his hands. "Voila! We'll have a nice fat fee in the bank and the rest of the afternoon off."

"We'll have the rest of the afternoon to spend in the office going through that correspondence you keep putting off." They had laughed together, knowing the truth of her statement.

At the same time she berated herself for not insisting on accompanying him, Ellen Thorne wondered when the two of them would laugh like that again.

"That's why the lieutenant called you," the officer apologized, breaking into her thoughts. "I'm sorry, Miss. This isn't any job for a woman – identifying a body."

She shrugged her shoulders, affecting nonchalance. "I've seen dead bodies before. As an attorney's secretary, I am often called upon to do… unpleasant tasks." Her words trailed off. As true as they were, she had never before been summoned to identify the body of a friend. A good friend.

A special friend. The kind that came along only once or twice in a lifetime.

"But this is different," the policeman stated, speaking louder now. He had lost the protection of his training, leaving him without back-up. "The corpse – it isn't a pleasant sight."

"So I have been told."

Brave words, gentle soul.

"You don't have to do this, you know. The lieutenant said that if it was too much for you, it could wait."

Ellen refused his offer with a casual wave of the hand she might have copied from a favorite actress. He nodded and led her down a corridor, opened and then entered the inner door of the City Morgue. She forgave him his lack of manners. In this instance, she did not mind him going first.

As the heavy barricade swished shut, sealing out the warmth of the day, Ellen was nearly overwhelmed with a sense of cold. She had forgotten how the sensation of refrigerated air affected her. Cold.

Death. Cold. And the smell; the faint tinge of formaldehyde and disinfectant. Like walking into a dentist's office, with the background whir of a drill mixed with the commingling of medical gasses, blood and spit.

"Are you all right?"

"Yes." The answer was reflexive, nothing more. She was not all right.

The sound of footsteps forced her head up. She recognized the man instantly but the wan, twisted appearance of his features under the unnatural overhead lighting gave him a ghoulish look. He misread her reaction.

"Lieutenant Henry Wade," he identified.

"Yes. Of course. We've met in court many times. And in the office." There was no need to specify which office.

"We're usually at cross-purposes," he tried. "Not this time." She had never heard softness in his voice before. Nor had he ever introduced himself by adding his first name. "I tried to contact –"

"Hugh. I know. He's in San Francisco. He should be back tonight. I scheduled him on the 9:15."

"If you'd rather we wait – the identification could be put off, but we have a murder on our hands and any delay might be costly. It really is… a man's job."

She bristled. "I can take it."

Wade motioned the policeman away and he disappeared as completely as though he had never existed.

"Then I have to prepare you. It won't be as easy as you think."

"I never thought it would be easy." Her words snapped into one another and she offered a weak gesture with her right hand as though to apologize.

"Identifying a body never is. That of a family member or a friend that much harder. Even seasoned police officers like myself find it disagreeable." He cleared his throat and then took a moment to wipe his forehead with a crumpled handkerchief extracted from a trouser pocket. They were all good at delaying tactics. "In this case, I'm afraid, your task will be complicated."

The friendliness had vanished, replaced with a professional's detachment.

"Why?"

He wrung his hands. The gesture made her want to scream.

"Perhaps you should sit down, Ellen."

The use of her first name came as a slap in the face. Not as an affront but as a dire warning. He had never used it before. She hoped to God he would never have occasion to use it again.

"Tell me." Despite the artificial coolness of the chamber a line of sweat trickled down his face. She affixed her eyes to it. "Tell me," she repeated.

"The body has been decapitated. We don't have the head."

She sensed there was more.

"Go on."

"The hands have been severed at the wrists, presumably so we couldn't make an identification through fingerprints. The soles of the feet have been seared for the same reason." She remained frozen. "A lab expert could use toe or feet prints in much the same manner as fingerprints... if we had some way of obtaining a copy of the deceased's prints. From the bathroom floor, perhaps. Whoever perpetrated this heinous crime thought of everything."

She expected cool detachment and heard only bitterness. For that she would be grateful the rest of her life.

Be calm. Put on your court face. You've watched Hugh do it countless times. Never let them know what you're thinking. He always says an attorney is part detective, part actor. When all eyes are on you the last thing you want to do is feed the fire. Make them think you have all the aces.

He never played poker. No one would play with him. Jack had once said Kerr could bluff a pair of deuces against a full house.

Jack.

"If there isn't any head and no hands, how do you know it – how do you know the body –" Not good enough. She re-wrote her lines as she spoke. "What makes you think it's Jack Merrick?"

Wade was gentle.

"We found a wallet nearby. It had been concealed, of course – tossed into some bushes. We might have overlooked it. Only found it by chance." Had they not been discussing the death of a friend, nothing on earth would have made him confess as much. "Inside was his driver's license, his private investigator's license. There was some money, too. Fifty-seven dollars in the billfold and change in his pocket."

"How much?" When she spoke, she heard Hugh's voice.

"Twenty-two cents."

"What else?"

"A pocket knife, a small pen flashlight, car keys. The motive wasn't robbery." He waited. She had no more questions to ask. "And another key ring: skeleton keys they call them in the trade. For illicitly opening doors. Illegal. Most PIs carry them. A matter of no consequence."

Not to the dead.

If Jack were alive, Wade would have rung him up on general principals. He was being generous for her benefit.

"May I show you, now?" he asked. She nodded and he put his hand around her arm. "The attendant has already pulled out the slab."

Slab. The word hit her like a sledge hammer.

Her knees buckled and suddenly her head felt as though it weighed two hundred pounds. Black spots swam before her eyes. With a cry of horror, Ellen Thorne, legal secretary and personal confidant to Hugh Kerr, Los Angeles' most prominent defense attorney, pulled free and ran back the way she had come, tears streaming from her eyes.

He walked with his hands in his pockets, the flaps of his calf-length coat flapping in motion to his long strides. Hat pulled low, head bowed, skirting the pools of light cast by the evenly spaced streetlamps, he might have been a fugitive from justice or a man on the take. The hour was late and the few stragglers on the street avoided him by ducking into shuttered entranceways or awkwardly crossing the street. Even the drunks wanted no part of the tall stranger who radiated the silent warning, *Leave me alone.*

With eyes cast on the pavement, another might have wandered a crooked line but Hugh Kerr walked the straight and true. He knew where he was going, could have walked it blindfolded, which, in a manner of speaking, he was. As a trial lawyer who specialized in murder cases, he was no stranger to the City Morgue, no more than he was to the law library, the crowded courtroom, or the local delicatessen where the bachelor took his meals on those evenings when he did not burn the midnight oil. To the old man who stood behind the counter and his daughter who served the hot, spicy food, he was always "Mr. Kerr," though he had known them for upwards of five years. They were not friends but acquaintances. The same held true for the elevator operator at his office building, the women at his answering service, the barber and shoe shine boy. He tipped well, spoke politely, made casual inquiries about the weather or their pets and kept his own council about matters that counted.

It was said of Hugh Kerr that he had only one love: the law. And that he had only two friends: his secretary, Ellen Thorne, and the man who performed his nefarious private investigations, Jack Merrick.

Tonight, so he had been told, that number had been reduced to one.

He had taken a yellow cab at the airport and dismissed it half a dozen blocks from his destination, preferring to walk the remaining distance. He had much to consider. Pacing helped him think. At the moment, however, he was thinking nothing at all.

As if counting the street lamps, he stopped at the seventh one, withdrew a packet of cigarettes and casually extracted one. His movements, like his pacing, were well calculated to eliminate excessive energy. With the cigarette between his lips, he struck a match, watched as the sulphur burned down, then touched it to the tip. A flame shot up and as quickly burned out, leaving only a red dot amid a cloud of smoke in the darkness.

The taste burned his tongue. Casting it to the ground in disgust, he crushed it with his shoe until the narrow white-papered stick bore no resemblance to its former shape. With a grunt of annoyance, he lit a second, inhaled deeply, then clasped it between pursed lips and resumed walking.

Coming to the well-worn steps of the City Morgue he turned sharply left and mounted, one, two, three, four, before taking a final drag and discarding the moist butt. This one he left to burn itself out.

Turning the door knob with a casualness that belied his inner turmoil, he stepped inside and paused to allow his dilated pupils to narrow and adjust themselves to the overhead light. His hand went to his pocket for another cigarette when a shadow crossed his path. It arrested his intent but did not compel him to raise his head.

"Hello, Hugh." A beat, then, more faintly, "I failed you."

"I told you to go home." No accusation, no recrimination. A statement of fact, like all the other statements of fact he had made in his career.

"I had to wait for you."

"I knew you would."

I expected it.

He spread his arms and Ellen Thorne slid between them. When they closed around her, she pressed her cheek to his chest. It was the first time she had felt warm in as long as she could remember. Longer, even, than the time Jack Merrick had been dead.

He patted her shoulder with an affection only two close friends could share. To the casual observer, had there been one, it might have appeared patronizing. To Ellen, it meant something else.

"I'm sorry, Hugh. I tried. I just couldn't face it. It was... too horrible. I didn't want to see..."

I didn't want to see Jack dead.

Between two confidants, there was no need to finish the sentence.

"I understand."

She reluctantly pulled away and made a vain attempt to brush away a strand of hair that had fallen across her brow.

"I failed you."

It did not sound any better the second time. He shook his head.

"You did not fail me."

"I failed Jack, then. I should have been braver."

"We don't know it is Jack."

"But they found his wallet."

"I lost a wallet once. That doesn't mean I was dead. It meant I was careless."

He made her smile.

"You, careless? You're making that up."

Kerr shrugged. The statement had served its purpose.

"Who's here?"

"Lieutenant Wade left several hours ago. I heard him leave orders to be called when you arrived."

"Then, someone should call him."

She pointed vaguely toward a side room. "There's a technician in there."

"I'll call him myself." The determination was spontaneous. "I need a pay phone."

Having spent hours alone in the House of the Dead, she had identified two. He started toward the booth before she pointed. He had known all along.

Without benefit of consulting the small black directory he kept in his pocket the way other men might carry a book of holy verse, or one listing the private numbers of their mistresses, Hugh inserted a coin in the slot and paused to listen to its faint tinkle before dialing the number. Ellen moved closer to hear the conversation. It was not eavesdropping. Had he wished to speak in private he would have closed the door.

"Police Department. Sergeant Hollis speaking."

"Lieutenant Wade, please."

"He's not on duty."

"I know he's there." Kerr's voice took on a sharp insistence. "Connect me."

The line clicked and in a moment was answered on another extension.

"Hello?" the voice growled. "I'm not here."

"Lieutenant, this is Hugh Kerr. I'm at the morgue."

"Oh. Kerr." From the other end of the phone Ellen heard the mumbled sound of annoyance. "Where the hell is the damn - *damned* morgue attendant? He was supposed to call me so I could be there when you arrived."

The lawyer nodded, appreciating the fact the officer had corrected his grammar. *Damned.* Not *damn.*

"I just got in."

"Then how did you know I wanted to be called?"

"Ellen told me."

"Oh." His voice sounded more contrite. "Miss Thorne is there with you, is she?"

"She waited."

He offered a third "Oh" and then paused. Longer this time. "Hell, Kerr, I'm sorry about that. She shouldn't have been called. That was my fault. I only wanted to hurry things up."

"I appreciate that. It's all right. She'll be fine. Good girl." He turned and nodded at Ellen. "How long will it take for you to get down here?"

"Ten minutes. Listen for the siren."

Kerr hung up the phone, then paused to inspect the return change compartment. His money had not slipped through. With a shrug, he took a dime from his pocket and placed it inside. Feeling her eyes on him, he hitched a shoulder.

"Wade likes his siren. Makes him feel important."

"The dime," she said.

"Oh, that. Times are hard. People are always looking to see if there's any money in the coin slot. If they find any – even if it's only ten cents – it makes them feel empowered. Like things have finally fallen their way."

"Do a good turn, get one in return. Put in another dime for me."

He fished in his pocket, took out a quarter and added it to the treasure trove.

"We're gonna need a lot of good turns before this is through."

"Are we fools or just superstitious?"

"We're gamblers, hedging our bets."

"You don't gamble."

Oh, I gamble, all right. But usually with other people's money. That's why it pays to have a rich clientele."

"We don't have a client tonight."

"Yes, we do." She arched an eyebrow in question. "Jack Merrick."

"He's not rich," she tried.

"I pay him enough that he ought to be."

Him and the tax man, they thought in mutual contemplation. Their private joke.

In precisely ten minutes they heard the scream of a police siren. Kerr checked his watch.

"Right on time."

The pair kept their own council, both wandering toward the front door. Kerr opened it and kept it ajar with the toe of his shoe. They watched as the car came to a screeching halt alongside a painted curb and a dented sign that read, "No Parking. Loading Zone." It required no imagination to deduce what was "loaded," or more appropriately," unloaded" in the zone.

Wade flew out the door, slammed it shut and took the stairs two at a time, legs pumping hard. As he approached the heavy outer door, the lawyer removed his foot, letting gravity close it in the lieutenant's face. Ellen shot him a quizzical look, wondering at the harshness of the action. What she saw stopped her cold.

Taking three steps back, Hugh Kerr used the precious seconds to put on his court face. Gone was the forced levity of a moment ago, replaced by a cold, hard, stony countenance that would have served him well when hearing the pronouncement of a death sentence on an innocent client. Lieutenant Wade, bursting through the barrier with the same question, expressed more harshly through blazing eyes, read the same story, nearly stopped dead in his tracks, then covered himself by removing his hat and fanning his flushed face.

"Driving like that always makes me…" Without an adequate finish, he lamely concluded, "hot. Winter, summer, same thing." He panted a moment before regrouping. "Glad to see you got back all right, Kerr. Don't like to fly, myself. Makes me air sick. It takes two shots of airline bourbon to settle my stomach. At a dollar a pop, too. Un-reimbursed by the Department."

Translated, he meant to convey the hope that the attorney had fortified himself for the ordeal.

The policeman's nose twitched. He did not smell alcohol.

"Thanks for coming. You didn't have to."

"Yes, I did. It's my job. I had to overlook the fact you're a practicing attorney, though. Always sitting on the other side of the court room."

Kerr nodded. "We both care about justice. We just go about it in different ways."

"Bartholomew says…" He did not finish the sentence. They both knew what the district attorney had said.

Tell Hugh I'm sorry. About Merrick, I mean.

"Let's get this over with."

"Sure. I talk too much."

"You're all right," Kerr stated and fell in line behind the officer. Ellen Thorne watched them go. She felt like a heel that her own courage had failed. She swore it would not happen again. The resolution brought no comfort.

Maybe it's not Jack. Hugh will come back and tell me it was a mistake. He can make anything right.

She had to believe that. So, she suspected, did Hugh Kerr.

Chapter 2

The morgue attendant heard them coming. He did not have to wait for either visual or verbal confirmation. No one else was expected. He had been given his orders in advance. Open the slab and make yourself scarce. He obeyed with alacrity, leaving the two men alone.

Silently debating whether to withdraw the sheet or allow Kerr to perform the solemn act, Wade's eyes snaked to the taller man's face. White, with a touch of red at the cheeks. Grim. Resolved.

Sad. With a trace of anger so deep it might have been drawn from a bottomless pit. Just this side of Hell.

Wade grabbed the corner of the sheet that draped over the shoulder, then hesitated as the gruesome shape of the headless corpse registered its full impact. A horrible lump of clay some talentless sculptor had abandoned as hopeless. He bit his lower lip and withdrew the medical covering. Kerr made no sound, gave no outward indication this was anything more than another routine murder case where he had been summoned to identify the body of a hooker, or a gambler who had failed to pay his debts.

Hugh Kerr did not blink. He unconsciously breathed through his mouth so as not to take in the odor of death. His chest moved slowly, lightly. Hands clenched inside his trouser pockets, he stared at the misshapen form that had once been human; once had a voice, a cheerful eye, a contemplative brow. Fingers that wrapped around a lock-pick or stirred ice in a glass of cheap Scotch.

He did not know how to identify a body that had no head, no hands. That course had not been offered at law school. Nor in the School of Hard Knocks. He had attended both and graduated with honors.

"Pull the sheet down all the way, if you please."

Wade's acute ear detected the trace of an accent in the whisper. Funny, he had never heard it before. He remembered that even actors who were used to altering their speech patterns were often unable to disguise their voice when whispering. Or singing. He stored the information away as all good cops did. One day he might need it. He doubted if he would ever hear Kerr sing.

If the corpse looked ugly half draped, its appearance fully naked did nothing to improve that impression.

The second hand on the wall clock affixed to the opposite corner swept around, impervious to the drama being played out. The clock had all the time in the world.

Finally, after an hour of seconds, Kerr sighed.

"The hair on the chest has been shaved."

"I believe the coroner said something about that."

"I wonder why."

Not why the coroner had made the observation, but why the murderer had bothered.

"What color was Merrick's hair?"

Wade knew as well as Kerr but it seemed a logical question under the circumstances.

"White blond."

Wade cleared his throat. "Did he have any distinguishing marks? Any scars, tattoos?"

Kerr expelled air through his nose.

How would I know?

"None that I can recall."

"Did he have a personal physician? Someone who would have made note of something like that?"

"I don't know. He was never sick. Well," he amended in the tone of voice a lawyer used when speculating to a jury, "the usual bumps and bruises and black eyes a PI is likely to get in the course of a routine investigation. Sniffles now and again."

"He was in the war, wasn't he? There must be medical records; routine physicals. Maybe he was shot. There'd be a record of that." No answer. "Did he have any next of kin?"

"He has a mother back east. I believe she's old. Elderly," he corrected. "He doesn't speak of her much. I think he went back to see her once. Maybe it was for her funeral. I've forgotten. Ellen would know."

"Anyone he was close to? I mean, besides you and… Miss Thorne? A girl, perhaps?"

Kerr shrugged. "Jack was very popular with the girls. He knew a lot of them. I don't know if any were special." His voice lowered. "Ellen might know."

"Well, we can ask her later. Tomorrow, maybe. Have you seen enough?"

"Not yet."

Kerr concentrated, this time with his eyes closed. He saw the image of a man. Tall: six foot three, with a mass of hair that looked grey in the shadows but wasn't. Appearances were deceiving. A lopsided grin. An easy slope of the shoulders. Quick to flop himself down in a chair, quicker to get up again. Nervous energy. A cigarette between his lips. Suntanned, even in the winter. He was a good swimmer. Liked to spend time at the ocean. They had once gone clamming together. Hugh remembered saying that no one ate Pacific clams; the best ones came from the cold water of the Atlantic. Jack had given him a blank stare. He was a California boy even if he had not been born in the state. "No one," he had told Hugh, "is born in California. We all migrate here. Like farm workers in the Great Depression. We find our niche and stay or we get homesick and leave."

Kerr opened his eyes to dispel the image of better times. He forced himself to stare at the body. Muscled arms; tight thighs. An athlete or someone who kept in shape. Like a private investigator.

He recalled the first time they had met. Jack's handshake had been firm. The dead man before him would never shake another hand. Not even when St. Peter came to raise him to glory.

"You looked for the head and hands, I presume? Nowhere to be found?"

"We searched the entire area."

"Was there a lot of blood? Had the body been killed and dismembered at the location where you found it?"

"No. It had been dumped there." Wade reconsidered. It did not sound right to speak of a man's friend as having been dumped. "Placed there." Kerr appreciated the consideration.

"You found a wallet, Ellen said? Personal effects?"

"Yes. I have the list for you." Wade pulled a piece of paper from his pocket and handed it to the lawyer. "You can inspect them if you want." He did not have to offer. Understanding how to mitigate the shock of death was part of his job. A professional courtesy.

"Yes. I will want to look at them." Retreating to routine made tragedy easier to bear. "Anything unusual – besides the fact the items were there at all?"

"What do you mean?"

"Someone went to a lot of trouble to prevent the authorities from positively identifying this man, and yet they left behind that which was certain to lead to an identification. It strikes me as odd."

"Yes. It is peculiar." Wade hesitated. "What do you make of it?"

"Someone doesn't want us to be sure. They want to torture us with the uncertainty of the situation. On one hand, they want us to *think* this is Jack Merrick and on the other, they want us to doubt."

"Why would anyone do that?"

"Isn't it obvious? To deepen the pain. To keep us guessing. To give us false hope."

The police officer stepped back. The smell of the autopsy room was giving him a headache.

"Hugh… have you seen enough?"

"I have."

Too much.

"Would you like to venture an opinion?"

Instead of answering, Kerr backtracked several steps as though it were a breach of etiquette to turn his back on the dead. He did not move again until Wade had replaced the sheet and motioned for the attendant to return the body to its lonely cold storage. As if that freed them from convention, they beat a hasty retreat into the outer chamber. Ellen watched with careful scrutiny as they approached.

Answering what he would not state to Lieutenant Wade, Hugh addressed his secretary.

"It is not Jack Merrick."

She knew him too well to accept the statement on face value. He spoke for the company who was not to be admitted into their private inner circle.

"I'm so relieved."

She knew how to play her part. Wade put a hand on Kerr's arm.

"Are you stating positively the body is not that of Jack Merrick? You're suggesting the wallet and personnel effects were planted to make us think it was?"

"I'm not suggesting anything. I am not making any statement, positive or otherwise. I am merely telling Miss Thorne that in my opinion it is not *yet* time to plan a funeral for an old friend."

"Damn it, Kerr, we're not in court now. You're not under oath. We're not playing chess. If you think it's Merrick, tell me. If you don't, I want a firm answer."

The attorney grabbed Ellen by the arm and squeezed with more strength than he realized. Setting his jaw, he caught the officer's eyes.

"I've said all I'm going to say. Come on, Ellen. We're both tired, we've both been under a strain and we both need a drink." After ushering her toward the door, he paused and looked back over his shoulder. "Would you care to come along?"

The offer was not meant to be accepted.

"No, thank you. I have work to do here. If this isn't Jack Merrick, then I have to find out who he is. I have a very brutal killer on the loose."

Not, *We have a very brutal killer on the loose.* His insinuation was taken.

"Good night, Lieutenant."

Keeping a grip on Ellen's arm, Kerr guided her through the door. They did not speak again until they had descended the steps and distanced themselves along the sidewalk. Only when they were free of inquisitive ears did she speak.

"Tell me the truth, Hugh. Was it Jack?"

She felt his body sag as he leaned against her.

"No." That was a lie. She waited for the mitigating circumstances before taking her conclusion further. "The hair on the chest had been shaved."

"Why?" she demanded in hurt shock as if that one factor alone represented a desecration worse than all the others.

"Perhaps because the dead man's hair was darker than Jack's. If he had a hairy chest, that would have told us right away it was a stranger."

"What about the wallet and the ID?"

"All that tells us is someone either robbed or kidnapped Jack. It isn't proof the body is his."

The statement left her with nothing else but another hollow, "Why?"

"That remains to be seen."

"All right." It was her turn to be brave. "My car is over there. Where are we going to go for that drink? The office? My place? Yours?"

"What time is it?"

She checked her watch. "Eleven-thirtyish."

"Good. The bars are still open. I don't think it would do either of us any good if we were to sit and stare at one another in an empty room until we're too soused to move."

His use of the vernacular made her smile.

"So we'll go out to a bar and drink until we're woozy and then you'll drive me home and get picked up for drunk driving."

He matched her expression with a grin. "I think in this case the police will let me off with a warning."

"Don't be too sure. Wade doesn't have that many good intentions in him."

"Then I'll appeal to the illustrious Defense Attorney, Bartholomew 'B.B.' Bond."

"How much did you have to drink on the plane?" she teased, waiting for him to open the driver's side door for her. He grunted and they left it at that.

When Hugh gave no indication which pub he preferred, Ellen drove several blocks and then deftly maneuvered her two-door blue Chevy sedan into a parking space behind a drinking saloon, half a block from the Executive Hotel Building where he lived. With a little luck and a stiff wind, she decided that after several shots of scotch, he would still be able to navigate the distance to his own apartment without being rolled, or running afoul of a foot cop. She did not doubt that the district attorney would enjoy bringing the renowned criminal attorney to trial on a charge of drunk and disorderly or at least, vagrancy.

"We're here, Hugh," she prodded when he made no move to stir. "Outside the Crowler's Pub." Although his eyes were closed his attitude of repose did not deceive her. She had known him too long to fall for pretense. "It *was* Jack, wasn't it?"

She knew and he knew that all the hooch in the world would not erase that fact, if indeed it were so.

A small, gentle smile curled along his otherwise pressed lips. "I told you no and I meant it."

"You weren't so confident with Wade."

"If I had been, he'd have stopped his investigation. I need him to harbor at least a little doubt." A tremor ran through his body. "We need his help, Ellen. We don't have the resources of the police department. He's got half a dozen men right now sitting in the back room playing cards. Let him put them to work checking missing persons reports; investigating any mob killings; looking to see if any recently released convict had a public grudge against one of his cohorts."

Without making any effort to disengage the car door, Kerr thoughtfully ran the thumbnail of his left hand under his teeth. Knowing that for a sign of deep distress, she affected a yawn.

"I say we both go to bed and sleep on it. Tomorrow our minds will be fresher and we'll have a new take on the matter." Turning the key in the ignition, she revved the engine and shifted into gear.

"Where are we going?" he suddenly demanded, sitting bolt upright. "I don't want to go to bed and 'sleep on it.' There's too much work to be done. We haven't a moment to lose. If Jack's – if the bastard who pulled this 'prank' has time, he'll get away before we can do anything about it. Hell, he may be hundreds of miles away right now."

"Who said anything about going to sleep?" she retorted with a scorn she knew would keep him awake for hours. "We're going to the office."

"What office?"

"The Merrick Detective Agency, where else? You said if Jack were kidnapped, we'd have to start by tracing him from his last known whereabouts."

Kerr looked confused. "I never said anything like that."

Taking a hand from the steering wheel, Ellen tapped his left temple. "You thought it. As your personal secretary, I'm expected to read your mind."

His eyes widened. "I hope you don't read it all the time."

"Only when it matters. Most of your private thoughts I leave alone."

"Most of?" he asked in the voice of a teenaged male caught staring up into the bedroom window of a high school girl.

Ellen laughed. Within that light-hearted sound lay power. It made her believe that if things were not exactly right with the world, she and the man beside her could change destiny to better suit themselves. And Jack Merrick.

Recovering his aplomb, Kerr pointed down the street. "Stop at the All-Nite Pharmacy on the corner. I'll call the Agency and have someone open the door for us." He hopped out as she slowed the car and disappeared inside. Watching through the plate glass window she saw him deposit a coin, dial a number and wait until someone on the other end picked up. He spoke briefly, nodded and replaced the handset. This time Hugh did not check for a returned coin nor did he leave one in its stead. Ellen nodded to herself as she whispered, "He's on the hunt."

Pausing only long enough to make a purchase she could not see, he hurried back, bag in hand. Slipping into the passenger seat with the grace uncommon in a tall man, he indicated his package.

"Doughnuts," he identified.

"I suppose this means you want me to make coffee when we get there."

"We could flip for it but if you leave it to me you'll be sorry."

"Do you even have a coffee pot in your apartment?"

He made a face. "Why should I? That's what cafes are for."

"What did you do when you were a law student? Or were you wealthy enough to frequent 'cafes' at Harvard?"

His choking sound was enough to convince her that such had not been the case.

"I worked two jobs besides clerking in the summer. And I didn't drink coffee then," he pouted.

"What did you drink? Boston Bootleg?"

"Tea."

Ellen made a sharp right-handed turn, causing him to roll in his seat.

"I've never seen you drink tea in my life. Not even iced tea."

"I gave it up the day I graduated law school."

"For aged scotch?"

"For coffee. The aged scotch came later."

"And you gave up tea because -?"

"It was part of my old life. I wanted to start a new one."

"What else did you give up?"

If she expected a glib answer to her leading question, she was disappointed.

"Poverty."

Marking the reply in her own imaginary little black book she kept on her employer, Ellen pressed the gas pedal to the floor. They had appointments to keep.

Driving through the heart of downtown Los Angeles, Ellen came up on the four-story office building Jack Merrick called home when he wasn't actually at home. On the cusp of respectability and second-class citizenship, the building, facetiously known in local parlance as "The Place," had seen better days but still maintained an address that included higher class establishments, and resided within a hop, skip and jump from the 25-story professional tower where Hugh Kerr maintained his office. Rather than park on the street, Ellen pulled into a one-way alley adjoining the deserted entranceway.

"To hide our movements," she explained. Agreeing with the concept he, too, would have employed, Hugh got out first and crossed to the driver's side to open her door. Waiting for Ellen to lock it, they walked side-by-side to the building entrance, entered and crossed the empty court to the elevator, accompanied by the sound of their footfalls echoing morosely against the locked and dark lower-level businesses. Riding the elevator to the 3rd floor feeling more like intruders than visitors on a mission, they turned left and found themselves at Suite 303, labeled on the exterior as belonging to the Merrick Detective Agency. A light shone above the transom.

For a second, the implication caused both their hearts to speed before Hugh explained with grim exactness, "John Cummings. He was on-call tonight. I asked him to meet us here."

She had forgotten. Or rather, she had wanted to forget. For as long as she had worked for Hugh Kerr, Jack Merrick had always been in his office when they needed him. Never more so than tonight. But as the hour struck midnight both knew such an expectation at present would only lead to bitter disappointment.

Hugh made a perfunctory knock on the door then tried the knob. It turned and they both entered. The private detective, who might have been John Smith or Raoul Andantes in another incarnation, hurried to meet them. It was obvious from his expression he was worried but had not been informed of the nature of their call.

"Mr. Kerr – glad to see you. You sounded urgent on the phone. What's up?"

"Jack Merrick is missing. I haven't been able to contact him all day."

The grim tone and ashen complexion of the attorney gave the PI a jolt and he asked, "Is he working on a special case?"

"That's for you to tell me. I want to know everything you can discover about his last known whereabouts. Everything," the lawyer underscored. "When was the last time he was actually eyeballed by anyone from the Agency. When was the last time anyone spoke to him on the phone. What, if any, case or cases he was involved in. It wasn't one of mine, so you can eliminate that. I also want a list of every client who has been in this office for the past week. Also, I need to know every active case you're handling. Names, addresses, phone numbers. Add to that anything suspicious any of you boys have noticed."

"About what?"

"About any of your clients, contacts. Any rumors they might have heard about a hit going down or being contracted. Grill the answering service people. I want to know if anyone called and asked for Jack, or if they had any call where the person sounded upset or angry or threatening – even if they hung up before speaking to anyone." He rattled on in shotgun fashion without taking a breath. "Next, I want a complete breakdown of Jack's whereabouts for the past seven days. When was he in the office, when was he at home? Anything and everything."

"What's this all about? You think something's happened to him?"

"I *know* something has happened to him. What I don't know is how much. The police have their ideas –"

"The police? Has he committed a crime?"

"Let's just say a crime has been committed on him. He's missing." This time he paused to swallow. "And presumed dead."

Cummings' head snapped up.

"Presumed dead? What the hell does that mean?" he demanded in rhetorical anger. "The cops haven't called here -"

Hugh held up a hand for silence.

"They found a body in an abandoned field this afternoon. The head and hands had been severed to prevent an easy identification. Jack's wallet and personnel effects were discovered nearby."

"So you don't know for sure it is Jack?" Kerr shook his head. "Then I don't believe it."

"Miss Thorne and I don't, either. Until proven beyond a shadow of a doubt, neither do you or any of the boys here. When the police call – and they will – give them whatever information you have. We need their help? Understand?"

"Yes, sir."

"Then start moving and get me the information I requested. Call in anyone and everyone; no holds barred. For the time being, you all report to me. I'll see that you're well paid."

The private investigator gritted his teeth.

"That won't be necessary, Mr. Kerr. Jack Merrick is the best boss any of us ever had. We'll work, all right, but on our own time."

Hugh considered, then accepted the offer.

"Good. Then come to me for any operating expenses you need."

"How will I get in touch with you?"

"We'll be in my office for the next few hours. When we get ready to leave I'll either call you or alert the answering service. And remember: no detail is too small or too insignificant. I want everything."

"Yes, sir." The man clenched his fists. "We'll get to the bottom of this. And the devil better be ready to accept whoever... pulled this dirty trick."

"No violence. Pass that order around. Until we find out what trickery this is, we stay calm and collected. Come on, Ellen." They reached the door before Hugh turned back. "Oh, and Cummings: two more things. Put a man on the morgue. If anyone comes in asking about the body or trying to claim it, I want to know. Immediately. Tail them when they leave. The same thing goes for phone calls. If anyone calls asking for Jack or questioning you about the case, get as much information from them as you can. From now on, nothing is to be considered routine."

"I'll be in touch."

Striding down the hall at his accustomed pace of a wolf on the scent, Ellen matched his tempo, two strides to one. Long used to his hyper activity, she had no trouble keeping up. The empty lift was still waiting and they entered, Hugh jamming the first floor button with a vengeance. When the doors slid open, he bolted out, Ellen on his heels. Once outside, he jerked his head to the right.

"We'll leave the car where it is and walk."

He did not ask if she were up to the trip and she didn't volunteer the information. Moving down the sidewalk, however, he more carefully matched his pace to hers and in five minutes they reached the Connor Building where he kept his office. At this time of night there was no doorman in attendance so Hugh pulled open the left-hand side of the double doors and stepped back, allowing Ellen to precede him.

Crossing the lobby and passing the familiar Cigar Stand, its glass counters covered with an off-white tarp, the lawyer waved a hand at the elderly man serving as a night watchman, then guided Ellen to the elevator. One of the three shuttered doors opened at his signal and they got inside. Ellen reached for No. 17 and the car moved upward.

"It's odd," she said to break the silence, "how different everything looks at night."

"That's because the lights are muted. It forces you to look more closely at things you've memorized and taken for granted during normal business hours when the light is brighter."

The lift made no stops and as the doors opened at the 17th floor they emerged together, turning right and moving silently down the corridor to the door marked "Hugh Kerr, Attorney at Law, Suite 1717."

Hugh unlocked the door, flicked up the light switch and began unbuttoning his topcoat. Ellen hurried through the reception area to his private office, turned on the desk lamp and flung her coat and hat onto the couch. She was standing at attention when he crossed the threshold.

"All right, Counselor. What's first?"

"We have two suppositions to begin with: either the killing was one of revenge directed at Jack, or it was planned to involve me – or us," he reluctantly added." I'm leaning toward the latter."

"Why?" she asked, taking out her notepad and writing down his thoughts in shorthand.

"An elaborate cover-up after a murder doesn't affect the deceased: he's already beyond appreciating the gory details. Mutilating a corpse is meant to warn or hurt those closest to him."

"Then you don't think it was done to delay a formal identification?"

"Of course, but my instincts tell me there was a larger issue." He crossed around the back of his desk and sat down. "Since half of Jack's work comes from us, we start with our own cases. We'll go through them, one-by-one."

"What are we looking for?"

His use of the word "our" made it easy and comfortable for her to adopt the inclusive "we" into her own sentence. That did not mean she took her confidential position with him for granted. Other secretaries of her acquaintance – those with more formal training or longer acquaintance with their employer – did not share the trust or private camaraderie she had with Hugh Kerr. That she treasured his confidence and occasionally his affection was a reward she had never anticipated and kept as close to her heart as was humanly possible.

"I don't know," he admitted, sounding suddenly tired and aged beyond his thirty-three years. "In this instance, Ellen, we're going to have to rely on intuition. Something that looks innocent enough but makes the hair on the back of your head stand on end. Maybe even a case we didn't take; someone who came in and their problem didn't click. Maybe someone we've dismissed from our minds but who comes back in our memory when we review your notes."

He poked around in the bag and withdrew half a dozen doughnuts that had stiffened since being taken from the deep fat fryer for the breakfast crowd nearly twenty-four hours ago. Without being asked, she dropped her pencil and went into the kitchen to make coffee.

"If it were someone obvious," Hugh pursued, raising his voice so she could hear him, "we would have remarked it at the time. You can't recall anyone like that, can you?"

"No. I've been running our clients through my mind all afternoon... since Lieutenant Wade called."

He waited to speak until she returned with two steaming cups of coffee.

"Not a pleasant task," he gently observed, noting tears at the corner of her eyes.

"No. But a necessary one." Her voice broke. "I want to help, Hugh. I want to find the devils who did this... who... played this rotten trick."

"Devils?" he picked up, noting the plural.

"Jack is a professional. No one man – or woman, for that matter – could take him unawares. Even if they had a gun I don't believe he would go without a fight. Unless they shot him in the back – which they didn't because we have the 'body' to substantiate that – there would have been a ruckus. A big one. With lots of blood."

"Devils, it is, then. Hired thugs?" he asked, taking a sip of the coffee and making a face. "Lobbies look different and coffee tastes worse at night."

"That's because your taste buds are jaded from eighteen hours of eating and drinking on the run," she retorted, divining his ploy to break the tension and responding in kind. "I suppose they could have been hired thugs," Ellen continued, returning to his interrogative. "Unless our mastermind is also some sort of Superman."

"Superman fights for justice," he pointed out. "And he also came from another planet. We have enough evil on Earth without importing any from another galaxy."

"How in the world do you know that? Don't tell me you read comic books as well as musty old law tomes."

"My tomes are not dusty –"

"I said 'musty,' not 'dusty.'"

"My mistake," he grunted, allowing himself the latitude to ignore her question. His subtly was not lost on her.

"I'll get the files. We'll start at the present and work back. All right?"

"You're the boss."

She took the comment for the praise it was meant to be.

They worked until 3:00 in the morning, discussing some cases, discarding others without comment. With red-rimmed eyes and dulled senses, Hugh finally heaved a sign, yawned, and pushed back from his desk.

"I can't think any more, Ellen. My eyes are running across the lines but I'm not comprehending a single word. I'm afraid I may overlook something important if I keep this up."

"It seems we were playing a game of chicken," she as readily confessed. "As to which of us would admit the truth first. My mind turned to mush an hour ago."

He shoved the papers back without bothering to pick up several that drifted to the floor. "Let's call it a night, then. We're not doing any good here. We need sleep and then a hot shower and a shave."

"I'll pass on the shave if you don't mind, but let's both go home and meet back here at..." She did a rapid calculation. "Nine o'clock tomorrow – or rather, this morning. That will give us about five hours rest. I'll notify Cummings we're leaving. If he finds anything that can't wait, I'll have him call me." Kerr raised an eyebrow. "Jack's men are used to calling me. I make the determination on the value of what they have and then call you if necessary. That's the routine. If we break it, the entire system may collapse. And we don't need any wasted effort. I'm the contact and you're the brains."

He shook his head. "Don't ever sell yourself short, Ellen. You have more intelligence than two-thirds of the attorneys in the state. If I had any sense, I'd send you to law school and make you a partner."

"I don't want to be a lawyer. I want to keep doing exactly what I'm doing. Besides, we make quite a good team the way we are."

"I'll say. But I take advantage of you."

"I'll let you know when you cross the line."

He debated how best to answer and Ellen could almost hear his say, *No, you won't,* but ultimately, he just pointed to the phone.

"If you call Cummings and tell him we're leaving, I'll go around and get your car. Stay inside the lobby and don't come out until you see me pull up."

She watched as he donned his outerwear and fitted his hat to his head before dialing the phone. Ten minutes later they were tucked inside Ellen's sedan heading down the deserted business street.

"Drive yourself home, and I'll keep my own car," she suggested. "That way, we'll both have our own 'wheels' if we need to follow different trails in the morning."

"I like the way you think, baby," he mumbled in imitation of a film character. "An attorney and his moll."

He winked at her and hit the gas pedal. In another five minutes he pulled alongside his apartment building and tiredly extracted himself from behind the wheel.

"Sure you're awake enough to drive home? I don't want you falling asleep."

"Why should I be any less tired than you? You're the one who worked all morning and then had to fly home. That, in itself, was a full day's work."

"It was supposed to be a fun day. Didn't work out that way."

Which was his way of expressing the Day from Hell.

Chapter 3

Ellen set her alarm clock for 7:30 and dropped into bed without bothering to change into a nightgown. She fell asleep before her head had settled on the pillow and rose like a shot when the bell exploded like a ten-alarm fire. Remembering his admonition that they both take a hot shower, she hurried into the bath, set the valves to as high a temperature as she could bear and stepped in. The steamy water cleared her pores if not sharpened her senses and by 7:55 she was dressed and out the door.

They had agreed to meet at 9 A.M. That gave her sixty-five minutes to accomplish her task and get to the office. She would have to hurry.

Taking liberties at several stop signs and running a yellow light that would have made her employer proud, Ellen parked across the street from the imposing City Morgue and dashed through a line of slow-moving early morning pedestrian traffic. Once up the concrete steps, she forced herself to turn the knob and pull open the door. Awash with a sense of déjà vu, she glanced through the window of the attendant's office, saw him tipped back in his chair, eyes closed, and rapped with enough nervous energy to wake the dead, a not inappropriate action considering her present location. Startled, the man's head shot up to attention.

Catching his eye, she made a demanding gesture. He pointed to the wall clock, implying the hour. Eyes narrowed in annoyance, she knocked a second time, pointing to her own wrist watch.

I have appointments to keep, too, buddy. I'm in a hurry, I don't want to be here and if you don't get up off your duff in five seconds I'm going to start screaming.

He reacted as if she really had spoken aloud and did have the power to wake the dead.

"All right, all right. I'm coming. Hold your horses." Cracking open the door, he peered at her through suspicious eyes. "What is it you want? We don't open for business until 9 A.M."

"I'm here to identify a body," she began with as brave a voice as she possessed. The idea had come to her during the long hours she and Hugh had labored over their case histories. Still burning with shame that her courage had failed, she had silently repeated his words, replayed his expressions, reviewed his body language.

It is not Jack Merrick.

If he had really been certain, he would have said, "Relax, Ellen. It's not Jack. It's some look-alike." He would have tilted back his head in that peculiar manner he had when revealing a bombshell piece of evidence to a packed courtroom and then offered a subtle smile of triumph to the district attorney. He had done none of those things.

Men did not know how to identify other men. They did not look at their bodies the way women did. Hugh Kerr was no different. She doubted he even knew the color of Jack's eyes; the length of his fingernails; the way his athletic body tanned in the sun. His skills of observation were directly solely toward clients and suspects. Take him out of his element, set him among friends or those unsuspected of crime, and he was just another man.

The task had been hers all along. She had known that yesterday. She had deferred to him on the chance he would have spotted an obvious flaw. He had not. Therefore, her turn had come again. This time, she could not fail. Her decision would determine whether they sought a murderer or a diabolical trickster.

"What body?"

"The one that was brought in yesterday afternoon. Police case."

Please don't make me say, 'The one without the head.'

He said it for her, which, had she the power, would have blasted him to hell.

"You mean the one without the head?"

Yes, damn you.

"Yes."

"It's already been identified."

Ellen had no compunction against lying.

"There's still a question of *positive* identification. Lieutenant Wade called me early this morning and asked me to come down and take a look. He is very anxious for me to report. He's waiting in his office now. By the phone."

If you don't believe me, you can call him.

And he hasn't had his coffee, yet.

She remembered Hugh Kerr and his tea. She would have that story out of him one day. When she and Jack and the attorney were sitting around a restaurant table, enjoying the contents of a bottle of aged champagne.

"All right; don't fluff your feathers." The attendant's eye squinted. "Say, you ain't pulling a fast one, are you?"

"Why do you say that?"

"What you're saying don't make a lot of sense. Why did Lieutenant Wade call you this morning when it was already positively ID'd last night?"

Flustered, she retorted, "Whoever he is, that poor man in there is not an 'it' – he was a living, breathing, loving, caring human being!"

Too late she realized she had subconsciously given the victim Jack's attributes and bit her lip. The attendant came to the same conclusion and seized his advantage, although until a minute ago he could not have cared less who the man had been.

"You sure you want to see it? It's ain't no sight for a lady."

She resented the tone. She knew it only too well.

You ain't a lady, you're a working gal. Ladies don't work. They marry wealthy men and stay home to keep house and mind the kiddies. They wear pearl necklaces and diamond earrings.

Ellen Thorne's mother had been a lady. Her daughter had inherited the title. Things had not worked out as planned. Had she a choice, Ellen wouldn't have changed a thing.

Except the expression on the attendant's face. But to alter that would delay her plans. And ultimately require the services of a lawyer to plead justifiable homicide. The fact she knew a defense attorney who would work *pro bono* delayed her decision a second longer than anticipated.

She pushed past the man and stormed into his cubbyhole office.

"What are you doing?" he demanded.

"Calling Lieutenant Hank Wade."

"You don't have his number," the man tried, less sure of himself.

"I not only have the phone number to the police department, I know his personal extension."

"All right, all right. I'll take you in the cooler. Don't know why you're in such a hurry. I told you: it ain't a pretty sight."

Repetition did not make the prospect more alluring. She pointed toward the morgue. He shrugged and led her across the corridor. They entered and he purposely shut the door behind them, locking in the cold and the odors. This time, they served to calm rather than rattle her nerves.

Once the body had been pulled out on the rollers, she took the sheet, lifted it to give herself a moment of silent meditation, then withdrew it past the tips of the toes. As she did so, her eyes caught a glimpse of the toe tag. The words, "John Doe" had been crossed out in blue ink, replaced with "Jack Merrick." Her lip curled in disdain.

She met the attendant's glare.

"Take a hike."

She expected him to obey and he did.

When alone with the corpse, if any living being could rightfully be said to be alone with a body whose spirit had fled, Ellen Thorne stared at the clay. Because she could not prevent her heart from pounding, she ignored it.

As promised, the body was not a pretty sight. The area around the neck where the head had been severed revealed a mass of dark, clotted blood. The remaining neck bone appeared to have been hacked, indicating the job had not been done with an eye toward neatness. What she presumed to be withered veins and arteries clung around it, deprived of purpose. The Adam's apple appeared more prominent than it had been in life. She did not know if that was normal or not.

The arms had been positioned at the sides of the body. Two bloody stumps lay at the ends. White bone protruded. These were more cleanly cut, she presumed with an axe, as there were no saw marks present. Passing over the mid-section for the moment, she studied the legs, then altered position to examine the soles of the feet. Purplish-red marks ran from the heels to the toe where the flesh had been scorched; blacker spots indicated areas where the skin had actually been burned. Only the small areas where the arches rose were untouched.

Overkill, she decided. Even if Jack had linoleum on his kitchen floor it was doubtful a usable set of prints could be lifted.

Having finished the first pass-over, Ellen began a second, more thorough examination. Without the head, she was forced to start at the neck.

Be calm. Logical. Visualize Jack at the beach. When was the last time we were together in Malibu? Labor Day. The office was closed for the holiday and Hugh said we ought to go down to the beach and get some swimming in before the weather turned cold. We made a fire on the sand: Hugh bought the steaks and we roasted potatoes and corn in the ashes.

She could taste the warmth of the red meat as it came off the grill Jack had rigged. They had forgotten to bring any sort of potholder and Jack took off his T-shirt. They had poked out the potatoes, rolled them into the shirt and wiped ashes off the skins with the sleeves.

Think about Jack bare-chested.

He had a good body and didn't mind showing it off. Muscular. Athletic. Tanned. Unlike most men who wore short-sleeved shirts in the summer and had a driver's tan covering only the lower two-thirds of their left arm that they hung out the open car window, Jack habitually wore a sport coat when he worked. He said it made him look more respectable when he interviewed witnesses. He was right and she had always admired him for his dress. Other private investigators of her professional acquaintance looked more like factory workers than white-collar businessmen.

Critically appraising the left arm of the deceased, she could not be certain whether he had an even tan or a driver's tan. The skin had a faint greenish sheen that made her assessment more difficult. If she had to guess, she would favor the latter. One mental check mark under the category, "Stranger."

Something else.... something I'm forgetting.

It did not come to her. She lowered her gaze. Hugh mentioned the chest had been shaven. The job had been quick: several cut marks showed around the nipples. They had not bled. The task had been completed post-mortem. Jack was not a hairy man; he had a thin line of hair running down his chest, thicker near his navel but not enough to draw attention.

With her gaze already in the area of his male anatomy, she blinked once and then concentrated on it. Ellen had never seen Jack naked which did not mean she had never considered it. A handsome man in bathing trunks invited comparisons with other men on the beach or around the pool. Women were no less shy than men in appraising the opposite sex. They were simply more subtle.

For a second she felt a pang of pity. No one ever imagined themselves lying buck naked on a morgue slab being stared at in stark appraisal. Jack was proud and equally vain. He would have preferred to be presented in his best light, not having his maleness limp and flaccid, his testicles shrunken like a pair of shelled nuts. What had he said once, when he came out of the ocean, shivering and half frozen and caught her eyes on him?

Turn your head, Starlet. Cold water turns a man's family jewels into pebbles.

They had laughed about it, then.

The dead man on the cold, unyielding shelf had small testicles and a penis that would have prevented him from saying any such thing.

A second check mark under "Stranger."

Yes, she decided. *Jack was better hung than this poor man.*

And what else? She would need something more definitive in her report to Hugh Kerr than "small balls, short dick." That would not go over well. He would immediately visualize his own dead body lying on a slab being appraised by the woman who had worked at his side for five years. She had never seen him naked, either, but like all men, he would find himself wanting in her eyes. That would embarrass him, even in imagined death. Without ever once being told, she knew his ego demanded he appear perfect in her eyes.

Stop it. Think about Jack. What will convince Hugh?

Ellen took her mind back to the beach. Nothing there. A pool. What pool?

The time all three of us went to that mansion in Beverly Hills. Hugh had won that case. The cards had been stacked against him but he had pulled a rabbit out of a hat. What was that client's name? She couldn't remember. But they had all gone to his home in the reclusive residential area of studio bosses and corporation presidents to celebrate. *An Olympic-sized pool. Jack said something. What was it?*

Think!

That was it! The St. Christopher metal. He was wearing a St. Christopher metal. Hugh had been surprised but Jack said he started wearing it in the war. For protection.

"A man learns not to take chances with the afterlife," Jack had joked. But he hadn't been joking.

What else did he say?

"The sun always makes the chain hot. If I stay out too long, it burns the back of my neck."

He had bent over and showed her. "Look at this. I got it in the Philippines. See that scar? It's from my St. Christopher chain. You'd think it was from the damn dog tags but it's not. We were working outdoors and the sun was so hot we damn near fried our brains out. We were stripped down to our skivvies and as red as lobsters. I kept swatting my neck thinking the bugs were biting the hell out of me. Which they were," he had groused with a long face. "But it wasn't them that irritated me. The chain was burning a line around my neck. Most of it eventually faded but this one spot."

Hugh had said, "Who knew you were marked by a saint, Jack?" and she and he had laughed. Jack had retorted that he tried to use the burn as an excuse to be sent to the hospital where they had all the pretty nurses, "but my CO nixed the idea." Hugh hadn't believed him but she had. Jack always had an eye for the girls.

Taking in a deep breath, then holding it, Ellen bent closer to the mangled corpse. Because the glare of the too bright overhead light cast shadows along the neck line, she could not determine whether there was a scar or not. Steeling and hating herself at the same time for fear of touching that which might be the remains of her dear friend, she carefully placed her hands under one shoulder and lifted. The body did not budge. She tried harder but with no greater success.

"Damn it!"

Ladies did not curse. She didn't give a *damn* and she supposed Jack Merrick would not have cared, either. His idea of a lady was a female who wore a skirt. Which was the same as saying he wasn't particular in his choice of dates.

"Warm and friendly," she had once heard him say in an undertone to Hugh.

"Damn it, Jack, move. And if you're not Jack, move anyway!"

She heaved a third time and felt her fingernails sink into pliant flesh. The sensation almost made her gag but she could not afford to be squeamish. Precious time was being wasted.

Wasted. I could use a drink about now."

The sentences came in Jack's voice, Hugh's or her own, Ellen could not be certain which.

Even if it meant she could be accused of talking to herself, she replied aloud, "You can say that, again!"

The shoulder and right side of the body rose just enough for her to examine the gruesome, purplish area that had once supported some man's head. There was no scar: at least none she could readily identify.

"Good enough."

She withdrew her hands and the body dropped like the dead weight it was. Stifling a scream, Ellen withdrew, wrung her hands in the air as if to decontaminate them, then hurried across the room. In one swift motion she yanked open the door and escaped.

Freedom never felt so good.

The attendant had positioned himself against the wall as though it were his job to hold it up. She knew he had been watching her through a crack in the door. As if to confirm her thought, he leered, "Heard you talking to yourself."

"Go to hell."

She knew Jack Merrick, who was neither in hell nor heaven, would approve. And he sure as *hell* owed her a drink. The kind served in a tall thin glass, bubbled over the top and cost $25 a bottle.

"Got a message for Lieutenant Wade?" he inquired, dragging out the rank. "Make a positive ID, did you?"

Ellen raked him with her eyes, finally settling at a point below his belt. She had nothing further to say. Her eyes, flashing a look of disdain, did the speaking for her. She knew that the attendant would spend his evening in the shower where a man could stare at himself without feeling guilty, trying to dispel the image she had conveyed of a very unimpressive manhood.

Ellen arrived at the office at exactly 9:15 A.M. carrying a box of doughnuts she had purchased to explain her tardiness. Plunking the box down on the lawyer's desk, she pretended to search in vain for coffee cups.

"I brought breakfast. What did you bring?"

"Myself," he answered, appraising her with hooded eyes. "Oversleep?"

"Yes."

"You did not. I called your apartment at 8:05 and you didn't pick up."

She had precisely two seconds to decide whether or not he was lying.

"It's not Jack."

He blinked.

"I told you that last night."

"No, you didn't. You conveyed to me your belief that it might not be Jack. You left open the door that it might be Jack."

He blinked a second time, then pried back the doughnut box lid and pretended to be looking over the selection for precisely the right pastry. The action did not cover the red blush that crept up his neck.

"Damn you, Miss Thorne."

"Proving, Mr. Kerr, that you are no lady."

He let it go. He knew a *touché* when he heard one.

"I told Geraldine to cancel today's appointments. Shall we get to work?"

"Not without coffee. Unless you'd rather have tea."

He grunted.

"You didn't get any doughnuts with sprinkles."

"That's because you don't like doughnuts with sprinkles. Unless that's another secret from your deep-down past. Try one of those filled with cream and covered with chocolate."

"It'll get my hands sticky."

"I think the *gentleman* who runs this office can afford napkins."

His gaze settled on her back as she marched into the kitchen, grabbed the coffee pot and filled it with water from the sink. She measured the grounds, dumped them in and set the machine to perk. When it finished, she poured two cups, added cream and sugar and returned, setting one mug on the coaster beside his right hand.

"How did you make that determination?" he asked, reverting to the question of identity.

"Women's intuition."

"You're not going to tell me any more than that?"

"I could, but I won't," she decided. "I'm pretty certain it would stand up in court but I wouldn't want to be cross-examined by our 'mutual friend,' district attorney Bartholomew Bond on it."

"Well," he sighed, taking out a cream-filled doughnut, "I accept your testimony."

"Thank you, Counsellor." She hesitated and then added, "But the name on the toe tag has been changed."

He appeared surprised.

"From what to what?"

"John Doe to Jack Merrick."

"Damn."

Neither pursued the subject and they worked for two hours in silence, alternately tossing case folders aside and drinking more coffee. By 11:30 Kerr rubbed his eyes and leaned discouragingly back in his chair.

"I keep finding my eyes going to Jack's chair," he indicated, nodding toward the bar stool reserved for the detective who was in the habit of twisting his long legs around it.

"Or listening for his wolf whistle," Ellen agreed. "Every time I hear anything remotely like those notes, I have to stop myself from looking up."

Having exhausted that stalling topic, they went back to the problem at hand.

"We're not going to find what we're looking for." Hugh hesitated then shoved back a pile of precipitously stacked Manila folders. "We're gone back nearly two years. We've identified those who've accused me of using dirty tricks to defend my clients and one or two who've hurled threats in my direction, but none of them dire enough to drive a man to torture. The physical torture," he continued, more to hear himself talk, Ellen suspected, than to arrive at any conclusions, "of, let us presume, some innocent victim who had the physical characteristics of Jack Merrick, and the mental agony he intended Jack's two best friends to endure. Speaking for one of them, I'd say the ploy's been pretty effective against us, to say nothing about the man who lost his life. Hopefully, he went pretty fast."

"I wonder who he was," she mused. "That's another mystery we're going to have to solve."

His head shot up and he drilled Ellen with a hard stare. When she met his look with one of defiance, Hugh lifted himself up with his arms and began to pace.

"So; you went to the morgue this morning. I've heard of hardened criminals, tough police officers and desensitized lawyers, but brazen secretaries?"

"I couldn't have lived with myself if I hadn't… We couldn't just order a closed casket and bury the body. Not knowing would haunt us the rest of our lives." Hugh turned in a loop and retraced his steps, working up steam like a railroad car. She watched him until her own head began to spin and then inquired, "Do you suppose that's what our antagonist wanted? To bestow on us a lifetime of uncertainty?"

Without losing a step, he nodded.

"He dealt himself two winning hands. In the first, he wins if we're forced to accept the preponderance of evidence and assume the body to be that of Jack Merrick. We mourn him while being plagued with doubt. In the second, he wins if we refuse to believe the scene he staged but are unable to prove otherwise."

Ellen riffled the sheaf of papers clutched in her hands.

"Assuming this is a set-up, that means Jack was kidnapped. That much we have to acknowledge because his wallet and other personal items were discovered by the body. Which reminds me," she suddenly remembered, snapping her fingers. "There wasn't a St. Christopher medal on the list the police showed you, was there?"

"Now that you mention it, there wasn't. Do we know he was still wearing it?"

"Once a person starts wearing a religious symbol they very rarely take it off."

Hugh put a hand to his neck as though to touch his own chain but knowing that he didn't wear one, Ellen could not place the need for such a gesture. Complicating her puzzlement, he whispered, "Sometimes they do."

Wondering if he had once worn one himself and some bitter circumstance had happened to alter his faith, Ellen persisted in her original statement.

"Jack wore his through the war. Nothing's changed that I know of to prompt him to abandon it."

He shrugged his shoulders in what she presumed to be resignation.

"Then the kidnappers overlooked it, I suppose, because they weren't expecting him to wear one. I'm not sure how significant it is but it's an interesting point."

Twirling her pencil back and forth between her fingers, Ellen shook her head.

"If someone had wanted to kill Jack, they would have. Instead, they opted for this elaborate deception. That indicates to me he's still alive. So the question becomes, for how long? How much time do we have to find him?"

She watched as Hugh bared his teeth and knew she had hit a nerve.

"How can I say? I have nothing to go on."

"Could they be holding him for ransom?"

He stopped pacing so suddenly she drew back as though his abrupt stop were an assault rather than the contrary.

"Ellen, the thought never occurred to me." Putting a fist to his forehead, he tapped it in annoyance. "All right, that's a possibility but it doesn't explain all this subterfuge. It's too elaborate, too… cruel. We don't need an incentive to –"

"Pay off?"

He grimaced and then shrugged.

"All right; to pay off." He shook his head and resumed pacing. "No, I can't buy that," he growled, missing the irony of the statement. "If someone wanted to shake me down for ransom, the obvious victim would be you."

Ellen flushed and looked down.

"Oh. Now I don't know whether to be flattered or the contrary."

Crossing to her, Hugh rested a gentle hand on her cheek.

"Be flattered," he whispered with meaning. She put her hand on his and they remained motionless for a moment while each tried to contain their emotions. He finally sighed and reluctantly withdrew. "This isn't about money. I only wish it were. It's far more insidious. Right now, I'm going on the assumption these men want to elicit our fears and lure us into some sort of trap. How we respond will determine Jack's fate."

Ellen tried a stiff upper lip on him.

"What you mean is that once they get you – or us – where they want us, Jack will no longer be necessary. They'll kill him for real this time, dump his body in the La Brea Tar Pits and be done with it."

"All three of us may end up in the La Brea Tar Pits if we're not careful." Stuffing his hands in his pockets to prevent himself from touching her again, Hugh backed off. "I think you ought to leave town. Right now. This minute. Before something else happens."

She ignored him and they lapsed into silence. Neither of them spoke for several minutes when Ellen finally broke the silence.

"Hugh, how much sleep did you get last night?"

"I didn't."

"Then why don't you lie down on the couch over there and close your eyes while I keep at the files?"

Hugh recommenced his pacing.

"Because I can't."

Temper rising, she snapped, "And you won't be able to tomorrow or the day after. You'll cancel your appointments, hand your active cases over to another lawyer, start drinking too much, become an alcoholic, ruin your reputation and end up a bum."

Her outburst startled him but his mind worked rapidly on the image she created.

"You paint a pretty picture. You'll stand by me, of course. Eventually I'll run out of money, give up this office, lose my lease at the apartment, grow a beard because my hand is too unsteady to shave, have holes in my shoes and live off your charity. You'll have to work two jobs but you'll keep changing employers because after a while their sympathy will turn to disgust. They'll make rude comments about how I dragged you into shanty town, suggest you abandon me to my well-deserved fate and --"

"Stop it! I started this and I'm sorry." Ellen sobbed. Abandoning his earlier reserve, Hugh quickly positioned himself in front of her. Wrapping her in his arms, he guided her head to his shoulder and kept it there a long beat, giving both a chance to recover and catch their breath. Reluctantly, Ellen finally looked up into his sad, searching eyes. "It's started already, hasn't it?"

He arched an eyebrow. "What this man wants. Exactly what I – what we just described. You said it, yourself. A trap: one in which we end up destroying ourselves. First mentally and then physically. We must guard against that, Hugh."

Clearly shaken, he backed off.

"You're right. It was too easy, wasn't it?"

"Yes. We can't let our hearts rule our minds. And we can't argue among ourselves." She tried a smile and poked him in the shoulder. "If you won't rest, then sit back down and pick up another stack of files." Pushing aside a strand of hair that had fallen over her face, Ellen pursed her lips. "I know what we're looking for is in here. I can almost remember the incident. It wasn't our client but someone you nailed in defense of a client."

"What makes you say that?" he asked, intrigued by her new assessment.

"You indicated there had been several times when you were threatened but there was one instance.... I thought I'd never forget it because I had just started working for you and I wasn't used to outbursts. This man.... What was his name?" She raised a hand. "Our mistake was starting with the most recent cases. I should have gone back to 1950 and worked our way forward."

"All right," he conceded. "It couldn't have been a capital case because the murderer wouldn't be out by now. Something less serious, then: an incidental embezzlement or a fraud or blackmail. A crime that would have sent him up for five or six years... maybe ten years and he's out on good behavior."

Ellen put a hand to her head.

"It's coming back to me. I can almost see his face."

As though privy to her vision, Kerr leaned forward. "Hold it. Hold it. I've almost got it." The flat of his hand shot down and smacked the desktop. "Carey Price! Bejesus, you've nailed him, Ellen!" Striding to the file cabinet, Kerr mumbled to himself as he flipped through the files in the drawer marked "1950."

"Ware, Waring, Whistler… Winston. This is it." Passing the folder to her, he recited as he resumed pacing. "Exactly correct: 1950. Allan Winston came to me because he was arrested for embezzlement. His initials were found on invoices for some expensive equipment -"

"Heavy industrial machinery," Ellen supplied after a rapid perusal of the papers. He snapped his fingers.

"That was never purchased. For some reason or other – I think he was applying for a rather substantial business loan - the owner had the books audited by an outside accounting firm and they uncovered an embezzlement scheme had been perpetrated for years, to the tune of a quarter of a million dollars. Winston was the head purchasing agent so his name appeared on all the transactions. The D.A. alleged he covered his crimes by making a paper transfer of the equipment he supposedly bought to outside contractors. By simply including them on the inventory every year it made it appear the trucks and cranes actually existed. It was neat and nearly foolproof."

"The prosecutor uncovered a private bank account in his name with deposits correlating to the 'purchases,'" she indicated, pointing to the case notes.

"That had been mysteriously emptied the week before he was arrested."

"The owner – a Mr. Clement Rutherford – begged the D.A. to offer Winston a deal if he'd return the money, but of course he couldn't because he didn't have it."

"He was looking at five years if he didn't confess –"

"But you found the hole in the set-up," she declared with pride. "The prosecutor put two bank tellers on the stand who positively identified Winston as the owner of the bank account. But you put Jack on the case and he came up with the vice president who had opened the account with 'Mr. Winston.' He had been retired for years and no one bothered to look back that far. Not when they had two clerks to testify."

Hugh nodded in satisfaction.

"*He* remembered the man very well. The original deposit was for fifty thousand dollars; that's why they called in an officer to set up the account. He positively remembered that the depositor had a lisp. In fact, he even wrote that salient detail on the signature card." He grinned in grim satisfaction. "The D.A. overlooked the clue because the officer's initials were 'L.S.P.' He simply assumed the carelessly penned word 'lisp' actually stood for 'L.S.P.'"

Ellen's trained eyes skimmed the almost forgotten report.

"Price was the chief engineer for the company. He was a brilliant man and well trusted. It wasn't unusual for him to put in requests for equipment and personally handle the transactions. When he received the checks from Winston he deposited them in the account of a dummy company. After they cleared he moved them into another account: one he established in Winston's name using false identity papers. He presumed that if anyone ever uncovered his scheme the money laundering could never be traced back to him since Winston signed off on the inventory."

Slowly closing the folder, Ellen shook her head in wonder.

"And considering Winston and Carey Price closely resembled each other, an innocent man would have been convicted. If it hadn't been for Jack's investigative work and your cleverness, no one would have discovered the duplicity." Crossing her arms across her chest, Ellen shivered. "I'll never forget that scene in the courtroom, Hugh. You called Price to the stand, but of course he was careful to articulate and it appeared his speech was normal. It was only after you started shouting and accused him of being the mastermind that he lost his temper and got angry Once he lost control, he mispronounces his 'S's' as "Th's." That proved to the jury he lisped and when he realized the trap you had set, he snapped like a brittle twig. His face turned purple and that evil stare of his would have burned you to ash had he the power."

The intensity of the scene came back to Hugh with vivid clarity and he quoted the criminal in the same intonation he had uttered his threat five years before.

"'I'll get you!' I'll make you *th-uffer*. When I get out I'll chase you to the *endths* of the earth and make you and your*th*s pay with more than your lives, *H-hughh Kerr!*'"

"Why is it the guilty blame those who catch them instead of their own greed?" Ellen asked, hugging herself more tightly.

"Because they feel entitled to do whatever they damn well please. Maybe they had a bad childhood; or maybe they feel their work has never been adequately compensated." Hugh shrugged. "Usually it's just that they think they're smarter than the rest of us and can get away with whatever crime they commit. When they find out they're not as smart as they thought they were they don't have the moral fiber to step back and see the flaws in their own character." He tapped his fingers on the desk. "It's always easier to blame someone else for your own failings, Ellen. That way, you never have to take responsibility for your own actions."

Heaving a sigh she forced herself to relax her arms.

"Do you think Price is our man?"

"How long was his sentence?"

Ellen went back to the folder to check. Her shoulders sagged and a look of discouragement settled over her face.

"After his frightening outburst in front of the jury, the judge ordered a psychiatric examination before sentencing. The doctor said he was sane in the sense he understood right from wrong, but he told the court Price was a maniac: one who suffers from fixed delusions." She met and held Hugh's gaze. "In the first instance, it was his belief he was superior to everyone and his devious mind had foreseen all impediments to success. The second was his maniacal determination to extract blind, unrelenting revenge on the man who had been his undoing."

"Directed against me... and mine," he whispered.

"That being the case – and his refusal to plea bargain by handing over the stolen money – the judge gave him seven years. They wouldn't let a man like that out on parole, would they?"

The lawyer crossed his arms and considered, finally conceding the point.

"Embezzlement is a non-violent crime. Notwithstanding his threats, he had no history of physical altercations. If he maintained a passive demeanor in prison, it's entirely possible."

"Shouldn't the authorities have notified you? After all, you were the object of his *monomania*."

"They should have but they didn't. For all we know, the prison psychiatrist gave him a clean bill of health." He shrugged but his expression of concern didn't lessen. "We'll have to check and see if he's been paroled. If that checks, we'll need to know everything there is about him. The address he gave his parole officer. Financial situation." He paused and let out a deep breath. "That should be easy: considering the state never recovered the embezzled money, he has two-hundred and fifty thousand dollars at his disposal."

"Would he dare use that?"

"It's untraceable, Ellen. No serial numbers were ever registered."

"But if he were caught, they'd send him back to prison."

"That's part of his obsession, isn't it? The belief he's more clever than anyone else. If Carey Price is behind this, I guarantee you he has no intention of being caught. He's disappeared and his parole office has no idea where he is. With a quarter of a million dollars at his disposal, he's going to be damned near impossible to find. Money covers a lot of tracks – and pays for a great deal of loyal blackguards to do his bidding."

"You mean the kind he'd meet in prison?"

"That's a major flaw in our correctional system, Ellen. It brings criminals together. Those who aren't capable of being rehabilitated end up making very dangerous contacts. We're going to have to assume that while Mr. Price was nurturing his hatred and plotting his revenge he recruited any number of men into his coterie. Not two or three but ten or twenty. Men who wouldn't think twice to… decapitate an innocent victim to further the 'cause.'"

She shuddered.

"The 'cause,' meaning you and me and Jack."

"If we're on the right track, yes."

"Will he try and kill us?"

This time it was Hugh who shivered.

"Dying may be the easy part."

Determined to be brave, she flashed him a reassuring smile.

"Then we'll have to stay one step ahead of him. If Carey Price is the one who had that man killed, we've already got a head start. We've identified him. We can call Lieutenant Wade and tell him –"

"Tell him what?" Hugh sharply interrupted. "We have no proof, only the vaguest of suppositions. The police work on facts, Ellen. Wade will listen to what we have to say; he may even put it on the back burner. But he's not going to go hell-bent-for-leather looking for an engineer out on parole. He's going to be methodical and slow. He's going to put tangible evidence together step-by-step. Right now, he doesn't even believe us when we say the body in the morgue isn't Jack Merrick. The name on the toe tag was changed, remember? It's no longer John Doe."

Her head shot up in surprise.

"You're right. I told you that, didn't I? But why did they change it if you didn't confirm the identity and neither did I?"

"I-don't-know." He gave her a bitter, compressed lips smile. "The preponderance of evidence? A wallet and a PI's license?"

Hardly convinced, Ellen made a negative gesture.

"Could one of Jack's men have identified the body?"

"I don't believe Wade would have given more credence to one of their opinions over my denial unless they produced something conclusive. And if they had, I'm certain he would have called me." Another unpleasant idea occurred to him and he caught Ellen's eye. "To be honest, I don't even know if Jack has a will, much less who would be the executor."

"Surely anyone who works in such a dangerous occupation would have a will," she weakly protested. "He never spoke to you about it? Asked you to draw one up?"

"No. But it doesn't have to be drafted by an attorney. Or he may have chosen another; it doesn't necessarily follow that he would ask me." Ellen opted not to comment, prompting him to ask, "Do you have a will?"

"No. I never really thought about it. Do you?"

He seemed more surprised by her interrogative than she had been of his and for some reason she could not fathom, required more time to answer.

"Yes."

"Well," Ellen tried with forced nonchalance, "You have more to bequeath than either Jack or I."

"Let's hope the issue doesn't become pressing."

She knew what that meant.

Someone's going to have to claim the body. If it is Jack, presumably that's you and me. And if we're not sure of its identity, that's you and me, again. If no will is found we're going to have to petition the court and claim the right of final disposition. In either case we won't find that pleasant.

She reached for the phone.

"The best place to start is with the Merrick Detective Agency."

"Have John begin an investigation of Carey Price. And have him ask around to see if any of them might possibly have identified the body."

"Right."

"Make sure he understands that he's to spare no expense. They're to drop whatever else they're working on and concentrate on this."

Ellen's fingers flew over the dial. Cummings answered the phone on the first ring and she explained the situation. Nodding in silent thanks, she hung up and looked at Hugh.

"He'll have a preliminary report ready in a few hours. And he said the job is on them."

"That gives us two hours to kill," the lawyer observed with a private emphasis on the final word. *Kill.* Not in, *Price has killed an innocent man,* or even, *Price has tried to kill our hearts.* More to the point, he was thinking, *If I ever get my hands on that bastard, I'll kill him myself.*

She did not have to be clairvoyant to read his mind. The awareness, however, brought no comfort for she believed it implicitly. It was said of Hugh Kerr that he acknowledged few boundaries, legal or moral, when it came to defending a client. Some who cherished that opinion held it as a strength, as it made him a formidable enemy to those he opposed, including the district attorney and the police. Others considered it a fatal flaw in his character; a weakness that made him susceptible to impulse and grandiose showmanship.

Standing between two opposing poles, Ellen Thorne made no judgment. At the moment, she was certain of only one fact: Jack Merrick had become Hugh Kerr's client.

Chapter 4

Collecting the empty coffee cups, the doughnut box with its mutilated contents and an ashtray filled with spent butts, Ellen tidied the office, speaking with her back to the attorney.

"We have two hours to kill. What are we going to do?"

"We're going to go to Jack's apartment and have a look around. Search for signs of a struggle. One thing is clear; if they took him by force, there would be one hell of a mess. And if someone called and made an appointment for him to meet them somewhere, he might have left a note."

Depositing the washables in the kitchen and the trash in the wastebasket, she kicked the can into the center of the room so the janitor would be sure to see and empty it before mold set in and poisoned the air. Picking up her purse she asked, "My car or yours?"

"Mine. I want to drive. I'm too jittery to sit still."

Allowing herself to be guided by his hand on her arm, the pair quietly escaped the confines of the office by the private rear door. Neither wished to be confronted by any one of several clients they heard in the waiting room being patiently but firmly informed by Geraldine, the receptionist, that, " Mr. Kerr is not in the office today and he is not expected in the rest of the week."

If either the attorney or the private secretary wondered if they would ever be back in the office again handling "business as usual," they did not voice their concerns.

Wasting little time, they settled into Kerr's stylish 1955 black convertible and arrived outside Jack's home by 2:30 P.M. Finding numerous parking spots along the curb of what had once been a predominately middle class neighborhood, they trod the familiar sidewalk and climbed the six steps to the landing of the former one-family dwelling. Over time, as the neighborhood changed, the building had passed through several hands before being converted into a six-unit "Rooms to Let." Out of habit, Kerr pushed the bell that rang inside apartment number 221. Realizing his mistake but loath to admit it, he hitched a shoulder.

"You never know who might be up there."

"Yes," Ellen agreed with a smile devoid of humor. "We would hate to disturb Jack in the shower; or walk in on one of his friends who just happened to be spending the night."

"I wish we would. Either or both scenarios would suit me just fine."

Depressing the bell to the manager's apartment, Kerr waited until a woman's voice replied "Yes," and then quickly offered his lie. "Good afternoon, Mrs. Owle. It's Hugh Kerr and Ellen Thorne. Jack asked us to stop by and pick up some notes he left on the table."

"Oh, Mr. Kerr! Just a moment."

Within seconds an elderly woman dressed in a housecoat and slippers made her appearance at the main entrance. She beamed at the attorney and nodded politely to his companion.

"So nice to see you again. I was wondering where Mr. Merrick had gotten to. He didn't come home last night."

"Out on a case," came the casual explanation. Standing aside to permit Miss Thorne first access to the foyer, Hugh turned on the charm that came naturally to him. "When was the last time you saw him, Mrs. Owle?"

"Oh, I never actually see him," she protested in girlish innocence.

"Then how do you know he wasn't here?"

"I hear him." She pointed to her own apartment immediately to the left of the door. "He always whistles when he skips up the steps. Well, sometimes he hums and when he's in a particularly good mood I've even heard him sing. Mr. Merrick has a very nice voice. I told him once he ought to try out for the picture shows. He's quite as good as Nelson Eddy. And just as handsome, if I do say so myself. I believe he and Ginger Rogers would make a very nice screen couple."

"I'm sure Jack would be flattered to hear you say that," Ellen offered after determining Hugh would let the comment go unremarked.

"So you didn't hear him come in yesterday? What time did he leave in the morning?"

"That I'm sure I couldn't say."

"He doesn't whistle when he goes out?"

"He hardly keeps banker's hours, Mr. Kerr. Weekdays, weekends, holidays, there's no telling. His job keeps him awfully busy." She sighed. "I suppose one day he'll get married and buy a house. The happy couple will move away and I'll lose one of my best tenants. He always pays on time, you know."

"If that blessed event ever happens," Hugh remarked in his courtroom voice, "I'm sure he'll invite you to the wedding. That ought to be some consolation."

"Yes," Ellen agreed, pushing him toward the carpeted stairs. "And with any luck, Nelson Eddy and Ginger Rogers will dance at the reception."

Mrs. Owle was clearly impressed. "Does he know them?"

"What he 'knows' I'm sure he wouldn't tell."

"Come on, Hugh. We have to get those papers. I hope they're on the table where Jack said he left them. But you know how he is. They might be anywhere. We may have to look for them."

She followed Hugh up the staircase before he could think of anything more useful to say. As they reached the upper landing he made a face.

"We should all live in houses. That way we wouldn't have any nosy managers to snoop."

Detecting the note of annoyance not common to him, Ellen offered a wan smile.

"Fine. The three of us can buy little box tract houses all in a row. You can be responsible for cutting the grass and trimming the trees. Jack can do the routine maintenance."

"And what assignment will you have?"

"Oh, Hugh. You left yourself open for that one. Snooping on both your nocturnal adventures."

He grunted and walked resolutely to the door marked 221. He tried the knob and found it locked.

"Now, how do we get in? I forgot to ask Mrs. Owle for her passkey."

"I know. That would have brought her up here with us and once inside, she would have insisted on helping us search for those papers."

"I would have given her five dollars and sent her on her way."

"Don't forget, Counselor, we're working on a murder case. The police apparently haven't been here, yet, but they will be. How would it look if we bribed our way inside?"

"Will it look any better after we beat the door down? Unless I'm very much mistaken, that's called 'breaking and entering.' Good for five-to-ten."

"Nonsense. Neither of us a criminal record. No more than two-to-three."

"And who was it who studied law?"

"You did." Fishing in her purse, Ellen removed a key ring and jingled it before his eyes. His mouth perceivably dropped.

"You have a key to Jack's apartment?"
"I also have one to yours."
If possible, his eyes grew wider.
"How - ?"
She winked. "Don't ask."
"Why didn't you ever tell me?"
"Because I was waiting for you to offer me one," she rakishly grinned. "That way, I could look pleased and surprised."
"*Why* do you have keys to our apartments?"
"For occasions just like this. As your secretary, I'm supposed to be efficient, aren't I?"
"I'd eat you alive on the witness stand," he groused and neither one of them believed it for a second.

Inserting the key, Ellen stepped back and allowed Hugh to enter ahead of her. Pausing to listen, he detected no sounds and flipped on the lights. Although both had been in Jack's apartment on numerous occasions, the room had a decidedly dead air as though it had been unoccupied for years and not merely a single night.

Ellen moved toward the window to open it on the hope a breeze would waft away the staleness but Hugh switched roles and stopped her.

"Better not. The less we disturb the better for us when we're questioned by Wade."

"But this isn't a crime scene," she mildly protested.

"We don't know that, yet. No worry about leaving fingerprints, but we don't want to overlay ours with those of someone who didn't belong here."

Ellen nodded. Leaving Hugh to inspect the living room, she wandered into the kitchen. The small room fronted the street, revealed by a curtain-less window over a narrow counter. A kettle sat on a hotplate beside a dented drip coffee pot, surrounded by four dirty mugs. She supposed that being a bachelor he only washed them when he ran out of clean ones. A set of four canisters completed the kitchen utensils. A check revealed three held coffee and the last was empty. In a bucket that doubled as a trash basket she counted two empty pizza boxes and three greasy paper bags that had once held burgers and fries. She shook her head.

"Potatoes might be vegetables, Jack, but once in a while you need something green."

"Haven't you ever wondered why fast food joints supply pickles on the side?" Hugh called, overhearing her soliloquy.

"That's a better answer than I thought I was going to get," she confessed. "But you didn't do Jack justice. He would have mentioned that mold was green."

She heard him hiss and knew she had gotten him.

Reading her thoughts, he called, "Right on both counts" as he disappeared into the small bedroom. Experiencing a peculiar sensation of being watched although she was now completely alone, Ellen crossed to the small desk Jack had set up by the wall, ironically in the same space Hugh had placed his own apartment desk. Sitting gingerly on the cheap, unpadded chair, she opened the top drawer and discovered a packet of letters held together with a rubber band. Briefly inspecting the outsides, she could not shake the feeling someone else was in the room with her and it was only after responding to a sudden compulsion to look up that she discovered the reason why. Pushed to the far corner of the desk was an unadorned picture frame. Although she recognized the subject immediately, the sight of it caused an instant electric shock to pass through her body.

Moving aside a dog-eared phone directory and an ashtray littered with unfiltered cigarette butts, Ellen picked up the photograph and brought it forward for closer inspection. What she beheld was a head-and-shoulders portrait of a youthful Jack Merrick, dressed in a dark grey suit coat, white shirt and slightly bowed necktie. While the pose, itself, was unusual, presenting the subject in stark profile, it was his expression which drew her breath away.

Oh, dear God, Jack, what are you thinking?

Not a sliver of a smile, revealing no trace of the humor Jack would later be known for, the boy in the image stared straight ahead, his mind fixated on a single thought.

Or, perhaps it's more than one thought. You're seeing something, Jack. Are you reviewing the past? Speculating on the future?

The cut of the suit and the smooth, guileless face made her guess he had posed for the photo sometime in the early 40s: 1940 or 1941. That would make him fifteen or sixteen years old. Since he wasn't wearing a military uniform, it couldn't have been taken any later than mid-1942; in all likelihood, she finally decided, he sat for the photographer when he was seventeen, just before he lied about his age and joined the Navy.

You don't know what's in store for you but you have a suspicion it won't be pleasant. Are you wondering whether you'll be killed in the war? Crippled? Dishonored?

No, you're not thinking that. You're determined to see this thing through no matter what the cost. How little you knew about life, Jack. Your innocence is palpable. Is that why you have this picture on your desk? To remind you what you've lost? Or what you've retained? I hope it's the latter, Jack, because you still have that youthful exuberance and love of life; your sense of fair play and decency.

Ellen closed her eyes and willed her prayer to reach the ears for who it was intended.

You're not alone, Jack. No matter where you are – whether in heaven or on earth – Hugh and I are here for you. We love you. You're the brother and best friend both of us need so badly. We'll find you, Jack and God willing, we'll save you. And if we can't, you wait for us because we're meant to be together. For ever and ever, Amen.

Wiping away tears, Ellen returned the photograph to its place on the desk, leaned back and waited for Hugh to finish what he was about.

Jack's bedroom was only large enough for a single bed, second-hand armoire, mismatched dresser and night stand on which sat a telephone and ashtray. Pausing a moment to contemplate the neatly-made bed, disturbed only by a pillow and a bathrobe hung over the top of a brass bedframe knob, Hugh decided the image was seemingly out of context with the rest of the "pad." The sharp military corners at the lower two ends of the mattress supplied the answer.

Although one glance had been enough to assure him the room had not been ransacked, Hugh opened the drawers of the dresser. In the top he found two dozen pair of socks rolled into balls and two piles of neatly laid-out handkerchiefs, cotton whites separated from the more formal colored pocket linen. The second drawer held jockey shorts and undershirts; the third a jumbled array of pajamas, swim trunks and lounging clothes. The last drawer contained half a dozen knives of various lengths, several styles of holsters, three boxes of assorted calibre bullets and odds and ends. No guns of any kind were present.

Crossing to the free-standing closet that stood a foot higher than the dresser, Kerr scanned the items displayed on top. Beside half a dozen different cologne bottles, he mentally itemized one straight razor and strop, a safety razor and a box of blades, a shaving mug and brush, comb, a military-style hairbrush, toothbrush resting inside a water glass, tooth powder, two jars of cream deodorant and a steel nail file. All items, including the top, were neatly dusted except for a wooden jewelry box shoved toward the back. After some hesitation, Hugh lifted the lid, revealing an open handkerchief containing four pair of expensive cufflinks, one of which had a Naval insignia, and several tie bars. Beside them rested a silver pocket watch with the initials "J.M." engraved on the cover. Gingerly removing it, Hugh depressed the barely discernible trigger to reveal the face. The time matched his wristwatch exactly. Beside it rested a small box that he examined with equal curiosity. Discovering it contained a Purple Heart decorated with an oak cluster, as well as the Navy Cross, both affixed to black velvet, his hand shook as he replaced the top.

Although not well versed in military awards, he knew the oak cluster affixed to the Purple Heart meant Jack had been wounded twice in the line of duty. The Navy Cross he had seen only once and that had been during his tenure as a law clerk in Washington. The soldier wearing it had been honored for extraordinary heroism. Jack had never let his possession of these awards slip. Not once.

Feeling less like an investigator taking inventory than a Peeping Tom, Kerr gingerly poked open the doors of the wardrobe with the tip of a pencil he had retrieved from his pocket. On the top shelf were towels, washcloths and bar soap. Formal suits and matching slacks hung from hangers curled around the bar. Situated furthest to the left, they were followed in descending order by business suits, sport jackets and four light, casual outer coats. He guessed Merrick had been wearing his winter coat when he left the flat. Black and brown formal and work shoes were arranged on the bottom along with an assortment of loafers, beach shoes and one pair of hiking boots.

After closing the doors, Hugh squatted on his haunches and peered under the bed. Besides a suitcase, nothing of interest met his gaze. Disappointed that not even a dust bunny remained to tell a tale, he straightened and returned to the living room.

His blue eyes had dissected this scene before. One couch that sagged in the middle; a duplicate end table to the one in the bedroom, holding a second telephone, a pencil, a glass and a bottle of Scotch and an ashtray, this one filled with butts. A small, roll-top desk with a lamp and an armless chair were situated opposite two overstuffed chairs for guests; a wood-slat upturned milk box on which sat five or six dog-eared detective magazines completed the furnishings. Following

Hugh's gaze, Ellen observed, "It looks as though he eats, drinks and sleeps his work."

"This place looks like it was furnished at a flea market. What does he do with his money? I pay him enough that he could live at the Biltmore."

"You're right," she agreed, sitting gingerly on the couch as if afraid to disturb ghosts. "We've been here before and I've always thought it had that homey feel. Just comfortable and lived in, if you know what I mean. But now..." She left the sentence unfinished and instead indicated the desk. "I looked inside. Nothing that might indicate what happened; pencils, pens, writing paper and envelopes, stamps. A few paid bills. Some letters."

His head perked up. "Opened or sealed?"

"Open."

"Did you read them?"

"No."

"Take down the return addresses?"

"No."

"They might be important."

"If they are, they're not to us."

"From a woman?" She shrugged. "A woman could be involved," he urged. "She might be a go-between. If Jack was lured somewhere, she might have been the bait."

"They had an out-of-state return address."

"So?"

He started to walk past her but Ellen stopped him.

"I'm not going to read them and you're not going to read them. If Jack really is dead and you're determined to be his executor, you'll have the right. But not until then. They're not clues."

"How do you know?"

"The same way you sense a client is lying or telling the truth."

"You can tell that by looking at envelopes?"

"I can."

"Then I defer to your judgment." He sighed and began pacing. Ellen offered a second opinion. "Whoever's responsible for Jack's disappearance lured him away. He didn't meet them here."

Kerr stopped and met her gaze with a questioning one of his own.

"Because the landlady would have seen them come in?" She shook her head. "Heard them arguing?"

"Because they burned the feet on the corpse." He looked toward the kitchen as she continued. "I thought so before and now I'm certain of it. If it were you or I they had mutilated, there might have been the slimmest chance footprints could have been lifted. Not from the linoleum in the kitchen – that space is too well-traveled. By the time the police finished their investigation, going in and out as many times as they're likely to, whatever prints existed would have been smudged beyond use."

Hugh snapped his fingers. "Good girl! You're right, of course. You and I both have private bathrooms in our apartments where they might have gotten foot impressions, but Jack uses a shared lavatory down the hall. Unless you had been here, you'd assume he had the same." Moving slowly, he tiptoed to the telephone. "Too bad the Agency didn't routinely tap his phone for security purposes. I'd give a lot to – Wait a minute! Look at this."

Grabbing a small spiral ring tablet he recovered from the floor under the phone stand, Hugh brought it over to the desk. After switching on the light he studied the blank top page with a critical eye.

"Can you make out what was written on it?" Ellen asked.

"Maybe."

Taking a sharpened pencil from a pencil cup, Hugh gently rubbed the lead sideways across the paper. Words appeared as if by magic.

"Directions?" she guessed, leaning over his shoulder.

"Yes. 'PCH N 20 r at Old Rat 10m l – wait.'"

"Pacific Coast Highway, north, 20 miles, turn right at 'Old Rat' something – a street name, probably – 10 miles along 'Old Rat,' turn left and wait there until someone shows," Ellen translated.

"Let's go."

There was no point wondering whether these directions were the ones that led Jack Merrick to the men who would eventually kidnap and perhaps kill him, or if they were a rendezvous for an old case. It was the only clue they had.

Nor did Ellen bother to ask Hugh if they ought to alert Lieutenant Wade. This was the lawyer's case and he was going to solve it. That, or die trying.

Cutting through the city of Los Angeles in pre-rush hour traffic was no easy feat in itself and by the time they reached Malibu shadows were already beginning to lean eastward from lonely telephone poles on their right and beach houses to the left. Had they been on a pleasure drive, the ocean waves lapping into shore, the cry of gulls, the prospect of a brilliant orange sunset and the smells wafting in from roadside restaurants would have made the trip a memorable one. Present circumstances, however, metamorphosed the shadows into wary adversaries, the silent stealth of birds ominous, the setting sun a hindrance and the odors of cooking sour and unappetizing.

With two hands on the wheel, eyes fixed ahead, Kerr concentrated on driving, occasionally stepping on the accelerator to pass a weary worker or a star-struck tourist. Once, he slid too near the edge of the pavement, scattering a handful of loose gravel. They shot into the distance, pinging off bare rock with the velocity of pistol shots. The similarity did not make their journey more relaxing.

A mile distant and Kerr hissed, "I should have brought a gun." And then with a lighter touch, "I don't suppose you thought to pack one."

"I would have ordered one at the deli but they don't come with pickles."

Her reference to a bachelor's diet and vegetables finally elicited a shallow grin.

"I owe you a steak dinner – with asparagus, baked potato with sour cream and chives and Brussels sprouts. With a salad and cream of broccoli soup."

"And pistachio ice cream for dessert," she rounded out the green recipe. "On Jack."

"We're taking him with us?"

"No, we're leaving him home to babysit the children. But the tab's on him."

"Children? Plural? You think it will be that long before I take you to the Ritz for a meal? You're talking -"

She petted his tense shoulder.

"Don't worry over the arithmetic, dear. 'Years' is more like it. Decades... centuries...."

"Will you settle for a raise?"

"No."

"Have we gone twenty miles?"

"Getting there. I have my eye out for 'Old Rat.'" In another five minutes, she tapped him a second time. "Up ahead. Old Rattan Highway. That's got to be it."

"I never heard of an Old Rattan Highway."

"That's because it probably doesn't lead anywhere. There are a lot of roads like that in Malibu; some contractor probably bought up this property," she explained, scanning the hilly terrain as he turned right and slowly maneuvered the automobile up the rutted, semi-paved trail. "With the idea of making private bungalows for the film people. Nice view of the ocean from the top but too long a distance to travel to the studio every morning; and too close to the city to hide from reporters' prying eyes."

The scattered remnants of isolated foundations, crumbled to ruin, confirmed her suspicion. Marking the odometer, he bypassed several even shabbier turnoffs before reaching the ten mile mark and pulling to a stop. The Old Rattan Highway petered out ahead of them with no evidence of any left-hand turn.

"Now what?"

"Shall we get out and walk around?"

"His note said 10 miles, left-hand turn. There are no turns. We haven't passed any for the last five minutes."

"Wait a minute, Hugh. Jack abbreviated, 'ten-m.' Maybe the 'm' stood for 'minutes,' rather than 'miles.'"

Shifting the car into reverse, Kerr made an awkward K-turn on the parched, uneven, shrub-encrusted ground, then slowly drove back the way they had come.

"We've been driving up this god-forsaken path for about fifteen minutes. Time me, Ellen. I'll try and keep the same pace. When five minutes have elapsed, we look for a right-hand turn." He banged his hand against the dash. "Damn it. If I had any sense, I would have been looking for tire tracks. It hasn't rained up here for months. If there had been traffic, we'd have been able to follow the tracks. Now it's getting too dusky to see."

"We'll be all right." With one eye on the road and the other on her watch, Ellen alerted him when time had expired. "Right about here."

Slowing their forward motion, both scanned the road. Finally Kerr gave a cry of relief.

"Here it is. How far does it say to go?"

"It doesn't. Jack just wrote, 'Wait.'"

"All right. We stop here and get out."

Switching into neutral and then turning off the engine, Kerr retrieved a flashlight from the glove compartment and then hopped out. Before he could reach the passenger side, Ellen had copied suit.

"You walk on one side of the road, I'll take the other. If you see anything, give a holler."

The area they found themselves in differed little from what they had encountered along the roadside on the way up. Patches of scrub brush were interspersed by wind-washed rock and shale devoid of sand or vegetation. One hundred yards beyond three bent trees huddled together, their leaves forming an irregular canopy that offered some protection from prying eyes. Without saying so, both worked their way up the path with that end in sight.

"I've got footprints over here, Hugh," Ellen called before she had quite reached the trees. He hurried over, shone the light where she indicated and nodded.

"Five or six pair: at least two men with feet smaller than mine and one with a larger shoe size. Those, presumably, are Jack's if we're in the right place."

Although spoken in the present tense, his tone reflected a trace of doubt. Working on a faith substantiated by nothing more than dubious proof, suspicion and intuition, the bleak scene, darkening sky and overwhelming dread cast a pall not easily dispersed by hope.

That mood only deepened when he played the beam over a large, irregular dark patch just beyond the trees. Hurrying toward it, they both drew the same instant conclusion.

"Blood."

"Enough to drain a man dry," Hugh bitterly deduced.

Scuffled footprints told the story of a life-and-death struggle that some man had lost. Dark spatter across an area extending at least ten feet indicated the tremendous force of blood being expelled when the head had been severed from the body.

"This is where Mr. X met his fate," he finished. "They executed him and the body fell here, where the blood is heaviest. Then they probably wrapped the body in a tarpaulin and shoved it into the trunk. From here they drove back to the outskirts of the city and dumped it where they knew it would be found."

Ellen swallowed hard.

"Shall we look around for the... head and hands?"

Kerr looked toward the setting sun, then shrugged.

"We're here. Might as well. For a few minutes. Before it gets too dark."

Four sentences where one would have done. She did not often hear the sound of defeat in his voice but she recognized it when she did. Hands in the pockets of her skirt, Ellen walked beyond the scene of carnage, wondering what Hugh had expected to find in this godforsaken spot. By rights, this is what they were looking for: Jack's last known "address." Where his own directions had led them. Interpreting the abbreviations correctly and finding a death scene put a final period on the trip.

Perhaps Hugh hadn't taken it any farther than merely finding the location. Or possibly he might have been more optimistic than that. Discovering Jack tired to a tree, waiting for them to release him.

What did I think?

Angrily kicking a small rock, Ellen turned and marched stiff-legged back to the trees.

I thought the same thing Hugh did. That we would find Jack tied to a tree, giving us a woeful expression and asking what took us so long to find him, "Since I left you all the clues you needed to rescue me."

Suddenly overcome by a sense of light-headedness, Ellen reached a hand out, steadying herself by holding onto the slim trunk for support. It swayed under her weight and her hand slid, stopping at the point where one branch shot out from the main body. The second her fingers touched a foreign object, her heart gave a leap.

"Hugh! Come quickly."

He was by her side before the words were spoken.

"What is it, Ellen? Are you all right?"

"By my hand. Something."

She felt the warmth of his flesh as his fingers rested briefly on hers and it gave her strength. Warmth was life. Grasping at the object, he dislodged two slips of paper and bent to scoop them up. Shoving the flashlight at her, he indicated she direct the beam toward the papers.

"What are they, Hugh? Tell me."

She could see for herself. The first scrap was the original directions Jack had written, the copy of which had directed them to this spot. Irrefutable proof Jack Merrick had been here. By itself, the clue was devastating.

"Jack's directions," he confirmed, turning it over to be certain nothing was written on the back. Seeing it was clean, he shoved it into his pocket as though it had actually revealed a black spot, reminiscent of Robert Louis Stevenson's mark of death, and needed to be hidden before the Grim Reaper caught them and completed its assignment.

"What about the other one?"

"It's a gasoline receipt."

"A gas receipt?" she repeated, trying to make sense of it.

"I'm sure Jack saved them as proof of a business expense."

"But why is it here with the directions?"

His voice sounded strained.

"I don't know. Maybe they were both in his pocket and when he pulled one out the other came with it."

"Did he leave it for us to find?"

"More likely when those assassins emptied his pockets to take out his wallet and keys, the papers flew out and weren't noticed or were considered insignificant."

"No, Hugh. Jack purposely placed them together in the crook of the tree." Taking the gas receipt from his curled fingers, she noted an indentation a quarter of an inch long. "Look."

"All right. I see it," he acknowledged. "A mark left when he… shoved it into the crook of the tree."

She knew he was parroting her words because he was floundering and she stiffened her own back to be brave for both of them.

"No. That's not what it is." With bravery came insight.

"Then what does it signify?"

"Give me your thumb." He obliged and she placed it against their copy of the directions. After driving his fingernail down as hard as she could, Ellen released the finger, displaying the mark it left. His eyebrows raised in surprise.

"An indentation exactly similar to the one on the gas receipt."

Satisfied that he had drawn the proper conclusion, she took both the gas receipt and Jack's original directions and held them together.

"They both have the exact indentation, proving it was made when both pieces of paper were pressed together. Don't you see? Jack wanted to them together. He didn't have tape and he didn't have a stapler, so he did the next best thing – he tried to fasten them together with his thumbnail."

"You've missed your calling, Miss Thorne. You should have been a detective."

"On the police force? Working with Lieutenant Wade and district attorney Bartholomew Bond? I don't think so."

"I was actually thinking of your being a private investigator."

"Working as one of Jack Merrick's agents? Do you want to carry that thought through to its logical conclusion, Mr. Kerr?"

He blushed.

"You're right. You're safer with me."

"Did I say I wanted to be safer with you?"

This time he coughed and laughed because they had rediscovered a cause for hope.

"Shine the light on this receipt again." Under the illumination, he made a second discovery. "Look, Ellen. He used his thumbnail to make a second mark. Not as deep as the other one – almost to bring attention to, or underline something."

"What 'something'?"

"The price." The moment he articulated the word chills ran down his spine. "Price, Ellen! Carey Price!"

"Jack was giving us the name of his kidnapper!"

No longer *murderer* but *abductor*. Jack had left a clue. It was enough to rekindle faith.

"You were right. Right as rain. You went through those files and you nailed the bastard. You have impressed me beyond words, Miss Thorne."

Ellen Thorne took a bow. If she lived to be one hundred, she would never receive higher praise. Nor treasure it more.

Chapter 5

Both the lawyer and his secretary frequented Malibu enough that had they stopped at one of the more popular "joints," either the staff or one of the patrons were sure to recognize them. They also had, at the moment, the disadvantage of knowing more than a few of the celebrities who resided along the coast or nestled in the hills. Not wishing to have their presence known, Hugh eschewed the brightly lit establishments and the warm comfort of a friend's home.

"This looks likely," he decided, hurriedly snapping down the turn signal and making a sharp left into a rather dull looking bar that promised "Live Music" with two exclamations points and "Cold Beer to Go," without any punctuation.

"Do you suppose they're mutually exclusive?" he asked, leaving the engine running as he slipped out the driver's side.

"As in, 'The music is so stale you'll prefer to drink your suds on the run?'"

"Something like that. I'll make some calls and be right back."

Striding up the gravel path, the lawyer yanked open the door and disappeared. Inside, a long-haired youth strummed a guitar, playing a strikingly original tune for his own benefit, as no patrons were present to appreciate the composition. He looked up at the man who could have been called nothing else but an intruder.

"Hi."

"Hi. Got a public phone I can use?"

"No. Just the one behind the bar. Local call?"

"Los Angeles. I'll be glad to pay you."

"No one is glad to pay."

Because the statement was spoken in a friendly way and also happened to be true, Hugh smiled. Taking a handful of change from his pocket that would have covered a person-to-person call to New York, he stepped behind the well-polished mahogany bar, deposited his money in a jar marked "Tips" and withdrew the black rotary phone. Knowing his party's number by rote, his finger made the dial spin. The call was answered before the first ring had finished.

"Merrick Detective Agency. Bill Daly speaking."

"It's Hugh Kerr. What have you got for me, Bill?"

"Enough, I hope. Your man Price spent four and a half years in the slammer and then got paroled."

Hugh's face remained impassive.

"How long has he been out?"

"A little over three months. He never checked in with his parole officer and no one's heard a peep from him since. I may have an address, though."

As though expecting a trap, Kerr demanded, "How'd you get it?"

"Got lucky. Did a quick check with one of the guards in Quentin who's worked for us before and he put us onto an inmate named Bradford. About four months ago he and Price were sitting side-by-side in the 'Meet and Greet' room. Bradford was talking to his lady friend while Price was conversing' with some guy in a three-piece. The guy was a little hard of hearing and spoke loud so he could hear himself. Our stoolie made lovey-dovey on the phone so it'd seem he wasn't listening but he got the gist of the conversation. Seems Three-Piece had arranged for a hideaway and gave Price directions. Guess Price figured Bradford heard too much because he got roughed up that night with a warning to keep his trap shut or else. Ended up in the infirmary and lucky for him he got reassigned to laundry duty or worse mighta happened. I sent one of our San Fran operatives over to see him with some comforts from home. For two cartons of cigs and six Hershey bars he got the story and the address Fancy Pants gave Price." Daly added, apologetically, "We haven't had time to confirm the locale."

"Give it to me and I'll confirm it."

"Mr. Kerr, excuse me for being blunt, but Price isn't the type of character you want to mess with. I said he got out on parole but it sure as hell wasn't for good behavior. He was involved in all sorts of behind-the-bars shenanigans."

"Such as?"

"He ran the protection racket up there. Pay through the nose or get your arm broken in a commissary accident. He put together a nasty little gang of thugs to do the enforcing for him. Whatever connections he - or they - had on the outside, he used to dig up dirt on the guards, even the warden, if rumors are true."

"What did he have on him?"

"Set him up with a dame, had some pretty lurid pictures taken. The kind the misses and the state authorities wouldn't like to see published." The agent snorted. "Appearances are, that's why they offered him parole – to get rid of him."

"And why no one notified me he was out," Hugh muttered.

"What was that?" the agent asked, not quite making out the words.

He shook his head in mute dismissal.

"Give me the address."

"There's more, Mr. Kerr."

"I'm listening."

"I told you he gathered a group of thugs – brutal men. Contacts he probably would have never made on the outside."

Hugh closed his eyes a moment and then set his jaw.

"Do you have a list?"

"I'm trying to put one together. Two or three of them got out around the same time Price did. Same deal: parole, but none of them ever reported to their parole officers. Dollars to doughnuts they're holed up with him in his hideaway. None of them would think twice to…" He hesitated, whether from delicacy of the lawyer's feelings or his own. "Do what they did to Jack. When we get ahold of them, I'm afraid you'll have to make yourself scarce, Mr. Kerr. We wouldn't want an officer of the court bearing witness to what we've got planned."

Hugh Kerr ground his foot into the floor the way a man would squash a particularly loathsome insect. Rather than argue the point, he ordered, instead, "No. You and the rest of the Agency are to stay out of it."

The man's voice sounded pained, tinged with an element of tightly guarded anger.

"Jack was more than a boss; he was a good friend. These bastards –"

"Then you know how I feel," Hugh briskly interrupted. "I told you: this is my fight. If you think I'm not capable of taking matters into my own hands, think again."

The coldness of what could have amounted to a threat did little to cool the operative.

"I told you: these are brutal men and Price is a devil out of hell. The guard told our operative he thought Price was insane the way he carried on. Cool as a cucumber when he was operating his protection racket but merciless when it came to getting his way. You saw what he did to Jack and he's the best in the business. How do you expect to defend yourself? When Price tracks you down he won't be throwing attorney's text books or law phrases at you, either."

This time Kerr made a low noise in his throat, a cross between a chuckle and a growl.

"If you imagine for one second I'm incapable of violent retribution, you're very much mistaken. You and I both have a score to settle, but right now you're working for me and I'm giving the orders. Once you give me the address, you and the others stay put. I don't want to have to worry about defending you boys on murder charges."

I'll have a hard enough time defending myself.

Taking a black notebook from his breast pocket, Kerr wrote down the address, added the directions Bill Daly supplied, then snapped the book shut.

"I want someone standing by the phone night and day. I'm not going back to my office but I'll try and call in as often as possible. I want to know everything else you can dig up on Price and his cohorts. Also, what, if anything, the police are doing. Got it?"

"Yes, sir. But, Mr. Kerr –"

Mr. Kerr hung up before hearing the last of what Bill Daly had to say. He was almost to the door when the youth with the guitar called after his back.

"Peace."

Which, to the attorney's mind, translated into "piece."

As in, pieces of Jack Merrick's body.

And as easily into, *pieces of Carey Price's body, scattered over the fiery pit of Hell*. With a capital "H" for emphasis.

Stepping out into the night air, Kerr took in a deep breath, paused to contemplate the scattering of stars that had broken through the cloud cover, then slid into the car through the door Ellen pushed open from the passenger's side.

"Price was paroled three months ago."

"Three months?" she demanded. "I wonder what he's been up to all this time?"

"I don't know," he admitted. "But I got an address where he might have established a hideout." Turning the ignition key then revving the engine, he added, "I'll take you to a cab stand and –"

She leaned forward so that her chin was within striking distance of his.

"No you won't. I'm not going home and you're not going anywhere alone."

"Ellen, Jack's man just about read me the riot act. These are dangerous men we're up against – men without a moral compass, directed by what can only be described as a self-delusional lunatic who acknowledges no boundaries."

"What's your point?"

Her question took him aback.

"I thought I had made my point."

"That your life is less valuable than mine?"

He faltered, trying to rearrange the question in his mind. The task proved more formidable than he would have imagined.

"No. Yes. Damn it, Ellen, you know what I mean and what I was trying to say: that your life *is* more valuable than mine. Yes," he finished with a flourish that made him feel foolish.

She did not blink nor did she withdraw her face from its close proximity to his.

"Why?" As he hesitated a second time, she made a gesture with the pointer and middle finger of her right hand. "Come on. I'm waiting to hear your explanation. Say it."

His eyes narrowed at the challenge.

"Because you're a woman."

The haughtiness of her expression cut through him like a knife.

"As I expected. That I am a woman I grant without argument and give you no points for the observation. I am twenty-five years old. I have a high school diploma and my higher education has nothing to do with my position as legal secretary. I am unmarried and have no children. I have less than five-thousand dollars in the bank. I own no stocks, bonds or property. You, on the other hand, are a man. Also unmarried and without children, so we can eliminate that from the equation. You are thirty-three years of age; the difference is negligible. No advantage or disadvantage there. You have both a Bachelor of Arts and a law degree from Harvard where you graduated magna cum laude. You are at the top of your profession as a criminal defense attorney. I don't know what you have in the bank, but let's just say one hundred thousand dollars for the sake of argument. What stocks, bonds and property you possess is also beyond my knowledge but suffice to say it is more than I have. Therefore, Mister Hugh Kerr, in the eyes of the world you are the more valuable of the two."

He started to protest but she pushed him back with the flat of her palm.

"If, on the other hand you are going to argue that this business is too dangerous for a *woman,* I will counter by saying it is too dangerous for a *man.* Again, we have reached a draw."

Leaning back against the car door, he shook his head in mute amazement.

"What then, Miss Thorne, is your ultimate conclusion? That we call the police and politely step aside?"

"Now that, sir, would be the sensible thing to do. But we already know the police think they have a positive ID on that body in the morgue. What we found on the hilltop will not convince them otherwise. They will merely conclude that's where Jack was killed. No amount of protest will convince them a gas receipt with a stray scratch under the dollar total is a clue, much less that it refers to a man named Price who swore to get revenge on you five years ago." She finally paused, searched his deep blue eyes and divining his tacit approval, continued. "You and I can both hear Bartholomew Bond now. 'Gosh, Hugh, there must have been dozens of men who swore vengeance against you during your career. In fact, you'd have to put me on that list because there's been many a time when I wanted to wring your neck!'"

Her uncanny mimic of the district attorney's voice and the accuracy of the statement she put on his lips, finally elicited a grin from the formerly stern countenance. Shifting the car into reverse, he backed out of the parking lot and quickly merged onto the highway.

"You, Miss Thorne, have a temper – and a very analytical mind."

"And you, Mr. Kerr, had better remember this conversation because we'll have it out again."

"When?" he asked in a tone that barely disguised his curiosity.

"If you can't figure it out, I'm not going to tell you."

He fired one last challenge.

"Do you know?"

"Yes."

Which ended the conversation. Or, more accurately, placed its denouement into the future.

They traveled in silence for fifteen minutes before Ellen broke it with a low sigh.

"You know, Hugh, I've been thinking."

"That you want to let me out at the first cab stand we pass?"

Proving he had failed to learn his lesson. She let it pass.

"I may have been wrong."

"Are we reasoning along the same lines?"

"I am afraid we may be. It doesn't bode well for our adventure. That is, if we don't find Jack."

He shifted his eyes from the highway to take in Ellen's profile.

"We're both thinking we've been set up." She nodded without enthusiasm. His hands gripped the steering wheel. "Those directions were definitely written by Jack. There's no doubt about that."

He ended the statement with a questioning inflection, prompting her to reply, "No, there isn't. I recognized his penmanship. Jack Merrick wrote them, all right. But why? He has an excellent memory."

"If we presume someone did call him on the phone and demanded a meeting, that person would certainly have recited directions."

"Granted, they were for an out-of-the-way locale, requiring various twists and turns. Just convoluted enough that a normal person would rather write them down than trust to memory."

"But not a private investigator. He's used to hearing something once and memorizing it."

Images of the detective, one leg twisted around the legs of his bar stool in the attorney's office, came to them with the vivid clarity of a shared mind's eye.

Here it is, Hugh. North on Pacific Coast Highway for 20 miles, turn right on Old Rattan, drive for 10 minutes then make a left and wait.

Tapping his noggin with a forefinger, Jack would offer them one of his lopsided grins.

A man in this business has to be quick and he has to be sharp. Lawyers can look things up in books and private secretaries take notes to cover the legal aspects, but us private 'dicks' as they call us in the paperbacks, commit details to memory.

Why is that, Jack? Ellen heard herself ask.

Because the cops aren't going to pinch a big wig or his assistant but they'll come after me like a hound dog after a 'coon. 'Let's just see what you have in your pocket, Merrick. What's this, now? A little black notebook.' 'It's just got girl's names and phone numbers in it, Lieutenant.' 'I see. You're dating a girl named Frederick Hank, are you, Merrick?' I hope she shaves before you pick her up for a hot evening.'

And then he would chuckle at his own joke. And Ellen would point out, *But you do carry a little black notebook, Jack.*

Yeah, but I only write things in it when I'm sure I'm safe. And I eat the page after I've given you the scoop.

"So... Jack felt safe at home," Hugh concluded for both of them. Ellen did not question how he had followed the conversation.

"And he did keep a pad of paper and a pencil by the phone for just that sort of call," she added for security. Kerr's fingers played a nervous rhythm on the steering wheel, prompting her to carry on the topic. "All right, let's assume both of our observations to be true. It still doesn't answer why he bothered writing the directions down in the first place when he had presumably memorized them."

"The man – or woman – on the other end told him to. 'Just to be sure,' he or she would say. 'I don't want you to make a mistake.'"

"Jack considers the request odd but not out of place. So he obeys instructions."

"He takes the top copy with him –"

"Leaving the rest of the pad behind."

"With just enough of an imprint for us to find. And correctly interpret."

"Which supposes we'd search Jack's apartment before the police did."

"I think that's a bet they were willing to take."

Kerr pressed his right foot to the floor and the car lunged ahead. Neither continued the discussion until he crossed a double yellow line and passed two vehicles traveling at the legal speed limit.

"Whoever called Jack wanted us to find those directions."

The attorney nodded. "They expected us to decipher Jack's code –"

"- not to alert the police –"

"- and to drive out to Old Rattan Highway."

Ellen asked "Why?" to give him the benefit of explaining.

"Because that is precisely the spot where our unidentified corpse was murdered and dismembered. It doesn't really matter who was killed there; the fact is, there's a body in the morgue and someone killed him. Murder is murder."

Ellen gasped in horror.

"Are you suggesting Carey Price is trying to pin the murder on you and me?" He hitched a shoulder and she leaned back against the seat cushions for support. "And we fell right into the trap. Do you suppose someone was hidden in the hills with a camera? There was probably just enough light to take a picture without a tell-tale flash.... Or they may have had special night film." Seeing his court-face, Ellen could almost hear him pleading their case before a jury. She had almost made up her mind to pursue the idea when he spoke. His voice sounded deep and distant.

"We left tire impressions that can be traced to this car and footprints that a rookie cop could match to our shoes. They don't need pictures."

"But the whole idea is preposterous! Why would we want to kill Jack? He works for you; he's our friend," she added to involve herself in the supposed plot.

"Stranger things have happened."

"None this side of lurid detective novels," Ellen scoffed.

"They sell, don't they?" he asked, this time in a voice as low as a whisper. "Besides, the charges don't have to be true, just sensational enough to ruin my reputation. Can't you see the newspaper headlines? 'Famous Criminal Attorney and his moll Dismember' – no," he corrected for effect, "'- behead Detective.' And beneath it, 'Jack Merrick, a renowned Los Angeles private investigator, was brutally assassinated and his body dismembered in the most heinous crime since the St. Valentine's Day Massacre. The District Attorney promises Hugh Kerr and Ellen Thorne will get the gas chamber –'"

"Stop it!" He silenced faster than if she had slapped him. Shocked at her own nerves, Ellen tried to mitigate the damage by adding, "Jack will be glad to know he is a 'renowned investigator,' although calling me a 'moll' is stretching it."

Dropping her eyes to her wrist watch, Ellen watched the minute hand move twice before she dared speak again.

"Hugh?"

"Yes?"

"You said you didn't believe the body in the morgue was that of Jack Merrick."

"That's right."

"When did you change your mind?"

Diverting his attention from the winding, single lane macadam to her face Kerr offered her a frown.

"I didn't. Why do you ask?"

"Sometime last night you called Wade and told him it was Jack. You waited until I was out of the way to spare my feelings and then you confirmed his identity."

"If I had done that, then why the hell did we drive out to 'Old Rattan Highway' to search for clues?"

The answer was perfectly clear.

"To find out who killed him."

"We went there to look for information on the assumption that's where he was kidnapped. The fact we also discovered the murder site of the body in the morgue was incidental."

"Then you really didn't call Lieutenant Wade after I went home?"

"I did not."

"Put your eyes back on the road before we really do kill someone."

He did as told, awkwardly jerking the automobile back into its proper lane.

"Someone called him. When I went to the morgue early this morning, 'John Doe' had been changed to 'Jack Merrick.' The attendant told me the body had been positively identified last night. I thought.... I mean, there's no one else."

Kerr took in a deep breath through his nose.

"No, Ellen. I would never deceive you like that. If I had changed my mind, I would have called you before I alerted the police. No, I take that back," he confessed, feeling his face grow red. "I would have driven to your apartment, even if it were at three o'clock in the morning, sat you down over a stiff double Scotch and told you that way. Never behind your back. Jack means too much to both of us."

She noted his present tense and smiled, despite herself.

"Then who identified the body?"

"I have no idea." His brows knit. "But I don't like it."

"Is it getting to the point we ought to call Lieutenant Wade? After all, it might be construed as concealing evidence if we don't report what we found."

"Yes, it is. And you're absolutely right. But if we call him now, he'll insist we meet him there. I have a feeling time is of the essence. I don't think we have two or three hours to waste going over the ground with the police."

Merging onto the freeway that would take them into the mountainous region where Jack Merrick's men indicated Carey Price had a hideout, Kerr rested a hand on Ellen.

"It's not too late for me to drop you off."

Looking out the window at the dry terrain along the side of the road and the lights of homes constructed along the distant perimeter of the great city, she pointed out a spot.

"Right up there will do fine, Mr. Kerr. Next to the trampled scrub grass and that pile of discarded beer bottles. Perhaps I can find some helpful tramp to take me home."

"I meant, I can turn off at the next exit and find a gas station or a restaurant. You can call a cab –"

"How would a working girl be able to afford a taxi ride all the way back to the city?"

"Put it on your expense account, of course –"

"Don't get too serious, Counselor. I'm giving you one of those 'supposes' that clever lawyers use to lure confessions from guilty parties. I'm going with you and you know it."

He grunted. "We'll call Wade once we get a look at Price's layout."

"That is, if we can't effect a rescue, ourselves."

"A dame and an attorney. I grant we don't look much like the cavalry."

"Speak for yourself. I'm a moll."

This time Hugh Kerr laughed.

Chapter 6

When they entered high hill country Kerr slowed the car so they could better observe their surroundings. Tall pines rose on either side of the narrow, twisting road, their branches occasionally forming an arch over their heads. The needles filtered the moonlight into obscure, twisted patches of light, adding a dimension of gloom to the claustrophobic roadway.

"Do you know this area?" Ellen asked as he slowed ahead of a sharp turn.

"I've been up here several times but not enough to say it looks familiar."

Staring down one long, lonely driveway, marked only by an unidentified post box, Ellen shivered.

"Pretty dismal. Who would want to live up here, anyway?"

"Don't let appearances fool you. Most of the property up here is owned by men of means. They've built very expensive hideaways for weekend excursions."

As if to belie his statement, they came upon what could not have been described otherwise, than as a shanty situated at the fork in the road. Several decrepit, rusting automobiles were parked in the front yard while a tire swing, held by a single, fraying rope, listed dangerously, testimony to long disuse.

"I see Mr. Vanderbilt is preparing for a yard sale," Ellen observed with a touch of dry humor. "Rumor has it he also sells moonshine in the back to business associates."

"Well, if he does, I hope he reports the income on his taxes," Kerr snorted in derision which only increased her merriment. Thereafter she devoted herself to pointing out other ramshackle cabins that had sprouted, like toadstools, amid the trees and unkempt brambles. It wasn't until their car bumped to the left and emerged through a tortuous turn that they came out at a spot overlooking a deep gorge. Miles below, illuminated by low landscape lighting, were magnificent pools, terraced backyards and widely-spaced multi-story habitats of the rich and famous.

"Oh, my," Ellen gasped. "If I hadn't seen it with my own eyes, I would never believe these private estates existed."

"You're not supposed to. They're not for the common folk like you and me."

"I would hardly call you common, Hugh. If they're beyond your means, then they're really exclusive. But we've come a long way up this road just to go down again. And I bet those villas are all gated."

"We're not going down. We're going further up."

"Into more exclusive territory?"

"More private, in any case."

"Then how can we expect to get past the guards?"

"Not by car, that's for sure. Once we find Price's hideout, we park and slip by the 'watchtower' on foot. I'm hoping the element of surprise will serve us well. After all, Price may have lured us to the murder scene but he can't have guessed we discovered his whereabouts. My hunch is he feels pretty secure up here."

"And if it turns out he's expecting us?"

"There may be three more corpses in the morgue before morning."

She did not have to ask the identity of the deceased.

Kerr. Thorne. And the real Jack Merrick.

When it became clear the road was petering out, Kerr dashed the headlights.

"This is it, Ellen. We've come as far as we dare in the car. I don't want them to hear the engine or the sound of tires on the pavement. Even rolling over a branch and snapping it may alert them."

Deftly maneuvering the convertible off the single lane road onto the narrow shoulder, Kerr made a K-turn and positioned the vehicle pointing back the way they had come.

"In case we have to make a fast getaway," he needlessly whispered as they caught one another's eyes. Ellen nodded. "We walk the rest of the way."

"I'm game if you are."

Slipping out either side with rapid movements to limit the time the dome light remained on, they quietly closed the doors then paused to listen. No one shouted alarm, no dog began to howl.

"So far, so good. The house can't be too far ahead."

His prediction proved correct. A brisk five-minute walk down the road took them to a gate that blocked further progress.

"End of the road. I was right when I assumed this place would be at the top."

"We hadn't passed a house or a driveway in half an hour," she agreed. "No neighbors, no one to track who comes and goes. But that gate looks rusty – nothing to indicate anyone has come this way in weeks."

"That's part of its beauty. The expensive cabins are all below us in that valley we saw. This place may actually have been constructed twenty or more years ago. And maybe it hasn't been used – at least not in the last five years."

After inspecting the padlock on the gate, Kerr moved to his left and appraised the iron railing that ran into a heavy growth of woods on either side.

"We'll have to scale it, but not here in the open. Look for a tree or a stump close enough that we can climb and jump over."

"I never thought I'd be grateful for my Girl Scout days."

Hugh's head snapped up and his eyes glinted.

"Breaking and entering was part of your outdoor survival training? Did they give badges for it?"

"No. But if you fall and break your leg, I can set it."

"How disappointing."

Ellen did not bother to follow up on whether his disappointment lay in the fact the Girl Scouts did not offer badges for criminal activities or that she had the skill to bind a splintered bone.

Picking their way, nearly blind, through the tangled mass of overgrowth, Ellen ran into Hugh's back as he came abruptly to a halt.

"Here we are! I'll give you a foot up to that branch. If you stand on tiptoe you ought to be able to reach the top of the fence and drop over."

Cupping his hands, she placed a foot in them and felt herself rising into the air. Grasping the branch, she scrambled atop it, bent over to try and determine exactly what she would land on and then threw herself down. He heard her fall with a soft "Humph!"

"You all right?"

"Yes. Hurry up."

Chinning himself on the branch, Hugh raised his feet, wrapped them around and worked himself in a sitting position on the crossbeam limb.

"Stand clear."

He jumped and landed beside her. A hand on his arm steadied his balance.

"Rather fun, isn't it?"

"You're crazy, you know."

"I've heard people say that but I don't know why."

"Now, you do."

Taking her hand with more warmth than the occasion required, Kerr led the way through the underbrush, occasionally striking his head or feeling a tweak at his ear as a stray branch scraped across his face. They worked their way slowly but after several minutes the dark outline of a low, two-story cabin took shape. One light shone through a lower window; none came from upstairs.

Suddenly confronted with the end of one adventure and the start of another, Ellen nudged him.

"Now what?"

"Now we peek through the window and see who's there. Come on."

Bent low to avoid making themselves a target, the pair crept toward the light. Hiding in the shadows and then dashing for a raggedy shrub, they paused to catch their breaths and still their racing hearts before the lawyer dared glance through the pane. He withdrew almost instantly.

"No one there."

"Then there's no point knocking."

He signed in pleasure. "Have I told you –"

Ellen put a finger to his lips.

"Not here. Not now."

He nodded and kissed her finger. She withdrew it rapidly and when she thought his attention had been diverted toward another lower level window, kissed it in return. Hugh did not have to see her act to know what she had done.

"Can't make anything out. This one has a drawn curtain but I don't hear anything."

After completing a circuit of the house, they ended up back where they started.

"I'm tempted to try the front door but I don't have the nerve," he confessed. "If I give you a lift, do you think you can see into that upper window?"

Ellen bit her lower lip. Despite their banter, she knew they were both afraid. Deathly frightened. That left her no alternative than to whisper, "If you're only suggesting this so you can look up my skirt, I'll make you regret it the longest day you live."

He almost laughed out loud and compensated by blushing.

"I'll close my eyes."

"No, you won't."

He bent over and with a little difficulty, augmented by the fact she did not want to lean against the side of the house, she managed to climb on his back and stand upright. Even balancing on tiptoe, she was just an inch short.

"A little higher."

Feeling him shift his weight, she altered her position so when he straightened, she stepped on his shoulders. Waiting until he righted himself, she grasped the window ledge for stability and peered inside. A sharp intake of breath told Hugh all he needed to know.

They had found Jack Merrick. In one fell swoop he thanked all the saints that protected attorneys, secretaries and fools.

Feeling his back about to give way, he tapped her ankle as a signal and lowered his precious burden to the ground. Ellen's eyes were ablaze with triumph.

"Quick. Give me your pocket knife."

He started to obey before common sense got the better of him.

"What are you going to do?"

"Jack's there, all right. He's tied to a chair. He's either asleep or unconscious because he didn't look up and he must have heard me."

"How does he look?"

"The worse for wear. His face had dried blood all over it and he has two black eyes and a swollen lip."

"That's our Jack." His voice quivered. "But I'm not sure about this, Ellen."

"We're both sure about it; we just don't like it. You and I both know there isn't time for us to get back to the car and drive down the mountain to find a phone and call the police. By the time they get here, the entire place will be aroused. Whoever's in there will get Jack out the back and have him disposed of in a matter of minutes."

"Even if you do get him untied there's no saying he'll have the strength to climb out the window, drop to the ground and hightail it out of here."

"Hightail it? They never taught you that word at Harvard."

"Their syllabus had a lot of holes," he tried with a grin. "OK, here goes."

He passed her his three-bladed, yellow-handled pocket knife then resumed the position of step ladder. Ellen climbed on his back, waited for him to straighten and awkwardly maneuvered back onto his shoulders. This time, her little tap dance was occasioned by the effort to open the window and when she sprang in, the sudden loss of weight nearly catapulted him forward. Gritting his teeth, he regained his balance, rubbed his spine and glanced upward, taking in the spectre of what his first impression styled the socket of an empty window.

Having already ascertained no one else resided in the room, Ellen slid across the hardwood floor. Afraid that the slightest touch would cause Jack to cry out, she waved a hand across his face, but his closed eyes did not flicker.

"Jack! Jack," she hissed. What that failed to elicit a response, Ellen crept nearer, hesitated, then clapped the flat of her palm across his mouth. His head snapped back, eyes wide with an anger tinged with disgust and a smaller element of fear. "Quiet! It's me – Ellen."

"Oh, dear God," he mumbled as she removed her hand, half afraid to believe the image before him. "Am I dreaming?"

"I doubt Hugh's aching back thinks so."

"Hugh? Is he here, too?"

"Outside, below the window."

Critically appraising his condition, Ellen wondered if Hugh had not been right when he questioned whether Jack would be capable of the arduous journey to freedom. Being associated with the lady for the past five years gave the detective the right to interpret her frown. To reassure her, he snapped, "Quick! Tell me one thing. Am I on the clock or has this whole adventure been on my time?"

"I don't know," she grinned, nudging him so she could sever the hemp rope that bound his wrists. "I work on salary so it sure isn't doing me any good."

"Starlet, you're on overtime and it's coming out of my pocket!"

Taking a brief moment to rub his chaffed wrists to restore circulation, Jack tested his legs. They remained steady but he doubled over as he took in a deep breath.

"Broken ribs for sure," he groaned. "God knows what else. They sure did a number on me. But I'll fly out of that damned window if I have to."

Holding onto her shoulder, Jack inched his way across the room. Peering down through the window he caught a glimpse of the lawyer's face staring up.

"Next to you, Ellen, that's the prettiest thing I've ever seen in my life."

"I won't tell him you said that."

"Thanks. You go down first. I'll hold you as long as I can and then drop you the rest of the way. It's not too far."

Ellen stepped up onto the sill, turned her back and lowered herself as far as Jack's arms could reach. Once she felt her legs dangle, she nodded and felt herself falling. In a second she dropped into Hugh's arms.

"He's all right, Hugh —"

The rest of her sentence was smothered by his lips and a tight, meaningful hug. Too soon he released her and motioned up to their friend. Jack acknowledged with a curt nod and dropped down, helped the last several feet by Kerr's powerful grip around his lower back. Once steadied, he gave a shaky thumps-up and the trio scampered away, using the shadows for cover.

Reaching the trees and out of direct sight from the cabin, Hugh and Ellen paused to let Jack catch his breath. Through painful heaves, he whispered, "How in the world did you find me? I thought I was a goner for sure."

Kerr grinned. "Ellen figured it out. We went through five years of cases until she hit on Carey Price. The rest was easy."

"And if you believe that," she warned, "I have some scrub land in Malibu to sell you."

"Right now, I'm buying whatever you two have for sale. Let's get out of here. They check on me every hour or so and once they find I'm gone there'll be hell to pay. You have a car?"

"Just past the gate."

"Thank goodness for that. I'm not sure how far I can walk. But I'll crawl if I have to. Lead the way."

With Kerr in front and Ellen behind Merrick to be sure he didn't stumble, they made their way back to the rusty, wrought iron fence. Jack's shoulders slumped as he used an unsteady hand to wipe away a sickly accumulation of sweat running into his eyes.

"I'm not sure I can make it over. My ribs are killing me and if my arm isn't broken it ought to be."

"I'll give you a leg up. Come on. We'll commiserate later."

Jack grasped one of the horizontal bars, placed a foot into Kerr's hands and waited for his friend to propel him upward. He failed to make it the first time, gritted his teeth and made a second attempt, this time succeeding in reaching the top.

"Bombs away."

He dropped like a sack of grain, groaned, clutched his sides and nodded.

"You're next, Ellen."

With strength summoned from muscles well-honed in his youth, Hugh hoisted his secretary up and held her steady until she was able to position herself on the top rung. Without looking down, she jumped. Once assured she was safe, Hugh grasped the bars and shimmied up. Motioning they stand back, he catapulted down, dropping to his knees as he hit the ground. Rising without ceremony, he assumed the lead and within minutes they reached the road.

"The car's just ahead, around that curve," he indicated. "Follow me."

They walked for what seemed like an age before Ellen's worried voice broke the silence.

"Surely we didn't park this far back, Hugh. You don't suppose Price's men found the car and moved it, do you?"

Proving he had already given the matter some thought, Kerr shook his head.

"I've been listening; haven't heard an engine start." He paused, stared into the darkness, then shrugged. "If they have, we'll just have to hide out in the woods until daylight and then make our way down to the nearest habitation and use the phone."

"They'll be waiting for us there," Jack grimly pointed out.

"All right; we make our way down to the tenth nearest house and use the phone. Unless they have bloodhounds, we ought to be able to hide until help arrives."

Noting the stress in his voice, neither Jack nor Ellen offered any further conversation and they picked up their slack, moving with a sense of purpose along the road. Another ten minutes hard walk took them around a second corner. Kerr's car sat along the right-hand side where they had left it.

"Why does the trip back always seems longer than the trip out?" Ellen asked to break the tension as they hurried forward.

"It's usually the other way around, isn't it?" Jack asked, responding to her offer.

Before they came within ten feet of the convertible, Hugh held out his hand, indicating they stop.

"I don't know. I think you're right, Ellen. I don't remember rounding two curves in the road when we approached the gate. Stay here." Patting his pockets, he made an annoyed face. "Wish I had thought to bring along a flashlight. Don't either of you move until I give the all-clear."

Hurrying ahead, he walked around the car, inspecting the tire impressions in the grass along the shoulder. Unable to tell much in the darkness he abandoned the effort and placed a hand on the front hood. It felt warm but not hot. If someone had tampered with the vehicle they had not taken it far.

Acutely aware that time was of the essence he slipped his fingers along the edge of the hood, found the latch and pulled it up. Without benefit of sight, he ran his hands over the battery and as much of the engine as he could identify without sight. All the cables appeared to be attached. Wiping his hands on his trousers, he took in a deep breath and opened the driver's side door. The dome light snapped on, temporarily blinding him. He made up his mind quickly.

"All right. Let's go."

Ellen and Jack came forward. She indicated he get in the back while she assumed the front passenger seat. As the doors shut, the overhead light went off, shrouding them once again in what seemed a preternatural blackness. Fumbling to insert the key, Kerr finally managed to slip it into the ignition.

"If this thing explodes, it's been nice knowing you both," he acknowledged in a courtroom voice.

"No last words," Ellen retorted. "Go!"

Obeying her command, Hugh Kerr turned the key and the engine roared to life. All three flinched, breathed out and reached for the door handles to steady themselves as the car bumped back onto the pavement and then raced down the lane. No one bothered to remind the driver they were on a one-way road and that if they came face-to-face with an oncoming vehicle the smash-up would be fatal.

Tearing down the poorly paved drive, careening around corners and occasionally rubbing the front fender against tree trunks growing too close to the edge, they raced away from one battlefield and into another. The difference being, the one they hurried to encounter was more occult and dangerous than the one they left behind.

No one spoke until the car reached the bottom of the mountainous area and pulled into the better lit and traveled highway. Surrounded by headlights, wayside businesses and the open road, two of the three heaved silent sighs of relief. Glad to be able to stretch her cramped muscles, Ellen craned her neck and checked on Jack.

"He's asleep, Hugh. We've got to get him to a hospital."

"I know. But not in Los Angeles."

The importance of his statement sent chills down her bones.

"The police -?" He did not answer. "Don't you think we ought to notify them that we found Jack alive?"

"Yes. But over the telephone."

"Why? They'll want to see him – they'll want proof. And Jack needs medical attention. More than you and I can give him. He may have a punctured lung, Hugh." Reaching back, Ellen rested the palm of her hand on the sleeping man's forehead. "And he has a fever."

"How hot is he?"

The urgency in Kerr's voice prompted her to overlook the double entendre.

"I'd say he has a temperature of at least 101; maybe higher."

"That's not so bad. It won't kill him."

"Not unless it goes higher, Dr. Kerr."

Taking his eyes off the ribbon of highway peeling away under the wheels of his speeding car, he sought her face.

"Ellen, there's too much going on that we don't know. I'm..." Loath to finish the sentence with, *I'm afraid,* he deftly corrected with, "I'm worried." He need not have bothered because she could read him like a book.

"All right: we're both *worried.* But I think we ought to alert the police that we found Jack – tell them that he's not dead. That way, they can't pin his murder on us."

"No. But that doesn't exonerate us from the murder of the man who is dead. For all I know, there may be some in the department who think this was all an exotic hoax."

"You mean, we pretend Jack has been murdered to hide our real crime of murdering Mr. X?" He shrugged. "I'm not particularly liked down there."

"They don't appreciate your tactics, Hugh. No one would consider you capable of murder."

"Anyone is capable of murder."

"All right. Call Lieutenant Wade. You may not want him as the best man at your wedding, but he's honest. He would never permit a miscarriage of justice."

Just as Ellen Thorne had avoided a risqué answer to his question about Jack Merrick's "hotness," so now he let pass asking who he might be marrying.

"I'll call."

Signaling a right turn off the closest exit ramp, Hugh scanned the area for a gas station or an all-night eatery. Finding one half a mile down the road, he pulled the car to a stop at the pump.

"Fill her up with high-test," he ordered to the sleepy attendant who came out rubbing his eyes. Reaching into his wallet, he offered Ellen a ten dollar bill. "Pay him; give him a tip but not enough to remember us by. And," he added, returning the wallet to his pocket, "have him check the oil and the air in the tires."

Pulling up the collar of his coat to protect against the late September chill, Kerr hurried to a stand-alone phone booth. Pulling the door shut behind him, the odor of dog urine proved too stifling and he bent the doors back a crack. Nose twisted in annoyance, he inserted a coin, waited for a dial tone, then dialed the number for the police precinct.

"Police. Sergeant Matheson speaking."

"I'd like to speak with Lieutenant Hank Wade; on a matter of some urgency."

As if resentful of the caller's use of the officer's first name, or just annoyed at the hour and the tone, Matheson snapped, "He is not on duty. Is this a matter concerning homicide, because if it isn't, I can –"

"Are you sure he's not there? Would you try his office just in case?"

The policeman's tone became more respectful. "Certainly, sir." The line went dead. After fifteen seconds the same voice came back on. "I'm sorry, sir. There's no answer in his office. Was he expecting you to call?"

"I believe he was."

"Is there someone else you would care to speak with?"

Kerr hesitated, torn between divulging too much or taking the change of withholding pertinent information in a homicide investigation. Without being sure, he opted on the side of the law which had been the life's blood of his professional career.

"Please listen carefully. This is Hugh Kerr –"

"The attorney?"

"That's right. Tell him I located Jack Merrick. He's alive."

"This is an open murder case, Mr. Kerr. I think you should come in immediately. The officer in charge will need to speak with you." All friendliness had disappeared from his voice.

Cold chills ran down the lawyer's back and his throat constricted.

"I can't do that. I'm on a county road and I have a flat tire. I'll have to call a repair truck because my spare isn't any good. It will probably take me... an hour and a half to get up and running again and then I'll have to drive back into the city. Can you have Lieutenant Wade there at..." He consulted his watch. "Four o'clock?"

"I think it would be easier if I sent a squad car out to assist you, Mr. Kerr."

"No. That's all right. I'll call back at 4 A.M."

Gritting his teeth, Kerr dropped the handset back and pushed past the half-open doors. By the time he reached the car the attendant had returned to the warmth of his office.

"All filled with gas, Hugh," Ellen informed him. "Windshield washed, oil and air checked. I gave him a dollar tip. He seemed satisfied."

"Good girl."

He slipped into the driver's seat, started the engine, checked the gas gauge to be sure he had a full tank, then shifted into gear.

"What did Wade say?"

"He wasn't there. At least, that's what the sergeant on duty said."

"It is late."

"Yes, but when he's on a case he seldom goes home. That's why homicide detectives should never be married. Their wives and kids have a hard time understanding why a cop can't work banker's hours. Do you have his home phone number?"

"No."

He started to say something, made a grimace and then shook his head.

"You purloined keys to mine and Jack's apartments but you don't have anything so simple as a homicide dick's home phone number?"

Ellen Thorne batted her eyes at him.

"I can see why I *might* want to get into either of your homes in the dead of night but I can't fathom why I would ever want to wake Wade up out of a sound sleep."

"Touché."

Pulling out into the deserted side street, Kerr followed the signs that directed him back onto the freeway.

"East?" she asked.

Checking the side and rear view mirror, Kerr changed lanes, got off at the first exit he came to, turned left, drove half a mile, then turned into a residential neighborhood. When it was clear no one was following them, he maneuvered into a driveway, used it to turn around and drove back to the thoroughfare by another series of side streets.

"Just to be sure we don't have a tail," he explained, finally settling down into the driver's seat for the long haul. "How's Jack's fever?"

Ellen felt his forehead then pressed her pointer and index fingers to the right side of his neck.

"He's still running a low grade temperature but it's no worse. His pulse is fast but regular."

Clearly impressed, he asked, "You learned how to be a nurse in the Girl Scouts, too?"

"Our motto is 'Be Prepared.'"

"That's the Boy Scouts." Kerr chuckled. "You were never in the Girl Scouts, were you?"

"No, Counselor. You caught me on cross-examination."

"Then how did you pick up all these useful attributes?"

"Who taught you how to shave? Or tie a tie?"

He considered. "Are you implying your parent taught you, are you soliciting information, or telling me it's none of my business?"

"My, you have a suspicious mind. You checked to see if we were being followed. That, I understand. But now we on the freeway heading *north*. That's away from the city. Let's be honest with one another, Hugh. We're both in this up to our necks. I want to know what you're thinking."

"I think we were damned lucky to get Jack out of there. We took a chance even professionals would hesitate to get involved in. If we had been caught, Price or one of his minions could have shot us as burglars and gotten away with it."

"I'm with you so far."

"I don't think that was his plan, but I suppose it would have done nearly as well. Having me – or *us* in this case – dead - would have satisfied his threat and thus his 'honor.'"

"What do you really think he wants?"

Kerr pulled into the fast lane and accelerated the car up to 70 miles per hour.

"If he wanted me dead, all he had to do was hire a hit man. I'm a public figure. I come and go to the office every day; my court cases are usually well publicized. At any given time, he could have someone hit-and-run me in my car or on the street. A man with a snub-nose in his pocket could come up behind me in a crowd, press the gun into my back, pull the trigger and be lost in the ensuing confusion before anyone got a good look at him. They could poison my food at a restaurant, sell me with a cigar filled with gunpowder, lock the door to the Turkish bath and parboil me."

"All right: I get the point. You're an easy target."

"He didn't choose any of those ways. We've discussed this before. He made it look as though my best friend had been murdered in a particularly gruesome way – that was to hurt my heart. Since I was out of town when he started his little game, I have to assume he wanted to involve you, too. I'm afraid, Ellen, you're guilty by association."

"Uh huh." She did not bother expressing the rest of her thought.

"He knew we wouldn't stand idly by and let Jack's murder go unavenged so he set us up by making sure we'd find the directions left in the apartment –"

"And knowing your penchant for getting involved, he gambled you – and I – would follow that clue ourselves, rather than alerting the police."

He nodded and gripped the steering wheel with both hands.

"That, of course, was our mistake. *My* mistake," he corrected, biting his lower lip. "I should have called Wade and filled him in –"

"But if you had, we never would have found the gas receipt."

Pressing the accelerator, the speedometer crept to 75 and then 80 miles per hour.

"Careful," she warned. "You don't want to get picked up for speeding."

It took a willful effort for him to ease up, but he managed to bring the car back into the legal limit.

"I wish I could say our clue was significant, but I can't. All it proved was that Jack was there. We jumped to the conclusion we wanted when the facts actually pointed in the opposite direction."

"That Jack actually had been the one murdered there? Yes, I thought of that, too." Ellen opened her purse, reached inside, removed a tissue and wiped her face. "Regardless of how we interpreted it, it set us on the right track. Without it, we might not have gone to the hideaway. And if we hadn't rescued Jack, he could be dead by now."

Even in the dim light she could see his face grow pale.

"No, Ellen. I made a grievous, arrogant mistake. By thinking I was more clever than the police I led us into a trap. One, I'm afraid, that may have very dire consequences." He pounded on the wheel in anger. "Carey Price wanted to get us to the scene so we'd be implicated in Jack's murder. What better way of exacting revenge on me than that? I suppose he's plotted some elaborate explanation why I would have done that."

Proving her mind had already worked along similar lines, she offered a rapid response.

"Not so elaborate, Hugh. I suppose he could use the oldest excuse in the world: jealousy." Taking a deep breath, she plunged ahead. "Despite the fact we've never actually been a couple, I've been seen in your company at social events enough to make it seem so. You thought Jack and I were having an affair; or that he had gotten fresh with me and you didn't like it."

His left eyebrow raised in surprise.

"I hadn't thought of that but it works."

"All right. So now the police can place us at the murder scene and they have a motive, however thin. If you were a seasoned detective like Wade, would you believe it? More to the point, if you were Bartholomew Bond, would you believe you had enough evidence to bring us to trial and get a conviction?"

"No on both counts. If we're correct in our assumptions so far, there has to be more: something we don't know, yet." He stretched the muscles in his back, trying unsuccessfully to unkink the knots. "My mind keeps going back to Wade. Someone convinced him the body in the morgue really was Jack Merrick, even after I told him it wasn't – and you would have corroborated my statement this morning."

"Does that matter, now? We found Jack."

"That wasn't part of Price's plan."

"So what is Plan B?"

"I'm only speculating, of course."

"Go on."

"He has to prevent us from bringing Jack in to the authorities at all costs."

"Then why are we heading north instead of back to Los Angeles?"

"Because that's what he expects us to do. Once he finds Jack's gone, he'll summon every man he has and put them on the roads. They'll cover hospitals, clinics and all the local police precincts in the hope of intercepting us."

"But you already notified the police he was alive."

"I didn't believe the officer when he told me Wade wasn't there. I think he was in his office."

"Then someone – or someones - in the department are working for Price."

"Why not? He's got a lot of ill-gotten gains to play with and apparently doesn't mind spending it. I have a feeling that Matheson isn't going to tell anyone I called. At least not until he has to. That gives Price's men four hours to find us."

"You didn't tell him where we were?"

"No. I said I'd call back at 4AM. That's why I had to be sure we weren't being followed. Until we reach Wade or B.B. Bond personally, we're still in trouble. And even that doesn't get us out of the woods until they actually see Jack."

"Wouldn't talking to him on the phone be just as good?"

"Neither one of them is going to *swear* in court it was Jack Merrick they were speaking with. They will say it *sounded like him* but that's not a positive ID. It will never stand up – especially when the DA – not Bond, because he's going to have to recuse himself – has evidence of us being at the murder scene."

"Why would B.B. have to recuse himself?"

"Because I'm going to insist on it."

"Certainly not on the grounds of friendship?"

"Well, we did go to a police charity picnic together once."

Ellen leaned back against the passenger side door and laughed until her sides shook.

"Oh, Hugh, I think that picnic was the first time I ever realized how truly wicked you are. B.B. was in the kissing booth and he refused your $5 so you went around telling everyone you offered him a $100 contribution for a peck on the cheek and he refused. The Commissioner got wind of the proposition and made him go through with it. And you just happened to have a photographer ready to preserve the moment for posterity."

"It was a damned expensive kiss," he admitted with a sly grin, "but worth every penny."

"And for a good cause," Ellen agreed. "And then you had the brass balls to have the picture framed and hung in the office. How much did he pay to make you take it down?"

"A matching donation to the police charity. What did you do with that photo, anyway?"

"Your ignorance, sir, does not speak well for your powers of observation. I have it hanging on my bedroom wall."

The car swerved and narrowly missed striking the median before Hugh brought it back under control.

"Observations, hell. I've never been in your bedroom, Miss Thorne."

Ellen winked. "I'm just trying to make a case for the defense, Mr. Attorney."

He rolled his eyes.

"I'm glad we're on the same side."

"So am I," she agreed, resting her hand on his. "We're both wicked in the same ways. Likes, as they say, attract."

Kerr could only nod in agreement and wonder where the long road they traveled would end.

Chapter 7

Approaching Santa Barbara, Ellen checked her wrist watch, using the vanity light above the sun visor for illumination.

"It's getting late, Hugh –"

"Actually," he observed, "it's getting early."

"You said you were going to call Lieutenant Wade back at 4 o'clock."

"Yeah," came a sleepy, atypically hushed voice from the rear seat. "And I could use a pit stop."

The driver and his passenger jumped from the unexpectedness of the interruption before Hugh agreed for himself and Ellen by confirming, "We all could."

"And some coffee, gas for the car and sleep. Not necessarily in that order," she completed.

Nodding in agreement, Hugh inspected his friend's wan countenance in the rear view mirror.

"How you feeling?"

"I've felt worse but I can't remember when. Those boys really gave me a working over." Shifting positions, Jack stifled a groan, then grasped his waist. "Can't get comfortable, can't take a deep breath. Classic symptoms of broken ribs. But I'm not spitting up any blood," he decided, rolling his tongue around in his mouth and then inspecting the saliva he collected on his finger. "That means my lungs aren't punctured."

"Jack," Ellen hastened to explain with a wink at the back, "was a boy scout."

"I'm surrounded by badge people," the lawyer groused. "I'm not sure which is worse – those tin stars they carry around in breast pockets or the little round appliques parents sew on sashes."

"Appliques?" Ellen asked in mock surprise. "I didn't think men knew such technical terms."

"Origin: circa 18th century France, *appliquer,* or 'apply,' from the Latin, *applicare.* Technically, ornamental needlework in which pieces of cloth are attached to one another, but in common usage, a badge meant to be attached to cloth, as in a sash."

"Do you know what he's talking about, Ellen?"

"I'm afraid I do. But he's being snobbish."

"Lawyers," Kerr imperiously informed his listeners, "are supposed to know French and Latin. As it happens, I am fluent in both."

"Snobbish," Jack agreed. "Why are we outside Santa Barbara?" he asked, catching sight of a highway sign. "Were all the bars in Los Angeles closed? And speaking of which –"

"We're on the lam," Ellen elucidated. "As a moll, I am entitled to use my own vocabulary. And no alcohol for you until we're sure you're going to be all right."

"Lam? Moll? 18th century? How long have I been out, or should I say, have I gone back in time? And if I have, let me remind you that a good shot or two of red eye was a marvelous cure for everything in those days."

"Actually, opium was the drug of choice; taken in liquid form it was called laudanum," Kerr offered.

"Well, I'd rather have some aged Scotch; or rum. Since I seem to have caught a chill," he added with a shiver, "a flagon of hot buttered rum would be swell right about now."

Kerr rolled down the window and stuck his arm out in a right angle, indicating a turn. The car eased smoothly off the highway but he bypassed the two nearest gas stations. Jack shook his leg.

"Say, if you're looking for the cheapest price, I'll add my two cents to the pile. Just stop, for Cripe's sake so I can use the little boy's room. Or am I going to have to raise my hand and ask for permission?"

Kerr's voice took on a serious tone.

"If, as I suspect, people are looking for us, I don't want to make it too easy to be found. Agents will ask at all the convenient gas stations but even the police won't have enough men to check all the outliers."

This caught the detective's attention and he did the best he could to straighten into a sitting position.

"Why are the police looking for us? You two didn't kill anyone you're not telling me about, did you? Because if you did and I'm caught in your company, there goes my PI license just like that." He snapped his fingers for emphasis.

"Yes, I'm afraid we did kill someone, Jack," Ellen sighed. "At least they think we did."

"OK, I'll bite. Who are you supposed to have killed?"

"You."

He fell back against the seat cushion.

"Great. They'll never renew the license of a dead man."

"Just be glad you're alive," Kerr advised.

"I'm glad, all right. But I don't understand any of this. Why would you two kill me and why am I still alive, then?"

"Jealousy," Ellen grinned. "You and I either had an affair or you forced yourself on me and Hugh flipped."

"You mean I missed all the fun? That doesn't seem fair."

"The 'fun' part was what you didn't miss."

"You mean the beating? That wasn't fun by any stretch of the imagination."

"Want to tell us about it?"

"Not especially. I-want-to-go-to-the-bathroom."

"All right; cross your legs. I'll pull into the next 'pit stop.'"

Kerr made several more twists and turns, passing two gas stations that were closed at the early hour before finding one with its lights on. He pulled up to the pump and turned off the engine.

"Ellen, if you don't mind, stay here until the attendant comes and keep an eye on him. If he looks as though he's interested in our license number, let me know." Taking the registration off the steering column, Hugh slipped it into his pocket and got out. Pushing back the driver's side seat, he gave Jack a hand out, then walked with him toward the men's restroom at the side of the building.

"Stay inside when you're done. I'll come and get you once I've telephoned Wade."

Waiting to be sure the detective's legs were steady enough to hold him as he slipped inside the one toilet/sink room, Hugh went to the telephone booth, set out a handful of change on the narrow ledge and dialed the Los Angeles number. Before the connection went through he was advised to deposit $1.50 in the coin slot. He did so and the call went through.

"Police precinct. Sergeant Matheson speaking."

"This is Hugh Kerr. I want to speak to Lieutenant Wade."

"Just a moment."

Keeping an eye on the second hand of his watch, Hugh counted the seconds before the detective's familiar voice came on the line.

"Kerr, where the hell are you?"

"Listen, I don't have much time. Jack Merrick wasn't killed, he was kidnapped."

"The hell you say."

Something in the tone sent cold shivers down Kerr's back.

"I've got him with me. He's in the car; badly wounded."

"He's in the morgue, Hugh and you and Miss Thorne had better turn yourselves in. The D.A. wants to see you. Badly."

"I tell you he's alive. Ellen and I rescued him."

"Then who's the stiff without the head?"

The crudeness of the question further alarmed the attorney.

"I don't know —"

"Listen to me, Kerr. You and Ellen are in a hell of a lot of trouble."

Hugh swallowed a mouthful of bile before speaking.

"Why?"

"First of all, you lied when you told me the body wasn't Merrick. That's giving a false statement to the police and by itself it's enough to get your law license suspended. Second, we have positive proof of the 'headless horseman's identity."

"What proof?"

"An inspector went back to the scene last night and recovered a St. Christopher's medal. It was positively ID'd by one of Merrick's men at 3 A.M. this morning." His voice turned sarcastic. "And what do you think the lab boys found on it?"

"I have no idea."

"Your thumb print on the back. Plain as day."

"What inspector?" Hugh demanded, trying to fight the vertigo Wade's information had given him.

"Louis Gray."

"I don't know him."

"Well, come on in and I'll introduce you."

"Who was the analyst?"

"Tucker Sweet."

Hugh's mouth went dry and he tried to swallow, nearly choking from the effort.

"I don't know him, either."

"They're on loan from the San Diego office. On the exchange program, you might say. You have a problem with that? Not that I think you'll be cross-examining them on their credentials anytime soon, Counselor."

"Hank —"

"Don't 'Hank' me, Kerr. Get your ass in here on the double because if I have to issue an all-points, it won't go well for you."

Seeing the second hand sweep toward the minute mark, Hugh put his hand up by the handset hook.

"I'll call you later. Maybe."

He depressed it quickly, stared at his shaking hand, then slammed the receiver down. Forgetting the rest of the unused coins, he grabbed the dog-eared yellow pages, flipped through it, found what he was looking for and tore out a page. Stuffing it in his pocket, he pushed away from the booth. The effort caused him to stumble and he regained his balance with difficulty. Walking slowly to the men's room he rejoined Jack. The detective, looking the worse for wear, nodded as he came up.

"Any luck?"

"Nothing you'd call luck."

"You going to tell me what this is all about?"

"Yes, but not here. We'll stop later and take a hotel room. Keep your back turned; I don't want that gas jockey getting a good look at you."

After using the restroom, Kerr, with Merrick in tow, returned to the car. Ellen hopped out to meet them.

"All clear, Hugh. I'll be right back. And let me drive for a while. You look done in."

Acknowledging her observation, Hugh let Jack in the back, then settled into the passenger's seat. Ellen returned five minutes later precipitously balancing three paper cups and a small brown bag. Handing them across to Kerr, she got behind the wheel and quickly drove back onto the street.

Hugh handed her one cup, gave the second to Jack and sipped greedily from the third.

"What's in the sack?" Jack sniffed.

"Stale crackers and cheese, six Hershey bars, a roll of adhesive tape and a bottle of aspirin. I'm sorry, Jack; that's the best I could do for now. Hugh, do you have a blanket or a jacket in the trunk?"

"Yes. Both."

Checking to see that no one was behind them, Ellen pulled over to the shoulder, switched off the ignition and handed him the keys.

"Get whatever is back there – any kind of cloth you can rip into strips and wrap around Jack's chest. That ought to ease his discomfort a little bit until we can find a drug store and buy something better."

Hugh popped out, opened the trunk and returned with two blankets, a sweater, a long-sleeve undershirt, an all-weather jacket and a fishing hat. Tossing the hat onto the front dash, he reached into the glove compartment for a black Swiss knife, then slammed the door and opened the one to the back. Crawling in beside Jack he gave Ellen the "all clear" and she guided the convertible back onto the road. Using the point of the knife to remove the sleeves of the under garment, he tore the body of cloth in one continual strip the way he might have peeled an orange.

"Pull up your shirt, Jack and I'll wrap this around you the best I can."

As Merrick obeyed, Kerr paused a moment to study the naked chest.

"What are you waiting for? I'm cold," Jack complained.

"I was just comparing your body to that which I tried to identify in the morgue."

"There's a cheerful thought. Are you two going to tell me about it?"

Finding nothing on the detective's chest that would have helped him had he remembered it, the attorney did the best he could, winding the strip twice around the ribs. Pulling it as tightly as possible, he affixed the ends with tape, then critically appraised his handiwork.

"I don't know if that will help or not."

"Feels some better," Jack admitted, trying a deep breath. While he flinched from the effort, he seemed to settle onto the back cushions with greater ease. Unscrewing the bottle of aspirin he gulped six down with hot coffee, made a face, then grabbed one of the candy bars.

"A man on the run's best friend," he acknowledged with a toothy grin. "Instant energy." He bit off half the bar and spoke with his mouth full. "A man on the run's second best friend: a bottle of cheap whisky. It not only gives energy but it warms his insides."

"We don't have any whisky. Put on the jacket."

Merrick did so and stuffed his hands in the pockets.

"Do I look like a lawyer?"

"No."

"Oh, well. Too heady a job for me. Whoever heard of speaking French and Latin, anyway? If you tried that on B.B. Bond he'd throw you out of court."

"Bartholomew Bond is a lawyer, too," came the dour retort.

"I rest my case."

After they finished the remainder of the food Ellen had purchased, Hugh consulted the local yellow page he had purloined from the phone book.

"Get off at the next stop," he directed. Turn right at the intersection and slow down."

"What are we looking for?"

"A used car lot."

"Are we going to split up?" Jack asked, taking more interest in the passing landscape.

"No. But we're going to ditch his car. I suspect before very long it and my licence plate are going to be very hot."

"Why, Hugh?" Ellen inquired with trepidation. "What did Wade tell you?"

"He explained why they changed the name of Mr. X to Jack Merrick. Some inspector 'on loan' to the department found Jack's St. Christopher medal and another new man in the lab found my fingerprint on it."

"How is that possible?" she gasped in horror.

"It isn't. Which means it's a plant, and one – probably both - of those officers are lying."

"But how could Price have gotten them into the force so soon?"

"It isn't exactly 'soon.' He's had three months to set this up, remember?"

"I did wonder what he was up to, didn't I?"

"Now we know. Spending a lot of time, energy and money putting people in place."

"But surely we can prove they're phonies –"

"Nothing is 'sure,' Ellen but –"

"Don't say it!"

She did not want to hear him articulate the rest of the phrase *death and taxes*. It would be a bad omen.

"I'm not sure they are phonies. It's easier just to buy the real deal. For a few thousand dollars I'm sure Mr. Price could buy the testimony of several fingerprint experts."

"But he'll have to show the medallion and a photograph of your fingerprint in court."

"I've been fingerprinted more times than I care to remember. All he has to do is pull a copy from the files and say it's the one he took off the medal. As for St. Christopher –" A thought suddenly occurred to him and he looked over his shoulder at Jack. "Do you still have yours, by the way, or did they remember to take it?"

"Someone came in late last night and ripped it off."

"There you go, Ellen. The medal is Jack's. They don't even have to lie about that."

"Which is why someone at the Agency was able to identify it."

"Then why didn't that someone call and tell us what they found?"

"For all I know, Inspector Gray told Wade he had already spoken to me."

Jack kicked the back of the seat in frustration.

"They know better than that. Never trust a cop; especially one you don't know. And speaking of which, Hugh, I've been thinking. Even if you trade in your car for another, once the paperwork goes through to motor vehicles, the cops'll realize what you did."

"That will take a week or more. By that time, I hope we have our problems resolved and can return to Los Angeles."

"But Hugh," Ellen objected. "You'll never get a decent exchange at a used car lot. Those places are scalpers –"

"Can't be helped."

"I see," the detective grinned, "you've learned a lot from representing criminals."

"The clients I represent are not criminals," Kerr retorted in a huff. "They are innocent victims of justice gone awry. If I believe someone is guilty, I won't defend them unless they agree to confess. Then, I'll try and get them whatever breaks they may deserve. But not otherwise. It's not a defense attorney's job to thwart the law." Peering at his two companions, he dryly added, "Present company excepted."

"Glad to know that," Jack sighed. "No one gets as close to skirting the law as you do. I'd hate to think you'd give up on yourself so easily."

"I meant," Hugh began, then stopped as Jack winked at Ellen. "I see. Very funny."

"Is this the place?" Ellen inquired, pointing to a large lot filled with automobiles and decorated with colored buntings strung over the entranceway on a taut wire. "Shall I pull in?"

"Keep going until we're out of sight and then pull over somewhere. You two are getting out. If the police are after us, they're looking for two men and a woman; or, one man and one woman, depending on what they believe. I'll look less suspicious if I'm alone."

The secretary pulled the car into the parking lot of a Mom and Pop eatery and maneuvered toward the back. Leaving the engine running, she and Jack got out. Hugh took her place and offered a curt wave.

"Hopefully, this won't take long."

Without waiting to see them safely into the restaurant, Kerr drove off, slowing only as he pulled into the lot of the used car dealership. He was greeted almost instantly by a salesman.

"Good morning, sir."

"Good morning," Kerr affably returned.

"What can I do for you?" Walking around the expensive black convertible, the man whistled. "Didn't come in to trade this beauty. Looking for a car for the wife?"

Hands in his pockets, Hugh Kerr shrugged.

"As a matter of fact, I did come in to trade it." He lowered his voice conspiratorially. "I'm going through a divorce and the court says I have to give one of my cars to my soon-to-be ex-spouse. I'm keeping the Cadillac for myself and I thought…"

"Say no more," the man agreed with a chuckle. "Been there, done that. You want something a bit less… ostentatious, shall we say?"

"Street-worthy but not flashy," the customer nodded. "Something –"

"Dull. What about a pick-up?"

"Not that boring or it will look as though I'm doing this on purpose. My shyster said to choose something that will make the neighbors believe she got the worst of the settlement. That'll keep away the fortune hunters. And if she wants to trade it in later, she'll have to pony up a small fortune for a red roadster. I'll just walk around and see what you have here."

"Certainly, sir. I'll be in the office if you need any help."

Having worked with the Merrick Detective Agency for the better part of a decade, Hugh Kerr had picked up more than a few tips from Jack and his operatives. The first two tenets they preached were to wear clothing that made them look like an everyday working man and the second was to drive a set of "wheels" that would be difficult to identify.

Crisscrossing several rows, he studied those available. While his preference would have been for an older auto, he couldn't take the chance of buying one that would break down twenty miles from the dealership. That meant a newer model with good tires and few, if any, dents. He considered a late model station wagon but afraid that a potential witness might be more likely to remember its details, he chose a blue, 1953 two-door Chevy sedan.

Deciding that represented vague Americana about as well as anything, he returned to the office and pointed out the car. The salesman flashed him a wide smile.

"She won't appreciate that, for sure. How soon do you want to pick it up?"

"I'd like to exchange it right now, if I can. I'm leaving town on a business trip and won't be back until the first of the week. I'm already cutting my time close because the court date is next Wednesday."

The man stroked his chin. "Your car is worth ten times what that one is and I don't have that much cash money on hand to make a fair swap, even giving myself a decent profit."

"Actually," the prospective divorcee decided, "I'm not as much interested in money as I am in making a point with her. How much money do you keep in your drawer?"

Having already anticipated the buyer's predicament, the salesman promptly offered, "Three hundred dollars."

Kerr whistled at his loss. "Good day for you... Bob," he added, reading the man's nameplate on his desk. "I'll make the trade on one condition. That you hold the paperwork up until Monday. I'll sign my ownership papers over to you now and you give me a bill of sale on the Chevy but don't register the transaction for a few days. That way, it won't look as though I'd thought this through but acted on the spur of the moment."

"For her own best interests," Bob agreed. "Sure, I can do that."

Having kept the registration papers in his pocket, Kerr signed them, then went to empty out his glove compartment and gather the rest of his personal belongings before returning to the office. Bob indicated where he was to sign, paid him $300 in cash and the two men shook hands.

Walking together to Kerr's new old car, Bob absently kicked a tire, then offered a pleasant nod.

"Say, if your ex comes in here looking for a red sports car, how will I recognize her?"

"She'll be the blonde wearing a fur stole and driving a blue Chevy."

They laughed together, Bob tossed himhe keys and Kerr drove away, hoping he had not made too much of an impression on the salesman and that he would hold the registration for several days at least.

Back at the restaurant, he gave a brief honk of the horn. Within minutes Ellen and Jack sauntered out, looking well fed if not any more rested.

"We played tourist," Ellen explained, holding up several fan-folded maps.

"And I took advantage of the hot running water in the men's room to freshen up a bit. Not much I can do about the bruises and cuts on my face but at least I got the blood and grime off. This jacket is ruined," he added, mournfully pointing to a blood stain, "but I brushed it off as best I could."

"I told him I didn't want to be seen in the company of a man fresh from a chain gang."

"She did, too," Jack agreed. "And I can't say I blame her. When the waitress gave me the once over, I whispered that my..." He cleared his throat. "...wife had given me a licking for coming home late from my night out with the boys."

Hugh beamed with pleasure. "So now we have an about-to-be-divorced man, as I presented myself to the used car salesman, a philanderer and a –"

"Bigamist," Ellen supplied. "Since I seem to be 'married' to both of you."

"I'm OK with that if you are, Hugh –"

"Oh, no, Ellen," Kerr reassured her. "The wife I'm ditching is a blonde."

"That probably saved your life."

He grinned and went to smack Jack Merrick when his eye caught a peculiar bulge under the detective's jacket.

"What's that?"

"I pilfered the yellow pages from the phone booth," Jack bragged. "It seemed to cover a pretty wide swath of the state and I thought it might be easier to look places up than try and find a booth that actually has a book in it. Can't tell you how many times I've been in a hurry, only to find the first seven telephone stands I came across devoid of anything but drunks or snarling curs. I've actually taken to carrying the local directories around with me in the car."

"Not a bad idea," Kerr agreed. "Your chariot, Madam," he invited, indicating Ellen drive while he sat beside her.

"Thank you, kind sir."

"I hope I sold the salesman my bill of goods," Kerr informed his companions as they stared at his new acquisition. "Made $300 on top of the exchange. Money that'll come in handy since we don't dare go to a bank."

"I'm proud of you, Hugh," Jack remarked, working his way awkwardly into the back. "This rig is plain, simple and ugly."

"Don't say that, Jack," Ellen protested. "It's a year newer than what I drive."

"Well, you're not a high tony lawyer. This sure is turning out to be an expensive trip for you, Hugh."

"It's only money, Jack. And if it keeps us alive and free, it's worth any price."

"He's only saying that because he's planning on putting this on my bill," the detective groused. "Good luck with that."

"You're the one who got kidnapped," Kerr reminded him.

"Which you still haven't told us about, Jack," Ellen added. The two passengers in the front seat waited for a reply, only to find Jack's answer came in the manner of a low snore.

Ellen drove for several more hours until it became apparent she and Hugh were going to need some serious sleep before going further north. Observing that he had closed his eyes, she gently nudged him with her elbow.

"Why don't you go through Jack's yellow pages and see if there's a motel up ahead? It's after 1:00 o'clock so we won't have to pay extra."

Kerr knuckled his eyes, then accepted the book and began scanning the entries under "Motels."

"Ah. This will do it," he finally decided. "Another twenty miles. The Sunshine Motel. It's off the highway a bit and if we're lucky there may be a drug store and maybe a decent restaurant within walking distance."

They reached their destination and wearily pulled into the parking lot, only to see a "No Vacancy" sign in the window.

"No vacancy?" Jack asked in disbelief. "How in the world could this place be filled up? What are they having – a convention of Martians? I can't think of any other visitors who would flock here."

Ellen pointed to her left at a poster affixed to a telephone pole.

"There's your answer: the good ol' boys are having a cock fight. 'Come one, come all,'" she read. "'Storm Tudor versus Boston John.

Fifty cents entrance fee. Other champion birds on the card and Fighting Birds of all Types for Sale. Refreshments.'"

"You have to be kidding me. Don't we have all the luck? This one-horse town is filled with clod-hoppers."

"Drive around, Ellen. See if we can get a room somewhere else."

A slow, ten minute drive through the main drag took them to the Smiley Face Motel. The sign read "Vacancy." Kerr wearily extracted himself, removed his coat and rolled up his sleeves to more closely resemble the men they had seen loitering on the sidewalks. Walking across the pavement, he pulled open the door to the office and entered. A clerk wearing a banker's visor appraised him with dull curiosity.

"I'd like three rooms, all with a private bath and –"

"Got one single left, mister. Been booked up for weeks. Wouldn't have this one but had a cancellation at the last minute. Fella's bird got its toe caught in the cage on the way down an' now it's too sore for it to fight."

Hugh Kerr pulled a long face.

"I hope it wasn't Lucius, that evil brown bird. I have ten dollars bet on him."

The answer seemed to appease the clerk. He shook his head.

"No, it were Cock 'N Bird."

"Not from Missouree, was it? Missouree has the best birds. I'm from Saint Louie. Joined up with some friends."

"Don't know. You want the one room?"

"Guess I'll have to take it."

Kerr pulled out the wad of $300 and peeled off two fives.

"This do it?"

"Right enough."

"Fine. We've been driving all night and day so we won't need anything else before tomorrow."

Taking the key, he noted the number, then walked around the sidewalk, checking numbers. Once he had located the room that happened to be on the lower level of the two-story lodge, he unlocked the door, made a quick inventory, then returned to the car.

"Follow me."

Ellen parked outside their door and Hugh held the seat back as Jack emerged. Once inside the room, the pair gave him a quizzical stare. He shrugged.

"This is all I could get."

"Which begs the question," Ellen stated with a deadpan monotone, "who gets the bed?"

"It ought to hold two," Jack helpfully suggested. "Heads it's mine, tails it's yours, Hugh. The loser can sleep on two chairs pushed together."

"Wait a minute, boys," Ellen objected. "I may be a 'bigamist,' but this is not my idea of a honeymoon suite. Jack, you take the bed. Your ribs can't hold up suspended between two chairs. Hugh, you can have them and I'll sleep on the floor. And since I'm being so accommodating, I get first dibs on the shower."

The two men exchanged glances.

"Lost opportunity, Hugh."

"I was thinking of peering through the keyhole."

"Too bad for both of you," Ellen informed them, straddling the space between the bedroom and bathroom. "There is no keyhole because there is no lock. I'll just take this," she demonstrated, grabbing one of two straight-back chairs, "and place it against the doorknob. From the inside," she added before they could offer her advice. "Jack, you lie down. Hugh, there's a radio on the nightstand. Why don't you see if you can find any local news?"

"You're pretty good at this 'moll' thing."

"I'm known by the company I keep," she retorted, taking the chair inside and shutting the door.

Hugh waited until Jack settled himself in bed, then padded back to the bathroom and tapped on the door.

"I'm going out to find a drugstore."

"All right," she called over the drone of running water. "Be careful."

He nodded and left the motel room. Walking to the Rexall he had seen on the way through town, he purchased a safety razor and blades, soap, shampoo and deodorant, toothpaste, three toothbrushes, a comb and a pack of playing cards. Bringing the purchases to the counter, Hugh reached into his pocket for some money when his eye caught a stack of newspapers. Casually picking one up, he scanned the folded half then flipped it over. His photograph was prominently positioned in the lower left-hand corner of the front page. Above it read, "Prominent Los Angeles Attorney Sought for Questioning in Horrific Murder Investigation."

Making a wry face, he tucked it under his arm, casually noting, "Add this to my tab."

By the time he returned to the motel Ellen had replaced the chair in the main room and was sitting on it, brushing her hair. Ignoring the newspaper he had transferred to his pocket, she eagerly inspected his purchases, selected several items and returned into the bathroom. Five minutes later she re-emerged looking more like her old self.

"I'm starting to feel human again."

"Did you leave any hot water for me?"

"Not intentionally." She nodded toward the sleeping form of Jack Merrick. "He's going to need more medical attention that we can give him. I'm not so sure about the punctured lung; he sounds wheezy to me."

"I thought so, too. In the morning we'll drive to San Francisco. I know several doctors there who run a private clinic. They can X-Ray him and administer whatever treatment he needs."

"What if they suggest hospitalization?"

"That's up to Jack, of course, but I wouldn't recommend it. I don't want to let him out of our sight." Sighing, he pulled up the other chair and sat beside her. "For Jack's sake as well as our own. He is, after all, the only proof we have that we didn't murder and dismember him."

Ellen continued brushing her hair to avoid meeting his eyes. Without verbalizing her concern over what the paper might contain, she asked, instead, "How much trouble are we really in? Level with me. I can take it."

"After what we've been through together these last few days, I'd say you can take anything, Miss Ellen Thorne. I should have told you before how impressed I am. You can think on your feet, you're cool under fire and your loyalty is beyond compare."

Overwhelmed by his compliments, she blushed and tried to cover up her discomfiture by asking, "You're just finding this out?"

"No. I'm just telling you now what I should have said years ago. It's just that... I'm not used to putting my appreciation or my feelings into words."

"I never expected you to."

"That makes you even more special." He rapped his fingers on his knee before continuing. "To answer your question, lest you think I was trying to avoid doing so, I really don't know how much trouble we're in – assuming you mean from the police." She nodded. "Obviously, we can prove Jack is alive. As for attaching us to the murder of Mr. X in the morgue, I don't believe Wade or Bond would consider bringing charges unless they had overwhelming evidence. As strange as it may seem to outsiders, I consider both of them my friends. And I think the feeling is mutual. All of us – you and me and Jack and Wade and Bart are on the side of right. We may not always see justice in the same light, but ultimately the end justifies the means. Therefore, they're not going to jump to conclusions."

Nervously getting to his feet, Kerr began to pace in a rhythm Ellen knew so well. Without intention, his actions belied his brave words.

"You suggested Price may have placed someone at the scene with a camera. It's possible; maybe even likely. But in any event, the police will match the tire impressions to my car –"

"The one you just traded in. That, in itself, is suspicious."

He grunted in annoyance.

"So it is. The police will eventually recover it. Damn!" he snarled. "I should have bought new tires before I traded it in. Well, never mind. What's done is done."

"By itself, that evidence doesn't actually prove any more than that we were at the scene," she reasoned, putting the brush in her purse. "After the fact." Having offered him time to bring the subject up, she asked, "What does the newspaper say?"

Hugh grimaced and retrieved it from his pocket. She took it and gave the photo a critical inspection.

"I've seen better," she finally decided. "You really must update your portfolio." Without reading it, Ellen handed it back. "Give me the lowdown. I don't think I have the stomach to read it."

"The reporter gave some facts about the body in the morgue and the supposition that it might be Jack. He connected Jack to me as someone I routinely employ and mentioned the rumor that 'undisclosed evidence' placed you and me at the scene. An unidentified source at the D.A.'s office mentioned the old chestnut about how a murderer – or murderers - always returns to the scene of the crime."

"Pretty careless of a criminal defense attorney and his secretary to clean up a murder site and leave such obvious clues behind."

Without losing stride, Kerr dug his hands into his pockets.

"All right: they can say we went back to recover Jack's medal." His face twitched and his eyes bore holes into the carpet. "And obviously didn't find it because 'Inspector Gray' had already picked it up. With my thumb print on it. That, I admit, is bad. I should have called Wade the moment we left. Whatever my reasons for not doing so, they won't sound good in court. Damn me, anyway, for always trying to solve things by myself."

"You weren't alone," she reminded him. "I was right there alongside you."

"But I took the responsibility. I wanted to play –"

"No, Hugh. You did not want to 'play' the hero. Time was of the essence and I thought at the time – and still think so – that if we had involved the police, Jack would never have gotten out of that house alive. I don't have any regrets and I don't want you to have any, either. We did what had to be done. And that doesn't change the fact you were in San Francisco taking a deposition when Mr. X was murdered."

"I thought of that but coroner's reports are always vague. I have no doubt he offered a wide latitude for the time of death. With several hours leeway, I – or you and I – could have killed and hacked him to pieces, dumped the body elsewhere, cleaned ourselves up and I still could have driven to the airport in time to catch my plane. In fact," he growled, "it could look as though we have planned the entire trip as an alibi. And since we were in such a hurry, that explains why we had to go back and straighten things out."

"I didn't go to San Francisco with you. Why couldn't I have gone back there alone?"

He gave her a fish-eyed stare.

"You're a woman."

"You mean I'm squeamish about blood after I just decapitated someone? That doesn't wash," she added, letting the pun stand. "So why did I stay behind?"

"Because you weren't needed at the deposition."

"That's the *real* reason. Oh, Hugh, if I had just killed someone and needed an alibi, wild horses couldn't have prevented me from going with you. After all, my ticket had already been purchased. If I wasn't needed at the lawyer's office, I could just as easily have gone shopping or sightseeing." She snapped her fingers. "And if I hadn't been so annoyed, that's exactly what I would have done. But that San Francisco attorney made it seem as though I were... superfluous. And that changed my mind."

Ellen got up and crossed to the bed. Gently rearranging the blanket around Jack's shoulders, she turned back to Kerr, eyes dark with anger. "If I had gone with you that would have messed up their timetable. We were planning on going the day ahead, having a sumptuous dinner, lingering over dessert and crème de menthe , staying the night in a first class hotel –"

"In separate rooms?" he interrupted.

Spinning her head around, she caught his eye before he managed to cover the sparkle.

"No, Counselor. We would *not* have eaten dinner in separate rooms. That would have been silly. It would have compelled me to pay for my own meal and that wouldn't have been easy on a working girl's salary."

She correctly interpreted his laugh to mean she had made a good point.

"I hadn't thought about that. Those were our plans, weren't they? Take the deposition the next morning and then return to L.A. on the commuter flight. Since you weren't going, I changed my ticket and ended up flying out that morning instead of the afternoon before."

She nodded in agreement.

"If we had been gone the entire 24 hours before the murder Price couldn't have pinned it on us. So he had to improvise to make his schedule work."

"Which means we'll have to get Jack – he better hurry up and get better – to investigate that San Francisco attorney. He's either involved or was compelled to insist on using his own secretary."

"Here I am on my death bed and you're still giving me assignments." Hugh and Ellen turned to their companion, who had managed to prop himself up on the pillows. "What is it this time?"

"Jack, I'm sorry we woke you up," she began but he waved down the apology.

"I'm in too much pain to do more than drift off for a few minutes. Besides, I want to hear what you two are discussing. And why are we headed north instead of back home?"

"Because the three of us are in serious trouble," Hugh bluntly admitted.

"From the police?"

"Yes. But they aren't likely to shoot first and ask questions later. Carey Price is. I never gave his original threats much credence because I supposed he'd be locked away a long time. Prison has a way of changing a man, tempering the threats he made in anger. In this instance I was wrong. Time made him worse, not better: his insane murder of 'Mr. X' proves that." He made a fist and as quickly released his tensed fingers, collapsing onto the chair as the physical and mental stress finally wore down his reserve strength. "He made one mistake by letting you slip through his fingers. We can't count on him making another. My assumption is he'll come after the three of us with guns blazing."

"Or," Ellen added, not entirely convinced cold-blooded murder was Price's only *modus operandi,* "he has something even more diabolical in mind."

Realizing that neither scenario bode well for their future, Jack kicked his foot in worried frustration.

"So you think we're more vulnerable in Los Angeles?"

"Of course we are. None of us can go home, so where do we stay? At a hotel? Even under assumed identities we won't be that difficult to find. Not by a credible detective agency. Local men know all the haunts and they have hundreds of contacts. Find Hugh Kerr and Ellen Thorne and Jack Merrick. We've had our pictures in the paper often enough that clerks or bell boys or taxi drivers or even hotel patrons might recognize one or all of us. And then we're shot or poisoned or murdered in any number of unpleasant ways."

"Every way to die is unpleasant," Jack clarified. "But what about police protection?"

"We could sit in jail until our legal troubles were cleared up," Hugh volunteered. "*If* we can prove ourselves innocent. That's not going to be easy. That damned thumb print –"

"Planted evidence," Ellen hissed in anger.

"But we can only establish that if we prove Gray and that lab man –" He fumbled for the name before remembering it. "- Sweet - were on Price's payroll. I don't imagine that's going to be easy." He despairingly shook his head. "Now, *that's* police work. And even if we got Bond to buy that theory and asked to be placed in protective custody, there's no reason to believe Price hasn't bribed half a dozen cops. Two or three get together, say we tried to escape and shoot us in self-defense. And then, of course, there's my personal favorite worst-case outcome: we're tried for the murder of Mr. X. Inspector Gray will come up with some far-fetched motive and involve you, too, Jack – we're convicted on the damning evidence of tire tracks and fingerprints – and sentenced to the gas chamber."

"Do we get to go side side-by-side or are we taken individually in alphabetical order?" Ellen quipped with false bravado.

"Cut it out, Starlet," Jack groaned. "I'm sick enough as it is."

"That's because you're an 'M' and you're in the middle. 'K' for Kerr comes first. I'm last. How lovely for me."

"They won't execute a woman," Jack snapped.

"Oh, yes, they will. I'll demand it. If you think I want to rot in a prison cell knowing you two are dead –"

"Stop it!" Hugh fairly screamed. "Enough! We're playing right into Price's hands. We're quibbling among ourselves. We can't do that. Not even in grim humor," he added as an appeasement.

"OK, OK," Jack grumbled, fumbling around in bed. "Which reminds me – Hugh, got a cigarette? Those bastards took everything I had out of my pockets."

"You're lucky you have pockets at all," Ellen pointed out, apologetically modulating her voice into a friendlier tone.

"What does that mean?"

"The body in the morgue was buck naked. The police recovered your clothing and personnel effects nearby so those can't be your clothes."

With a grunt of surprise, Jack examined his wardrobe.

"Holy smokes, Ellen, you're right. In all the excitement I never realized it. These aren't my clothes. Not a bad fit, but not mine. Just as well – I bled all over them. Say," he perked up as Hugh lit a cigarette and handed it to him. "Can I put a new suit on my expense account?"

"You weren't working for me at the time, were you?"

"Geez, now he gets cheap on me."

Jack dropped onto the pillow, took a deep drag on the cigarette and then ground it out on the cheap tin ashtray resting on the lamp-stand. "Good night, you two. Work out the sleeping arrangements any way you want. This bed is big enough for three if we all squeeze together. It's gotta beat sleeping on the floor."

Hugh headed for the bathroom.

"Ellen, you can do whatever you want. I'm going to take a shower." He paused at the door and forced a grin. "Shall I take the chair in with me and prop it up against the knob for privacy?"

"Yes," she decided. "You better."

He believed her.

Chapter 8

By the time Hugh came out of the shower, two things struck him as immediately obvious: Ellen was neither asleep on the straight-back chairs nor was she curled up in a blanket on the floor. She was, he discovered without much effort, catching her beauty rest in the bed, a pillow judiciously positioned between her and the slumbering Jack Merrick.

His first thought was to smile at the two innocent countenances. His second, ramrodding in on the other, was.... Face furiously turning red to the tips of his ears, he turned his back on the pair and walked to the window. Withdrawing the curtain no further than half an inch, he pretended to scan the parking lot.

Am I jealous? he demanded of himself in actual surprise. The answer should have come as no surprise.

Hell, yes, I'm jealous!

While his eagle eyes sought license plates and memorized them for future reference, this required no cognitive direction. The task was performed on a subliminal level and only as an excuse not to concentrate on his raging emotions.

The high-priced criminal attorney did not fool himself although he would have sworn otherwise.

I should have made Jack go into the shower before me. That way...
"California TXR 467."
That way, Ellen and I could have squeezed in bed together...
"California, SAJ 360."
... leaving enough room for Jack to get in my side when he was dry.
"Utah, PYI 784."
Leaving me in the middle and Ellen on the other side. Would she have agreed to that?
"Arizona, silver pick-up with a spare thrown in the back. And an empty chicken cage."
Why not? His leg shook. We're too tired to contemplate...
"California, GHS 928."
In bed with Ellen. She and I, with Jack in the shower. What would we do? Would I have kissed her? I've kissed her before. Passionately. He wiped away a roll of sweat trickling down his neck. *Well, what's wrong with that? We've worked together for five years. We're friends.*
"South Dakota, something, something B 632."

All right, we're more than friends. More than friends but less than... lovers. Do I love her? Does Ellen love me? Could I really be jealous enough of Jack to shoot him? How far-fetched was Price's scheme, anyway?

"New York, HLK 229. That's a long way to come to bet on a chicken."

"Rooster."

He spun around as if he had actually heard the discharge of a hand gun. Ellen met his open-mouthed gaze with a tender smile.

"What?"

"They're fighting cocks – the male of the species. Not chickens."

"I was speaking figuratively."

He had not realized he had been articulating aloud.

"I know." She knew more than she said and he knew she knew. "A dangerous habit, carrying on a one-sided conversation."

"But I wasn't answering myself. Otherwise, the police psychiatrist would diagnose me as crazy and put me in a cell next to Carey Price."

"He's out, remember? And no, you weren't answering yourself. Your real thoughts were miles away."

Miles, measured in feet.

"I wasn't speaking those out loud, I hope."

"I heard them clear enough."

"Then what's the answer?" he challenged, calling her bluff.

Her smile softened, almost to the point of sadness.

"To which one?"

"All of them."

"You know, Hugh," she began, taking his hand and joining him at the window. He dropped the curtain back and cradled his free hand on top of hers. "When I was a little girl my brothers and I had a Ouija board. When we thought our parents were asleep we put a blanket by the door to block out the light and took it out. We set it up on Tom's bed and then Tom and Walter and I sat cross-legged, Indian-style, around it. We each put a finger on the director, or pointer, or whatever you call it, and asked questions."

"They have to be yes or no questions, don't they?"

"That's correct."

They leaned together against the wall, shoulders touching.

"My brothers asked all the usual questions: will I be an engineer when I grow up? Will I be rich? Does this girl like me? Should I use my savings to buy that used sports car Mr. Henning is selling?"

"What did you ask?"

Ellen's hand tightened around his.

"I didn't ask it anything."

"Nothing?" He sounded surprised. "Because you didn't believe in Ouija boards?"

Her face assumed a thoughtful expression.

"I don't know whether I believed in it or not. What I didn't want to know was the future. I guess I wanted to be surprised by it. Or, rather, I wanted to make my own future. I didn't want to be influenced; I didn't want the spirit world to tell me if I was going to grow up to be rich and famous, or if some boy liked me or not. I wanted to read it in his eyes."

Hugh drew his face closer to hers and their gaze locked.

"What do these eyes tell you?"

In a second their lips met and they kissed, long and intensely. Still holding one hand in hers, Hugh wrapped his other around Ellen's back, pulling her closer. Their kiss became more passionate, more urgent. Without breaking contact, they embraced, arms encircling one another's backs. Only the necessity for air forced them apart. When Ellen spoke, she breathed into his mouth.

"There you have it, Hugh Kerr. I have answered your question."

"Which one?"

"All of them, sir."

This time he grinned and held her close, running his fingers through her dark, shiny hair.

"Does this mean I don't have to shoot Jack?"

"Yes," she whispered into his ear. "But I hope you don't blame me if I think about it once in a while and treasure the thought."

"Ellen, I will never blame you for anything."

"That, Hugh, is a promise I won't hold you to."

Breaking the embrace, she performed an exaggerated yawn.

"You and I really have to get some sleep."

"Sleep?"

She ignored the suggestion in his voice.

"The Sand Man is beating both our eyelids shut. We have a long drive ahead of us in the morning."

"Damnation!"

"We're too close to that with the police and Price's men on our heels. Think of something else to say."

"Good night, Ellen."

And thank you for answering my questions.

"Good night, Hugh."

You're welcome.

Jack Merrick was the first to wake. Groaning in pain as he tried to lift himself up by his elbows, his mind filled with momentary panic when he discovered himself pinned to the bed. As his mind reverted to the last time he had been in such a predicament, its recent memory brought all the agony and sensations of terror to the forefront. Kicking violently with his foot to free it from its restraints, Jack had the satisfaction of hearing a cry of surprise.

"Son of a bitch!" Feeling movement to his right, he pushed his arm out, hoping to inflict more damage. "What the hell are you doing?"

Another voice broke into his hazy consciousness.

"Jack! Jack, it's all right. You're with friends."

"Don't try that old trick on me," he warned, turning shuddered eyes toward the new speaker.

"Jack, it's Ellen. Hugh is on your other side. You're safe."

"Safe?" he yelled, and then, softer, as his fevered brain replayed the sentences, "Ellen?"

"Yes, Jack. It's Ellen. I'm right here."

"What the hell are you doing in my nightmare?"

"You're not having a nightmare, Jack. You're wide awake."

"Then why can't I see anything?"

"Because your eyes are shut." Pressing his hand, she ordered, "Open your eyes, Jack."

He hesitated, then peered out at her from beneath half-closed lids.

"Sweet Jesus," he intoned with reverence. "I thought I was having a nightmare and now I find I've woken up to one. What the hell are you and I doing in bed together? Did we go on a bender and get hitched?"

"If you did, then I went along for the ride," Hugh pleasantly observed, swinging his legs over the side of the bed.

"Oh, no! Are you going to kill me?"

"A question – or rather the probability of one – I was pondering as I fell asleep," Kerr agreed.

"What did you conclude?" Jack demanded, still not fully awake and alert.

"I didn't."

The detective sunk back on the pillows, moaning aloud.

"Where am I – where are we?" he paraphrased, "And why do I hurt? I feel as if I'd been run over by a Mack truck. Did you do this to me?" he asked suspiciously.

"No. As a matter of fact, Ellen and I were hoping you'd tell us. As best we can determine, you were lured out to Malibu and assaulted."

"Yeah. Now it's coming back." His leg shook nervously and Ellen helped him rearrange the pillow. "That's right. I got a phone call from some guy who wanted to hire me. He offered a big retainer. I wanted him to meet me at the office, but he was adamant. Couldn't go there. Was afraid of being seen. He said he was out at some property of his where we could talk without any chance of being overheard. I'll say." His eyes fluttered shut as the memory weighed them down. "I bet I screamed loud enough to wake the dead."

"What happened?"

"First, I broke my own cardinal rule of never going off to some strange location without backup, or at least telling someone where I was going. The guy sounded so insistent and so sincere, I took him on face value. He took me for a sucker and you know who won that bet."

"What did he say he wanted?"

"A business partner of his shadowed. Real urgent. Thought the guy had embezzled some money and was making a break for it. No time to waste."

"Did he give you a name?"

"Rudolph K. Abernathy. Does it mean anything to you?"

"No. It was obviously a pseudonym."

"Hindsight is 20-20," Jack sighed. "So he starts rambling off these directions and I said, 'Wait a minute, repeat that.' So he insists, 'Write them down, they're complicated and I don't want you getting lost.' I was a little hot under the collar at that point, but I wrote them down, stuck them in my pocket and hurried out. I drove like hell getting out there and I wasn't too careful when I finally located the spot. I got out of the car, saw a man standing in the open, and went up to meet him. Didn't see his thugs hiding behind some trees. As soon as my back was turned they jumped me."

"How many were there?"

"Three – with Abernathy – or Price, as it turned out – that made three. I never had a chance."

"What happened?"

Jack looked from Ellen to Hugh, appealing with his eyes.

"It isn't very pretty."

Ellen answered for herself. "Go ahead, Jack. We already know the outcome; we just need to know how it got to that point from your perspective."

"All right." He sounded less than convinced. "Once they had me nearly out for the count, the first man I saw pulled my head back and shoved his face in mine. By the looks of him he was half mad. Mad," he clarified, "as in nutzoid. He asked if I had any idea who he was. I said no and he slapped me – jarred every tooth in my head."

Gently rubbing his jaw, Jack ruefully tested the stability of his teeth. "He said, 'My name is Carey Price. Does that mean anything to you?' and I said, 'Oh, yeah. You're the guy with the two gorillas.' Guess he didn't like my answer because he put a knee in my crotch. I can't say I appreciated it but it did give me the satisfaction of puking all over him." Jack whistled. "I'm not sure which of us was more T'd off."

"I'm sorry, Jack," Kerr apologized but the detective shook his head.

"I'm not finished, yet. He started doing some sort of a war dance – arms waving and feet jerking like he'd landed barefoot on hot cement. 'Hugh Kerr took away five years of my life and I swore revenge.' What could I say, but, 'You got the wrong guy, bubba. My name is Jack Merrick.'"

"You mean, he thought you were Hugh?" Ellen asked in incongruity.

"No. He knew who I was all right. 'You work for that shyster, and I'm gonna rip his heart out,' he said. So I kicked him where the sun don't shine and he set his gorillas on me again until I was pretty close to wishing I was dead. I figured he was gonna kill me anyway, so I said, 'I've had worse than this from wizened old men wearing Japanese uniforms,' and I think they would have finished me off right then and there, but Big Britches stopped them. His thugs tied me to a tree and they went and got this poor fellow –"

Kerr quickly interjected, "What did he look like?"

"My size and shape. I think he must have been drugged because when they brought him out from a car, he seemed pretty dazed. Just as well." Merrick closed his eyes to regain his composure before continuing. "Before either he or I knew what was coming, one of the men came at him from behind with a sickle or a scythe and lopped his head off." He shook and wrapped his arms around his chest. "Only it wasn't quite as easy as that. It took two or three hacks. It was the most brutal thing I had ever seen. Right out of a war movie but it was real. Blood spurting everywhere, the body twitching on the ground, the head rolled off a few feet."

"You didn't recognize him?"

"I didn't have much time to ID him. Don't think I ever saw him before. At the time, all I could think was that this Price guy was enacting a scene he really wanted to play on you."

"He had something else in store for me. Then what happened?"

"The men took out hacksaws and severed the poor sod's hands off. Then they ripped off his shoes and socks and burned the bottoms of his feet. Sure glad he was long dead by that time because I've heard of some fellas living through that kind of torture." Jack's voice choked and he dropped his head in shame. "Hugh, if I had any idea they were going to murder him, I would have tried harder to stop them but before I put two and two together, it was too late."

Hugh sat on the bed and put his arms around his friend. "It's all right, Jack. There's nothing you could have done to prevent it."

"What the hell was it all about?"

"That victim – whoever he was – was selected purposely to look like you. He was beheaded and his hands removed to prevent identification. Price must have exchanged his clothes with yours and dumped the body where it would be found fairly quickly. When it was, your personal possessions were located nearby."

"You mean… they wanted it to look like I was the dead guy?"

"That's right. I was in San Francisco so Wade called Ellen to identify you…"

His voice dropped off and she picked up the thread.

"But I couldn't face it. So when Hugh returned, he went to the morgue."

"Christ; that must have been pleasant."

"It wasn't. It was one of the hardest things I have ever been called upon to do. Price told you he wanted to rip my heart out and he did."

"I don't get it. Why didn't he just kill me, then? What was all this murderous play acting for?"

"I suppose so he could leave just enough doubt –"

"Or hope," Ellen added.

"So that he could do it again."

"And this time, kill you for real, so we would have to go through losing you all over again."

"And then what?"

"Either frame me for one or both murders or ruin my reputation so I would never be able to practice law again. You know, once the public takes it into their heads that I'm a murderer, even if I'm acquitted, they'll never seek out my services as an attorney."

"Jeez, Hugh, I'm sorry."

"Nothing for you to be sorry about. You, too, were an innocent victim."

Merrick rested his head against his friend's shoulder.

"First time I've ever been accused of that."

Ellen sat next to him and put a hand on his arm.

"We're just glad you're all right, Jack. And we found that clue you left."

His eyes brightened.

"The gas receipt? You figured out what I was trying to get across?"

"*Price.*"

"My God, you're good. I sure didn't have much hope but it was all I could think of."

"Pretty darned clever, these Three Musketeers," Ellen decided.

"But how did you ever find that canyon location?"

"You wrote the directions down on the tablet by your phone. We used the old standby of rubbing a graphite pencil over the blank page to bring out your handwriting."

"Wow!" Breathing through his lopsided nose, he paused, then asked, "You interpreted my hieroglyphics?"

"That was the easy part."

"But why didn't Price's ruse work? I'm not even sure *I* could have identified a torso as my own. Didn't you think… that I was dead?"

This time it was Kerr's turn to hang his head.

"I… wasn't sure," he admitted in a hushed voice. "It was Ellen who was so positive it wasn't you."

Merrick's eyes snaked over to the woman at his side.

"How did you know? Without a face or fingerprints…?"

"Small balls."

When the significance of her tawdry observation sunk in, Jack blushed like a school boy.

"Now I wish I was dead!"

"That was supposed to be a compliment," Ellen reminded him, playfully putting her hand on his tussled hair.

"I got that…. But it's a mixed bag." The inadvertent double entendre deepened his reddened face. "OK, I'm ready to ditch this place and hit the road."

"Not before you take a shower," Kerr warned. "You've got to get cleaned up and I've got to buy you a more presentable wardrobe. We've gotten away with that bloodied jacket and trousers long enough. It wouldn't do to be stopped by some police officer inquiring what barroom you tore up and whose face you blackened."

"Wish there was a tub," Jack sighed. "I'm not sure how long I can stand."

"I'll stand outside the stall if you want."

"Geez, and have you report to Ellen on the size of my… anatomy? No, thanks. I think I'll be OK. But if I get woozy, I'll holler."

Rolling off the edge of the bed, Jack steadied himself, took in several shallow breaths and then shuffled into the coffin-sized bathroom. Ellen glanced worriedly at Hugh.

"Maybe you should stay with him. He doesn't look very steady."

Hugh stared wistfully at the bed and shrugged.

"I had other things in mind."

So did I.

Her verbal answer was longer in coming.

"Yes, well…"

"This isn't the place or the time," he finished for her with a grin that was meant to dispel their rising passions. She grinned back.

"We'll leave it at that. You move the chair over by the door and listen. If he starts to groan or cry out, you can get inside in a second. I'll go shopping. There has to be a men's clothier in town; I'll bring back a change of clothes for Jack. Do you want me to buy anything for you?"

Kerr reached into his wallet and took out five twenty dollar bills.

"We have the three hundred dollars I got for the car plus whatever I had in my wallet. That should carry us for a while. Buy what you have to; better get some luggage, too, so we don't look like vagabonds. And get whatever you need for yourself. And keep the change," he added. "If, for any reason we get separated, I don't want you to be short on money."

"I learned a long time ago always to carry money with me," she said, putting the cash in her purse. "Being your private secretary and Gal Friday, I never know when I'll find myself taking a taxi to the moon or bribing a public official."

He raised an eyebrow in feigned surprise.

"Really? Have I ever asked you to do anything as extreme as that?"

"Nooo," Ellen drawled. "Our adventures of the past seventy-two hours have only included a visit to the morgue, breaking and entering, inspection of a murder scene, the break-out of a hostage and flight to avoid prosecution. Just another day at the office."

"Fairly routine," he agreed.

Ellen crossed to him, kissed him lightly on the forehead and slipped outside, leaving Hugh feeling desperately lonely and somehow vulnerable, two emotions that were nearly as foreign to him as losing an important court case.

In order to stop his leg from shaking in agitation, he retrieved the pack of playing cards he had bought at the emporium and rearranged the room so that he could sit by the bathroom door and deal out the cards on the cheap, three-drawer dresser. After riffling them several times, he commenced playing solitaire. So engrossed was he in the game that he did not notice a towel-draped Jack Merrick standing behind him.

"That's called cheating, you know."

Kerr looked up, more surprised at the comment than the fact Jack had come out of the bathroom without his noticing.

"What is?"

"You had two jacks showing and peeked under each one before determining your move."

"Why is that cheating? I'm just trying to get an edge."

"Solitaire is not legal courtroom wrangling, Hugh. You're supposed to play by the rules."

"What rules? Who made them up?"

Taken aback by the other's vehement argument, Jack arched his head back.

"I don't know who made them up; whoever created the game, I suppose. Way back when."

"Why do I have to follow them?" Kerr demanded, dealing out three cards and placing a black king over a red queen. After dealing three more and seeing a second black king appear on top, he lifted the card to see an ace beneath. Taking back the previous hand, he bypassed the first king and played the second, promptly placing the ace above the seven piles in play.

"You have to follow them so everyone who plays the game has the same advantages and disadvantages; so all players are on an even playing field."

"I don't believe in that. I play to win."

"Tell that to the bouncers in Las Vegas and see how far it gets you." Hugh's eyes twinkled.

"Where will it get me?"

"In an alley with two broken legs – if you're lucky."

"I'm not playing in Las Vegas; at the moment, I'm playing in a flea trap motel in California."

"So you're playing to please yourself? Altering the odds just so you can win? What good is that?"

"I find it satisfying – when I win, that is. I don't always win."

Jack leaned against the wall, watched him deal another three cards, then began drying his hair.

"It seems to me that if you're going to cheat, you ought to win every game."

"It's not cheating. I'm outmaneuvering my opponent."

"Hugh, you're playing by yourself. Solitaire. Get it? Alone."

"I'm playing against the person who made up the rules so that the game is almost impossible to win on a consistent basis. He – or she – stacked the odds against me. I'm just creating that 'level playing field' you mentioned."

The door opened and both men looked quickly to appraise the intruder. Seeing it was no one more dangerous than Ellen, the lawyer went back to his game.

"Ellen," Jack acknowledged by way of greeting. "Hugh's cheating at solitaire."

Shocked to see the deep purple bruises and fresh wounds on his bare chest and arms, she caught her breath before asking, "Is he winning?"

Jack examined the money cards stacked on the aces and nodded.

"Looks like it. He's up to $55 profit this hand and he isn't through yet."

"That's good."

She deposited a number of parcels and boxes on the bed and began unwrapping them.

"What do you mean, 'that's good'? You know he cheats at cards?"

"He isn't cheating, he's amending –"

"– the mistakes of fortune. Yeah, yeah, I get it. Does that mean you approve?"

"Come see what I have bought. You, too, Mr. Kerr."

"I'm not through, yet."

"You're through."

"Yes, ma'am."

He scooped up the cards, replaced them in the pack and joined Jack at the bedside. Ellen rapidly began distributing articles of clothing.

"Underwear, socks, trousers, shirts – I bought you each a white business shirt and a casual sport shirt, have your pick." She tossed a linen clothing bag out for their perusal. "Put your dirty clothes in here; if we stay on the lam long enough, we'll have to find a Laundromat."

"What did you buy for yourself?" Kerr inquired, attempting to peek into the one unopened bag. Ellen snatched it away before his curious fingers could widen the top.

"Never you mind. And a gentleman knows better than to ask."

Taking his new possessions with him, Jack retreated toward the bathroom.

"A man who cheats at cards is no gentleman."

Hugh winked at Ellen as the door slammed shut.

"Since Mr. Merrick, Esquire, has commandeered the only place of privacy, what do you say we each turn our backs and change clothes?"

She raised her own eyebrow in response.

"To quote the illustrious Jack Merrick, Esquire, a man who cheats at cards is no gentleman. I therefore demurely refuse your offer."

Gathering in his own belongings, Mr. Kerr sat on the edge of the bed and pouted. He did not have long to console himself as Jack popped out of the bathroom, jauntily attired in his new wardrobe.

"It's not exactly Sax Fifth Avenue but a perfect fit. Say, how did you guess my size?"

Kerr held up his hand in warning, quickly pleading, "Don't ask," but Ellen was faster.

"From the critical appraisal of a corpse."

Jack groaned and the lawyer hurried off into the lavatory. From behind the closed door he called, "Did you buy pajamas?"

"I did not. Which means," she hastened to add, "the next motel we stop at had better have three rooms."

"Pretty light-hearted banter from someone on the run."

"Oh, Jack and I aren't worried. We figure a man who cheats at cards has any number of tricks up his sleeve."

Hugh Kerr's comment was to flush the toilet.

Chapter 9

As they reached the environs of San Francisco, Kerr diverted into the area known as Chinatown, drove around until he found a shop displaying a blue and white telephone sign and hastily double-parked.

"Be right back. Ellen, slide over to the driver's side in case a meter maid walks by. If you have to, drive around the corner and come back. I should only be a minute."

Hurrying inside, he used the pay phone to call a private physician of his acquaintance. Explaining the need for secrecy as well as urgency, the doctor agreed to see Jack at his private clinic within the next half hour. Once back in the car, Hugh shifted into gear and carefully maneuvered the narrow side streets until finally stopping outside a newly refurbished building bearing the sign, "Free Clinic. Walk-Ins Welcome. No One Turned Away" in both English and Chinese.

"You go in by yourself, Jack," he informed the detective. "I don't want to go with you in case one of Dr. Wong's staff recognizes me."

"What he means," Ellen explained, "is that he's one of the largest donators to Dr. Wong's clinic and his photograph probably hangs on the wall."

"Oh. I get it. Like one of those Veterans' Hospitals where the picture of the President is prominently displayed by the main entrance."

"Something like that," Ellen acknowledged with a smile. Kerr grunted in disapproval.

"How will I get in touch with you?"

"We'll take a room – three rooms," Kerr amended, "probably get a bite to eat and be back here in an hour. Here," he added as an afterthought. "Take twenty dollars. Leave ten and keep ten for yourself. If we're not back when you get out, buy something 'touristy' and sit on the bus bench over there. Try and look inconspicuous."

"Inconspicuous is my middle name. See you."

Hugh waited until Jack disappeared inside, then pulled out into traffic.

"Look for another pay phone. I'll call Los Angeles and see if I can get Lieutenant Wade on the phone."

Ellen spotted an empty booth on a side street directly in front of a green grocer. Kerr maneuvered the car into an empty parking spot and dashed out. He was back in thirty seconds.

"Got any change?"

She dug into her purse, opened the coin compartment and emptied it into his hand. He nodded thanks and returned to the booth, this time closing the door to be sure no one overheard his conversation. The phone at the precinct rang twice before it was answered. This time when he asked for the officer he was put directly through.

"Wade speaking."

"It's Hugh Kerr."

After a moment to absorb the shock, Wade spoke quickly.

"Kerr? Where the devil are you?"

"I prefer not to say."

"What does that mean? You know we're looking for you. Come in and –"

"Listen. Im pressed for time." He checked the second hand on his wrist watch and kept an eye on it as he talked. "I'm afraid this call is being traced."

"The hell you say –"

"Never mind. I'm calling to reconfirm my previous statement: I have Jack Merrick with me. Ellen and I rescued him from a cabin up in the hills owned by a man named Carey Price."

"Alive? Put him on the phone!"

"I can't. He's being checked out by a doctor. He was pretty badly injured."

"Kerr, this better not be one of your tricks –"

"You know it isn't."

"Where-are-you?"

"Hiding out. We left the city for safety's sake."

"We? You mean you and Jack Merrick? And I suppose Miss Thorne is with you, too."

"Yes."

Wade modulated his voice, instilling in it a tone of fatherly concern.

"Hugh, listen to me. There are all sorts of accusations flying around here. We got a tip that you and Ellen were seen at the scene of a murder. Bond wants to put out an APB on you. I've been trying to delay on that, but eventually I'm going to have to act. Real soon," he underscored.

"Please. Hold off as long as you can. I can't afford to have the state police looking for me as well as Carey Price and his thugs."

"Who the devil is Carey Price?"

"An ex-con who's behind this whole damned scheme. Five years ago he was sent up for embezzlement; he blamed me and swore vengeance. He's been out about three months. He kidnapped Jack and then had another man killed to make it look as though the body belonged to Merrick. That's the body in the morgue."

"Who is it, really?"

"I don't know. Ellen and I were set up. We traced Jack to an out-of-the-way place on Old Rattan Highway; it's off 101 in Malibu. That's where Mr. X was killed. Whoever tipped you off about us being at the scene is likely on Price's payroll. I'd keep a very steady eye on him because you may be able to shake him down."

"Don't tell me what to do."

"All right, I'm sorry," he said and meant it. "After we left there we drove up into the mountains where Price was hiding."

"How the hell did you find that out?"

"The Merrick Detective Agency got it from a con who Price had roughed up. Talk to Bill Daly. He'll confirm the details. We found Jack there and managed to get him out. Then we started running because I was worried if we stuck around, sooner or later they'd hit us."

"You know, Hugh, if you'd let the police do the work the public pays us for, you wouldn't be in this fix. And don't get me wrong – you and Miss Thorne are in a fix. Tell me where you are and I'll meet you, myself."

Kerr swallowed hard.

"I'm telling you, I'm afraid. I have Ellen and Jack to worry about. Give me a chance to work through this. Please, Wade. On the basis of our –"

"Don't say friendship, whatever you do. Are you trying to ruin my career?" He sighed again. "All right. I'll speak to Bond."

"Privately. Don't use the phone and don't put anything in writing. I have a sick feeling there are more than two men in the 'exchange program' who are actually on Price's payroll." The second hand swept past the second minute. "Give me your home phone number. I'll call you there."

"My what? Oh, hell. Metropolitan 57893."

"Gotta go."

Hugh slammed the handset down, hoping that he had ended the call before anyone had time to trace it. Taking a deep breath to calm his shaken nerves, he ran his fingers through his wavy black hair and returned to the car. He need not have bothered. One look at his stone-faced ashen complexion told Ellen all she needed to know.

"You got Wade and we're in over our heads," she surmised, sliding back to the passenger's side so he could get in behind the wheel. He hesitated, realized it was too late to lie and nodded.

"Metropolitan 57893. That's his home phone number. In case we get separated."

She wrote it down.

"You told him the story?" He nodded. "Wade didn't believe you?"

"I think he wanted to. That's more than I had a right to expect."

She surprised him by putting her hand on his.

"No, Hugh. It's exactly what you have a right to expect. Remember what you told me. Just because the newspapers and the popular rags make a big deal out of your courtroom 'antics,' and how you're always getting the better of the district attorney's office, you and Bartholomew Bond and Hank Wade are all on the side of right. None of you want to see a miscarriage of justice. If you 'win' and they 'lose,' that's because you have the brains and the brass to do whatever it takes to protect your clients. If you're well paid for your work, that's your good fortune. It's not a reason to consider you a natural enemy – or to mistrust your word."

"Tell them that," he retorted with a bitterness she had not anticipated.

"Lieutenant Wade has dedicated his life to police work because that was his calling; Bartholomew Bond chose public service for the same reason. Your calling was as a defense attorney. All three of you made choices and you have to live with them. I expect them to act as honorable men and if they don't, by God, I'll give an interview that will resound all the way to the state capital." He stared at her a long time and then finally permitted a fleeting smile to cross his otherwise hardened expression. She rightly interpreted his thoughts. "Yes, I've made choices in life, too. I don't envy you your wealth, Wade his authority or Bond his status. I'm satisfied with what I've accomplished and although it wasn't how I expected my career path to turn out, I have no regrets."

"What did you expect?" he asked in a voice so low she had to read his lips to get the full import of the question.

"That if I am arrested for murder, a famous criminal attorney will get me off. Not because he's famous or wealthy but because I am innocent. And at the same time," she added, working the hand crank to unroll the window for some fresh air, "I expect him to get himself off, as well."

"Hand-in-hand. Right you are. What do you say we get a hotel room?"

"Three."

"Three," he agreed and started the car.

At the appointed time Hugh and Ellen arrived outside the Free Clinic. Failing to spot their colleague, they parked the car and canvassed the sidewalks. To their shared relief they found Jack inside a small Oriental shop. He waved in greeting.

"Hello, you two. Look at all the interesting stuff in here."

Appraising the contents of the store, which turned out to be the equivalent of a Chinese apothecary, Ellen nodded in appreciation.

"Yes, I see. Dried bat's wings, rattlesnake venom, eye of newt –"

"Shrunken heads, chicken blood, virgin –" Hugh offered. Ellen cut him off before he could finish.

"What are you doing in here, Jack?"

"... olive oil," Kerr concluded with a grin. Ellen rolled her eyes.

"Dr. Wong sent me. With a prescription."

"A prescription? For what?"

He shrugged. "I don't know. It was written in that funny hieroglyphics of theirs."

"Very powerful and ancient Chinese remedy," an elderly Chinaman remarked, emerging through a curtain that separated the front from the rear of the shop. Holding out a white paper bag neatly folded at the top, he added, "Twenty-five cents, please."

"Whatever it is, at least it's cheap," Jack opined, handing over the coins. "Here you are: two bits. Did Dr. Wong say how often I was to take it?"

"Five... pills... twice a day until gone."

"Oh. That's a lot. I don't like to swallow pills –"

"Not swallow whole. Chew."

"Chew? What kind of medicine is that?"

Opening the bag, the patient stared inside, poked his finger around the contents, then looked up and grinned.

"Say, what do you call this?"

"Chinese gumdrops," the apothecary elucidated. "Sweet and pleasant tasting. Guaranteed to take your mind off your troubles."

"Then you better give us two more prescriptions, Doctor," Hugh observed. "We could all use that in spades." Pulling out a dollar bill, he offered it to the proprietor. "Make ours double."

The man nodded and disappeared behind the curtain to fill the order.

"Gumdrops! Well, how do you like that?"

"What did Dr. Wong tell you, Jack?" Ellen interjected. "Are you all right?"

"Four broken ribs and chest contusions but no punctured lungs. Broken nose, displaced jaw that he righted – very painful," the patient added, ruefully rubbing his chin, "innumerable cuts, some of which were deep enough to be stitched but he said it was too late for that – and a concussion. He gave me a shot of penicillin, taped my ribs up like a mummy, told to me take it easy for a couple of weeks, take two aspirin and –"

"– call him in the morning. Got it."

"Could have been worse," Kerr decided in relief.

"You're telling me. I told him to send you the bill, by the way."

"I see. And what did he say?"

"He only gave me one of those inscrutable Chinese smiles and said he'd be sure to do that."

"I think that's one bill you won't mind paying," Ellen observed.

"What does she mean?" Jack asked when Kerr made no reply.

"He isn't going to send one."

Carefully counting out five gumdrops, Merrick stuffed them into his mouth.

"Why don't I have any friends like that?"

"You do," the lawyer finished, taking the over-large bag from the proprietor. "Thank you." Guiding his companions outside, he concluded the thought. "Your friends risked their lives, their professional careers and possibly their freedom to save you. Not bad, I'd say."

"Ok, you got me there. And if I didn't express my appreciation, I'm doing so now. Dr. Wong said I was beaten within an inch of my life and if I hadn't gotten out when I did, that would have been the end of me. He was sure right, too, because I had the very distinct impression I wasn't long for the world."

"You weren't. And neither will Ellen or I be if we don't get moving. Even though I don't think we are, I just can't shake the idea we're being watched."

"Yeah. I got the creeps, too. Let's go."

They hurried back to the car, piled in and Kerr drove them to the motel rooms he and Ellen had secured earlier. After looking over the three inter-connecting apartments, they settled into the middle one.

"Jack, why don't you lie down," Ellen suggested.

"Don't mind if I do. I'm all done in." Kicking off his shoes, he lay down on the bed, grunted, and sat back up. "Lumpy. And my back is killing me. No, take that back," he quickly amended. "My back hurts like the devil."

"Have some more gumdrops."

"They taste all right, but they don't do anything for pain." Taking out the bottle of aspirin, Jack dropped four pills into his hand, made a face, then swallowed them without benefit of water. "What's the plan, Hugh?"

Kicking off his own shoes, Kerr pulled up a bamboo chair, settled into it and propped his feet on the edge of the bed. Ellen brought in another chair from the far room and joined them.

"I don't know. I need some time to think – to work through all this." Too restless to remain in a comfortable position, he dropped his legs and glanced over his shoulder at the window. "We all need some rest and a chance to recover our aplomb, but this place isn't it. I hoped I'd get over this uneasiness –"

"But every shadow makes you jump," Jack finished. "Me, too. Say, why don't we call the Agency and have them send some men up here to watch our backs?"

"I'd like to but you can bet Wade has half a dozen men watching every move they make. I just can't take the chance."

"What about calling in some local boys? I have connections here."

"So do I, but at the moment I don't trust anyone. What's more, anyone we contact may be subject to prosecution."

"Aiding and abetting," Ellen promptly supplied.

"Presuming she and I are brought up on charges. It wouldn't be right to involve them. Calling in the doctor was bad enough. No one else." He slammed his right fist into his left palm. "I need to think; to lay all the facts out just as if I were working on a court case, which, in fact, I guess I am. But there are too many variables and my mind's all tensed up." His hand slapped his thigh in frustration. "I'm not used to this! Damn it, everything keeps going around in circles. Something's wrong with me."

"What's 'wrong,' Counselor, is that you're accustomed to working on problems in a safe, protected place. Somewhere you're used to; where you're free to open your mind and let it wander without fear of interruption. No one can be creative when you're jumping at shadows."

"I don't know, Ellen. I'd like to think you're right but there's nowhere for us to go and feel safe. There are any number of first class hotels where we'd be a hell of a lot more comfortable and I have friends in the city who would loan us the use of their apartments, but my thoughts keep going back to Carey Price. He's clearly done his homework – for all we know, he's investigated my comings and goings with a fine-toothed comb. I think we did a pretty good job covering our tracks, but if he's got an entire detective force out looking for me, they'd eventually uncover my usual haunts."

"We could drive up into Canada," Merrick suggested.

"We could," Kerr agreed somewhat hesitantly, "but that's crossing an international boundary. If Bond does put out that APB, then my license is really in trouble."

Ellen had heard enough. "All right, boys," she declared, getting to her feet. "Let's go."

"Go? Go where?" Jack demanded, already reaching for his shoes.

"Mr. Price may be looking for you, Hugh, but he's not looking for me. I'm only a mere woman, after all and he'll expect you to make all the decisions. He'll have his detectives root out your favorite hotels and even your friends, but he's under a serious time constraint and all the king's horses and all the king's men can't investigate every hiding place, even assuming they're looking in San Francisco. I know somewhere we can go and I think we'll be safe there for at least a week. That ought to be enough time for us to come up with a plan."

Kerr and Merrick exchanged looks, nodded and retrieved the luggage they had not unpacked.

"After you, Starlet," Jack said, buttoning his jacket.

While she appreciated the compliment, it was the respect in his voice that meant more to Ellen than all the king's horses and all the king's men.

Any king.

"I'll drive."

So saying, Ellen took the wheel and headed due north. Neither of the men made any comment and settled back to enjoy, as best they could, the ride. After an hour, she turned off onto a less-traveled highway that eventually gave way to a two-lane road. Bypassing Lodi, another half hour brought them into the countryside, dotted by large, landed properties, widely separated from one another. As the sun began to set in the west, they came over a slight elevation and looked out across a wide expanse, a portion of which was fenced. Driving through a wide, open gate, she maneuvered down a dirt road that terminated in the front yard of a three-story mansion of the last century. Although the house showed its age, it was well maintained and offered a neat, familiar appearance of old fashioned wealth and comfort.

"Here we are," Miss Thorne declared, turning off the engine with the sort of finality typically reserved for coming home after a long and tiring journey. When Hugh opted not to speak, Jack took up the slack.

"Where is 'here,' exactly?"

"Home."

"Home?" he asked in wonder and surprise. "Your home?"

"That's right. Or did you think I sprang up out of the highways and byways of Los Angeles?"

"I guess I never gave it a thought.... All right, yes, I did think that."

"Well, you were wrong. I'm a country girl."

"Nice country."

"Thank you."

Opening the door, she got out and surveyed the homestead with an emotion akin to pride, while her companions got out, stretched their cramped legs and took in deep breaths of fresh air. Before they could question her further, if such were their intent, the front door opened and a remarkably well-preserved, middle-aged woman with only a few strands of grey in her hair and the hint of wrinkles around her eyes came flying out the door.

"Ellen!" she cried, engulfing the young woman in her arms. "Why didn't you let me know you were coming? I haven't received a letter from you in weeks!"

"We came on the spur of the moment, Mother. Let me introduce –"

"Why, one of you must be Mr. Hugh Kerr," Mrs. Thorne exclaimed. "That must be you, sir," she decided after running a sharp, quizzical eye over the men.

"I am he," Kerr acknowledged, offering her a small bow.

"My daughter has told me so much about you, sir. I would know you anywhere from your piercing blue eyes Ellen has described so well.

And you, sir," she continued, turning to Jack, "must be Mr. Jack Merrick." Her expression as quickly turned to one of concern. "You are ill?"

"Yes, mother," Ellen interjected. "He has been in an accident. Mr. Kerr and I thought a rest cure in the country would be just the thing for him."

"And so it shall be. Come inside, all of you. Oh, Ellen, I wish I had known you were bringing such distinguished guests so I could have prepared something special."

"No need to go to any trouble on our account, Mrs. Thorne," Jack politely offered, clearly uncomfortable with the domestic scene. "But if you've got any cold cuts or some soup, that would be great. I'm starving."

"Then I shall feed you." Taking Merrick's hand as though he were a child, she led them through the door and into the parlor. "Make yourself comfortable. My home is now your home. Would you like a fire? Of course," she answered for him. "You look as though you have a chill. Mr. Kerr, sit here in this chair; it is for the master of the house. My husband used to sit here and read by the fire when he came home from the office. He would be honored if you were to take it. After all, it is to your generosity I owe so much."

"No, indeed, Mrs. Thorne. It is Ellen whom you must thank. After all, I am merely the intermediary. She and I...discussed the arrangements at some length." Carefully avoiding Ellen's surprised countenance, he finished, "We agreed that instead of adding her *quarterly* raise to her weekly paycheck, I would forward it to you."

"What is my 'weekly contribution' up to?" Ellen asked her mother in some consternation.

"Bi-weekly, dear," Mrs. Thorne corrected. "Fifty dollars. Without it, I could hardly maintain this old house. The extra money has been a godsend."

"I am so relieved to hear it." Ellen smiled while drilling a hole through Hugh's chest. "So thoughtful of him to mail the check himself. That way, I never have to bother myself about remembering."

"That is exactly what he wrote me three years ago. I have saved all his letters; they are as dear to me as those from you and your brothers. And if it weren't for Mr. Kerr, I would hardly know what you are up to. I have never known an employer to take such an interest in his employees."

Reining in her shock if not her annoyance, Ellen grabbed her mother by the arm.

"Let's go into the kitchen, mother. *Mr. Kerr* and Mr. Merrick are hungry. And after they fall asleep by the fire, perhaps you'd like to tell me more about how *Mr. Kerr* writes you a letter and encloses a check *every two weeks*. I'd just *love* to see them and read about what I've been up to."

"I'm sure you know, Ellen."

"I'm sure I don't, mother."

Without letting the conversation degenerate further, Ellen led Mrs. Thorne away. When they had gone, Jack settled into a chair and whistled.

"If I had great legs and a pretty face, would you mail me one hundred extra bucks every month?"

"No."

"Well, suffice it to say there's one person left in the world who isn't out to get you." He crossed his legs and stretched them to full length on the ottoman. "Although on second thought, it sounds like Mrs. Thorne's got you sized up for a tux and a wedding march down the aisle with her daughter. And you have no one to blame but yourself. And to think, I always imagined you and I as perpetual bachelors."

"You and I and Ellen?" he asked with some curiosity.

"Well, I don't know about that. I figured with your cold feet and long hours at the office some nice fella would come into her life when you weren't looking and snatch her away."

"Really?"

Jack looked surprised.

"Really."

"Oh. Nice to know your opinion."

"I had Ellen pegged for three kids, a dog, two cats, a hamster and a guy with a nine-to-five. Why? What did you think?"

"I didn't," Kerr muttered and Jack closed his eyes.

"Oh, brother."

Hugh Kerr might have asked him to elucidate but didn't.

A young servant girl with plain features and a guileless face came in and without introducing herself, adeptly made a fire and departed without saying a word. Although curious about the strangers, she had evidently been warned against engaging them in conversation and followed her instructions implicitly.

Moving their chairs closer to the spreading warmth, the detective basked in the heat, while the lawyer wandered up to the mantle, carefully studying a framed yellowed photograph of a stern-looking gentleman dressed in a business suit, and two framed college diplomas belonging to Thomas and Walter Thorne. Less interested in the Thorne family history, Jack spoke again.

"So, the old lady needs dough, ugh?" Kerr shrugged. "How did you know? You doing investigative work on your own, now?"

"That was years ago. You must have been busy on some other case."

"Didn't want to share your Good Samaritan Award, that it? Or were you determined to keep Ellen's background a secret?"

"Neither. And as far as Ellen's 'background' is concerned, I know as little as you. I wasn't investigating her or her mother, as you so indelicately put it. I just happened to overhear a conversation one evening and divined the gist of it. I knew Ellen wouldn't take any money for her mother and the one time I offered her a substantial raise, I did it rather clumsily and she refused."

"Who in their right mind ever refuses money?"

"Ellen did."

"Clumsy? You must have been tripping over your feet."

"All right; I put it awkwardly, then."

"Same difference. When we get back to L.A. I'm going to up my fees ten percent."

"No, you're not."

Merrick yawned. "Is that a threat?"

"You make yourself too expensive and you'll spend your time dogging famous actors for jealous wives and working for insurance companies."

"It pays the bills."

"Which reminds me," Hugh interjected, raising his palms, open-faced, toward the flames licking the dry logs. "Why in the world do you live in such a small, shabby apartment without a private bath and with all the amenities of an 1870s frontier hotel?"

Jack chuckled at Kerr's description, thought a moment, then got up and stamped out an ember that had escaped to the hearth rug.

"I appreciate bright light and glitter and Oriental rugs when I'm out in society, but when I go home I want it simple, quiet and uncomplicated. Besides, what more do I need? I don't cook so I don't need a fancy kitchen. If I want to appreciate the fine points of a

Rembrandt, I go to a museum. I get all the classical music I need when I take a date to the symphony. Animals are OK in the zoo, behind bars, and I can mix my own Martinis with a jigger and ice they don't taste any better in Waterford crystal than they do in a glass pinched from the Tropicana. Belleek vases just beg to break and anyway, I don't buy myself flowers."

"What about a private bath? Most people don't consider that a luxury."

"There's a tub down the hall that a baby elephant could swim in, enough hot water for ten men and a boy to bathe in and everyone in the building goes to bed by 10 P.M. The landlady knows when to keep her mouth shut, she discretely looks the other way if I bring a visitor home and she signs for my mail."

"What do you do with all your money – and the ten percent extra you're going to charge me when we get back?"

"I'm saving it for my retirement."

"You'll never retire."

"You'll never retire, old boy. Now me, that's another story. A little villa on the French Riviera, a Mexican cottage on some private beach, or my own gondola in Venice. Or maybe I'll buy a piece of a sports franchise and drive around in a fancy sports car waving at the envious."

"Is that so?"

"Sounds good, doesn't it?"

"Where's the challenge? Doing crossword puzzles in your private box?"

"You just don't get it, do you? Well, your lordship, when you're confirmed to the Supreme Court, send me a ticket."

"Now, that would be boring."

"Yeah, but it would give you a chance to have the whole country hate you instead of just a measly little city."

"Now you're talking."

Jack reseated himself and stared at his friend.

"Hugh, just once in your life wouldn't you want to be loved?"

"My clients appreciate me."

"After you've worked your butt off for them and they can go back to their comfortable lives and forget about their harrowing, near-death experiences."

"All right, then *I* love me. That is, I love what I do."

"Two different things, old buddy."

They were interrupted by the return of Ellen and her mother, wheeling in a wooden cart laden with foodstuffs. Warm smells immediately filled the room.

"Mrs. Thorne," Kerr protested, rising out of politeness, "There was no need for you to bring the food to us. We will be more than happy to eat in your dining room or the kitchen."

"Oh, no, Mr. Kerr, I want you to relax here by the fire."

Giving him a motherly pat on the shoulder to indicate he re-seat himself, she retrieved a small three-legged tray from a closet and set it up before him. After performing the same task for Jack, she set out plates, bowls and silverware.

"Ellen, dear, serve the soup."

Although Ellen and her mother had clearly had a conversation in the kitchen, whatever the younger had said clearly had not curbed the elder's enthusiasm for playing hostess. While her daughter ladled steaming tomato soup into the bowls, she offered fresh bread and butter to each man.

"Mr. Kerr, would you take a glass of sherry with your meal? Or some wine, perhaps?"

Reseating himself, Hugh tried to catch Ellen's eye and failed.

"I most certainly do not wish you to go to any trouble, Mrs. Thorne."

"No trouble at all. It is a pleasure to have such distinguished guests." Making up her own mind, the matron hurriedly brought out two small crystal sherry glasses and filled them from a vintage bottle. "This was Mr. Thorne's favorite; I hope you like it."

"I am sure I shall." Sipping the beverage, he nodded in satisfaction. "Excellent. But won't you please sit down? And Ellen," he added more forcibly, placing a hand over her wrist before she could withdraw. "You're as tired and hungry as we are. You drove all the way here. Sit down and join us. *I insist.*"

"Mr. Kerr," Mrs. Thorne began, but he assumed the liberty of speaking over her.

"You must not consider us as strangers, but as friends of the family. And being such, neither Jack nor I wish any special treatment. And we don't wish to be deprived of yours or Ellen's company."

Quickly rising, he guided Ellen into the chair he vacated and put a spoon in her hand.

"Hugh –"

"I will sit closer to the fire; by your mother."

Indicating that she remain seated, he casually disappeared into the kitchen and returned with two more soup bowls and bread plates. Placing the first on a silver charger, he added food and brought it to Mrs. Thorne. Once she accepted it, he did the same for himself, and, sherry glass in hand, seated himself on the couch. Holding it up, he inspected it against the light, and then nodded toward the lady of the house.

"Shall we have a toast at this, our first meal together? To old – and new friends."

"You are too kind, Mr. Kerr."

"Not at all. It is only to be regretted that I have known Ellen five years and the four of us are only now becoming acquainted."

They ate the rest of the meal in silence and it was only after the dishes had been removed and the sherry glasses refilled that Mrs. Thorne reopened the conversation.

"You are in a very prestigious and exacting line of work, Mr. Kerr."

"It can be. I find it very challenging and rewarding."

"And you must meet such interesting people. Ellen tells me something about it but of course I understand the details must remain confidential. I have saved all the clippings from the newspapers she sends. I have always wondered, Mr. Kerr, whether you ever worry that you have prevented a guilty person from being punished for a crime they actually committed?"

"Being on either side of the case – as a defense attorney or as a public prosecutor – your question would be equally apt," he began, crossing his legs as a sign he could talk forever on the subject. "It is the goal of both sides that a fair and impartial justice be achieved. I trust my clients when they tell me they are not guilty; were it otherwise, I could not honestly defend them. Some lawyers will argue a spirited defense no matter the guilt or innocence of their client, but I could not. My job is not to thwart justice but to serve as an officer of the court to preserve it."

Demurely repositioning her long skirt so that her ankles were covered, Mrs. Thorne gave Kerr a long, hard look. When she spoke her tone was not accusatory, but rather one of long deliberation.

"What would you do if you discovered your client lied to you?"

"And was actually guilty?" She nodded. He signed and drummed his fingers on the arm of the chair. "I would then present him or her with one of two options: I could either withdraw and allow them to retain other council or I would argue for extenuating circumstances and do my best to get them the least punishment allowable."

"Then you are an ethical man, sir. Like my late husband."

He nodded out of politeness.

"I appreciate the compliment. For a lawyer to do otherwise would be to break his oath to uphold the law. It is a common misconception that it is the obligation of defense attorneys to do whatever it takes to free those he represents, whether he knows them to be guilty or not. Such is not the case. It is his obligation to see they get a fair trial and to use his skill for their benefit – at times," he added, winking at Ellen, "with courtroom theatrics, but never to become an accessory to a crime, which he would be committing, were he to free a guilty party."

"My daughter is helpful to you?"

Wondering whether her questions had been cleverly directed to maneuver him to this point, he nodded with easy affirmation and spoke with an admiration not to be mistaken.

"Ellen is vital to me. She and Jack and I work as a team. I depend on her analytical mind and her insight, just as I need Mr. Merrick to investigate conflicting circumstances. I have the easy role of putting together the facts and presenting them to a jury in plain terms they can understand."

"Facts would seem to be facts."

He smiled. "Truth, it is said, is stranger than fiction. What people do, how they think under pressure, the ways they react, are not always logical. But if I can lay them out in such a way that a reasonable person can understand them, I have a good chance of winning the case."

"And sometimes, mother, it is just easier for Mr. Kerr to solve the crime himself. That, Hugh Kerr," she completed with a smile of her own, "is what you are known for."

"And why the police department is not overly fond of Mr. Kerr," Jack added with good humor. "Their case may be solid and fit the evidence, but Hugh delves into the emotional side. That's one thing I've learned from him – passion clouds judgment. Don't jump to conclusions until you've walked a mile in their moccasins."

He yawned, belatedly put a hand over his mouth and grinned. "Gosh, your sherry seems to have made me sleepy."

Glancing at a majestic grandfather clock, Mrs. Thorne stood, hands clasped together.

"Of course you are tired. You have had a long drive. Let me show you to your rooms; they have been prepared for you."

Hugh, who had stood with Mrs. Thorne, readily seconded the motion.

"Please don't bother. Ellen can do the honors while I get our luggage from the car."

As they went their separate ways, the servant hurried in the clear away the dishes. By the time Kerr got back, Ellen was waiting for him at the foot of the stairs.

"This way, Counselor," she indicated, leading the way. He followed, Ellen speaking as they walked. "My mother sleeps on the second story. There are three other bedrooms on this level that my brothers and I used when we were younger. In those days we had five servants and they stayed upstairs. But after my father died, my mother let all but one go and the three of us moved up into the third level."

"To escape the prying eyes of a watchful parent?" he teased.

"Something like that."

Bypassing the middle level, they came out on the top landing.

"My room is that one," she indicated. "I put Jack in Walter's room and you in Tom's. Mother wanted you to take one of the lower bedrooms but I convinced her you would feel more comfortable being nearer to Jack in case he needs anything during the night. He certainly did look all in."

"A concussion is nothing to sneeze at. We've pushed him pretty hard as it is. A few days here is just what he needs."

Opening the door to the bedroom, Ellen held back as he entered.

"The common bathroom is through there," she indicated.

His eyes twinkled.

"That ought to make Jack feel right at home."

She nodded at their shared remembrance.

"The house was remodeled in the 40s. My father was very successful during the early part of the war and he demanded a full staff attend him when he was home in his kingdom. The lower bedrooms all had private baths installed but no one was particularly concerned about the servants' convenience."

Placing the suitcase on the bed, he stared curiously around the room that still held the remnants of a young man's taste.

"I'm sorry about your father. When did he die?"

"1945. It came as a great shock. He had a massive heart attack."

Turning his back to her, Hugh observed a number of paintings on the wall that depicted World War II airplanes in various modes of attack. Ellen's silence was palpable.

"Things didn't go well for the family after that?"

"No." She hesitated, then added, "You impressed my mother."

He turned and offered a patented smile.

"I'm used to impressing people."

Clearly disinclined to continue the conversation, Ellen backed out.

"Sleep as long as you like. I hope the bed is comfortable. These rooms have been closed up for years but the linen is fresh and there are plenty of towels if you want to shower in the morning."

It did not take a brilliant mind to determine her reluctance and he graciously acceded to her tacit wishes, but not without one try at expressing his feelings.

"Thank you for bringing us here. Whatever it cost you I hope I can repay some day."

"You've pre-paid, Hugh: one hundred dollars a month for God-knows how many years." Tears came into her eyes. "Why didn't you tell me?"

"Because I was afraid you'd refuse."

"But why did you do it?"

Hands in his pockets, he went back to examining the water colors.

"Because I'm not very good at expressing my appreciation. I may 'delve into the emotional side' of my clients as Jack expressed it, but when it comes to my own feelings, I have very little experience."

He waited a moment and when he turned around, Ellen had vanished.

Into the thin air of her past.

And their shared present.

Chapter 10

"Mr. Kerr must have found your brother's bed very comfortable," Mrs. Thorne observed to her daughter. Ellen cast her a mild expression of surprise.

"What do you mean?"

"It is 10 o'clock and he has not yet come down. I held breakfast as long as I could and then prepared Mr. Merrick his meal. You are late, yourself," she scolded. "Big city people keep big city hours?"

Although she had been up since dawn, Ellen demurred and went into the living room to see Jack.

"Good morning," he greeted, offering her a cheerful wave and omitting his customary compliment out of deference to listening ears.

Moving over to take his hand, she gave him a thorough once-over.

"You look better. How do you feel?"

"Headache's fading and my strength is coming back. It's amazing what a good night's rest in a secure place will do. Where's Hugh, by the way? Your mother has been fussing around the stairs like a cat. It occurred to me she had a brass band or something waiting. He must really be catching some Z's."

"I heard him get up about 6 A.M. and go out."

"Out? Where, out?"

"I don't know."

A look of concern flashed across Merrick's newly shaven face.

"You don't suppose something is wrong, do you? You think he heard or saw someone lurking about?"

"No. I think he's restless and didn't want to disturb anybody by pacing up and down in his room."

"Oh. You're probably right at that. You going to have some breakfast? The bacon and eggs were out of this world. I'd forgotten what real home cooking tastes like. I've eaten in so many 'Ma and Pa' restaurants that serve the same grub I can get at any greasy spoon, the distinction has blurred."

Ellen patted him reassuringly.

"That's because you don't cook for yourself. I do."

"Well, when we get back, you'll have to make me a breakfast some Saturday when his Majesty is out of town so we won't be disturbed until our second cup of coffee."

"It's a date," she promised. "Try and keep as quiet as you can today, and tomorrow maybe you can get out and walk around."

"You don't have any cows to milk, do you? Or eggs to ferret out? I'm not a country boy, you know. Those creatures make me nervous."

Already half way across the room she turned an arched an eyebrow. "Why is that?"

"Because they suppose you know what you're doing. And when they find out you're a tenderfoot, they kick and bite."

"Peck," Ellen corrected. "Cows kick and hens peck. No: this isn't a farm. And besides, mother would never permit a guest to help around the house. Why don't you turn on the television? It's Saturday and the cartoons are on."

"Good idea."

As Jack shuffled toward the television set, Ellen slipped quietly away. Outside a stiff breeze blew hair in her face, forcing her to brush back the long brown locks before scanning the horizon. When she detected no movement or any shape that might be construed as a human form, the private secretary concentrated on the problem at hand. Three compass points to the east, south and west comprised unbroken, gently rolling flatland; only the area to the north held a stand of wood. Making a quick determination that was really no choice at all, she stooped under the rope clothesline and headed toward the trees.

Half an hour's brisk walk took her to the first line of low-growth bushes; beyond lay saplings before the older trees took precedence. Moving into the woods to no greater depth than that which was required to hide her from prying eyes, she made her way east for another quarter of an hour before coming to a steep rise and open ground strewn with rocks. As she paused to contemplate, a cheery voice hailed her from the heights.

"Hallo!" Following the sound, Ellen stared up at the rocks and beheld a familiar face. Catching her eye, Hugh waved. "Come on up."

"I won't if I'm intruding."

"Not a bit. Need a hand?"

"I could climb this hill blindfolded."

As good as her word, within five minutes Ellen had scaled the ancient boulders and joined him at the top.

Hair tussled by the wind, face reddened by the cool air and wearing only a loose-fitting shirt open at the collar, and the weekend pants she had bought at their last tarrying place, Ellen was taken aback by how different he looked. Gone was the expensive business suit, the tailor-made white shirt, the freshly shined shoes and the impeccable grooming that characterized his business presentation. And while she had certainly seen him in casual attire, his aura at the moment struck her with an awe she could not readily explain.

"How did you find me?" he asked, either oblivious to her surprise or opting not to pursue it.

"That was easy. I know you too well. You needed somewhere you could think; to pace around like a caged mountain lion. So you walked to the woods. But one does not prowl through underbrush and around trees, so you kelp walking until you found the summit here."

"But I wasn't pacing; I was sitting," he protested.

"Granted. But you had found an elevation where you could look out upon the land and that was good enough to let your mind wander."

"Come here. I want to show you something."

Taking her hand for guidance, they scrambled down the other side of the hill. A few minutesquestion walk took them to a small stream and a stand of white birch. Before he could show her what he had found, Ellen chuckled.

"You have detective blood in you, Mr. Kerr."

But she followed as he pointed to the bark on one of the taller trees.

"T.T.; W.T.; E.T."

"Tom, Walter and Ellen," she translated. "My brothers and I carved our initials on that trunk many years ago before we all left home."

"It's amazing."

"What is?" she asked, detecting the same sort of awe in his voice that she, herself, had felt a moment before.

He shrugged suddenly and sagged as though the air had gone out of his balloon body.

"I don't know." Leaving her standing by the initialed tree, he stomped away, hands behind his back. "I'm confused, Ellen. My mind is all tangled; I can't get anything straight." He stopped and turned on her in sudden savageness. "I'm not used to this. I feel as though – I were a writer with writer's block." His face twisted in wry agony. "I can't see the forest for the trees. The harder I concentrate the more muddled I become."

"Give it time, Hugh. We're safe here –"

His voice rose. "For how long? A day, a week? Then what? We've been framed for murder, I can't trust the cops because at least two we know of are on the take, we're being hunted like rabbits and one of the hunters is likely going to shoot to kill."

Shocked by his use of the word "cops" instead of the more formal and respectful "police," she shuddered.

"I thought you said Price would be satisfied ruining your reputation."

"I said he wanted to hurt my heart; after that comes my reputation, if they're not, in fact, the same thing. He threatened revenge. He kidnapped Jack and very nearly killed him. He would have gotten around to that if we hadn't interceded. We know he's capable of cold blooded murder. What next?"

Slapping both hands to his head, then balling his fists and grinding them into his temples, he growled in fury.

"I've got to get him before he gets us, but how? I can't think! What's the matter with me, Ellen? I've never felt so... damned... tense in my life. Like I'm going to explode."

"I think we ought to try calling Lieutenant Wade again. It's Saturday and there's a chance he'll be at home."

"What good will that do?"

"For all we know he's located Price and had him arrested. Or maybe there's been a shootout. Or Price has tipped his hand and the police have stopped looking for us. After all, Hugh, we didn't kill that man; Price did. You gave Wade his name; they've surely investigated him. Maybe they've uncovered more information about the whole scheme. We won't know until we ask."

Her logic carried the argument and he heaved a sigh.

"I apologize for my language. I'm not being a very good influence on you, am I?"

"Good Lord, Hugh. I grew up with two brothers and for a period in their lives swearing was an absolute necessity; a ritual to manhood, you could say. Not around our parents, you can be sure, but there was a time or two when they were locked in their rooms for a very long weekend. Come on. We'll get in the car and drive into town and find a pay phone." When he hesitated, she added, "Won't you come? Or shall I call Wade myself?"

"All right."

Hands once more jammed into his pockets, Hugh led the way. Ellen walked by his side.

Without bothering to tell anyone where they were going, the pair got into the car and drove off, leaving, for the moment, the old homestead behind in the proverbial dust.

"Which way?" Hugh asked as they reached the first fork in the road.

"Turn left; and take it slow. The county doesn't spend a lot of money repairing these old back roads."

They traveled a mile or more before he broke the silence.

"Pretty country. How long has it been since you've been home?"

Turning her head to stare at the landscape, Ellen was forced to consider before answering.

"A year or two, I guess. Probably the Christmas of '53."

"That was the year I went to Scotland for the holidays."

"Was it? I'd forgotten."

"You don't have to put off visiting the old homestead until I leave the country, you know."

"I'd rather spend the holidays… in the city." She left unspoken but not unexpressed, *I'd rather spend the holidays with you.*

"You mother seems very nice." Another pause. "You've never been close?"

If he expected her to answer the interrogative, he was mistaken.

"You didn't go to Scotland, either. You went to Canada."

This time it was his turn to obfuscate the truth. When he spoke, his voice was stilted.

"Did I? What makes you say that?"

"You cancelled the reservations I scheduled and made new ones at the airport. You had a refund coming; the airline mailed it to the office."

"I don't recall seeing that check."

"Rather than bother you, I put it into the petty cash fund."

"Oh. Good thought. Careless of me."

"We've both been keeping secrets from one another."

"So we have."

"Turn left here."

He applied the brake, slowed and made the turn onto a wider road. His leg shook in nervous agitation.

"I know so little about you, Ellen; I mean, your early life."

"Didn't my mother tell you?"

"She never wrote back; I didn't expect her to. I wasn't prying. I thought one day you would tell me."

Pointing to an old brick building with an empty parking lot, she began speaking.

"That's where my brothers and I went to high school."

Almost accusatorily, he demanded, "They went to college."

Debating how much to say, she sighed.

"All three of us were to go. Tom graduated first and went to the state university. Walter went two years later. They both studied engineering. Tom took his degree but Walter dropped out in his third year to get married. He eventually changed his major, finished college and went into banking like my father." She finally turned to face him. Kerr kept his eyes on the road. "They both do very well for themselves and either one could afford to send mother money every month. They don't, and she would never ask."

He grunted, not in the least surprised.

"What about Tom? Did he marry?"

"Yes. He has a lovely wife. They have two children. Walter has three, all boys."

"No lack of grandchildren, then. Where do they live?"

"Tom moved to Phoenix and Walter lives in San Francisco."

Quietly appraising the empty school, Hugh asked, "What about you? You said all three of you were meant to go to college."

"By the time I graduated, there wasn't enough money to send me. I had already been accepted into the art program at Berkley but I turned it down and got a job to help mother. I lived at home and commuted to work in Lodi." Ellen cleared her throat and indicated a vague area in the town they approached. "I was more fortunate than I realized. A lawyer by the name of Eugene Mattingly needed clerical help so I went to work for him. There really wasn't that much for me to do, so I started reading his law books when he was in court." She finally laughed and the gloomy mood in the car significantly lightened. "He caught me at it one day and said if I was that interested, he'd teach me."

"Good for him!"

"He let me go with him to court after that, and that's how I picked up my legal knowledge."

"What type of law did he practice?"

"He was what's known as a country lawyer, Hugh. A little of this and a little of that. Whatever came his way, really: wills, deeds, property settlements, probate. Once in a while he'd use his influence to fix a speeding ticket; defend the mayor's son on a drunk and disorderly. Petty theft cases."

"He should have sent you to law school; you could have become his partner."

"He might have. But I didn't want to be a lawyer; I wanted to be an artist."

"Those were your water colors in Tom's bedroom, weren't they? They were very good. You captured a brilliant arrangement of detail with vague lines that drew me in and kept me at a distance at the same time, as though I were both a pilot and an observer."

"Thank you."

"Why didn't I see any of your paintings over the mantel?" She shrugged. "I imagine if Tom or Walter had created that artwork they would have been there."

"Boys have their place and girls have theirs."

"That's what we call – outside the law – separate but unequal." She made no reply. "How did you end up in Los Angeles?"

"Mr. Mattingly was an old man when I went to work with him. When he died, I had the choice of working for the lawyer who came into town and bought his practice from the estate or striking off on my own. By that time, I was ready to fly. L.A. appealed to me because I thought if I got a good job I could afford to take art classes at night."

"Then why didn't you?"

"I did."

Hugh was so surprised he nearly clipped a telephone pole.

"When was this?"

"About a year after I became secretary to a young, ambitions defense attorney named Hugh Kerr. Ever heard of him? He's known to be a little outlandish in court but he can win a case like nobody's business."

"And how is it I – Mr. Kerr – never knew you were attending college?"

"I suppose because he never made it his business to ask what I did with my evenings."

"A serious deficiency for which I chide him unmercifully. And what about these art classes?"

"I eventually earned my Bachelor of Arts and was working on my Master's."

He stopped the car at a red light and stared at her in stark wonder. "Good God. Why wasn't Mr. Kerr ever invited to your graduation?"

"Because the degree didn't mean to me what it once might have."

"What are you going to do with your B.A.?"

Clutching her hands together, Ellen replied firmly, "Cherish it."

"As well you should. But -"

She interrupted him with finality.

"I am the private legal secretary to the greatest lawyer in the state - probably the entire country. He trusts me and relies on me and I am content."

A car behind them honked and he rolled through the green light.

"What about the Master's?"

"I stopped going to class."

"Why?"

"Because as Mr. Kerr's case load grew, I had more and more work to do. He was called at all hours of the day and night and so was I. We never knew from one minute to the next who would walk through the office door needing your help; plans were set aside, personal appointments cancelled. I no longer had the time – or the inclination – to pursue my studies."

"Ellen, if I had only known –"

"Yes, Hugh. If you had only known. Which is precisely why I didn't tell you. I wanted to be there for you; I *enjoyed* the challenge and the responsibility. I had found my true calling."

"But your art work –"

"I sketch and paint in my spare time. That satisfies me."

"That is not an acceptable answer. You must go to Europe and study; to Paris and Rome."

"You don't have a license to practice law in those cities."

"The hell with me, Ellen. What have I done for you? Gotten you involved in a murder case, nearly killed, chased by the police –"

She let out a breath and leaned back against the cushion.

"It's fun, isn't it?"

Anticipating a different answer, Kerr nearly choked as he stumbled to turn an agreement into a denial. First sputtering, then gagging and finally coughing, he took a long moment to contain himself before growling, "Yes. But that isn't the point."

"If it isn't, I don't know what is."

Stepping on the accelerator, Hugh sped through town, blowing through yellow-red lights and ignoring stop signs. Adjusting the rearview mirror to catch her reflection, he explained his driving skill by mumbling, "If I get stopped by one of your local cops, I'll hire myself a local attorney and get the ticket fixed."

"I knew I shouldn't have told you that."

Reaching the outskirts of town, their phone call to Lieutenant Wade forgotten, he made a wide, looping U-turn and started back.

"The best lawyer in the state, hell."

"I said, 'the greatest lawyer in the country," she easily corrected. He pounded a fist on the steering wheel. The car jumped the curb.

"Damn!" Maneuvering the vehicle back onto the blacktop, he blew through another traffic sign. "Hell's bells!" he cursed a second time. "Why the hell are their so many stop signs in this hick town, anyway? Whose brother-in-law owns the municipal contract?"

"We may have occasion to find out."

"Well, I'm sure as hell not going to defend myself. My brain is so damned muddled I might turn a $5 citation into a 5-year prison rap. I can't make sense of anything. Ideas are spinning around in my head but none of them will settle down; as soon as I fix on one, ten more drown it out. I've never felt this fucking wretched in my whole life."

Anticipating his barrage of off-color language, Ellen casually readjusted the rear view mirror to prevent him from watching her when his eyes should be on the road.

"I know what you're doing. Put it back, by God, or I'll drive this broken-down jalopy off the nearest son-of-a-bitch cliff." She ignored the salty command.

"Turn right at the next intersection."

"I will, like hell."

She did not have to see him to know he was pouting. Nor could she ignore the perspiration streaming down his face, or the red that had seeped into his cheeks.

He turned right at the intersection and a mile down the road took them off the main thoroughfare.

"Where the hell are we going?"

"To the nearest cliff. Or a reasonable facsimile thereof, Counselor."

"Good. I meant what I said." When she didn't follow up, he added, "You believe me, don't you?"

"I believe everything you say."

"Oh, fuck!"

This time she laughed out loud. His ire increased.

"You don't even have a will."

"How do you know?"

"You never asked me to draw one for you."

"Oh, I'd get another attorney for that. It's way too personal for you to handle."

"Why? Did you leave me all your worldly possessions?"

"What if I did?"

He slammed his foot on the brake and they both catapulted forward, bouncing off the dashboard.

"Now see what you did," he groused. "I don't want your worldly possessions, damn it."

"What do you want?" The question was so pointed he began to shake. "Turn right here."

He did as she ordered and the car rolled down a narrow dirt lane that terminated at a dead end surrounded by a dense cluster of trees. Beyond the foliage lay a deep, wide, man-made depression.

"What is this?"

"We call it the sand pit. It was excavated decades ago for some reason or other and then abandoned. There's a small pond at the bottom where rainwater gathers. It's not very deep but it swells pretty nicely after a storm. The moon glints off it at night."

"You want me to plunge down, or glint at the moonlight?"

"To answer your question, this place is where the local kids come to make out."

"You want me to flatten a few erstwhile lovers on the way down?"

"No, that wasn't what I had in mind."

"What, then?"

"Don't you know... Hugh?"

"Oh, Jesus."

Stealing a surreptitious glance around to be certain they were alone, he slid over the seat and grabbed her. Wrapping his hands around Ellen's shoulders, he drew her close and pressed his lips against hers. They kissed passionately, broke for breath and then repeated the act before his face slipped lower so he could kiss her neck. The warmth of her skin, the heat of his own body and the suddenly incessant need for physical contact drove his hands to her breasts.

Eyes closed, touching what had hitherto been forbidden territory, Hugh moaned and plied the responsive flesh with eager fingers. She allowed him to explore her body and then unbuttoned the top several fastenings of her blouse to ease the transition from fabric to flesh.

"Ellen.... Ellen. We should get married."

After running her fingers lovingly through his hair, she playfully tugged his earlobe, forcing him to open his eyes and stare into hers. He did so with hopeful urgency.

"I told you we would have this conversation again, didn't I?"

"Yes, Ellen, you did."

Fully cognizant of the fact he was not then capable of a deep philosophical discussion, she poked his nose. He blinked in incomprehension.

"You're supposed to say, 'beep.'"

"Beep." She pressed his nose a second time. Proving he was a fast learner, he "beeped." "Good boy."

This time, she took the initiative, grabbed the sides of his jaws to hold his face steady, and planted her lips onto his. As psychic explosions shattered his mind and starbursts crackled before his eyes, he pressed back, kissing, making low crying noises and kissing again. When a pressure of a far different sort than that which had been plaguing him for days became his guiding light, Hugh tucked his hands behind her back with the intention of repositioning her body back against the seat.

Having anticipated his desire and his unreasoned intention, she wiggled free and held him back by placing the flat of her hand on his chest. Confused, hurt and demanding, he began, "Ellen, I –" but she stopped him by placing the fingers of her other hand against his mouth.

"Shhhh, Hugh. Not here; not now." He wiggled in insistence, eyes pooling with emotion. "Wait, baby. Can you wait a moment?" He nodded, quickly down, and more slowly up. "What we have between us is precious. We have been carefully weaving our lives together for years, but we have been very cautious. Haven't we?"

Less an interrogative than a statement, he whispered, "Yes, Ellen. We have."

"We've been careful for a reason. Those reasons have not yet been resolved. If you ask me to marry you now, I will say no. I am not your equal and in what should be an equal partnership, I will not be subservient."

"I never intended that –"

"Hush. I told you to listen. Are you listening?"

"Yes, Ellen."

The quiet, respectful, *loving* whisper almost broke her heart. But she was not to be swayed. While his mind had been muddled, hers had been crystal clear. She had taken them this far and she would take them further. But on her own terms.

"If we make love now, we make a commitment neither of us can back away from. It will interrupt the tapestry we've created, and ruin the pattern before it is properly finished." She finally smiled. Disentangling herself from his stiff arms, she reluctantly pushed him back, so that he nearly lay on his back. "I have a better idea." She winked and he flushed. "One that will speed the process along but carry no shame."

He did not understand but she had no intention of leaving him in the dark. With swift, knowing fingers, she rested her hand on the fly of his trousers. Just as her breasts had felt foreign and stimulating to him, so his hardened penis conveyed a world of urgency and desire to her pounding heart. With the timeless sensations of curiosity and eagerness propelling her forward, Ellen deftly drew down the zipper and slipped her warm hand onto the inflamed organ. Feeling the instant arch of flesh that was not bone but felt transformed into a substance of like strength, she grabbed and tugged with joyous disregard for any existence outside their small living space.

Hugh's hips gyrated upward, straining to mesh with the encircled fingers of Ellen's hand. Thrashing and then stomping with his feet, he strained into the pull of her body, harder when her other hand caressed and then squeezed his testicles. Neck muscles taut, head pressed back against the seat cushion, eyes closed, he willed his consciousness to absorb the floating euphoria and demanded deeper penetration. Wild, madly unconscious of any thought, greedily straining, he released semen into her hand, nearly drawing blood as teeth clenched over compressed lips.

Falling into the natural rhythm of his thrusts, Ellen rocked back and forth with him, bonded and yet separate, sharing the experience of foreplay and mating without crossing the boundary of ultimate morality by tarnishing the golden ring of marriage.

Holding her hands in place in order to indulge in the luxury of newness, exploration and assimilation, she draped over his chest, found his lips and kissed him. Registering the complexities of his own insatiable craving, the desire to sustain the pulsing, throbbing sensations in his groin and the insane lightheadedness of passion, Hugh caught her, engulfed her in his arms, returned her kisses, then smothered his face between her breasts, infant, boy, man and soul sharing a physical love of this earth and beyond that no flights of fancy or learned contemplation had prepared him for.

Covered in sweat, heaving for air, smeared by the shared fluids of passion and love, they steamed the windows so that if any errant passerby had dared cast a glance their way, all he would see was a car and two shadowy shapes. What he would surmise was another matter entirely.

When they finally caught their breaths, Hugh's eyes caught Ellen's and he gasped, "Good God!"

The innocence of his exclamation caught the woman, who thought she had anticipated everything, momentarily off guard.

"Hugh, do you mean to tell me…?" She faltered for lack of a proper way to express her surprise. Eyes now sharp and bright, he offered up a lopsided grin.

"I mean to tell you."

Brushing strands of hair from her face, Ellen tucked one behind her ear and matched his boyish expression with one of girlish delight.

"Never?"

He blushed. "Never. Why? Did you have a contrary opinion?"

"Of course I 'thought otherwise,' Mr. Kerr," she retorted, which was only half a falsehood.

Using a weak and shaky hand to wipe his own brow, he raised an eyebrow.

"The fact you had considered my… experiences at all, Miss Thorne, surprises me no end."

"That, sir, is a bald-face lie. And I suppose *you* never considered *my* experiences?"

The red in his cheeks deepened.

"Maybe just a little."

"And what did you conclude, *Counselor*?"

"I am embarrassed to tell you."

Snuggling up under his arm, she filled her lungs with the smells of his body that would resonate within her the rest of her life, separating him from every other male on planet Earth or any other.

"Tell me, anyway."

"Some... nights I supposed you had and some days I supposed you hadn't."

"A politically correct reply," she decided.

"And what is yours?" he demanded, thrilling to the sensation of rubbing his stubbled chin against her cheek.

"I have already confessed, although I like your answer better." He poked her and she leaned closer. His hand rested casually against her breasts and played with the unfastened buttons of her blouse. "How was I to think otherwise? You are a wickedly handsome man, sir. There must have been any number of high school and co-eds who threw themselves at you. You surely law-clerked with some famous attorney, putting you smack-dab," she teased, "into the middle of high society. I suppose there you were introduced to wealthy young heiresses and..." She deepened her voice, "more mature women of wealth and power. Both single and married."

He guffawed.

"Suppose that's true."

"It could hardly be otherwise."

"And suppose I told you my one true love was the law? That nothing diverted me from the course I had set for myself. If I wasn't blind to their offers, I was true to myself." Turning her face to his, Hugh opened his eyes and for the first time in his life, withdrew the shield from his inner soul. Ellen locked her orbs into those blue windows and delved into the depths of the man who would nevermore be a stranger. He did not speak again until she finally blinked. "I was holding myself true for a woman I knew existed, but not her name. I know, now. For you, Ellen."

"And I for you, Hugh."

Both inexplicably frightened by where their conversation had taken them, they withdrew their emotional, if not their physical, contact. Slipping on his courtroom demeanor, the defense attorney went on the playful attack.

"If that be true, Miss Thorne, how is it you were so well... versed... it what has so recently passed between us?"

"Oh, Mr. Kerr," she drawled in an enticing voice used so well by attractive women on the witness stand, "you forget, sir. I grew up with two older brothers. And while I was never, myself, intimately involved in the activities of youth exploring the wonders of budding manhood, I was not, shall we say, ignorant of their activities." On his startled look, she casually explained, "I stared through the keyhole."

"You didn't."

"I most certainly did."

"But… how did you know… when to look…?"

"They-were-hardly-subtle. Or quiet. One of the advantages of sleeping a floor away from disapproving parents."

This time he laughed loud and merrily.

"And if you ever confessed that 'sin' to said brothers, one, or several of you would most certainly have needed the services of a good defense attorney."

Her eyes twinkled.

"Murder or blackmail?"

"I was thinking of murder, but either crime will suffice."

"There you go, again. Always drumming up business."

They hugged and dared kiss one last time before both knew they would have to retreat from the intimacy of the hour.

"Miss Thorne."

"Yes, Mr. Kerr?"

"I am in need of a telephone. I have a call to make to Lieutenant Wade. And then we have one evening to spend in northern California before returning to Los Angeles. I have devised a plan."

"I knew you would."

And so she had. That had been her plan all along.

With benefits.

Chapter 11

"Where in the hell are you, Kerr?" Lieutenant Hank Wade screamed into the phone. "My men have been trying to locate you. And where is Jack Merrick? Put him on the phone – if he's really there with you as you claimed the last time we had an abbreviated conversation."

"He is alive but he could hardly fit into this phone booth with me."

"Then step out and put him on. I want to speak to your walking corpse."

"I left him behind; he's suffering from several broken ribs and a concussion."

"Had him checked out? Where? By a real doctor or some gas station attendant? Or perhaps Miss Thorne did the nursing. Where is Ellen, by the way, Hugh?"

The more familiar use of first names and the softer tone alerted Kerr that Wade was attempting to pacify him. He grinned and winked at Ellen, who, being less bulky than Jack, just managed to fit snuggly between the narrow sides of the phone booth.

"Tut tut, Hank," he chided in a voice calculated to raise ire. "I'm not going to talk long enough for you to trace this call and you know it. Put 'Bartholomew' on the phone."

The sputtering of muffled curse words assured him he had achieved the requisite consternation.

"What makes you think Bart – District Attorney Bond is here with me?" Without bothering for a reply, he grumbled, "Never mind," and handed the phone to his associate.

"Hugh, this is Bartholomew," the suave, steady voice of his long-time opponent came over the line. "You have exactly two minutes and twelve seconds before we make a trace, so listen carefully."

"Two minutes and one second," Kerr corrected, having already done the calculation in his mind. Bond sighed.

"Kerr, I'm not trying to trick you. But you've got to turn yourself in. You and Ellen are wanted in connection with a murder – possibly two, if Jack Merrick is really dead."

"He's not."

"All right, I'll take your word on that. But I have witnesses and photographic evidence that places you at the scene of *one* murder. You know we released that body and it was buried at the expense of the Merrick Detective Agency."

"Jack won't like that."

"All right: he can put in a claim on the city when he gets back. Who was the dead man, anyway?"

"Bart, I don't know."

"Don't 'Bart' me." Exasperation crept into his voice. "You do know. And you better know this as well – if you don't present yourself, Miss Thorne, and Merrick to police headquarters within the next two hours, I'm going to order every cop in the state to look for you. And when they stop you, they won't be very polite about it. You'll be charged as murderers running from justice. Anyone who aids you will be charged as accessories. I mean it, Hugh. For the sake of our friendship, I don't want to do this to you, but you're giving me no choice."

Holding the phone away from his ear so Ellen could follow the conversation, he directed his ad lib to her.

"You did try and convince me 'Bartholomew' and I were friends, but you did say I didn't have to ask him to be my best man."

"I was speaking of Hank Wade," Ellen corrected.

An explosion of noise forced Kerr to extend his hand away from his ear.

"What do you mean, best man? Are you and Ellen getting married? You'd better think twice about that – at least for right now. A husband and wife can't testify against one another. How will that look to a jury?" He answered his own question. "Guilty as sin."

"I'm speaking figuratively." Checking the second hand sweeping around the face of the dial, Hugh's tone grew more serious. "We can't be there in two hours. You have to give me more time."

"How much?"

"Thirty hours."

"Twelve –"

"I'm not negotiating. Thirty hours precisely and the three of us will show up at police headquarters."

Bond hesitated, placed his hand over the mouthpiece of the phone, held a whispered conversation with Wade then directed his words back to the listener.

"All right, but you owe me. And God help you if you're lying about any of this."

"I'm not. And I have your word? You take no action against us until… exactly 5 P.M. tomorrow afternoon?"

"Five P.M. But if the three of you aren't in Wade's office – alive, I might add – by five o'clock *precisely,* by five-o-one the entire police force will be breathing hell fire to bring you in. And after that – *no deals.* Do you get that, Kerr? Cross me and that's the end of it." He hesitated, not from kindness but for emphasis, and added, "Forever."

"Got it. Bye." He slammed the receiver back onto the hook and checked his watch. Taking a deep breath, he nodded at Ellen. "Made it by twenty seconds."

"Then we're all right?"

"I wouldn't go that far, but we beat the trace."

Reaching over her, Hugh pushed open the door, took in a deep breath and pushed past. Once he had extricated himself, she followed. Straightening a wrinkle in her skirt, she grinned.

"Piece of cake. I must be getting used to close quarters. Now what do we do?"

He chuckled and directed her back toward the car.

"We return to your mother's house, have a nice dinner and relax watching television. It's Saturday night: *Gunsmoke* is on."

"Just so long as you know I'm rooting for Miss Kitty."

"You watch *Gunsmoke*?" he hopefully inquired.

"Uh huh. Although," she added, opening the door and getting into the passenger side, "Marshal Dillon is a mighty fine-looking man. But he sure gets himself into a heap of trouble. Like someone I know."

"He always gets out of it." Inserting the key, he started the engine, shifted gears of the standard, and rolled out into the road. "Think those two will ever get married?"

"No," she sourly retorted. "Not if the show runs twenty years."

"Too bad."

"Who you telling?" Observing his raised eyebrow, Ellen Thorne finished her thought. "Kitty Russell has more to lose than I do. She owns the Long Branch Saloon. She'll never be beholden to the Marshal."

"Have to give up her sideline, though."

Shocked at his implication that Kitty Russell sold more than redeye whisky and watered beer, Ellen balled her fist and hit him on the arm.

"You, sir, have an awful mind."

"I didn't say I disapproved – about Miss Kitty."

"Prostitution is against the law, Mr. Kerr.and you're an officer of the court."

"Not in 1873, I'm not."

"Are you saying you *do* approve? Prostitution was against the law in 1873, just like it is now."

He frowned. "How do you know?"

"I told you, I read Mr. Mattingly's old law books. A lot of them went back a long way."

Hugh paused in thoughtful contemplation before speaking.

"Prohibition made drinking illegal and people disregarded it with bemusement."

"So, you're making a distinction between good laws and bad laws?"

"What I'm saying is that to be effective, the vast majority of citizens have to support a law. I don't believe that was the case in either instance." His voice grew more reflective. "What I'm really expressing is my belief that: one; I regret the need for punishing the victim, and two; civilizations have never successfully legislated morality. Doing both creates terrible wrongs."

Ellen stared at him a long moment before settling back into the seat.

"The world needs more people like you, Hugh."

Greatly touched, he kept his eyes on the road.

"Thank you, Ellen. That means more to me than I can say." Realizing he had become too contemplative, he added, "And no, I've never visited a prostitute."

"Marshal Dillon will be glad to know that."

And he isn't the only one.

As the car pulled to a stop outside the house, Jack Merrick came up to meet them with a broad, relieved grin.

"Where did you two go? I've been worried sick that you might have gotten picked up."

"And leave you here, alone? No such luck. I would have sent the police to get you so the three of us could enjoy being handcuffed in the back of a patrol car all the way to Los Angeles."

Whistling a happy tune, Hugh tipped a finger to his forehead in salute and sauntered into the house. Merrick stared after the retreating figure in amazement.

"What got into him? Last night he was as glum as a convict doing thirty to life."

Ellen's eyes sparkled and she answered him with distinctly enunciated words.

"I cleaned his clock."

Blushing furiously, eyes wide in disbelief, Jack withdrew faster than if she had snapped a whip.

"Huh?"

"I 'polished his knob.' Does that make it any clearer for you, Mr. Merrick?"

"Perfectly," he gulped. "Sorry I asked."

She knew he wasn't and that made it all the better.

Things were returning to normal and their shared world had finally righted itself.

Matt Dillon and Kitty Russell would never marry, even if it took twenty years. But that was another story, entirely.

That evening after dinner, the three fugitives and Mrs. Thorne settled down before a fire, sipped Crème de menthe and watched *Gunsmoke*. Half of the audience secretly wished the lawman and the saloon keeper would write their own happy ending. The characters, it was obvious from the outset, had a better grasp of what they wanted than did – or would – *most* of the writers.

Watching the story of a kidnapping unfold, Hugh, Ellen and Jack's uncomfortable identification with the victim, who unfortunately died from a wound sustained while trying to escape, brought little mental relief. The unusual twist of having the outlaws make Doc Adams swear he would never reveal their identities added another level of unease, so by the time the story ended and after the credits rolled, they made their good-nights and trudged wearily upstairs to the much looked-for sanctuary on the third floor. Yawning broadly and without benefit of manners, Jack mumbled something neither Hugh nor Ellen caught and slipped into Walter's former bedroom. Waiting until they heard the sound of bed creaks, Hugh slipped his arm around Ellen's back and kissed her lightly on the cheek.

"It was a good day," he whispered. "One I will always cherish."

"That's only because Bartholomew Bond was nice to you on the phone and gave us a break." He started to protest but she put a finger to his lips. "That's just my way of agreeing with you without getting overly sentimental."

Tearing his soft blue eyes from her face, Hugh stared wistfully at the door to her bedroom, then nervously shook his leg.

"Thank you for everything, Ellen. You are a treasure beyond compare." Afraid of her own emotions, she backed away until pressed against the door. He started to follow, thought better of it and grinned. "A time for everything and everything in its place."

"Words of wisdom, *Hugh.*"

Normally she would have said, *Words of wisdom, Counselor,* but for the first time in their relationship, Ellen Thorne opted for the more *equal* use of his first name. That he fully comprehended and approved her thought was demonstrated by the slight bow he made before backstepping toward the door of Tom's former bedroom.

"Nighty-night."

"Sleep tight."

"Do not let the bedbugs bite."

Another shared familiarity.

Going into her own former, and at the moment, current bedroom, Ellen gently closed the door, switched on the bedside lamp and changed into a flannel nightgown she found in the dresser. Wrapping her arms around herself, she ran her eyes over the familiar objects, viewing them now as a past rapidly dissociating from her present.

How many times have I sat on this bed and wondered what the future held? she asked herself. *Childhood fancies, dreams of going to college and the bitter disappointment of being left behind when Tom and Walter left.... Imagining myself a great artist and then having to settle for a secretarial position in a little... podunk office in a rural town in Northern California no one outside the county ever heard of.*

She smiled because "podunk" was one of Jack Merrick's disparaging descriptions.

How could I have known what awaited me? That one dream would be substituted for another of greater worth. How all the pieces of my life would fall in place and leave me happier than I ever thought possible.

He loves me. That strange quiet, intensely personal man who adopts the persona of a brash genius without a doubt in the world; one for whom the worst odds present his most exciting challenges.

She stopped herself, cocked her ear toward the wall and listened. It took her a moment to place the muffled sound.

Hugh Kerr madly slapping cards down, playing solitaire. She found the action strangely comforting.

No, she corrected herself, reverting back to her pervious thoughts. *He does not adopt the persona. It's not a façade but part of what makes him who he is. Hugh Kerr isn't one man but two, living in the same*

skin. Even he doesn't know who he is, sometimes. Maybe he doesn't have to know; maybe he doesn't see the contradictions. Probably he doesn't care. But I do. Because if we ever take our relationship further, someone's going to have to stitch the halves together.
Do I have the right to do that? Do I even want to?

Drawing back the spread, she had almost finished readjusting the pillows when she heard a low, almost inaudible whistle. For a moment her heart pounded and as quickly quieted as she placed the coded "wolf" call.

"Come in, Jack."

A wide-eyed Jack Merrick stuck his head in through the narrow opening.

"Hugh's cheating at cards, again, Ellen!"

She almost laughed.

"How do you know he's cheating?"

"He's playing, isn't he? And you know Hugh. Nothing is ever a game with him."

"I know Hugh," she agreed. "And I wouldn't change a thing about him."

Which came close to answering another conundrum.

"Sheesh. Good night, Ellen."

"Good night, Jack."

He retreated as quietly as he had come, leaving her alone. But not really alone. Not any more.

Maybe we're all two people. Maybe relationships are only meaningful when we stitch ourselves together, not into two separate people but into two people with separate halves.

That was an idea to dream on.

The following morning after breakfast Hugh announced they were leaving. Mrs. Thorne, who had anticipated a longer stay, grabbed his hands and offered him a hopeful expression.

"You'll come back, won't you, Mr. Kerr?"

"Of course I will. But remember, I told you to call me Hugh."

"I know you did," she confessed, dropping her head. "But you're such a great man and that seems so informal. Mr. Thorne always said that a person could never err on the side of formality."

"Then he was a very wise man. But you have received Jack and me as virtual members of the family and being such, we ought to be on a first name basis. Besides," he protested, "if you continue to flatter me, these two will tease me all the way back to Los Angeles."

Growing serious, the matron cast a sidelong glance at "these two."

"I hope that is not true, Mr. Kerr. Certainly not in Ellen's case."

"Oh, especially Ellen." He made an obvious wink in her direction. "But remember what I said: in a sense, we're a family. A working one, if you wish, but my success as an attorney is predicated on Ellen and Jack's contributions. People who work and function in a relaxed atmosphere are happier and more dedicated to what are often very difficult tasks."

"I see what you mean. But you will come back?"

Releasing himself from her grasp, he cast an arm around the room.

"Ellen has been filling my head with all the camping and fishing opportunities you have up here. One day I'll just throw all my gear into the back of the car and come up to spend a week trying my hand at fly fishing."

"That would be wonderful. And as a man of your word, I shall hold you to it, sir. But kindly wait until I pack you a lunch. It is, as you say, a long drive, and I don't want you to have to eat at one of those terrible cafes along the side of the road."

"Please don't go to any trouble," Jack offered, but she was off on her mission, leaving the three alone. After packing their few belongings, they tarried outside.

"So, you're going to come up here and go fishing, are you? Because I filled your head with the wonders of Northern California?"

He offered a placid smile.

"That's right."

"I don't recall mentioning a single thing about fishing." Walking around the side of the car, she stared off into the trees. "In fact, it would never occur to me to discuss fishing with you at all."

He pretended offense.

"Why is that? I have half a dozen fishing poles and a box full of expensive, hand-tied flies."

"You might as well have said you'll drive up here for deer season. If I'm not mistaken, you have a deer rifle and probably even a shotgun powerful enough to take down a bear."

"That's right. I do."

She quickly doused his smug grin.

"Then why is it you've never been known to come back with a deer or a bear, or even a fish? And don't tell me because you've given the antlers or the claws or the filets to one of the other men. You're a phony, Hugh Kerr. You never go into the Great Outdoors with any other than a few drinking buddies and the only thing you've ever caught is a cold."

Jack guffawed and hid his grin behind a judiciously placed hand. Hugh stomped his foot.

"Then I've spent an awfully lot of money for nothing."

"Oh," Ellen continued, on a roll, "I suppose you boys get out the rags and the oil and clean your guns and tell all sorts of stories about the ones that got away. You probably swap flies, try your hands at tying some new ones and traipse around the cabin once or twice to get mud on your boots. You play mountain men for a week and come home when you get sick of your own cooking."

"Last year... or was it the year before...?" Kerr reminisced, "I'm sure I brought you home four or five pounds of fresh, cleaned and boned trout."

"You'd have done better if you had remembered to take the price tag off the butcher paper."

This time Jack laughed out loud.

"She's got you there, Hugh. Even I spotted that dead giveaway."

Snorting in annoyance, he stomped back into the house. Finding Mrs. Thorne just packing their picnic in a basket, he lowered his voice conspiratorially.

"Mrs. Thorne, there is one huge favor you could do for me."

"Anything."

"There are two paintings upstairs in the room that used to be Tom's."

"The airplanes?"

"Yes. The next time I come, I'd like to see them framed and hung over the mantel. I'm sure you can rearrange the diplomas to make room for them."

"If you like."

"I would like it very much. And if you happen to have any other of Ellen's work around the house – perhaps saved in a trunk – I'd appreciate it if you would carefully pack them and send them to me. Don't mind the expense. I will promptly reimburse you."

Not quite sure how to respond, she nodded.

"I will look for you, Mr. Kerr."

This time he did not correct her use of his title and surname.

"I'll carry the basket."

Taking the wicker hamper, he led the way outside and placed it in the back seat.

"All right, you two: let's go. Thank you for your hospitality, Mrs. Thorne. It was a pleasure meeting you."

"And you and Mr. Merrick, to be sure. Safe journey."

Kissing her daughter on the cheek, she waved a handkerchief as they drove off. Ellen waved out the window while Jack peeked under the checkered covering.

"When do we get to eat?"

Which seemed as good a question as any to ponder before the miles dwindled and their minds turned to more unpleasant matters.

They drove several hours in relative silence before Jack reached across the seat and tugged Hugh's sleeve.

"See that gas station up ahead? Pull up there, will you? Fill up the tank; keep the guy talking. Ellen, you go inside the shop and engage the cashier in small talk."

Kerr turned on the blinker and slowed the car.

"Another short trip? So soon? And you have to do it in such privacy?"

"Yes. Yes. And yes."

Without offering further details, Jack escaped as the attendant came up, and sauntered toward the public restroom. Neither of his cohorts noticed that he bypassed the door and kept on going. Ten minutes later, the detective returned, grinning sheepishly. Ellen rejoined them just as the gas jockey finished checking the balloon spare.

"Boy, Montezuma's Revenge sure got me," Merrick declared, rubbing his stomach. "That Mexican chili we ate at the last stop tore my insides up." He did not explain until they were half a mile down the road. "O.K., Hugh. Pull over here."

Without asking why, Kerr rolled the car to a stop along a wider section of ground. Jack carefully extracted two small, flat panels from beneath his shirt.

"License plates!" Ellen identified.

"I've had my eyes peeled for an old abandoned vehicle ever since we left San Francisco. There were half a dozen parked behind that last gas station. By the looks of them, they've been there for some while and it isn't likely anyone will notice I removed the tags. Be right back."

Using a dime as a screwdriver, Jack exchanged the plates on the car they were driving with those he had stolen. Crossing around to the driver's side, he opened the door. "Let me get behind the wheel; it's your turn to sit in the back."

"That's my reward for having you further obscure our identity?"

"No. It's *my* reward. Maybe Wade will keep his word and maybe he won't. But on the off chance there is an APB out on us and that salesman didn't wait to submit the paperwork, I don't see any point taking chances. If the coppers got wind we switched cars and have a description of this one, the closer we get to home, the more likely it is we'll be spotted. They may identify the make and model but when they see the plate numbers don't match, we may get a free pass. It isn't foolproof but it's an edge."

"Good thought." Hugh got in the back and promptly drew back the checkered cloth on the picnic basket. "But you didn't think it through quite well enough. Now *I'm* in charge of the food."

"Bitch!" And then in a contrite voice, "Excuse my French, Miss Thorne."

"You're excused. Hugh, what time is it?"

"Twelve-o-one."

"All right. We can eat."

"Is that some etiquette rule I don't know? Hedda Hopper says Edward G. Robinson and his two thugs can't partake of nourishment before *High Noon*?"

"Gary Cooper," Jack supplied.

"What?"

"Gary Cooper starred in *High Noon*."

"You really should widen your horizons, Mr. Kerr," Ellen chided. "There are more movie genres than horror flicks. But that's not *precisely* what I meant. Knowing my mother, she put beer in the basket along with lunch food and cake. I'm sure Miss Hopper would want us to wait until *post meridian* before chugging it."

Staring at her in stark amazement, Hugh laughed and immediately tore through the contents. At the bottom, carefully wrapped in wet towels to keep them cool, were two bottles of beer. After searching for a third, he came up empty.

"She may know her movies, but she can't count. There are three of us."

Even Jack knew the solution to that puzzle.

"Ladies don't drink beer."

"I…" Proving his mind had returned to its normal state of efficiency, Kerr cut off his sentence before getting himself in trouble, quickly amending it to, "I found a bottle opener!"

Nodding at his prowess, Ellen poked Jack in the arm.

"Without discounting my mother's etiquette, *I* have something to say, and that is, 'drivers don't drink.' If you wish to imbibe, pull over and switch places with me."

"Aw, come on. It's only beer!"

"Tell that to Eliot Ness and the Prohibition boys."

Grousing language unbefitting a gentleman that concluded with, "Prohibition's over," Jack signaled right and hopped out of the driver's side. Ellen took the wheel and sped them back into the lane of traffic.

Hugh handed out fried chicken and when the trio had consumed all there was, they feasted on hard-boiled eggs, potato salad and an assortment of pickles and olives. After the boys washed their meal down with beer, deftly opened by the lawyer without too much spillage, they ate chocolate cake and licked their fingers.

Patting his stomach in satisfaction, Hugh leaned forward, resting his chin on the back of Jack's seat.

"All right. We've had our well-deserved and well-needed R&R and now it's time to put our minds to the prospects at hand. We have to report to Wade at police headquarters at precisely 5 P.M. There's no getting around that."

The sudden inflection of finality caused Ellen to turn her head so she could view his stern countenance.

"What kind of trouble are you anticipating?"

Jack had his own question ready.

"Assuming Price has been informed of our ETA by one of his paid informants on the force, do you think there's any chance he'll ambush us outside the station?"

Kerr's voice grew thoughtful.

"That's certainly something I've considered. I believe if he had found us on the road or in San Francisco that would have been the case, because he would have derived a great deal of instant gratification from our bloody and vicious murders. He might even have tried to make it look as though we had a murderous quarrel, with the 'last one standing' taking his or her life. But we were too clever for him and he missed his chance. So, yes, I think that's possible."

Taking out a cigarette, he offered one to Merrick and took another for himself. Lighting both from the same match, he tossed the spent wooden sliver out the window, then contemplated the curling smoke a long beat.

"Where do I come in, anyway? I didn't have anything to do with his original conviction" Jack interrupted, taking a deep drag on the cigarette to punctuate the question.

"Sure you did," Ellen supplied. "It was your investigation that gave Hugh the information to use against him."

"Oh, great. I knew I should have stayed in the Navy. It was a lot less dangerous than hanging out with a defense attorney and his moll."

Kerr ignored the comment, thinking aloud.

"Price's first plan was to get rid of Ellen and me courtesy of the gas chamber. Once our fate was settled, you'd become superfluous and he'd have you killed. If we weren't convicted for whatever reason, he'd still have a damned good shot at ruining my reputation, either from adverse publicity or by holding you over our heads. Who knows? Like we just saw on *Gunsmoke,* to earn your freedom maybe he forces me to make the one concession I otherwise wouldn't: never to practice law again."

Finished with his smoke, Jack disgustedly heaved the butt out the window.

"Nice and neat. Just like the corners on a military cot."

"Helping you escape, Jack, put a crimp in that plan."

"You don't think Bond will hold us?" Ellen asked.

He hesitated before answering.

"I'm not sure. It's a sticky situation. Ordinarily I'd say no because it's going to look like showboating on his part when we're released. On the other hand, he has enough evidence to make a case. One the grand jury would be hard-pressed to ignore."

"Us being at the scene and your fingerprint on the St. Christopher medal?"

"Yes."

Ellen's chin jutted in defiance.

"All we have to do is prove the fingerprint was planted."

"To do that, we need to establish at least two ranking officers on the police force are on Price's payroll. An inspector and a lab technician, no less. And even if we can, there's still your Mr. X. And he's still dead. We don't know who he is, and the odds on us ever identifying him are next to none."

"Unless Price happened to have picked up an old, disgruntled client of yours and has Police Inspector What's-His-Name from San Diego miraculously discover the head and hands. Then, they'll have a face and fingerprints," Jack noted.

Kerr and Ellen stiffened at the horror of the thought. After a long, uncomfortable pause, she unfroze first.

"I have to believe that's too intricate even for Carey Price. Let's stick to the fact we can certainly prove we didn't kill Jack because he's still alive. And he's an eyewitness to the murder of Mr. X," she hopefully added.

"Even I know how dicey that is, Starlet," Jack interjected. "Considering how intricately I'm involved in this caper, my testimony can be construed as coming under the heading of self-serving."

She threw up her hands in exasperation.

"What's our motive, for goodness sake? Why in the world would we kill someone and then make it appear as though you were the victim?"

"So Hugh can get his name in the paper?" Jack speculated, eying the attorney. "Everyone knows, or thinks they know, you're a publicity hound. You get your picture in the papers more often than the Queen of England." When the attorney made no comment, he pursued the idea. "How's business been lately, pal? Can your accounts stand a police audit? You spend money like a drunken sailor. Or how about this? You're crazy as a loon."

"Jack," Ellen warned but Hugh waved her off.

"Perhaps I am. But I don't need to pull off a real murder so I can be charged with a pretend one to antagonize the police, get myself – and Ellen – charged with a capital crime, spend time in jail and defend us at trial, only to prove our innocence by producing the supposedly dead body just before the case goes to jury. Although," he added with a wry smile, "the idea does have its appeal."

"Oh, please. See what I mean, Ellen? It may help a defense lawyer but it'll be murder for my business," Jack added with an emphasis on *my*, then made quote marks with his fingers. "'Corpse of brassy-balls detective turns out to be tainted evidence.' Think what a field day the newspapers will have with that!"

"I'm thinking precisely that," the lawyer confessed.

"You are?" came the suspicious inquiry.

"Yes. Newspapers. Publicity. Lots of it."

"Oh, lord, he's at it again, Ellen."

"Which reminds me, Miss Thorne. How much does a new hairdo and a glamorous outfit cost?"

"For you or for me?"

"I know what my suits cost. For you, of course."

"How glamorous?"

"Plenty."

Jack sank back into the seat cushion, holding his hands over his face as she glibly responded, "One hundred and fifty dollars. With gratuities."

"OK. We'll put it on the expense account. And yours, too, Jack."

"I don't need a new hairdo and while I have sexy legs, I'm not sure I could ever meet anyone's expectations of 'glamorous,'" he groused through splayed fingers.

"We haven't got time for a custom-made suit, but one nicely tailored out to do the trick. I'll need one, too."

"Do-the-trick-for-what? Are you planning on holding a fashion show before we're incarcerated in the hoosegow?"

"No. But I want us to look nice when we have our photographs taken."

"No-one-looks-nice-in-a-mug-shot."

"Not mug shots, Jack. On the front pages of the Los Angeles *Times*."

"All right, Hugh," Ellen sighed. "Just where are you going with this?"

"I said it was a distinct possibility Price could have us assassinated; that's why we fled L.A. in the first place. Now, we're compelled to return. Therefore, we need protection. What better bodyguards are there than a host of reporters and photographers hovering around us like bees after nectar?"

"And just how are the schmos going to know anything about our predicament?"

"We're going to tell them, of course."

"Oh, God. Good for you as an attorney; bad for me as a detective," Jack moaned. "I can see it now. There I am, out on assignment trying to look inconspicuous like an average, everyday Joe and some floozy or pencil-pusher comes up to me and says, 'Say, you're a private dick, aren't you? I saw your picture in the paper. What are you doing around here? Who you investigating?'"

"Well," Kerr considered, "Ellen and I can take the spotlight and you can hang around the rear." Merrick started to nod when Hugh finished the thought. "And get a knife stuck between your ribs. Ellen and I have already seen you at the morgue once; a second time ought to be easier. And as the Merrick Detective Agency has already buried you, I guess we can throw the real body into the Los Angeles River and be done with it."

"There isn't any water in the Los Angeles River. And what do you mean, the Merrick Detective Agency already buried me? Who gave the eulogy? And more to the point, who paid for it?"

Hugh answered the first statement and ignored the interrogatives.

"The rats won't care. They'll eat you wet or dry."

"OK, Hugh, you've made your point. But you get my point."

Kerr finished the last of his beer and stared longingly at the remainder in Merrick's bottle.

"Just keep in mind that in most instances there's nothing more fleeting than cheap publicity. In a week, you can go right back to being your old, anonymous self."

"Hugh and I will think of you as a one-hit wonder, Jack," Ellen chimed in. "if that's any consolation."

"It isn't, but thanks just the same. And what do you mean by 'old'?"

Hugh and Ellen laughed and Jack finished his beer. Caught in an unexpected burp, he excused himself and stared morosely out the window.

"I'm getting this creepy feeling again that Price's boys are patrolling the highway. While machine guns went out with Frank Nitti, I wouldn't want to have to race past black sedans filled with pistol-toting thugs."

"I agree; they're out here, all right. Maybe not waiting in ambush but to follow us and report our whereabouts to the boss," Kerr agreed. "We have an advantage in driving a car they're not looking for and you switched the tags. Getting through L.A. is another matter, entirely. We don't dare go home or to the office because those places will surely be covered. Therefore, we fool them by going someplace conspicuous. Even if they had it in their minds to… wipe us out, we'll do our level best to ensure they can't."

"Someplace like where?"

"You'll see."

Twenty miles outside the city a pair of nondescript cars fell in behind them. Jack nudged Hugh.

"Looks like we've got a tail."

"We'll find out in a minute. Slow down, Ellen. Give them a chance to pass." She obeyed and the two cars fell back. "All right; speed up." Again, the cars matched their pace. "Looks like you're right, Jack."

"Real subtle. If they worked for me, they wouldn't be."

"I suppose they're just following orders," Ellen suggested. She turned to Hugh. "Shall we be worried?"

"Nope. Just drop back down and follow the speed limit. The one thing I don't want right now is to be picked up by the highway patrol for a traffic violation."

The two cars followed them into the city limits and then dropped out of sight. Jack quickly identified two new tails. Kerr shrugged and gave Ellen directions. In a quarter of an hour they reached his destination in plenty of time for the stage to be set.

"The Golden Bear Hotel!" Ellen gasped. "You mean we're going to stay here?"

"That's right," a smug Hugh Kerr agreed.

"Home of internationally famous actors, wealthy foreign dignitaries and world-renown business executives. I've never had the nerve to set foot in the lobby before."

"That's all about to change. And about time, too."

Ignoring the raised eyebrows of the courtier who dubiously came up and opened the door for Miss Thorne to alight, the three wearily traipsed inside. Surrounded by the opulence of glittering gold-plated fixtures, decorative lighting and even more decorative people, Hugh led the trio to the front desk. Giving the clerk his most affable smile, he reached into his pocket and produced a wad of bills.

"Good afternoon," he began, nodding politely to a woman dressed in a full-length mink coat standing to his right. To the clerk he explained, "My name is Hugh Kerr, the defense attorney. I require three of your best rooms; the penthouse will do nicely if it has three consecutive suites."

The flash of cold, hard cash and the familiar name brightened the clerk's countenance considerably.

"Certainly, Mr. Kerr. The Golden Bear is happy to accommodate you. How long will you be staying, sir?"

"That depends entirely upon circumstances. Let's say a week." Peeling off a number of high denomination bills, he set them on the counter. "If that is too much, consider it a gratuity for yourself and the bellhop."

"Thank you, sir!" Kerr signed the register for Ellen and Jack while the clerk rang the bell for assistance. A smart-looking youth dressed in livery appeared at the urgent summons. Correctly divining they had live ones, he tipped his cap as the clerk asked, "Have you any luggage, Mr. Kerr?"

"No, we plan on using the resources of the hotel. Have a hairdresser and a clothier for Miss Thorne meet her upstairs in half an hour; Mr. Merrick and I require the services of a barber and a tailor."

"Certainly, sir!" Passing three keys to the bell boy, he admonished him with an officious and unnecessary, "Hop to it!"

The boy made a deep bow before backing up.

"Right this way, if you please."

Making a surreptitious sweep of the lobby with his keen eyes to be certain they would have no trouble, Kerr took Ellen's arm. Pressing tightly against him, she looked up and smiled, eyes glittering in excitement.

"I feel like a movie star."

"You look like one, too."

For the moment, at least, they were embarking on an exciting and opportune adventure.

Chapter 12

"Oh, Hugh, will you look at this?"

Arms wide, Ellen made a circuit of the main room in the suite, brushing past half a dozen vases filled with fresh flowers, a three-tier box of French chocolates displayed on an end table within easy reach of a luxurious brocaded armchair and a silver bucket filled with ice that contained an unopened bottle of champagne. Beside it were two narrow crystal glasses. Kerr extracted the bottle, inspected the label and carefully replaced it.

"A vintage year."

"And look at this – two thick terrycloth robes bordered with satin in the bathroom! And the tub – deep enough to soak in up your nose." Taking more delight in watching her amazement than in itemizing the wonders of the room, he followed at a respectful distance, a hint of a smile playing across his compressed lips.

"Triple milled French soap!" she continued, tearing around the bath like a child inspecting the contents of Santa Claus' sack. Lifting one of the bars, Ellen brought it to her nose and sniffed. "Rose; and others scented with lavender and Lily of the Valley."

"See what's in the cabinet," he suggested.

Hardly daring to look, Ellen gingerly drew back the mirrored door. The sight of two shelves filled with perfumes took her breath away. Quickly inspecting the atomizers, she sprayed one on her wrist, rubbed it in and gentle inhaled.

"Rose. How wonderful; my favorite. And look – matching powder! It's all coordinated." Crossing to him, she extended her hand so he could appraise the perfume. As he nodded in approval she asked, "Is this really how the other half lives?"

"I suppose it is."

Frowning a moment, she realized her mistake and grinned.

"Oh, well, you wouldn't know about what ladies like in their *boudoir,* but I mean –"

"I know what you mean," he laughed. She playfully pushed him away and went back "on tour." After sitting and then bouncing on the bed, Ellen pulled down the soft, peach-colored comforter.

"Feather-down pillows, satin sheets, and look, Hugh! There's a mint under the pillow! Do they really do this? I thought it was only true in romance novels."

"I see," he said, hands in his pockets. "Flowers, champagne, milled soap and you're most impressed with the mint under the pillow."

"Remember it," she winked. "I'm a simple girl."

"On the contrary, Miss Thorne: you are the most complex – and beautiful – women I have ever known."

Obviously flattered and caught momentarily off-guard, she warned, "Stop it," before a polite knock on the door prevented further conversation.

"Come in."

A woman wheeling a cart full of hair products and blow dryers entered. Behind her stood another woman holding tape measures and several dresses. Reluctantly realizing their time together had been interrupted, Hugh hastily made his way toward the door.

"I'll be back in an hour. Is that enough time?"

"Combien de temps avez-vous, monsieur?" the hairdresser answered in French.

Checking his watch, Kerr replied without thinking, *"Je vous prie m'excuser, mais par le temps. L'heure, c'est tout ce que je peux de recharge."*

"Ensuite, tout sera pret dans une heure."

"Merci."

Quietly observing his spontaneity and perfect French, Ellen asked, "What did you say to her?"

"Have everything ready in an hour." He offered a grin. "I've got some telephoning to do and then I'm going down and sit in the steam room for a quarter of an hour. Then a shave and a quick change of clothes. I should be back just about the time you're ready. Have fun."

"I will."

He waved a happy good-bye and disappeared. Ellen watched him go, feeling the room suddenly grow colder and less exciting without his presence. Letting it serve as a reminder that the most precious things in life were better shared, she gave herself over to the artisans with a shrug half of resignation and half of eagerness.

When Hugh Kerr returned exactly sixty minutes later, he beheld a transformed woman. Hair shampooed, dried and styled and dressed in an exquisite emerald-green gown that accentuated her form, he stepped back in surprise, huffed and then broke out into a boyish grin.

"Wow!"

"You like?" she asked, failing to hide the blush of pleasure at his obvious approval.

"I like."

"And you, sir, look like a million dollars, yourself."

Tilting back her head, she took in the fine cut of the formal blue suit that looked as though it had been tailored made for him on the spot, the matching tie and the gold tie bar. Beneath it, he wore a white shirt with French cuffs and cufflinks that coordinated with the tie bar. Smooth-cheeked, his wavy black hair neatly brushed and sporting a subtle lime cologne, he nearly took her breath away.

"You look as though you ought to be posing for the cover of a 'Man of the Year' spread."

Keeping their distance for the moment, they appraised one another with a curiosity heightened not only by the handsome wardrobes but from a relationship that had grown deeper, more meaningful and decidedly more intimate over the past six days.

Words failed and it was not until Hugh made the first move by holding out his arms that Ellen hurried into them. Hugging with rising passion, their cheeks rubbed together, nuzzled and simultaneously their heads turned until they faced one another, eyes sparkling in anticipation. As their lips met, their first kiss explored, questioned, and blossomed into an evolving expression of power, respect and love.

Trembling in excitement, Hugh pressed closer, absorbing the warmth of her body, the curves of her flesh, the taste of her lips. Eyes closed, he kissed her a second time and then a third, each longer and more demanding than the last. She responded with an eagerness that should have surprised him and did not.

Lingering over the fourth kiss, Ellen gently inhaled his breath, rested her head on his shoulder to quiet her pounding heart, then held back her head to forever etch his likeness into her soul.

"Hugh…"

"Yes?" he whispered, allowing her to take the lead.

"I've been thinking."

"Me, too."

Her voice choked. "If something happens… something terrible this evening… We don't know. We can't be sure."

"I won't let it happen."

"You mustn't say that." He held her closer as though afraid of what she would say and she struggled against herself to speak. "That puts the responsibility on you. I won't have that." He tried to argue but with tears glistening in her eyes, she stopped him by freeing an arm and placing a finger against his lips. He kissed it and she ignored him because she had to. "I'm afraid."

"Ellen –"

"– afraid that we may never have this time again. We… can't afford to waste it. Do you…" Her voice lowered. "Do you understand what I'm saying?"

"Then let me get on my knees."

"No, Hugh. I'm not ready for that. That has to be for another time and another place. When you have a ring in your pocket, and we're alone and safe. This is different."

Freeing his own arm, he fished in his pocket and removed something he kept covered in his palm.

"I was thinking the same… exact thing. And if you think I'm not afraid, you would be wrong. I am. We're taking a big gamble, and I don't want… to spoil other moments we have together."

He started to open his hand and she stopped him. Divining her thoughts, he sheepishly grinned and shook his head. Puzzled, she abandoned her protest and he revealed what he held. It was not a diamond ring but a small, round package the size of a fifty cent piece. The significance of it froze her mouth in a small "O" for a second before she found the power to speak.

"A condom. No, Hugh – there's no need for that. I don't want our first time -"

He shook his head as his hand found her wrist and applied pressure.

"There is a need. We're both adults, Ellen. We both understand the consequences of what we're contemplating. A man and a woman may consummate their love without a wedding ring but if they do, the chance they take is a great one." His voice hardened. "I don't want people counting on their fingers; *we* don't want to engender a life before everything is right and proper."

"It's all right –"

"Mistakes happen. Between us, we don't want to commit that kind of an error. We've been too careful, too respectful of one another. If we make love now, there must be no shadow of doubt; no shame. No fear. No holding our child and thinking it was conceived as a bastard. I couldn't do that to you; or to myself. What we have is too precious to taint with the selfishness of a moment."

Tears rolled down her cheeks.

"Hugh, no man ever worries about that.... Only you. Only you would think those things."

"I love you, Ellen. Know that, before anything else."

"I love you, Hugh. More than any words can ever convey. I think I've always loved you... even before we ever met. Does that make sense?"

She expected him to laugh but instead his face turned thoughtful.

"I know exactly what you mean. For as long as I can remember... from the time I was a small child, in my darkest, loneliest moments when I didn't have a friend in the world, I knew... perhaps I should say I *divined* someone special was out there." His hand shook as he attempted to make a sweeping motion across the universe of his past, present and future. "You couldn't even have been born yet, Ellen...."

"But I was watching. And hurrying to catch up."

"Thank God you did. The first time I laid eyes on you, I felt as though my feet had been knocked out from under me."

"Not the most romantic way of expressing it," she teased, wiping her eyes, "but exactly right."

Placing trembling hands on his face, she sought his orbs, held them, sent her mind through the swirling emotions of his conscious and subconscious essence.

"Take me to bed," she whispered into his ear.

He held her, lifted her up, walked on lover's air across the room. It was a long walk and a short walk, an eternity and the millionth of a second. But when he put her down and sat beside her, they shared an aching awareness that the moment had passed. Or perhaps it had never been, for they had played their game knowing they were destined to lose. For a minute or two or ten they had dared step out of time and enter a dimension where only lovers lived. Taking their physical intimacy as far as they could, their challenge to fate had failed. Or rather, time had resumed its brutal, worldly insistence.

The second hand stole their attention as it swept around the clock face. Entwined in each other's arms they waited in dread anticipation for the inevitable. It came in the form of what could be called music only in the ear of the beholder: two notes, the second held longer than the first.

Jack Merrick's familiar wolf whistle.

"Anyone home?"

Reality had come calling.

They had known it all along.

And damned that fate which frightened them and kept them apart.

It had not been time.

Two lovers, playing with shadows of what might have been.

Biting his lip, Hugh slipped the condom back in his pocket.

"I've never actually used one of those," he grinned as a rivulet of perspiration the composition of tears rolled down his forehead. "You were going to have to help me, anyway. I don't think they come with instructions."

"Where did you get it, anyway?"

"I gave the bellhop five dollars."

She giggled.

"That must have been embarrassing."

"It was and it wasn't."

She gave him a fist on the arm.

"My hair and make-up, you know. They wouldn't have survived."

He stiffly nodded.

"We have to have our pictures taken."

"And Jack's waiting."

On cue, the detective called through the closed door, "The reporters are here."

"Coming," Ellen and Hugh replied in unison. At least they had done that together.

Neither was sure it represented a consolation.

Waiting patiently while Ellen wiped lipstick from his face, Hugh straightened his tie and walked casually to the door. Opening it with a flourish, he noted approvingly that Jack had kept the newspapermen at bay.

"Where are they?"

"Downstairs in the lobby. Geez, Hugh, you must have called every rag in town."

"The more the merrier. Go down and gather them together; see if management will give us a conference room."

"That's nothing. The way those boys are bellying up to the bar, I wouldn't doubt the management would put the three of us up for free for as long as we want to stay. Right now, we're a better attraction than a post-Academy Awards party."

"Everyone loves a winner, Jack."

"What have we won?"

"Our lives – I hope."

"That's better than a gold-plated statuette any day."

Merrick touched a finger to his forehead and disappeared. Kerr turned to Ellen.

"We'll give him five minutes to get everything settled and then make our grand entrance."

Crossing to him, she rested a hand on his arm.

"What in the world do you think Bartholomew Bond and Lieutenant Wade will think of all this?"

"They don't concern me. It's how Carey Price reacts that matters."

"How will he react?"

He shrugged, stared at the ceiling for a moment, then took out a pack of cigarettes, tapped one out and lit it. Taking a deep drag, he averted his head so as to avoid blowing smoke in her direction.

"That depends on what he wants – and how soon. But he sure as hell can't get at us with all those people around." On her look he added, "Well, he could but I'm betting very high stakes he won't."

"I'll go with that."

Ellen reluctantly broke away, quickly ran a brush through her hair, reapplied lipstick and joined him at the door. Hand-in-hand they left the room, walked to the elevator and rode down to Ellen Thorne's first press conference.

It was turning into a day of firsts – and almost firsts.

Already aware of what was transpiring, the elevator operator stopped on the mezzanine level and indicated the direction.

"Right down that way, Mr. Kerr."

"Thank you."

Directed by the sounds of voices raised in eager anticipation, the pair casually strolled along the plush carpet. As the reporters recognized the defense attorney, they readily made way for the pair.

"What's it all about, Hugh?" one called, waving a press badge for identification.

"Hold it, Mr. Kerr," another called, holding up his camera. "Smile, Miss Thorne."

The couple obligingly paused for photographs, allowing ample opportunities until red dots popped behind their eyes from the brightness of the flash bulbs. Waving they had had enough, the press men backed away and they continued their journey through the crowded room.

"What about the murder charge you're being investigated on, Mr. Kerr?"

"Are the police going to crash your party?"

"Someone said drinks were on you, Hugh! Is that true? That's what we really want to know."

"All in good time, boys."

Carefully climbing the three steps to a permanent speaker's platform, Kerr summoned Jack Merrick, smiled in casual anticipation and then held up his arms for silence. The room hushed.

"First of all, for those who don't know me, I am Hugh Kerr, the defense attorney. I'd like to thank you all for coming." He waited for the good-natured cheering to die down before continuing. Looking out over the sea of perhaps fifty faces, many of whom he recognized and knew by first name, the lawyer appraised them as he would a jury for a closing argument. Those who covered the law courts would later write that he was a man in his element; a man who knew how to work the crowds.

"I'll cut right to the chase: yes, the bar tab is on me. Those who have already paid can claim restitution at my office tomorrow morning. But be sure to send along your receipts; no double-dipping on your expense accounts."

The cheers and hand-clapping were louder and more raucous.

"Aw, you know us, Hugh! Would we do that?"

Making an ambiguous gesture, his face grew reflective.

"No more than I – or Ellen Thorne – would commit murder." He let the statement sink in before continuing. "Especially if the victim was Jack Merrick, who just happens to be standing alongside us." The abrupt change of subject and the seriousness of the charge immediately quieted the initial twittering. "By this time all of you know – and have printed in your newspapers - that the police are looking for Miss Thorne and myself on a charge of first degree murder." His voice lowered an octave to underscore the importance of what he was saying. "We are accused not only of murdering our colleague and friend, but of decapitating his body and savagely severing both his hands to eliminate the possibility of the corpse being identified by fingerprints. Makes for good, front page headlines, doesn't it?"

"Is that really Jack Merrick?" a man from the back called out.

"Yes, it is."

"Have him step forward, Mr. Kerr."

Hugh nodded and Jack Merrick separated himself from the others by a foot or two. Those in the audience who recognized him let out a yell of relief and approval.

"Hey, Jack, is that really you?" one teased. "We thought for sure the rumors of your demise were true when we didn't see you at the open bar."

Jack grinned although both Ellen and Hugh felt his unease and appreciated his performance.

"That's because Mr. Kerr didn't make the announcement until a moment ago. With the prices they charge here, I didn't want to take any chances – especially knowing it wouldn't be allowed on *my* expense account."

"Did you ask?" a short man with wire-framed glasses and a receding hairline standing in the second row quipped.

"You bet."

Kerr waited for the chuckles to subside before regaining control of the informal press conference.

"As you can clearly see, Jack Merrick is alive."

"And to think I went to his funeral," one of the reporters complained. "And a dry affair it was, too."

"I hope you mean 'dry,' as in no liquor was served, as opposed to 'dry eyed,'" Jack quipped, doing his best to hold up his end of the interview.

"The boys from your Agency were sobbing, all right – because they were all out of a job!"

Another of the press corps took up the thread.

"Then how can you and Miss Thorne be charged with his murder, Hugh?" The lawyer shrugged.

"I presume the police have changed the name of the deceased."

"Who was killed, then?"

"I don't know," Kerr replied with charming innocence. "An individual who had a strikingly remarkable physical similarity to Mr. Merrick."

"But why? What's it all about?"

Pencils poised above notepads, the reporters waited for the news scoop that would make the evening headlines.

"It is my contention that a person – or persons unknown - deliberately staged Jack Merrick's murder. First, to cause Miss Thorne and me considerable emotional distress occasioned by the death of a close friend. And second, to frame us for the murder."

"How could they do that?"

"By setting a clever trap: leaving clues behind so that we would follow them to the murder scene – inadvertently leaving evidence of our having been there - so when the police later investigated, they would be found and identified. The same individual responsible for the murder also saw to it that my fingerprint was planted on a crucial piece of evidence to further implicate me."

"Who is it, Kerr – who set you and Miss Thorne up? Surely you have an idea."

"Yes," he conceded, casually walking a few steps closer to the end of the raised apron. "I know who it is, but I can hardly give you his name. That will have to come out if and when there is an indictment and a grand jury is convened."

"Tell us, anyway. We won't spread the news."

Kerr waited until the catcalls and smiles faded.

"The hell you won't," he began, playing down to the level of a murder suspect with a sly smile.

"Can we quote you on that?"

Hands in his pockets, the lawyer assumed an "Aw shucks" posture. A reporter wearing a tan trench coat waved his hand for recognition.

"What's the mystery with Merrick? If he wasn't really dead as his presence here attests, where was he?"

Jack spoke for himself. "I was lured out to some private location, beaten within an inch of my life and kidnapped. If it hadn't been for my two loyal and very brave friends here, I'd really be dead by now. And all you boys would be going to a second funeral." The impact of his avowal caused a momentary lull before another question rang out from the side.

"If you and Miss Thorne are innocent of complicity at the very least, why did you run? I heard when the cops started looking for you to ask questions, you had disappeared. As a law-abiding citizen and a member of the Bar, wasn't it your duty to report what you knew to the police?"

"I made several attempts to do just that," he easily agreed without going into further detail.

"But as it was readily apparent that after failing to involve us in Jack Merrick's murder the perpetrator of the real crime would come after us in another way – one most likely involving violence against me and very possibly against Miss Thorne – our best and safest course of action was to go underground until we felt it safe to return."

"What makes you feel safe now? What happened to change your mind?"

As though finishing a summation to the jury, Hugh Kerr took in a deep breath and took the time to make eye contact with as many of the reporters as he could without causing an undue delay.

"You – all of you here – changed my mind."

A low undercurrent of shock and surprise rumbled through the room. Finally, one intrepid fellow inquired for the rest, "What do you mean, sir?"

"I believe it's called safety in numbers. With all you boys around us – and I invite all of you to accompany us to the police station, where, incidentally we are to report by 5 o'clock sharp – it will be difficult and I hope impossible – for anyone to take shots at us, run our car down or employ any of the sundry methods killers use in their unsavory trade."

The import of his statement finally shattered whatever calm had been maintained. Some raised their fists, others cheered in recognition of the role in which they were being asked to participate.

"Let's hear it for the Fourth Estate!"

Kerr sagely nodded. "First the Church, second the nobility, third the people and fourth the press. Not necessarily my numerical arrangement; let me say at the moment, you fellows constitute my First Estate."

Jack Merrick took in the scene, marveled at Kerr's almost magical handling of the situation, then quietly edged nearer the master, touching the pointer finger of his right hand to the face plate of his wrist watch. Understanding the implication, the lawyer called for silence.

"I'm sorry, boys, but it's time to take the show on the road. Those who want to be part of history – albeit a small piece of it – are invited to come along and provide cover for Miss Thorne, Mr. Merrick and myself. But I warn you – and all kidding aside – the element of danger is very real."

"O.K., Hugh, we'll check with our mommies and get permission."

Kerr laughed. "You do that." He had set the scene and he had anticipated the question: all with an eye toward getting what he needed. While he would not have agreed with Jack that he had a magical touch, he might have conceded the point that he had skillfully maneuvered the crowd. But the play was far from over and he very much suspected the worst was yet to come.

On his signal the crowd parted and the three fugitives from justice made their way out the room and through the crowded lobby. Outside, the parking valet greeted them a slight bow and a smile.

"I have your car ready, sir. I took the liberty of having the tank filled and the oil checked."

"Thank you." Kerr took a $5 bill from his pocket and exchanged it for the keys. "I wish you'd drive, Jack," he added, taking Ellen by the arm to be certain they were not separated in the outpouring of reporters and spectators into the drive.

"I was going to volunteer," Merrick replied, waving away the keys. "But not that auto." Standing on tiptoe he scanned over the heads of the swirling crowd, saw what he wanted and offered a curt motion with his hand. "This way."

Letting Jack clear a path, Hugh and Ellen followed behind. At the end of the drive Jack suddenly raised a hand and was answered by a middle-aged, smallish man wearing a shabby tweed coat and a low-riding, broad-brimmed hat. It was not until he disappeared inside a waiting car and drove it toward them that Kerr recognized him as one of the Merrick Detective Agency operatives. Putting the vehicle into neutral, the detective jumped out and embraced the taller man.

"I never thought I'd see you again this side of the Great Beyond, Boss!" he cried in utter joy. "What happened? Why didn't you call, let someone know? We chipped in our own money to give you a send-off —"

"I know, I know," Jack remarked, giving the man a bear hug then directing him aside. "I'll fill you in later. Here: take this key. It belongs to a blue 1955 Chevy, California license 2XG 187. It's up by the front door. Drive it back and park it in the alley by the office."

"Sure thing, Boss."

Jack grabbed him by the arm before he scampered away.

"Give it a thorough going over before you turn the ignition, Bill. I don't have a good feeling about it."

"Sure thing."

Touching a forefinger to the rim of his hat, the operative slipped away. Hugh and Ellen both got into the back seat of the Agency vehicle while Jack climbed into the driver's side. Before the doors were fully shut, he had shifted gear and turned the snub-nosed compact around.

"What was that all about, Jack?" Ellen asked, turning around to watch as a train of reporters' cars fell in behind them. Unrolling the window, Merrick signaled the first half dozen pull ahead of them, then settled back to drive.

"The valet, for one thing. He wasn't the same man we met on the way in and it wasn't time for change of shift. General precautionary measures for the second. We were in the hotel a good two hours – plenty of time for word to get to Price and have him send one of his thugs out here to do a little job."

"How did your man know to meet you here?"

Checking the rear view mirror to ascertain they were still in the middle of the convoy, Jack shrugged.

"Hell, Hugh, you were telling the world where we were, so I thought it was safe to call the office and get someone over here. No sense being penny wise and pound foolish –"

His sentence was cut off by the sound of a thunderous explosion. Although muffled by the distance of half a mile there was no mistaking the cause. The color drained from Jack's face and his eyelids closed for half a second in grief. When he opened them again, the orbs reflected a hatred as intense as ever his two friends had ever witnessed. Kerr immediately leaned forward, his own face lined with sorrow and intensity.

"It wasn't your fault, Jack. You warned him to be careful."

"Not well enough, apparently. Jesus, Hugh, you can forget taking that bastard Price to trial. If I ever get my hands on him, he's dead meat."

Wise enough not to argue, Kerr settled back and let out a deep breath.

"I'm sorry. I'll try and make it up to his family –"

"He doesn't have a family and it doesn't matter if he did. *You're* not making anything up to anyone. It wasn't your fault and it wasn't mine. We know whose fault it was and he's gonna pay, believe you me."

Hugh Kerr and Ellen Thorne had nothing further to say.

They believed him implicitly.

Chapter 13

At 4:55 P.M. Jack Merrick pulled the agency man's car up to the curb outside police headquarters and killed the engine. Removing the key from the ignition Merrick squeezed it in his hand a moment then jammed it in his pocket.

"Looks like the band's all here," he remarked to cover his momentary weakness.

Motioning Hugh and Ellen to wait, Jack slipped out, made a quick survey of the area, then crossed to Kerr's side of the car and opened the door.

"Keep low. I think there's too many people around for someone to take a shot at you, but you never know. You too, Ellen. I'll be right behind you and I'm a bigger target."

She started to argue then thought better of it, nodded and ducked out of the car. Sandwiched between the two men and surrounded by twenty or more reporters, they made their way up the steps and into the precinct. Standing just inside the front door stood Lieutenant Hank Wade. Giving them a quick once-over, he asked, "What happened at the hotel? Whose car blew up?"

"Hugh Kerr's car," Merrick answered with chipped efficiency. "One of my operatives was inside. We exchanged cars with him at the last minute. Other than hearing the explosion, I don't know what happened to him."

"He's dead. What was his name?"

"Bill Mulcahy."

"All right. Enough of these pleasantries. Follow me."

"Wait a minute, Lieutenant. I have reason to believe one or more of your men may be channeling information to Carey Price. They may even be paid to kill us –"

Wade raised an eyebrow in mock concern. "What's the matter with you, Kerr? What's the murder of a private eye between friends? You going soft on me?"

"Maybe I am."

Not expecting that answer, and uncomfortable enough with his own hand-boiled attitude, Wade abruptly spun on his heel and led them down the corridor. Outside the first office on the right stood a uniformed female policewoman. Wade turned his attention to Ellen.

"Right in there, Miss Thorne. Someone will be in to speak to you shortly."

Hugh responded before she could obey the command. Blocking the door with his wide shoulders, face flushed with anger, he bore beady eyes on the officer.

"Wait a minute, Wade. You're not going to separate us –"

"You don't give orders here, Kerr," came the sharp rejoinder. "You're not an attorney on your high horse down here, you're a suspect and I'll do whatever I damn-well please with you. Right in there, Miss Thorne," he concluded, regaining a polite, if terse composure. Ellen hesitated only long enough to catch Hugh's eye.

"I'll be all right."

Grinding his foot into the floor as if attempting to eradicate the tile, he stiffly nodded. Damning himself because he had meant to take the time during the ride to the station to go over what she and Jack were to say, the car bombing had shattered those plans and he had remained mute the entire trip. Too late to rectify matters, he tried a weak smile.

"You have nothing to fear, Ellen." Only too well aware of Merrick's loss, he added, "There have been *five* victims in this plot. None of us have done anything wrong and Lieutenant Wade knows that."

"Lieutenant Wade knows nothing of the sort. Keep moving."

Ordinarily, he policeman would have shoved the suspect down the corridor but he refrained from doing so, not the least of which because he sensed Kerr was seriously strung out and he did not want to add assault and battery of a law enforcement official to other pending charges. He owed him that much for *Auld Lang Syne*.

Jack Merrick was ushered into the next room and Kerr was taken to the interrogation chamber on the right. Opening the door, Wade stood back. Kerr hesitated at the last door, taking stock of the plain room which contained a table upon which sat an ashtray, a pitcher and a tumbler, and three straight-back chairs. Biting his lip he entered. Directing his glare toward a black-glass window, behind which he presumed Bartholomew Bond to be standing, he purposely took the chair situated with its back to the one-way mirror.

"Take this one," Wade ordered, indicating the one with its back to the door and facing the mirror. Kerr obliged. Reaching into his pocket, he hesitated, then turned to his adversary.

"Mind if I smoke?"

"Not at all."

Taking out a cigarette, he offered one to Wade out of habit. When the policeman refused, he struck a match, touched the flame to the tip, drew in a mouthful of smoke, then tossed the spent stick into the ashtray. The chair squeaked as he settled in.

"I'll be right back," Wade advised, sidling toward the door. "Make yourself comfortable. If there's anything you want, just ring for room service. And Hugh – don't try to escape."

Kerr nodded and offered the other a cursory dismissal. When the door closed behind him, he did not move but sat watching the smoke curl upward from the end of the cigarette. Acid churned his insides. The sarcasm had hurt – more than he dared admit. While he had not expected Wade to offer him the fatted calf, he had not anticipated a cold, stiff reception. He had known the man professionally for seven years, only two years longer than he had known Ellen Thorne. While they had never become close friends, he would have classified their relationship as cordial, even friendly and certainly respectful. He admired the way Wade went about his business and he had supposed the older man felt the same about him. While they had not always seen eye-to-eye, they represented two sides of the law and the aim of both was to uphold justice. Just as Wade had never knowingly arrested an innocent man, so too had Kerr never worked the system to prevent a guilty client from receiving fair punishment.

Suddenly realizing his cigarette had burned down without his having taken more than one puff, he crushed the butt into the ashtray and lit another. This one he made an attempt to smoke, although it was tasteless and hot against his tongue. Finishing that one, he lit a third and this time made a concentrated effort to smoke slowly. He did not want to appear nervous to the district attorney and whomever else stood with him behind the cover of black glass.

But he was nervous and the longer he sat the more uncomfortable he became. Although he had been in countless rooms like the one he presently occupied – and in fact had been in the exact same room dozens of times – it had always been as an attorney. No one had ever said to him, "Don't try to escape." Innocent enough on the face of it, the words rang in his ears.

Don't try to escape.

No car waited outside to take him home. No desk officer would give him a polite, "Good night, Mr. Kerr" on his way out. If he attempted to leave, he would find himself in handcuffs.

What the hell is the matter with me? I've got to get a grip on myself. I haven't done anything wrong. I'm the innocent victim in all of this.

Startled to hear his own words to Ellen Thorne slightly amended and re-directed at himself, he shook as though waking from a reverie.

Calm down. They're watching.

What the hell do they mean by watching me, anyway, damn it! This whole thing is a sham. They know I didn't kill anyone. They know Ellen didn't kill anyone.

Ellen.

The word cut him to the quick. Whether intended or not, he had gotten her involved, dragged her through hell, landed her in a police station on the wrong side of the interrogation table. She hadn't asked for any of this; she didn't deserve it.

Let Ellen go, for God's sake! I'll tell you all you need to know.

As the words formed on his lips, it required all his willpower to stop from saying them aloud. What good would it do? It would only make him sound guilty; make it appear he was in a vulnerable position, willing to make a deal to save his...

His what? His moll? He almost smiled at the thought. How proud she had been when accused of being such a thug.

Thug.

A Jack Merrick word. He didn't belong in an interrogation room, either. His only crime had been to be beaten within an inch of his life and kidnapped.

Hugh's mind wandered. They had played games in law school. It was Professor Langley's idea, to give his students a real taste of what it felt like to be interrogated. One of the boys had been a *cop* and the other a suspect. They were to make up the story as they went along; it had been up to the "suspect" to decide whether or not he was guilty and incumbent on the policeman to get the truth. There were twelve students in the class and each had taken his turn.

The boys were awkward and embarrassed at playing such a game but Hugh had readily volunteered to be the first suspect. He had done his homework with enthusiasm, creating a scenario and preparing his dialogue around a predetermined crime, daring the other boy to tear his statements apart. They had turned their classroom into a mock interrogation chamber. While the professor and the rest of the class watched, Hugh had stood fast to his protestation of innocence, carefully leading the other down a trail of twisted facts and carefully contrived details, purposely making small mistakes and then correcting them.

They had been given one hour for their performance. Hugh's enactment had been allowed an extra sixty minutes. The youth playing the detective went at him with fired enthusiasm and intensity, determined to get the better of the class star. At the conclusion, the class voted on whether the policeman had extracted enough detail to charge him with a crime or declare him *not guilty* and let him go. The decision of the students had been unanimous: guilty. When they unsealed the plan Hugh had written, explaining how he perceived an *innocent* man would react when faced with a hostile interrogator; how he could be tripped up, confused and ultimately scared enough to agree to explanations that bore no relation to what actually happened, they had been flabbergast.

Hugh Kerr had been the only one to receive an "A" for the class and he had remembered the lesson, reminding himself time after time when he spoke with his own clients how intimidating such a situation could be. He had silently given them the benefit of the doubt, trusting to his own perceptions and gut feelings as to their true guilt or guiltlessness. To his credit, he had been correct nearly 90 percent of the time. Possessing that knack and believing in himself had made him the most respected defense attorney in the state.

Probably in the entire country.

Sitting alone in a room similar to that in which he had once played an innocent victim wrongly accused, Hugh Kerr's confidence waivered. He *thought* he knew what it felt like to be unjustly charged and convicted by a "jury" of his peers but he had been wrong.

Dead wrong.

Between pretend and reality lay a universe of fear.

Such fear that not even being the greatest defense attorney in the entire country saved him from.

His eyes closed and the burning cigarette, reaching his fingers, singed his flesh. With a cry of dismay, he dropped the butt, shook his hand, and then furiously swept it off the table.

Behind the black glass Lieutenant Hank Wade and District Attorney Bartholomew Bond exchanged glances. Neither had been in Hugh Kerr's law school class but they knew a guilty reaction when they saw one. It presented them with a dilemma: whether to be satisfied or the contrary.

Was Hugh Kerr a friend or an enemy?

Knowing the man and his values, the pair had been willing to give their courtroom adversary the benefit of the doubt. They were no longer feeling that charitable.

Ellen Thorne sat with her hands folded and her head slightly bowed. Dark circles had appeared under her eyes and her once bright, steady countenance had faded to one of tired resignation. She had been in detention six hours and it felt like six years. There had been two detectives interrogating her. The first had stayed two hours, hammering her with questions, pounding the table, bringing his face so close to hers they almost touched. The last time he tried that she had cried in frustration and pulled away, bringing up a hand to protect herself. He left shortly after that and fifteen minutes later another detective had come in. This one smiled and offered her coffee. She had refused and told him she understood the good cop-bad cop technique.

He had made her go over the same details she had outlined to the first detective, asking different questions but amounting to the same thing. She had answered them as truthfully as she could. Hugh had not told her to do otherwise and she could see no reason why she shouldn't be completely truthful. After an hour of mind-numbing cross-examination she had agreed to accept a cup of coffee because she supposed it was expected of her. When a female warder brought it, however, she could not compel herself to take a sip. For some reason she could not get it out of her mind that it was either poisoned or contained some sort of truth serum.

Her head hurt, her eyes were almost bleary and she felt desensitized to the point of resignation. That dullness of spirit left her with only one recurring, devastating thought.

Carey Price has gotten his wish. He has brought us to our knees. He has made good his vow.

He was guilty and we are innocent.

It isn't fair.

She might have cried but could not summon the intensity of emotion to do so.

She worried about Hugh. She wanted to see him, to have him hold her in his arms, wink with that all-knowing humor of his and whisper, *It's going to be all right, Ellen. I have this one in the bag.*

When the door opened, she did not bother looking up. Lifting her head was too much effort. If they wanted her attention, they would have to pull her head back by the hair that until recently had been so carefully coffered.

"Hello, Ellen."

The soft, friendly voice and the familiarity had nearly the same effect. With a low cry, she turned to face the speaker.

"Oh, Lieutenant Wade!" This time, tears found a way of leaking from the corners of her eyes. "I'm so relieved to see you." Without thinking, she stood, tottered a moment, then rushed into his arms. "I was afraid... someone had taken you off the case. Thank God you're here."

Wade's aged face, a moment ago bland and controlled, metamorphosed into a warm, fatherly expression. He hugged her the way he might comfort his own daughter, then gently guided her back into the chair.

"Sit down, Ellen. You look so pale and weak."

"I am," she confessed, wiping her eyes. He withdrew a handkerchief from his pocket and handed it to her. She used it, then clutched it in her hand as though it offered some protection from the horrors to come. "It's so good to see you. Have you spoken to Hugh? Is he all right?"

"At the moment he's doing exactly what you're doing: just sitting in a chair."

"They haven't been mean to him, have they? They haven't hurt him?"

"Now, Ellen, you know that's not my way. It's not allowed," he added. Giving her time to control herself, he continued with an obvious twinkle in his eye, "I understand you told Detective Rollins you knew the bad cop-good cop routine."

"Oh, that," she dismissed, almost laughing in relief. "I'm a legal secretary. I've been with Hugh – with Mr. Kerr," she awkwardly corrected, "hundreds of times when that sort of thing was played out on one of our clients. Well, not exactly there, but afterwards –"

"I know," he grinned, holding up his hands in surrender. "Of course you do; and well you should. And please don't bother correcting yourself. Calling your employer 'Hugh' is quite acceptable. I do it myself, as you know."

"I just don't want to say anything wrong... to give the wrong impression."

"I understand."

"I... hoped you would. Thank you, sir."

Wade took the chair opposite her and leaned back as though they were having a casual conversation at the coffee shop across the street from the county court house.

"I like you, Ellen. I always have. And, I must confess, there's been a time or two when I considered you the brains of the outfit. You're sharp and you're intuitive."

If he meant to shock her, Wade succeeded.

"Oh, no, Lieutenant. You mustn't say that. It isn't true. I may have an idea or two but Hugh is the one who puts everything together."

"I see."

Running a hand through her hair, Ellen sought his eyes, finding an intensity behind the fatherly front.

"Will we be able to go home soon?"

"Do you want to go home?"

"Yes! Well, not 'home,' exactly. Hugh said it isn't safe." Relieved to be speaking of matters other than those on which the first two detectives grilled her, she took in a deep breath and forced herself to relax. "That's why he took Jack and me to the Golden Bear."

"Tell me about that, Ellen."

"The whole time – after we rescued Jack, that is – he was worried Price would have us followed. That somehow they'd get on our tail and finish his original threat –"

"Which was?" he interjected.

"To destroy Hugh. That's what he threatened in court when he was convicted... or sentenced." Starting to shake, Ellen wrapped her arms around herself. "I'm sorry, Lieutenant. I'm not thinking very clearly right now. I'm so tired and worried."

"About yourself?"

"Well, yes, but about Hugh."

Wade smiled. "Why Hugh? Don't you think he's big enough and strong enough to take care of himself?"

"I don't know." Her voice lowered to a hush. "He's been under such a strain. Seeing Jack's body in the morgue – well, it wasn't Jack, but we couldn't be sure –"

"You went back," he reminded her.

Ellen's face flushed.

"I had to. I knew no matter what he said, Hugh wasn't positive about the identification –"

"About it not being the body of Jack Merrick -?"

She nodded. "Yes. He and Jack and I are very close. In his heart I think he knew it wasn't Jack but he couldn't convince his mind. After all, they had Jack's wallet and the items from his pockets. There was no mistaking that."

"No. There was no mistaking that."

"I let him do the dirty work the first time but I couldn't live with myself not knowing. So I went back, because…"

"Because?" he prodded.

"Women are better at these things than men."

"All right."

She began to tremble. "It was horrible. That body… so mutilated. The poor man."

"Who was he, Ellen?"

"I don't know. Someone who was chosen because he had the physical attributes of Jack. But after I forced myself to study the corpse, I knew it wasn't Jack and that someone was playing a horrible hoax on us."

"What made you come to that conclusion?"

Foregoing her initial observations, Ellen replied, "There was no scar on the neck. I remembered something Jack had said once – about being burned by a chain he wore; his St. Christopher medal. In the war. It was so hot, the metal burned him and it left a mark. I looked and I didn't see it. So I knew it wasn't Jack."

"And then what did you do?"

"I went to the office and told Hugh."

"What did he say?"

She gave out a low cry of frustration.

"Oh, Lieutenant Wade, I don't remember. Something like, 'I knew it all the time,' or some such words."

"All right, all right, Ellen. It was a trying time. Then what happened?"

"We put our heads together to try and figure out who would do something like that; what enemies Hugh may have had."

"Just a minute before you go on. Do you recall whether Hugh had to be in court that morning? Did you cancel appointments?"

Her face turned white.

"Honestly, I can't remember whether we discussed that or not. I hope he didn't miss a court date. You don't happen to know, do you, because –"

"No. I don't happen to know. I was just curious."

"Well, if he did it was my fault and I'll have to make it right somehow. I will apologize to the judge and Mr. Bond. You don't think he'll hold it against Hugh, do you, when it was my fault? Everything was so stressful. I just didn't think."

Wade passed by her question.

"What about appointments? Did you have to reschedule any?"

"If he wasn't in court then he had a full slate for the day; he almost always does. Maybe I asked Geraldine to cancel them… or maybe Hugh did. He arrived at the office before me that morning."

"Because you stopped by the morgue, first?"

"Yes, and –" It came back to her and her head shot up in triumph. "And I stopped on my way over to buy doughnuts. I knew we'd be working all day and…"

"Yes? Go on."

"I needed an excuse why I was late. I'm never late and I didn't want to confess I had been to examine the body."

"So you came in late with doughnuts and –"

"I made coffee… or I may have bought coffee with the doughnuts. And I told Hugh the body wasn't Jack Merrick's and –"

"Wait a minute. What did he say to that? Did he guess you had made a side trip that morning?"

"Yes. It's very hard to keep a secret from him –"

"But he was under a great deal of stress?"

"We both were. And I think he felt better after I told him it certainly wasn't Jack's body and then I had this idea that whoever did this was someone who had sworn a vendetta against him and it came to me there had been one time when a man threatened him," she finished in a rush. "I couldn't remember his name but I thought it had been an embezzlement case. Hugh's client had been charged with the crime and two bank tellers positively identified him as having opened a very large account. But Jack dug up the original officer who had opened the account and he ID'd the chief engineer of the firm. The men resembled one another and that explained the initial confusion"

Pausing to catch her breath, Ellen started to cough. Wade snapped his fingers and the door opened.

"Bring Miss Thorne some water. Or would you prefer coffee, Ellen?"

Remembering her last experience with coffee, she shook her head.

"Water would be fine."

They waited until the female officer returned with a pitcher and glass. Setting the items on the table she quietly backed away, closing the door behind her. Wade took the initiative to pour Ellen a glass. She took it gratefully, drank deeply, then nodded.

"Thank you."

"You're welcome. Now go on. You were saying about the embezzler?"

"The engineer's name was Carey Price. Once Hugh proved he had been the one who had cooked the books, Hugh's client was exonerated and Price was charged with the crime. He was some sort of an ego maniac and was terribly angry at his sentencing. He stood up and shook his fist at Hugh and said he would get him – make him pay if it was the last thing he ever did."

"Surely a man of Kerr's status gets several threats like that a year. What made you take this one seriously?"

Her answer was terse and uncompromising.

"Because he was evil."

"Evil? What do you mean, evil?"

"Hateful. And very, very serious. Someone may scream out a threat in the heat of passion but this man was different. He was cold and calculating. You don't forget someone like that."

"And yet you did forget him. Years went by and you put his threat out of your mind."

"*Five years*, Lieutenant. I suppose we should have been more careful – asked the court to notify the office when he was released, but we didn't. Or maybe we did and they just forgot. It had been a long time."

"How did you come up with his name? You did come up with it, didn't you?"

"I described what I remembered to Hugh and he recalled the name of his client. We pulled his file and there it was. 1950. Of course we couldn't be certain it was this Carey Price. We were only guessing."

"So then what did you do?"

"We put the Merrick Detective Agency on the case. They found out Price had recently been released from prison."

"Why didn't you call me for help?"

"Because we had no real evidence to go on, only a hunch."

"It would have been the smart thing to do – and a safe one."

"I know we should have. But…"

Ellen hung her head. To cover her discomfiture, she poured more water into the glass and sipped from it.

"But, what?"

"Hugh and I agreed that you would think we were off on a wild goose chase."

"You mean Hugh thought that and you went along."

Her eyes hardened and her fingers clutched the handkerchief Wade had given her.

"I mean what I said: Hugh and I both thought you'd tell us to stay out of things and let the police handle the investigation."

"Ah." He smiled. "That is precisely what I would have said. And I would have been right, too, wouldn't I, Miss Thorne?"

She surprised him with her answer.

"No."

"No?"

"No."

Hank Wade pressed his fingertips together in momentary contemplation.

"Why 'no?'"

"First of all because it was a matter of deep personal interest to us. And since we were already involved – you did that by asking us to view the body –"

"A routine procedure –"

She brushed aside his protest.

"And since Jack was an associate *and* a close personal friend, *and* since by your own admission you might not have taken our lead seriously, we decided to investigate it, ourselves."

Wade's back stiffened.

"Being an attorney and a legal secretary does not give either one of you the right or the authority to stick your noses in a murder case."

"Not a legal right. This was a moral duty."

"Claiming that can often get people in a great deal of trouble." When she opted not to pursue his lead, Wade went on. "All right. So you had a name. What happened next?"

"We went to Jack's apartment."

"To look for clues."

"Yes."

"How did you get in?"

"I had a key."

Clearly surprised, Wade arched an eyebrow then thought better of asking the obvious question and settled for, "I won't ask how you got it."

"It's as well you don't because I wouldn't tell you."

"All right. Go on. You went into Merrick's apartment."

"Yes. And looked around. If you want to charge us with breaking and entering, I'm sure Jack will tell you he won't press charges."

"No, no. Not if you had a key. That implies tacit permission. So, you looked around."

"And found a pad of paper by the phone. Hugh rubbed a pencil across the top page and that brought out the wording. A type of shorthand. I deciphered it; it was directions to someplace on Pacific Coast Highway."

"You deciphered it."

"That's right. I'm familiar with Jack's abbreviations. I've typed enough of his notes to pretty well be able to read whatever he jots down."

"And off you went. Again without calling the police."

"What would have been the point? We really didn't have any more then than we did earlier in the day. We didn't know whether the directions were for Jack to meet a client or…" Her eyes narrowed. "A girl."

"I see. It may surprise you to know, Miss Thorne, that the citizens of this state pay a great deal of money so they can maintain an efficient police force. We do like to earn our keep, you know. Makes us feel useful and not a drag on society."

"I told you it was personal."

"They call that vigilante law, you know." He heaved a tired sign and waved her on. "Go ahead. What happened next?"

"Besides," she pursued, "Hugh was beginning to suspect some of your officers had been gotten to by Price."

"What led him to that conclusion?"

"He tried to call you and the sergeant on duty wouldn't put him through; he said you weren't there when Hugh was convinced you were. And then there was the issue of those two men being transferred from San Diego; the first one finding the St. Christopher medal and the other identifying Hugh's fingerprint on the back. Since he knew that evidence had to be planted it appeared all three men were on Price's payroll."

"That's a pretty tall order, slipping in three decoys."

"Not when you have a quarter of a million dollars to spend, it isn't." Her back straightened and she met his eyes. "Who was in such a hurry to claim 'Jack's' body and why was it released? As his executor," she lied without conscience, "no one had a right to it but Hugh."

The lieutenant rubbed his jaw, debating how much to say. He finally let his hand slip over to his earlobe. Giving it a decided tug he replied, "Someone from the Merrick Detective Agency brought in an individual claiming to be a cousin. We had no reason to disbelieve him."

Turning the tables, Ellen Thorne leaned forward, resting her forearms on the table.

"Yes, you did. Nothing was really certain at that point. You owed it to Hugh – and to me – to wait until matters were settled and we had a chance to present Jack's will."

The accusation hurt and Wade flinched.

"That was my doing. Later that day the funeral home called. The coroner had already performed an autopsy and I didn't see any reason to hold onto it so I gave permission for it to be released to the family."

"We're Jack's family." When he didn't answer, she added, "Someone sure buried the body in quite a hurry."

"So they did," he agreed. "But it was paid up front – in cash – and all the boys from the Agency were there. Bartholomew Bond and I were there, as well."

"No one thought that Hugh and I would have liked to be there, too, to pay our respects?"

"No one could locate you. Remember?"

Ellen's pulled back, eyes narrowed.

"Forgive me if I'm leading with my jaw, Lieutenant Wade, but I think you ought to look into who exactly this Agency man was. And investigate the 'cousin,' as well. I don't know how he would have heard about the death, even if he were really related. Which he wasn't," she added with finality.

"I'll just do that, Miss Thorne. Now you want to tell me the rest of the story?"

Head throbbing, muscles tense and her brain beginning to jump with nervous energy, the last thing Ellen wanted was to tell the rest of the story. What she really desired was to get Hugh and Jack and go somewhere to hide; preferably on the dark side of the moon.

"Hugh got Carey Price's address from one of Jack's boys... one of his *real* boys and we drove up into the mountains looking for the hideout. I presume you've been there?" He nodded.

"After the fact. And you approved of this late light Don Quixote escapade? It didn't occur to you that it was dangerous? That one or both of you might get killed? To say nothing of that little old thing called breaking and entering? This time, a legitimate charge?"

"Time was of the essence."

"You deduced that?"

"We *knew* it. We also knew that if we waited for the police to make a proper search – even presuming they would have – all the noise and bustle would alert the – thugs – inside the house. They would have gotten Jack out of there in a hurry, killed him and buried him somewhere so remote no one would have ever found the body."

"That's why we have cadaver dogs."

"All right!" she cried, feeling the weight of the world on her shoulders. "Stop it! We didn't want cadaver dogs finding the body. We wanted Jack alive." On the verge of hysterical exhaustion, Ellen pushed back in the chair, get up, paused to let the feeling return to her legs, then moved as far away from Wade as the four walls of the cell allowed.

Realizing he had pushed too hard, Wade also got up but she backed away from him the way a cornered animal flattened itself against a cliff wall.

"I'm sorry, Ellen. I know you're tired and upset. I hate to put you through this, but I have to ask these questions. It's my job. Won't you sit back down?"

Rather than respond to the friendliness in his voice which she suspected was also "part of his job," she returned to the chair because if she did not she suspected his attitude would harden. And that, she knew, she couldn't face. If Wade turned on her, then she would be really alone.

"That's better," he tried, rejoining her at the table. "Now, would you like a cigarette?"

"I don't smoke."

But Hugh does. Have they taken those away from him to break him down? Who's talking with him if Wade is here? Bartholomew Bond? What is he saying? Is he trying to destroy him? Don't they know we're innocent? What's the matter with these people? They must know Hugh and I didn't kill anyone. That evidence was obviously planted.

They have to know that.

"Some coffee, then? How do you like it? Black? Cream and sugar? Let me get you some."

Acting as though he were glad to get away, the officer walked slowly toward the door. She watched him. His age showed. He shuffled slightly when he was tired. She seemed to remember Hugh telling her once he had been wounded in the line of duty. A long time ago. Shot in the knee. Clearly the wound hadn't healed correctly. Or he had developed arthritis in the joint.

She tried to feel sympathy for Hank Wade and could not.

Hugh, Hugh, where are you? What are they doing to you? Don't let them break you down.

"Never fear, Ellen, when the truth is on your side."

He had said that to her once.

Once, she had believed him.

Chapter 14

Wade returned with a tray. On it were two white mugs similar to those used in greasy spoons, a battered sugar bowl and a small ceramic pitcher with faded blue violets on the sides. She supposed someone had brought it from home. Someone since retired and forgotten. Or someone maimed in the line of duty.

She did not want coffee.

"When can I go home?"

"Oh, soon, soon. Cream and sugar?"

She nodded. It didn't matter.

He prepared her coffee and pushed the cup toward her.

"Drink up."

"Thank you."

She refused to touch it. Wade blew a stream of air over the top of his cup, then sipped the steaming black liquid. On her dull stare, he observed, "Policemen always drink their coffee black. We save the condiments for company."

Ellen presumed he was attempting to be humorous and smiled.

"So how," he continued after a prepared pause, "did you rescue the estimable Jack Merrick?" Astutely observing her flinch, he hastily added, "I meant that as a compliment. If Hugh didn't have Jack so occupied, I'd offer him a job on the force. Of course," he reflected, "we don't pay as well."

"No," she agreed. "You don't," resenting the fact he had used Jack's first name.

Dropping her head back, Ellen rested it on her shoulders. Eyes closed, her mind wandered into what might have been a waking sleep, revisiting a time late in the summer of 1950. She had only been working for Hugh three or four months. Bartholomew Bond, the newly elected district attorney, had come onto the scene, as Hugh described, "like gangbusters," eager to prove his worth as Los Angeles' principal prosecutor. Bright, eager and ambitious, he and Hugh had faced one another before but not since Bond's election. The first case he prosecuted as D.A. was the murder of a wealthy, well-known elderly businessman. The outcome had seemed apparent; eyewitnesses pointed the finger at the victim's grandson, a ne'r-do-well who, it was supposed, killed his maternal grandfather for an early inheritance. Bond anticipated a quick strike and an easy conviction, establishing his credibility and his prowess in such an important case where the upper crust of society would be summoned to testify.

The youth's mother had called Hugh and asked him to defend her son. Her choice of an attorney was peculiar. While Mr. Kerr had the reputation as an up-and-comer, he had only been in Los Angeles four years and was considered too young, too flamboyant and too unconventional to handle the family's dirty linen with discretion. Even Ellen had been surprised, but Hugh had laughed in that unique way of his when things fell into place just the way he anticipated.

"I expected her to call," he explained, running his fingers through a pair of suspenders that she had always suspected were more prop than convenience.

"But why? The newspapers say the family has always been represented by Fitch and Franklin. They've been around for years and have a big, impressive office downtown. They handle," she had said, lowering her voice, "all the wealthy clients in this town."

"So they do," he readily agreed. "They do a thorough, steady job. All of the preliminary work is done by their associates and law clerks. Those fellows put the case together and the two old partners present it in court. I could have worked for them if I had wanted."

"Really? When was this?"

"In 1946 when I first blew into town with my Harvard law degree, the ink still fresh on my diploma. I told them if they wanted to rename the firm 'Kerr, Fitch and Franklin' I'd consider it, but otherwise, they could go fly a kite."

"You didn't," she exclaimed, clasping her hands, half in pleasure, half in shock.

"I did. I was out to make a name for myself and I didn't want to be buried in an old, established firm where I'd always be a junior partner – at least until the two of them died, and probably not even then. No, Ellen. I'm not one to work under anyone's thumb or by anyone's rules. I have to be myself and do things my way. I'm a fighter. No one tells me when to stop and take a plea. No one tells me who I can and cannot represent. If I want to defend a kid who got caught roller-skating across wet cement, I will."

"But isn't the fee important to you?"

"Hell, yes, the fee is important to me. I never said I didn't want money; lots of it. I want to live in style, Ellen. But not at the expense of justice and fair-play."

"All right," she had conceded. "But that doesn't explain why Mrs. Hagle came to you instead of the family retainers."

"Because, Miss Thorne, those old windbags wouldn't touch that case with a ten-foot pole. Not when they know they're going to lose. That boy looks guilty as sin and their reputation means more to them than a generous settlement. Prestigious law firms," he continued, "don't *ever* lose. They can't afford to, or their wealthy clientele flock somewhere else."

"But no one wins all the time."

"They do if they only take on cases they're assured of winning. The old open-and-shut type. Oh, their minions play it up, make a lot of noise, feed the press boys a story about how hopeless things look, and then the partners present a case based on plain ol' obvious facts – and it gets played up big in the newspapers. I'm the only damned attorney in the city," he bragged, "with the brass balls to take on a hopeless case. I'm the magician who astonishes with smoke and mirrors, and before anyone can recover from my theatrics, I drive home my points with real legwork and deduction. That's why she came to me."

"It will be hopeless," she dared point out, "if you lose."

"I won't lose."

"But the newspapers say eyewitnesses saw him commit the murder."

"And who told the newspapers?"

"I don't know. The police?"

"Sure. To make it look as though they had really done some stand-up detective work. And then the D.A. himself announces he'll prosecute young Hagle. Everyone will be following the case and if he wins, Bond will be a big man in this city."

She easily picked up on his qualifying word, "If."

"You think you can win?"

"Sure."

"But why? When everyone else is so sure he's guilty."

"Because he's innocent."

"How-do-you-know?"

"Because I feel it. Now all I have to do is prove it."

Hugh Kerr had been right, too. By discrediting the eyewitnesses and providing an alternate theory of how the crime was committed – and then pointing the finger at the guilty party – he not only defeated the new district attorney, but the grateful mother paid him in what the press styled "gold bullion." She and Hugh and Jack Merrick had been celebrating at one of the local hot spots when they were accosted by Bartholomew Bond. Still stinging from his defeat, he waited until she and Hugh finished dancing before slipping up behind the defense attorney at their table and muttering, "Enjoy your big pay day, Mr. Kerr."

"I am enjoying the triumph of justice, Mr. Bond. There is nothing sweeter."

"But I imagine the taste of it goes down pretty well with caviar and aged champagne."

"That it does. See you in court."

Ellen did not put it all together until they were standing outside waiting for the valet to bring around Hugh's car.

"He wasn't here eating, was he? He only came in to see how you celebrated. He's jealous, Hugh. Not just of your prowess but of your money. You earned it –"

"Never mind, Ellen," he interrupted, opening the door for her. "Prosecutors sometimes forget why they chose their avocation. When they look at their paychecks – which the citizens of the state think a fair and equitable remuneration – and compare it to my fees – the highly publicized ones – it's understandable. But what they also have to take into consideration is their original trade-off: forgoing the remuneration of a successful defense attorney for the benefits of public office. Bond became a prosecutor and then ran for election as district attorney because he's ambitious. He has his own dreams which involve prestige, power and wealth. I wish him well with those aspirations – but not against my clients."

Is that why we're being held? Because Bartholomew Bond is jealous? Is this his way of paying Hugh back for being wealthy and successful?

Does Hank Wade feel the same way?

What's a lieutenant's salary? Has he saved enough to retire on?

Ellen's head snapped up in anger.

"No. I can't believe that."

The officer stared at her in some surprise. Although divining her mind had wandered, he had no way of telling where or why.

"I wasn't following your train of thought."

"Never mind. What was it you asked me?"

This time Wade did not make the mistake of embellishing the private investigator with a word of questionable praise. Nor did he use both first and last names, opting for a friendlier and less formal way of expressing his question.

"How did you manage to rescue Jack?" Seeing her hesitate he added with what might have been construed as a touch of pride, "It couldn't have been easy."

Responding to his tone more eagerly than she realized, or perhaps would have cared, Ellen offered an emphatic nod.

"It wasn't. On one hand it was terribly exciting because I'd never been involved in anything like that before. Oh, I may have played that type of game with my brothers when I was a girl, but when you grow up, all of a sudden men think of you as delicate and weak. Maybe that's what most women want but it isn't what I want. I want to be an equal. Why should Hugh risk his life while I cowered in the car? Or allowed myself to be sent home on some pretext or other?"

Wade stroked his chin thoughtfully. There came a point in any good interrogation when the invisible barriers broke down and the answers came almost before the questions were asked. Sometimes that point was reached by careful, well-planned manipulation. More often, however, it was reached by a combination of weariness, a desire on the part of the suspect to explain his or her actions, as an unintended response to sympathy or a kind word and the stroke of luck.

Ellen Thorne had reached that point. In a self-effacing moment Hank Wade realized he had achieved that goal by the wanderings of Ellen's own memory and a carefully rephrased statement. Leaning back, eyes half closed but as sharp and piercing as those of a raptor, he settled in to allow his subject to talk.

Along the way he almost sadly realized he would learn more about the woman with whom he had been cordial, even friendly with for the better part of half a decade, but with whom he had developed no more than a causal relationship. The loss pained him more than he would have thought possible.

"I'm getting ahead of myself," she began, inadvertently correcting his oversight, which, when he realized it, Wade covered by a small cough. "We followed Jack's directions down the Pacific Coast Highway and up into the mountains. We drove past the turnoff once – that was my fault." She paused to wipe her forehead with a shaky hand. "'M' for minutes, not miles. So we had to turn the car around and go back. We didn't find Jack but we found the spot where he'd been kidnapped."

She looked around the room, seeing the dry, deserted area before her eyes. "There was no mistaking it: there was blood everywhere. Signs of a terrible struggle. Of course we had no way of knowing whether it was Jack's blood or that belonging to the poor man in the morgue. As it turned out, it belonged to both of them."

"How did you come to that conclusion?"

"Jack told us. But that didn't come until later. After we had gotten him away from that house of hell."

He shuddered at her expression, partially because he had never heard the lady use such language and partly from his own recollection of the scene, so recently visited.

"Go on. Please."

Growing calmer, Ellen recounted the experience as though relaying details of a particularly vivid story she had just read.

"I don't know what we hoped to find: Jack, I guess," she sighed. "We didn't, of course. We looked around a bit for the... head and hands, but didn't find them. I guess they were taken away. But I did find a clue." Her eyes grew in intensity. "Ask me what kind of a clue."

"What kind of a clue did you find?"

"A receipt shoved into the crook of a tree. Where Jack had stashed it. A gas receipt. There was a mark on it, little more than a scratch, or an indentation you might say. And then I got goose bumps because I realized what it meant."

Wade leaned forward.

"Tell me."

"It was under the price. Don't you get it? Price, Carey Price!"

"I get it, Ellen," he begrudgingly acknowledged. "But that's a pretty good stretch."

"Of course it is! That's why Hugh and I had to follow the clue ourselves. No judge would give you a search warrant on such evidence. I'm not even sure you would have believed us if we had told you."

"I feel quite certain I wouldn't have. But then, I don't know Jack the way you and Hugh do."

"Precisely! So when Hugh got the address where Price was staying – where we hoped he was staying – we had to track him down ourselves."

"Just a minute, Ellen. You didn't say anything about the St. Christopher medal."

She looked confused.

"You mean about the scar on his neck? The one that wasn't there on the corpse?"

"No," he gently corrected. "About finding it at the scene."

In her extreme tiredness, she remained unable to follow his thought.

"It wasn't with his belongings."

"No, it wasn't. It was recovered at the scene."

"Oh." Her memory slowly returned. "You mean the one that was found with Hugh's fingerprint on it?" He nodded. "We didn't find any sort of chain or medal there." Her shoulders sagged. "I think if we had, we would have been terribly discouraged. That would have..." Ellen debated how best to continue but even in retrospect the idea of verbalizing it risked changing history. "... pointed to his death." She heaved a sigh. "Even the discovery of the gas receipt *could have* indicated the same thing but we were desperate to believe, don't you see?"

He did see.

"How long were you there?"

"Fifteen minutes. Maybe less. We walked around, but Hugh said not to touch anything. I can't remember if we did or didn't. Only the receipt."

"Did you take it with you? You still have it?"

"I... I don't know. Maybe I put it in my purse. Or maybe Hugh took it."

Observing that she was becoming agitated, he gently guided her on.

"All right. We'll look for it later. Then what?"

"We stopped at some bar along the highway. To use the telephone. Hugh went inside and I stayed in the car."

"What was the name of the bar?"

"I... don't know. Hugh would remember. Ask him." An idea came to her and she hurried on. "You could speak with the bartender couldn't you? He'd remember seeing Hugh. That would prove the time, wouldn't it? That we were there late Wednesday afternoon, not Tuesday, the day of the murder."

"It would prove you were there Wednesday. Not that you weren't there Tuesday morning before Hugh went to the airport."

The realization seemed to deflate her.

"Oh. I see. But Hugh said..."

She lost her train of thought. He quietly prodded her.

"What did Hugh say?"

"Something.... That's it! The client he went to see. I was supposed to go to San Francisco with him and take the deposition at a lawyer's office but at the last moment the attorney decided to use his own secretary. If I had gone, our plan was to fly up Monday, see the sights, take the deposition Tuesday and fly back later that day. Hugh figured that would have ruined Price's timetable because we would have been out of the city when the murder was committed so he put pressure on the lawyer to insist on using his own secretary."

"How would Price have known where you two were going and what your plans were?"

"I suppose because he was monitoring our activities," she cried in despair. "It wasn't done in secret. For all I know he might have gotten the information from Geraldine. Or even set the whole trip up."

"Possibly. Go on. You were going to Price's hideout."

She hurriedly took up the thread, eager to tell him the rest.

"Hugh wanted me to go back to the office and wait for him there but I refused. I'd gone that far with him. I was the one who deciphered the clue on the gas receipt. Two minds work better than one." That distant look came back into her eyes. "Besides, if he was going to get himself killed up there, I wanted to be by his side."

"So you could get yourself killed, too?"

Her orbs sharpened back into the present.

"Yes, Lieutenant. Condemn me if you will, but if Jack was really dead and they killed Hugh, what was there left for me? Men are always so self-righteous with their lives, thinking how noble they are to save their womenfolk. But has any one of them ever stopped to think what they're leaving their wives and sweethearts to? A life of bitter loneliness. An empty house and an empty bed. Maybe she has children – what of them?" She turned to stare into Hank Wade's blue eyes. "What of her hopes and dreams? The path she had hoped to follow through life? Which is crueler? To take her with you and allow her a death with meaning and dignity, or leave her behind to mourn and suffer alone?"

"I have never thought of it in just that way."

"If a woman can't be equal and share equally in life's adventures, however dangerous, then relationships and marriage are inherently unequal. I couldn't stand for that. So I told him I was going and I went."

"Good for you, Ellen Thorne," he said and wished she were his daughter.

"We drove into the mountains looking for Price's hideaway. By this time we found the address it was dark. Hugh helped me over a fence and we crept up to the house. We didn't see anyone in the lower level so Hugh lifted me up and I peered through a window on the second story." Her voice took on an expression of pride. "I saw Jack tied to a chair. I could tell he had been badly beaten because there was dried blood all over him."

Pausing to catch her breath, Ellen saw the coffee, reached for it and took a deep drink of the now cold beverage. Hungrily, greedily, she finished the entire cup before continuing.

"I managed to get the window open and I crawled through. Something Hugh couldn't have done on his own. I cut the rope and untied Jack, got him across the room and I guess he either jumped or just tumbled out and hit the ground. I followed him and we ran like the wind through the woods and back to the car."

"Maybe," Wade decided, playing with the buttons on his coat sleeve, "I should have said, I ought to ask *you* to join the police force."

She smiled gratefully at his compliment.

"I've never been more frightened in my life."

"Don't mistake, Miss Thorne. Hugh was just as frightened as you were. And if I had been there, I wouldn't have been any braver."

"All right, the three of us were scared. But, we did what we had to and got away."

Following her lead, the lieutenant drank his own cold coffee. In all honesty he did not note the temperature one way or the other. Had it been scalding, he would have swallowed it just the same.

"And so you -?"

"Escaped. Once Price realized we rescued Jack, it would have been clear to him we had most of the pieces of the puzzle and that he would most certainly be indicted for murder, kidnapping and assault. To save himself and his dirty plan of revenge he'd have to catch us and stop us from ever telling the story to the police. Since he had already proven he wouldn't stop at murder – and as we were assured he had detectives – or *thugs* at his service - Hugh was afraid we would be too easy to track down if we took Jack to a local hospital – or even to the precinct. Even now I'm not sure we're safe. You are watching Hugh and Jack, aren't you? With men you know and trust?"

She started to get up but Wade restrained her with a gentle hand.

"They're being watched. Believe me."

"But you don't know…. One of them could say Hugh tried to escape and he had to shoot him!"

The note of hysteria in her voice betrayed the terrible strain beginning to overtake her resolve.

"No, Ellen. I promise you."

"Go and see, won't you? Please? Just to be sure. Don't let anyone with a gun near them. That man Price has a lot of money. I'm telling you he can buy murder right under your nose."

He nodded. "I'll just go and have a look at them."

"Let me go with you."

Wade shook his head. "You stay here. I'll be right back."

Rising to his feet, the policeman fell into his accustomed shuffle as he left the room. Without his presence, the temperature seemed to grow colder and Ellen hugged herself for warmth. As tired as she was, she could not permit herself to remain seated so she got up, stretched cramped muscles and began making an uneasy circuit around the room. She had just completed the second go-round when he returned.

"They're all right," he said, gently closing the door behind him.

She hurried up.

"You saw them? Both of them?" He nodded. "Thank God. But they must be awfully tired. When can we go home?" She misinterpreted his pained expression. "I mean, it's not safe to go home. I understand that. Back to the hotel, then. Are the reporters still outside? Hugh said they would protect us." Feeling suddenly faint, she leaned against Wade and he put his arms around her shoulders to steady her. "That poor man – Jack's agent." She sobbed quietly. "We never meant to put anyone in danger. The car… Jack was right. Something had been done to it. He warned him but he didn't listen." She wiped her eyes. "You see what I mean? Carey Price will stop at nothing to hurt us."

"Believe me, Ellen. No one is going to hurt you or Hugh or Jack. You're in my care, now. Please – sit back down. We're almost through."

She allowed herself to be directed back into the chair. He followed suit, moving closer to her so that they almost brushed shoulders.

"Tell me the rest of it. Where did you go?"

"We drove north to San Francisco. Along the way we stopped and Hugh traded in his car for another one so we'd be less conspicuous."

"That was good thinking. Kept the police off your track, too."

"That was the idea," Ellen bluntly agreed. "We didn't want anyone to catch us until we had it worked out."

"I thought you said you had most of the pieces of the puzzle."

"I should have said we needed to prove what we knew." She ticked off the items on her fingers. "That Carey Price was the one who killed, or had killed, that man in the morgue. That he was responsible for savagely beating Jack and kidnapping him. That his motive was vengeance against Hugh for discovering his embezzlement scheme and sending him to prison." She took in a deep breath, slowly expelled it and then started at the officer. "We needed proof that we weren't involved – that we had been set up, right from the beginning."

"Why would we think that, Ellen?"

The question rubbed her the wrong way and she withdrew as though suddenly realizing they weren't on the same side after all.

"You're the one who told Hugh we were in a lot of trouble. He, and I suppose me, too, were accused of falsely identifying a body. We were identified as being at the scene of the murder when there was no… logical way we could have known the location unless we were involved. And then there was the little matter of the fingerprint on the St. Christopher medal."

"Did you really expect us to believe that?"

Her answer was straightforward and terse.

"Yes."

"That doesn't say very much for me. Or Bartholomew Bond."

Her voice turned acerbic.

"We're here now, aren't we?"

Wade flinched. "But you haven't been charged with anything, have you?"

"I want to see Hugh. I want to see my lawyer."

He held up his hands in concession.

"All right. But just finish the story and you can go… see him."

She was not fooled. Being over-tired sometimes had the ironic twist of sharpening the senses.

"There's nothing left to tell. We drove to San Francisco and took Jack to a doctor. He said he had a concussion and broken ribs and a broken nose. We took a room –"

"Where?"

"In Chinatown."

"Go on."

"And got some sleep. We talked it over and left this morning after *Bond* gave us the mandate to return."

Wade casually leaned away from her.

"I'm going to ask you something and I want a straight answer."

"I'm listening."

"Were you and Hugh married within the past week or two?"

Ellen recoiled in shock at his audacity.

"How dare you? That's none of your business."

"A wife can't testify against her husband, you know."

"So if we had, that makes us guilty?"

"Did-you-get-married?"

"No."

The detective bit a hangnail to avoid meeting her glare.

"Now that's odd. Because Hugh said you did."

She gasped and nearly fell over backward. He attempted to help her but she recoiled from his touch.

"Oh, my God. Hugh told you that?" Wade nodded. The color rushed to Ellen's face as she fought the sensation of acute consternation. "That's because… because Hugh Kerr is a gentleman. He didn't mean it literally."

"How did he mean it? Figuratively?"

Responding on instinct, Ellen slapped him. Wade's head snapped back as though he had been hit by machine gun barrage.

"You have no right to insinuate anything."

"I'm sorry, Ellen. I had to ask and I have to be sure."

The small hairs on the back of her neck stood on end.

"Whether we were married or not is none of your affair. And it doesn't mean a *damn* thing to me whether a wife can't testify against her husband or not, because married or single, there's no way on earth I would ever testify *against* Hugh Kerr. Throw me in jail for contempt of court and throw away the *damned* key, for all I care. Now are you sure?"

"Now, I'm sure."

Pushing away, Ellen stood on her own two legs and pointed to the door.

"I want to see my attorney. I demand to be taken to Hugh Kerr. Now. If you don't take me, I'll charge you and Bartholomew Bond with every crime in the book and I'll kick down that *damned* door and find him, myself. Is *that* clear?"

"That's clear, too."

"Then do as I demand before one of us regrets it."

Rubbing his chin that still bore the red welt from Ellen's slap, he rose to his feet and indicated she do the same. Moving with a real or exaggerated shuffle, he crossed to the door, opened it and spoke *sotto voce* to the female attendant. She nodded and disappeared, leaving the lieutenant to lead Ellen down the corridor. Bypassing the last door on the right, he rounded the curve in the hall. It wound around to the back, so that when he opened the first door of the second corridor they emerged into a room that abutted the chamber on the opposite side.

Pushing past him, Ellen found herself in a small, dark chamber about the size of a walk-in closet. To either side were bare walls. Dominating the scene was a large window constructed into the far wall which she immediately recognized as the business end of a dark mirror. Bartholomew Bond stood on the far right facing the glass; opposite him was an individual she didn't recognize.

She had no trouble identifying the occupant in the observation cell. Heart sinking, Ellen gave a cry of despair and raced forward, attempting to press her hands against the cold, unyielding glass.

"Hugh!" she cried. "Hugh, it's Ellen!"

The stranger responded with alacrity, grabbing her arms and pulling them back. Without thinking, Ellen kicked him, eliciting a curse. Not content, she bit his hand and refused to let go as the taste of warm blood filled her mouth. Wade jumped forward to pry her loose, but it was Bond's cold, calm voice that worked its own form of violence.

"Let him go, Ellen."

Nearly insane with fury, she glowered at him, teeth bared.

"Do not take the liberty of calling me by my first name. You and I are not on such terms."

"I beg your pardon, Miss Thorne. Kindly let the officer go."

"Why should I?"

"Because it won't do you or... Mr. Kerr any good and it may do some harm."

Hissing under her breath, she pulled away but remained in an offensive position, ready to attack again if the situation warranted.

"That's better," Wade soothed. "We're friends here... Ellen."

"What we were and what we are remains to be seen... Hank." With exaggerated friendliness, she turned to the district attorney. "So good to see you again, Bartholomew. *Hugh* and I deeply regret that either of us has imposed on your leisure time. It is after-hours and on a Sunday, too. What a pity. The roast will be cold and the French Burgundy over-decanted. A fine year, was it? 1940 or 1941?" While she had little reason to suppose either was a "fine year," her sarcasm carried the point. "Perhaps we should ask *Mr. Kerr*. As a highly successful defense attorney of note and wealth, I feel quite certain he could elucidate us, Hank and I being only working stiffs."

Clearly taken aback not only by her physical display but from her ill-controlled bitterness, Bond shook his head slowly in a gesture she adroitly interpreted as being a stall for time while he controlled his thoughts. Rudely interrupting them, she continued.

"I have not studied you in the court room these five years for nothing, Bartholomew. I know your *tactics*. What did you think? That I would be quiet and docile? I presume Hank warned you on his extended trip for coffee that I was becoming agitated; that his Father Christmas routine was growing stale."

"Ellen... Miss Thorne, please," Bond pleaded. But his jury of one was unresponsive. He tried harder. "I have to get to the bottom of all this – mess. I can't afford to treat you or... Hugh Kerr any different than I would any –"

"Common criminals? Suspected murderers?" He shrugged with an exaggerated, ill-at-ease gesture as his face reflected true discomfiture.

"Oh, I see. The boys from the Press will go hard on you, is that it?" She glanced around the room. "Well, I don't see any of them here. The Mayor? I always supposed your position was more or less autonomous. Who, exactly, are you trying to impress? Lieutenant Wade? I would have imagined the opposite. You are the city's district attorney, after all. A position with a great deal of authority and power." Her lips curled in a snarl as she recalled a previous conversation with a man who had defended the prosecutor. "As a compensation, I presume, for earning a civil servant's salary." She pointed at the stranger who was still shaking his hand. A drop of blood had soaked into the sleeve of his suit jacket. She hoped it would not come out during the dry cleaning process. "This gentleman? Who is he? We have not been introduced."

Repositioning herself so that she could keep Hugh in view, she held out her hand.

"So pleased to meet you, sir. My name is Ellen Thorne, private secretary to Mister Hugh Kerr, attorney at law, and present murder suspect. You are, perhaps, the State Executioner? Here for an early assessment of your subjects?"

"Ellen: stop it!"

"Be careful with your familiarity, Mr. Bond. Someone might tell the newspapers that you treated Mr. Kerr with kid gloves because you have worked alongside him for five years and are well versed in his humanity, sympathy, kindness –"

"I'm warning you –"

"– and known throughout the state of California as an honorable man, incapable of the murder of a friend – that would be Jack Merrick – or of a stranger – that would be the recently buried corpse – or of perpetrating any crime so heinous as to involve decapitation or dismemberment." She threw back her head in haughty superiority. "*If* Hugh Kerr ever contemplated murder and *if* he ever committed such an act, I assure you that he would perpetrate the crime with such skill and finesse that neither you nor anyone else would ever suspect him." She inhaled deeply and jutted out her chin. "But then, you would not be called upon to investigate the deed. Hugh Kerr would present himself to police headquarters and confess before the body was cold. 'I am not above the law,' he would say. 'I believe justice must be fairly administered to the weak and the poor, the wealthy and the famous. Lock me up, gentlemen. I will represent myself, plead guilty and accept my punishment.' Can any of you say the same?"

The unnamed man scowled at Wade.

"Why did you bring this woman in here?"

"This *woman*? I am no more or less guilty, no more or less deserving of respect than any *man*. I resent the implication that I am *merely* a woman, beneath contempt."

"Ellen, he didn't mean that –"

"Of course he did. And I'm *god-damned* sick and tired of it. Hugh Kerr is a gentleman. What is this man?"

The stranger's scowl deepened until the age lines deepened around his chin and his eyes smoldered.

"Take her away."

"She demanded to see her lawyer," Wade protested. "Kerr is a lawyer and he is undoubtedly *her* lawyer."

The stranger debated, then stepped aside.

"All right. Let her *see* him." He pointed toward the darkened window. "There he is."

Barely controlling her rage, Ellen brushed past him and pressed her nose against the glass.

Let her see him.

What she saw was nearly enough to break down her barriers and make her cry.

Chapter 15

Hugh Kerr sat in the narrow, straight-backed, un-upholstered chair. Just as Wade had positioned him, he faced the one-way black mirror. Rather than stare into the glass, let his eyes wander around the room or nod off with lids closed, his attention was fixed on the table. More specifically, his orbs were riveted on the game of solitaire he had just dealt himself.

Quickly scanning the line of seven stacked cards in concert with the player, Ellen read: 9 of spades, 7 of hearts, 8 of clubs, 4 of clubs, Jack of hearts, 7 of diamonds and the Ace of spades. She could have duplicated his first moves without looking.

Ace of spades to the upper line, far right. That revealed the Queen of spades.

Peek under the 7 of hearts; underneath was a 3 of diamonds. Play the 7 on the 8 of clubs, and the 3 of diamonds on the 4 of clubs. Under the 3 was a 10 of hearts. Taking back these moves, Kerr peeked under the 7 of diamonds; underneath was the ace of hearts. He moved that to the top left, two spaces before the ace of spades.

The stranger prodded Bond.

"You can't look under the 7 of hearts, play it, change your mind and then play the 7 of diamonds. He's cheating."

The district attorney shrugged.

"I know. Look at what we've learned so far: Hugh Kerr cheats at solitaire. Who would have guessed?"

"That's my point," the stranger slowly articulated, belying the prosecutor's intent. "Who *would* have guessed? The fact presents an interesting psychological look into the inner workings of his conscience. A man who would cheat at a meaningless game certainly has the propensity to cheat when the stakes account for something. I'm just trying to point out that none of you knew him as well as you thought."

"Since we've watched him play a hundred games – two hundred in the last six and a half hours," Bond sighed, "I think we can all pretty well agree that the noted counselor for the defense is highly adept at cheating at solitaire."

"But then some would argue," Wade interjected, "there is a wide berth between amusing yourself playing cards and murdering a man, doctor."

Shocked and dismayed to hear the stranger referred to as "doctor," Ellen tore her attention from the window, redirecting her focus on the man she now presumed to be a police psychologist. The object of her curiosity paid no heed to her heightened scrutiny. His interest lay squarely on the subject in the adjoining room.

"Not as wide apart as you may think. Psychologically speaking, there is a close connection between the two. A man with the mental deficiency to cozen a mere game might very well see nothing amiss with bending other rules, even ones as sacrosanct as the taking of human life."

Rubbing his back the way a man would when suffering from a steady but not excruciating pain, Wade casually placed himself between Ellen and the psychologist. The act served to seal her lips from an angry outburst and she returned her attention to the window.

Six and a half hours. The strain has taken its toll. He looks so tired... so introverted.

Is he concentrating on the cards because he dares not think of the dire situation we're in?

"There," the doctor snarled, his tone laced with contempt. "He's doing it again: putting the red king on the black queen, instead of the other way around. I will say it once more: he has no respect for rules; he makes his own. That, gentlemen, is considered psychotic; a disassociation with reality and the civilization in which he lives."

The crimson of shame and humiliation crept up Ellen neck and spread up her cheeks.

Oh, my God, Hugh, I'm so sorry.

Leaning against the wall for support, the images around her faded, replaced by those of a different place and a past time. Five years ago, although it seemed almost yesterday....

"What are you doing, Ellen?"

Caught off guard because she had not heard him come in, Ellen looked up at the man towering over her. Instead of a scowl, she found his expression one of soft, puzzled curiosity. Face reddening from embarrassment, she assumed a casual air.

"Playing solitaire."

"I can see that. But why did you place the king on the queen?"

"Isn't it obvious?"

Eyes rounding in quiet amusement, Hugh Kerr shook his head.

"May I sit?"

"Of course."

He drew up a chair in the small office kitchenette and settled down. Resting his elbows on the table, he inadvertently caused it to tip. Grunting in annoyance, Hugh looked around, reached for a paper napkin, carefully folded it into a small square and leaned down. Lifting up the rickety table, he played the paper under the short leg then straightened, tested it and found the problem at least temporarily solved.

"That better?"

"At least until the janitor comes in this evening, sees the napkin on the floor and removes it."

He matched her grin.

"You're probably right. Can't we petition for a new table?" On her look, he shook his head. "Never mind. Two or three more successful cases like the one we just finished and we can pack up and move out of here. To a high-rise penthouse. One where there's a staff commissary in a room the size of a restaurant kitchen. With an icebox – a refrigerator," he corrected, "an oven and some nice couches where a person can read a good book while they wait for their meal to digest."

He had corrected "ice-box" for the more urbane "refrigerator," but had apparently seen nothing wrong with the inclusive word, "we."

"... like the one we just finished."

In her professional experience, Ellen had never known a secretary to be included in "successful cases." They were, after all, only hired help.

His familiarity allowed her to take the liberty of asking, "What good books do you like to read, sir?"

"No 'sir' about it, Miss Thorne. If I call you 'Ellen,' you must call me 'Hugh.' At least in private. 'Sir' makes me sound…"

Old, she silently surmised as he paused to consider. His reply crossed her up.

"Like someone from the British peerage. That would be presumptuous."

"I use it as a term of respect. You are my employer."

"And therefore worthy of respect?" He grinned in esoteric amusement. "You might find a great number of employees who don't feel that way for their 'boss.' And rightfully so." Leaning back in the chair so that it balanced on two legs, his grin turned reflective and then solemn. "But we were speaking of good books. Let us say, good works of fiction? I suppose Jack London is my favorite author."

Clearly surprised, she asked, "Really? Why?"

"For the pure simplicity of his language and the vividness of his prose. Because he understood nature and how often it is cruel." Leaning further back, he thought a moment, then shook his head. "That is, cruel as in unsentimental, as opposed to morally deviant. A man struggles to survive against innumerable odds and just when he may have achieved that goal –"

"A clump of snow falls on his fire and extinguishes it, thus sealing his fate."

Letting the two suspended chair legs thump back onto the floor, he slapped his palm on the table.

"You have it, Miss Thorne!"

"Ellen," she hesitantly corrected.

"You have it, Ellen!"

"And who else do you read… Hugh?"

"Poe. Melville. Dostoyevsky. Because they all understood the workings of the mind. The demons of humanity."

Eagerly, for the subject fascinated her, not only on its own merits but for how they pertained to him, she inquired, "And how they relate to crime?"

"I suppose you could say that. We all have devils, Ellen. Some to a greater or lesser degree, but they're there. Whether they're related to trauma or alcohol or financial concerns or personality or voices in the head, they effect what we think, how we react. To defend a client, a lawyer has to come to grips not only with the motives and emotions of the person he's defending, but his own, as well."

"Give me an example."

His fingers drummed on the table.

"An alcoholic lawyer may have no sympathy for a client who's also an alcoholic because inwardly he believes that individual is weak and unworthy. He presses his own fears and doubts on another and is thus subconsciously incapable of defending him, although he cries to the rafters that he did his best when the outcome is unfavorable."

"I never thought of it like that."

"Have you read Poe and Melville and Dostoyevsky?"

Not as much as I will.

Taking her pause as an affirmative, he redirected his attention toward the cards.

"So: why the king on the queen? No," he as quickly amended. "'*Isn't it obvious?* Of course! In your game of solitaire, the Queen rules the King; therefore, she is on top. Good girl! I like that. It demonstrates an amazing self-reliance and confidence."

"Which I have admired in you... Hugh."

"Ah ha! Almost caught you and that damned 'sir.' Banish that from your vocabulary. Or better yet, save it for others we are intent on flattering, and it will be a code word between us."

"Meaning?" she teased.

"The bloke is 'a idiot.' An old fuss-and-feathers who preens in the mirror –"

"– and complains when his wife does the same."

"Now you have it! And what do you have for lunch?" he inquired with shameless inquisitiveness, poking his finger into her brown bag and then peering inside.

"A bologna sandwich and an apple."

His nose wrinkled in disgust.

"That's prison fare. I cannot allow ... an employee of mine to eat such unappetizing and uninspired food. What you need is a good meal to sustain not only your body but your mind for the rest of the day. Come on. Get up."

"Where are we going?"

"Out to eat! At a fine restaurant where the word 'bologna' is entirely unknown."

"But my lunch hour is almost up –"

"Nonsense. You've only just sat down and besides, I have taken up your time."

"You have clients scheduled for one o'clock. And besides, Mr. Kerr, I saw you go out. You have already dined."

"Not a bit of it, Miss Thorne," he countered tit-for-tat. "I went out to see my banker. Very dull business but it has caused me to work up a tremendous appetite. I suppose our clients will wait if we are half an hour – or an hour – late. And if they don't, that's their loss."

Taking her arm, Hugh guided Ellen to her feet and out the door for the first lunch they ever shared. They did not return to the office until three o'clock, by which time, they found it packed with agitated litigants. They worked until well past dark and by the time the hour hand reached nine, they put out the lights and left the building together. Parting in the garage with a hand wave, Ellen drove home with the calm assurance that the headlights in her rear view mirror were following her to be certain she reached her destination in safety.

That expanded lunch hour had taught Ellen Thorne many things but the one she treasured most was the fact Hugh Kerr lied poorly when the situation became purely personal.

He had forgotten she made his reservation for lunch.

And she had taught him how to play solitaire by promoting the queen to the top ranked royal card. A style he had henceforth incorporated into his own play.

Which made him, in the eyes of a psychologist, *a psychotic: a man who disassociated reality from the civilization in which he lived.*

Hugh reshuffled the cards and dealt himself another hand. From what Bartholomew Bond said, Ellen guessed he had played one hundred, perhaps two hundred games since being incarcerated in that small, barren room. A crumpled cigarette packet lay discarded by his right hand. He was no longer smoking and she deduced he had run out of cigarettes. Her heart hardened. At least Wade had brought her coffee. No one had seen fit to bring Hugh anything.

Nor had they bothered to interrogate him. From what she gathered by listening to the three men behind the dark mirror, Bond and the doctor had done nothing more than watch him.

Toward what end? What can they possibly hope to gain by observing him play cards? Am I the only one they questioned? Why? Because they think I'm the weak link?

The thought humiliated her but offered no rational explanation. If the authorities wished to see if she, Hugh and Jack had conflicting statements, they achieved nothing by interrogating only one of three.

Are they trying to break him by keeping him in solitary confinement? Do they think loneliness or the uncertainty of the situation will shatter his reserves? Are they waiting until he is too tired to put up a defense? Can Wade and Bond actually believe we're guilty?

Clutching her hands together, Ellen was no longer sure of anything. She had no doubt that if the district attorney broke the news to the press that the famous Hugh Kerr was being held on a charge of murder, the sensationalism would be immediate and far-reaching. Papers around the country would carry the story as front page news. All the salacious gossip known or imagined about him would be dug up and spread across 50-point headlines. Bylines by everyone from investigative reporters to society columnists would offer opinions, speculate on cause and effect and universally delight in the destruction of a paragon of the legal system.

The psychologist, whatever his name, would be in great demand from radio and television stations across the country. Such venues would allow him to discourse on what pressures, emotions and jealousies would prompt such a prominent citizen to commit an atrocious murder. He would say cheating at solitaire was an indication of instability, or the "win at any cost" mentality.

Having already inferred Hugh was a menace to society, what else would he question?

At 33 years of age, why is he still a bachelor? What romances had he been involved in? Was his relationship with his secretary, Ellen Thorne, unrequited? Did he see Jack Merrick as a rival? Were his parents too strict? Too lenient? What of his brothers and sisters? What sort of a complex did he have toward his mother?

If he cheated at cards, did he cheat in law school? What did his professors have to say about him? His fellow students? The lawyers he clerked for. Did they suspect his mentality was such that one day he would commit a heinous crime? Did they ever suspect him of being unstable? Did he believe in God? What, if any, were his religious affiliations?

The more questions she imagined, the more distraught she became. Her Hugh Kerr was an intensely private man. Aside from the fact he had graduated from Harvard College and Harvard Law School *magna cum laude,* she had little inkling of his personal life. She did not know if his mother and father were still living, what relationship, if any, he had with them, or if he had siblings. She would have bet her life he never cheated but the past seven hours had proven what little worth her opinion had to the outside world.

He had friends, but most of them were either fellow professionals or those he had met in the course of conducting business. No one had ever called who claimed to be a boyhood pal and he had never spoken about his relationship with other women.

Or with God.

Ellen did not need to know the answers to any of those questions. She knew the man.

Others, however, would not be as discreet.

After a particularly arduous and challenging case where the client's bohemian lifestyle had been used against him, Hugh had sunk into his chair and said to her, "No one can ever assess the thoughts in a person's mind. They are private and utterly confidential. A man may think one thing and do another. He may be quiet on the outside and raging on the inside. All the psychiatrists in the world can add two and two together and they will never get four." When she had asked him why, he replied, "Every person wears many masks: one they put on at work, one they wear at home, another at the barber shop and a fourth in the theatre. A person is all of those things, not one of them, and the sum total is obscure, even to the individual. There is no equation known to science or the arts that can sum up a complex life, predict cause and effect or justify actions."

But that was just what the authorities, the press and the public were about to do with Hugh Kerr, a technique known in religious circles as "crucifixion."

She did not think he could survive the onslaught.

"How much longer are we going to stand here?" Bartholomew Bond asked. He sounded tired. His voice held a peculiar quality Ellen could not quite place. Something between annoyance and pique, perhaps.

"Not much longer. I am almost through. Very soon I will have the mental profile I need."

Wade hissed under his breath.

"Without ever having spoken one word to the man?"

"That is correct, Lieutenant."

"This is the damndest interrogation I've ever witnessed."

"It is not an interrogation, per se. Think of it more like a psychological examination."

"It seems more like torture to me. I'd just as soon beat the tar out of criminal than put him through this. And I'd get a damn site more information."

The doctor turned to Wade, eyebrow arched.

"You wish to beat him?"

Wade stiffened and his eyes narrowed in anger.

"I'd never lay a hand on Hugh Kerr even if an avenging angel came down and ordered me to do so."

The doctor smiled. Ellen hated him.

"You're getting soft, Wade. I'd bet you've conducted more than your fair share of bloody third-degrees in your career."

Unaccountably cowed by the statement, the officer stepped back as though too close contact with the doctor might provide the temptation to pummel the hell out of him. Bond reached out and placed a restraining hand on Wade although Ellen could see no reason for the action.

"We're all getting tired. Are you ready to make a recommendation on his sanity?"

Ellen clutched her stomach as the question struck her with more force than an actual blow.

"Oh, he's quite sane."

"Then you're recommending we charge him with first degree murder?"

"In a moment. See for yourself." He pointed at the window. Bond and Wade inched closer. "He has lost his composure. For the past hour he has been misplacing cards –"

"Not that damned king on the queen," Bond protested.

"I mean, he has not seen opportunities: there. He should have played the black five on the six yet he did not see it. And during the last hand, he turned over an ace and never placed it on top before ending the game." Unthinkingly, the man rubbed his thumb and forefinger together. "Quite a bit of luck, giving him those playing cards. Which of you came up with that idea?"

The D.A. glanced furtively at the policeman, then shrugged.

"He had them in his pocket."

"Ah. I offer you a compliment and you refuse it. Why?"

"I don't want your damn compliment," Wade snarled. "I want to get this over with."

Again, Bond went to quiet him but Wade batted the hand away. The doctor smiled and turned back to the window.

Ellen gave the psychologist no credit for his observations. She, too, had seen Hugh miss the ace and fail to play the five on the six. He had also put a black ten on a black jack and had stopped peering under cards of the same color and number to determine which offered him the best opportunity for winning. For a while he had slowed the tempo of his play but as if hearing his interlopers speak, he had begun dealing with ever faster intensity, at times playing only half the cards before scooping them up, performing a brief shuffle and re-dealing.

His play did not surprise her. He was a habitual solitaire player, often remarking that he needed to do something mindless while his mind worked in the background on pressing matters. She had often watched him at the game for hours, ultimately making the same mistakes he did now, until she could feel his hands going numb and his mental capacity face. And just as suddenly, his head would snap up, the light would come back into his eyes and he would declare, "I've got it, Ellen! I've figured it out!" And they would be on their way, either to court with a new tactic or dashing off to investigate a sudden clue he had remembered or interpreted.

She had the sinking feeling that this time, his mind would not wake up from its lethargy.

Or worse, there would be no need, as he would be tarred and feathered by a legal system manipulated by his enemies.

She would – and had – thought better of the district attorney and the lieutenant.

Reluctantly returning her attention to Hugh, Ellen watched as he interrupted play half way through a game he had been winning, half-heartedly shuffled the cards, started to deal them again, and then, with a cry of utter frustration, swept them off the table. Dropping his head down, he cradled it on an outstretched arm and began to shake. That served as Ellen's cue to action.

"For God's sake, you're torturing him!"

The fingers of her right hand balled into a fist as she made a move toward the doctor, intending to flatten his nose and then strangle him. Reacting nearly as fast as she, Wade intercepted her. Finding he could not easily control her fury, he absorbed the blows meant for the doctor.

"Get out of my way, damn it!" she screamed, pummeling his chest and then jamming her shoulder against him in an attempt to get by. Nearly startled out of his own skin by the sudden frenzied activity, Bart Bond crossed behind her and encircled her in his arms. Dropping his head down, he pressed his lips to her ear.

"Let it go, Ellen!"

"Go to hell!"

"Let-it-go! Do as I say and keep your mouth shut. Don't say any more."

Catching the doctor staring at them, Ellen responded by an instinct older than conscious thought. Elbowing the D.A. away, she cried, "Bond bit my ear!"

A moment of stunned silence was followed by a loud, almost dirty belly laugh from the physician. Although Bart had done no such thing, Ellen slapped a hand to the side of her head, rubbed it and then pretended to be staring at crimson liquid.

"I'm bleeding," she cried.

"By God, Bond," the doctor gasped between laughs, "you bit her ear. Now there's a manly attack if ever I saw one."

"It worked, didn't it?" he lied by following Ellen's lead.

"Get her out of here. I've seen enough." While Ellen allowed Bond to draw her toward the door, the doctor addressed Wade. "There's no question in my mind that Kerr is sane and that he is laboring under the guilt of a capital murder. With Miss Thorne as his cohort," he added, sharply appraising the woman who had frozen to hear his pronouncement. "I have more than enough material for a psychological profile. My testimony alone is enough for the Grand Jury to indict and my analysis in court will solidify your case, Mr. Bond."

Wade indicated he understood the implications.

"What about Jack Merrick?"

"I would indict him, too, on conspiracy charges. That's enough to hold him for now. Eventually, I believe you can develop the case and charge him with being a co-conspirator. I doubt Kerr and Thorne had the strength or the stomach to kill our un-named victim. It is my contention that Merrick was the one who actually perpetrated the murder and the dismemberment, although Kerr and/or Thorne probably lured him out to the canyon. In any case, their plot to frame Mr. Carey Price has been un-raveled and they'll pay the – price – for it."

Brushing by the lieutenant, he approached the door. Although her arms were pinned by Bond, she lashed out a foot, striking the doctor in the leg. He pulled back, started to say something, then thought better of it and quickly departed. Neither of the three remaining participants moved a muscle or made a sound until they were quite sure the fading footsteps had taken the man out of earshot. Ellen reacted first, but Bond put a finger to his lips. When he saw she would not speak, he directed his order to Wade.

"Go. Now."

Wade nodded and hurried away, leaving the district attorney alone with the private secretary. She eyed him with bitter scrutiny.

"Congratulations."

"Not now, Ellen." Opening the door, he peered down the hallway, saw a uniformed policeman and indicated he come forward. "Take Miss Thorne back to the interrogation room and hold her there. Make sure she has something to eat. If she needs a blanket, give her one."

"If I'm to be locked up, I want to be with Hugh – and Jack." Her voice dripped with sarcasm. "So we can plot our defense against the capital crime we're being charged with. I hope you burn in hell, Bartholomew."

Struck by the vehemence, Bond hesitated, then grabbed her once again by the arms. Pressing his face close to hers, their eyes locked.

"You can't see Hugh just now. Wait, Ellen. It won't be much longer. More than that, I can't say."

"Can't – or won't?"

"Daren't." To the policeman, he said, "Take her away."

Debating whether or not to fight, Ellen shot a look of anger at the uniformed policeman. In a second she recognized him as one of the men Jack occasionally hired to do off-duty work.

"You're David Kelly."

"Yes, Miss Thorne."

"I've met you before."

"Yes, ma'am. At the Merrick Detective Agency. But I'm not supposed to say that in front of Mr. Bond."

"Mr. Bond," the D.A. mumbled, "didn't hear it. But he doesn't like it, anyway. Get moving."

More confused than scared and uncertain who, if anyone to trust, Ellen reluctantly went with Officer Kelly. Walking around the corridor, she balked at the door to the interrogation room.

"Won't you please take me to Mr. Kerr?"

"I can't, ma'am."

"Can you bring him to me, then? Or Jack? Where is Jack? Have they hurt him?"

"No one's been hurt, Miss Thorne. That isn't police procedure."

"None of this is right. Won't you please help me?"

"Miss Thorne, trust me. Go inside and wait."

"Wait for what? A cell? The gas chamber?"

He made no reply and Ellen walked inside, head held high. She would not for the world let anyone see the tears rolling down her cheeks.

Chapter 16

A low, hesitant knock on the door alerted Hugh that he had visitors. Wearily rubbing his blood-shot eyes without dispelling his trance-like mental musings, he looked up with little curiosity. Nor did that emotion sharpen when he beheld Bartholomew Bond standing in the door frame.

"Hello, Hugh," the district attorney greeted in a voice so hesitant the defense attorney would not have recognized it had he not been looking straight into his face.

"Hello, Bartholomew."

"I have something I want you to take."

The D. A. held out his hand and Kerr identified four small white pills cradled in the palm.

"What is this – cyanide? The modern-day equivalent of falling on my sword? Are you trying to save me the humiliation of a jury trial or yourself from prosecuting me in court?"

Bond scuffed his foot along the floor.

"Neither, although I deserve – I deserve *some* of your bitterness."

"In this case, I'll be the judge of that."

"Come on; we haven't much time. Wade is waiting for us."

"The charge must be pretty serious if it got you out of bed at this hour. Delivering it personally? Really, B. B. –"

"The newspaper boys are still out front. That's *your* fault. *You* brought them with you. They'll have a story, all right, but not the one they thought they were going to get. We have to go out the back so they won't see us."

Kerr's expression turned to inflexible granite.

"You're not whisking me off to some out-of-the-way hiding place where you can grill me until the cows come home. Nor will I allow you to separate me from Ellen Thorne and Jack Merrick."

"Just for a little while. Now take these and let's get going. Time is of the essence."

"You may be able to threaten some downtrodden and cowering murder suspect, but –"

"Damn it, Kerr. I'll explain it all later. These are wake-up pills. I want you alert. You'll want to have all your wits about you, too."

"What-for?"

Bond stamped his foot in frustration. Kerr hesitated, debated the consequences of disobeying the order and then decided he didn't care what happened to himself. Rising awkwardly to his feet, he paused a second to fight a wave of vertigo occasioned by long inactivity, inhaled a deep breath and reached for the pills. Giving them no more than a once-over, he threw them into his mouth and swallowed without benefit of water.

"All right, I've taken your pills – whatever the hell they are. Now what?"

"I told you: Wade is waiting. Follow me: and be quiet about it."

Without waiting to see whether Hugh would obey, Bond turned and scurried out. Less energetic and far less eager, the prisoner trudged after him, fighting waving sensations of having the floor sway beneath his feet. Although Hugh knew the layout of the police station by heart, one turn around a corner left him adrift and frightened as though he had somehow been transported to an alien landscape.

Trailing down a long corridor with closed doors on either side, he finally found Bond and Wade standing in the communications center. Shielding his eyes from the bright overhead lighting, Hugh beheld a row of telephones hastily connected by a jumble of wires and cables strung across the wall. Several uniformed men sat by the phones. Seeing him enter, the lieutenant bounced on his toes in eager anticipation.

"Good to see you again, Kerr," he greeted.

The lawyer shrugged, blinking his eyes from the profusion of light streaming in a series of red, blue and yellow flashes. When opening and closing his orbs failed to dispel the colored display he made a low moaning sound and turned away.

"That's the effect of the caffeine and the narcotic starting to act on your brain," Wade explained. "It'll wear off in a few minutes. You'll feel a bit jittery but otherwise wide awake."

It took a moment for Hugh to work through the grogginess before he felt secure enough to speak.

"What, exactly, am I supposed to be wide awake for?"

The surly, almost bitter question did not faze Wade.

"How much did you hear in the interrogation room?"

"Voices." Kerr tried to concentrate but an assault of dizziness complicated his efforts. "Three voices: you and Bond and another man." The harder he concentrated, the more he confused the recent with the more distant past. One image, however, took shape before his otherwise clouded mind's eye. "Ellen." In rising panic he demanded, "Where's Ellen? What have you done with her?"

Wade opted to answer by rephrasing his question.

"Could you make out what we were saying?"

"Not much. You were whispering. I decided I didn't care."

"Never mind. It doesn't matter. The third man was a psychologist by the name of Charles Dunning. Ever heard of him?"

Dropping his hand from his eyes, Hugh rubbed his temple in an effort to concentrate.

"Have I? The name sounds vaguely familiar. In court?"

"Yes." To Bond, Wade remarked, "He's waking up, now. The pills are doing their little trick. I knew they would." To Hugh he added, "That's right. We use him occasionally to testify about the mental stability – or lack thereof – of suspects."

Kerr's eyebrows came together.

"What did he say about me?"

This time, Wade grinned.

"Oh, he said you were quite sane."

Kerr instantly caught the drift.

"Sane enough to stand trial? How gratifying."

"Actually, that's what we wanted him to say but not for the reasons you think," Bond interjected. "Once Dunning offered his professional opinion your actions were consistent with a man who had committed a capital crime, Wade took him outside and told him I would charge you, Miss Thorne and Jack Merrick with first degree murder. Now wait a minute," he warned, hurrying to finish the explanation, "That's what Wade *told* him."

When Hugh gave no outward sign of comprehension, the district attorney hurried on. "I was in a hell of a predicament. You're a big man in this town, Hugh, and after the press got wind of Merrick's murder and your possible involvement, the politicians came down pretty hard on me. They didn't want there to be any hint of coddling on the part of the prosecutor's office. If we hadn't played hardball, the reporters would have ridden the story for all it was worth." Receiving no reply he blurted, "You wouldn't come in and it didn't look good."

Reading Hugh's confusion, Hank Wade suddenly realized they had pushed the lawyer too far. Putting a hand on his arm, he waited until the other's eyes refocused.

"It's all right, son," he comforted in a slow, calming voice. "I took your advice and checked on those two transfer officers from San Diego. They *were* on the take as you suspected. The fingerprint on the St. Christopher medal was phony. So was the operative from the Merrick Detective Agency and the man claiming to be Merrick's cousin. You were way ahead of us on this one."

Staggered by the confession, Hugh made a valiant effort to assimilate all he had been told.

"What you just put us through –?"

"We needed Ellen to fill in the pieces of the puzzle we didn't have."

"And me?" he whispered.

"Your… silent interrogation was for Dunning's benefit."

"I… don't understand."

"I'll let Wade explain," Bond indicated, bowing out of the conversation. Hugh's sad eyes shifted slowly toward the detective.

"When Lieutenant Gray recommended we bring Dr. Dunning in to administer psychological evaluations, I couldn't figure out his angle. My first instinct was to outright refuse, but then I got to thinking that if Dunning had a connection to Gray and Gray was on the take from Carey Price, this might be our chance to wrap them up together in one neat package. I went to Mr. Bond, here, and put it to him."

His direct stare at the district attorney forced him to take up the thread.

"I called the doctor on the phone and gave him a brief outline of the situation. He agreed to come in readily enough and when he did we sat down and discussed matters. At this point, Hugh, you have to understand I wasn't completely convinced he was involved. For Christ's sake, we'd used his expertise before. When he agreed not to give you the third degree or use any harsh tactics, I consented."

"There are many ways to torture a man," Hugh whispered, perhaps too low to be readily comprehended.

"I didn't see any harm. If he were on the up-and-up I thought his evaluation would satisfy my superiors that I wasn't giving you any special breaks. And if Wade's investigation proved he was somehow connected to Price, we'd have an opportunity to trace Price through him."

Staring glumly at Wade, he waved an impatient hand for him to continue.

"My theory held that Dunning's job was to convince Bond the three of you were psychologically capable of cold-blooded murder. He said as much when he left the observation chamber. Based on that professional assessment, I told him the D.A. would summon a grand jury to indict you. If my suspicion was correct, I knew he'd want to report the news to Mr. Price as soon as possible. The easiest way was by telephone." He permitted himself a grim smile of satisfaction. "To be on the safe side I made sure all the telephones in the precinct were occupied. That forced him to go across the street to use a pay phone. One I had bugged as soon as I knew you three were coming in. He did exactly what I anticipated."

A sudden sharpness came into Hugh Kerr's eyes.

"Who did he call?"

"Who do you think?"

"Carey Price."

"That's right, Hugh. That's exactly who he called. He reported everything he had seen and heard and then offered his opinion that based on his testimony and the *planted evidence* no jury in the world would fail to convict you."

This time when Hugh's eyes closed, it was from an insurmountable weight being lifted from his heart.

"Good God."

Bartholomew Bond reached out his arms to steady the man he was not going to prosecute in court.

"We traced the call. Wade and I thought... you might like to be in on the... kill. We have several unmarked police cars standing by. There's room for you if you want to go." Hugh slowly re-opened his eyes and bore them into those of the district attorney. Bond held the stare a half second before adding, "We owe you than much, at least."

"Did you ever consider for one moment that Ellen and I killed Jack; or that the three of us concocted some far-fetched conspiracy to murder a man for reason or reasons unknown?"

Bond gave a practiced laugh, proving he had been a successful prosecutor for many years.

"Now Hugh, you know me better than that. I admit, *Wade* did entertain some doubts, but I never suspected you for one minute. Are you ready to go?"

Which Hugh Kerr interpreted as, *Wade never believed it but I had my doubts,* adding in his mind for good measure, *The evidence was stacked against you and I could have made out a pretty damned good case. Everyone knows you're a bit on the wild side and Ellen would do anything you asked. Who knows what may have pushed you over the edge? Besides, it would have been interesting having you across the aisle as a defendant rather than an opponent.*

As depressing and dispiriting as the implied answer was, Kerr put it aside. If he had not, he never would have been able to face Bond in a court of law again. And that would have forced one of them out of Dodge.

On the next stage.

"Yes. We shall go."

Which Bartholomew Bond adroitly translated as, *I won't forgive you but I'll overlook it.*

Proving that life as they knew it could continue as usual.

Lieutenant Hank Wade, coming out of the conflict slightly better than the district attorney, led the way out of the communications room and down the corridor. Before they were half way down the hall, Kerr stopped dead in his tracks, causing Bond, who pulled up the rear, to run smack into him. He bounced back and rubbed his nose in annoyance.

"Now what?"

"I want Ellen and Jack to go with me."

"Kerr, I'm not organizing a parade! This is official police business. And it may be damned dangerous. You ought to know that."

"It can't be more dangerous than the last week from hell we've lived through. They have the right. And if you don't agree, I'm not going."

"All right. Stay here and sulk. I was only trying to do you a favor."

Bond attempted to move past him but Hugh's hand shot out, wrapping his fingers around the other's arm with a vice-like grasp of deadly intent.

"I've just been judged capable of first degree murder. If you want a confirmation of the fact, I'll be glad to demonstrate. Bartholomew, my nerves are frayed, I haven't had any sleep and your Dr. Dunning has just spent the last eight or ten or however-the-hell many hours it's been grinding my soul down to nothing. You've given me a narcotic, my head is swimming and there's nothing I'd like better than to rip someone to shreds. I want Ellen Thorne and Jack Merrick released. Now. This instant. If they're not, Los Angeles will have the biggest lawsuit rendered against it in the history of the state. Don't think I won't win."

Clearly shocked, Bond mumbled, "Oh. So it's all about the money –"

"No, Mr. Bond. It's all about your re-election."

"Screw you, Hugh." Stomping his foot in annoyance, the D.A. looked at the lieutenant for help. Wade jerked his head, then started walking toward the rear entrance. He called over his shoulder, "I don't know about you, Bartholomew, but I'm not ready to retire. And personally, I don't like the idea of Kerr breathing down my neck in that cab he's sure to find outside the precinct. The fool's likely to get his head blown off. Think of the headlines, then."

Bond threw up his hands.

"You're all crazy as bedbugs! Sometimes I think I'm the only sane one around here."

"Then heaven help the city."

The comment could have come from either the policeman or the defense attorney.

"I should have known better than to give you a break. Sweet Jesus, Kerr, you never give an inch." To which "Kerr" had nothing to say. "All right. You," Bond pointed to the female warder standing outside the door to one of the interrogation rooms. "Let Miss Thorne out. And you," he called in a louder voice, indicating a uniformed man down the corridor. "Let Merrick go."

The recipients of his imperial commands jumped with alacrity. Two doors were jerked open; two recent suspects flew the coop. Seeing his friends run toward him, Hugh's eyes rolled to the top of his head. Fighting the sudden, vicious attack of vertigo, he leaned against Ellen as she flew into his arms. Feeling his weakness transmitted to her through the close contact, she braced her legs, grasped her hands around the back of his neck and drew his face down. Daring to kiss him in public, she used the embrace to let him gather his thoughts.

The ploy, which was only half a ploy, worked, and after returning her kiss and gathering his strength, Hugh looked up, displaying a calmer, stronger demeanor.

"Let's go, starlet," he directed to Jack. And to Ellen, "O.K. handsome, you're both coming with me."

Having witnessed the display of emotion but missing the secondary issue, Bond groaned and dashed after Wade, muttering, "The lunatics are running the asylum."

"That's gotta be a good thing, right Hugh?" Jack asked, loping toward his friend.

"Right."

Placing her hand in his, Ellen looked for instructions.

"Where we going, Counselor?"

"To nail a bastard to the cross."

"You mean it's all over?"

"I mean," he declared, re-working his courtroom presence, "we have been declared 'not guilty,' which is a legal term meaning we have been exonerated. In the eyes of the district attorney it does not mean 'innocent.'"

"And what, exactly, does the difference signify?" Jack asked, falling into line as Hugh led Ellen after the two vanishing authority figures.

Kerr offered a grim assessment decorated with a sloppy grin and a chuckle.

"Bartholomew Bond lost his chance to screw us."

"What a hell of a picture that conjures," the detective groaned.

Ellen's groan came inwardly. Not only did she recognize a stage chuckle when she heard one, she knew it to be a lie. She had seen what they had done to Hugh. "Screw" was as good a word as any. Even if they had never laid a hand on him.

Hurrying to catch up, they made it outside just as Bond was preparing to shut the front passenger door of the unmarked, four-door car. He offered them the kind of wild-eyed stare he used in court to express an unanticipated move by the defense attorney but his tone sounded surprisingly conciliatory as he motioned they hurry inside.

"Come on, come on." Hugh entered the back seat first, followed by Ellen; Jack slid beside her so that he was positioned directly behind the district attorney. Before the three had time to adjust to the cramped space, Bond motioned madly to the plainclothes police driver wearing a dark jacket and a baseball cap pulled over his eyes. "Keep those two cars ahead of us in sight, but don't tag along too close. We don't want this to look like a Foreign Legion assault – just in case Carey Price has the route lined with spies."

"Right, sir."

The passengers were jerked backward as the car roared into the street. Rounding the corner on two wheels, they just had time to catch a glimpse of the squad of reporters hanging around the front of the precinct as they sped away.

"Those boys will sure be mad they missed out on the action," Jack observed. "They've been waiting for hours. Say, what time is it, anyway?"

"What's the matter? You have to take a pill?" Bond asked. Although he attempted to make it sound as though he were making a joke, his voice betrayed a latent nervousness. The three in the back needed no explanation. He had a lot riding on a successful outcome – and a quick, neat prosecution.

"Where are we going?" Kerr asked to break the tension. "Not up to his mountain hideaway?"

"No. Wade has staked out that place since we got the address from Merrick's men and no one has gone near it."

"But you did have it searched?"

Bond sniffed in indignation.

"There wasn't a damn thing in there; not one single stick of furniture. The windows were all boarded; nailed shut. Someone went to a lot of trouble to make it look as though the house hadn't been opened for months. They had even scattered dust across the upstairs and downstairs floors."

Hugh shrugged as though the information struck him as irrelevant. He debated whether or not to pursue the subject, then muttered, "Fireplace ash most likely. A lab analysis ought to confirm that."

"Let's hope so. The way it stood, it didn't do a lot to substantiate your story."

"Well, we're past that," Ellen decided, wondering what the professional and personal relationship between the two men would be like when the matter was finally settled. But she wouldn't have bet a plugged nickel it would substantially improve over the course of their careers.

Nor was she sure she wanted it to.

The unmarked car slowed as it approached a stop sign, then rolled through it. Traveling two blocks further, they were caught at a traffic signal and the driver stopped. By the time it changed to green they found themselves alone on the street. The driver progressed along the main thoroughfare, then suddenly veered to the right and directed the vehicle down a residential street. At this time of night most of the lower middle class, single family dwellings were dark and shuttered. Cars parked at irregular intervals along both sides of the curbs reduced the road to a single lane, forcing a careful maneuver between them, while even more treacherous shadows, cast into existence by the headlamps, seemed to bear an ominous life of their own.

"I don't see the other police cars," Bond whispered to the driver as though afraid to raise his voice for fear of being overheard. "You're not lost, are you?"

"No, sir. We got held up at the red light and the other two cars went ahead. Good thing I have the address. And I know the neighborhood. I'm cutting through this way because it's a more direct route. We'll catch up in a few minutes."

"All right."

Jack Merrick stifled a yawn, making a lame attempt at covering his mouth.

"I sure hope it doesn't take long. I've forgotten how bad a concussion can be. The symptoms creep on you when you're least expecting them. My head feels as if I had been kicked by an elephant and I can't keep my eyes open. Those damn thugs really did a number on me." He shook his arm. "My hand is getting numb, too."

Ellen slid closer to him.

"Rest your head on my shoulder, Jack, and close your eyes."

"Yeah. Maybe I will. Thanks."

In a moment the low sound of his deep breathing filled the otherwise still car.

Hugh stared at his friend a long beat before shifting his gaze out the side window. The cheap bungalows had given way to larger and more widely spaced commercial property, representing, if possible, a darker aspect than the shabby neighborhood. Before he had time to contemplate their ultimate destination, the driver made a sharp left-hand turn and drove down a narrow alley flanked by silent brick buildings.

"We'll come out on another street and be back on track," he reassured the four passengers. "It isn't much farther; we're almost there."

As if on cue, a loud, sharp retort shattered the night stillness. Bond leaned forward, eyes riveted ahead.

"Was that gunfire? Wade must have encountered resistance. Hurry up!"

"Car backfiring," Kerr corrected.

"No, sir," the driver protested. "Mr. Bond is correct. That was a shot. And very close. This is as far as we go." Shoving the gear into neutral, he held a finger to his lips and snapped open the door. Because of the close quarters, the edge banged dully against the brick warehouse wall as he slipped out and stepped back. "Quiet," he whispered. "Danger. You'll be all right, *thur*," he added, addressing Bond with growing agitation. "I'll protect you."

"You'll protect all of us –" the district attorney corrected before stopping short as the barrel of the driver's service revolver was pointed directly at him. "What the -?"

"Hell," the driver finished. "What the hell? An apt expression." Removing his baseball cap and flinging it aside, he bent down to stare through the window at the passenger sitting directly behind the driver's side. "Recognize me now, Mis*th*er Kerr?"

Hugh's voice was calm.

"No."

"Take another look."

"I don't have to. I don't recognize you." Ellen started to move but he stilled her with pressure from his leg. "Should I?"

"Don't you know who I am? Can't you guess?"

"I can make an inference."

"Then do so."

"Allen Dunlap, the –"

The gunman cut him off with a sharp, angry shout.

"No, you fool. I am your arch enemy –"

"Don't tell me you're from the IRS?" Kerr inquired without the least levity. "In which case I can explain –"

Face red with fury, the gunman pulled the trigger, sending a bullet screaming just over Kerr's head. The missile tore through the rear window, sending a million chards across the seat and out into the alleyway. Reacting instinctively, although he would have been too late if the bullet had been accurately fired, Hugh shoved Ellen down. While still on top of her, he clicked back the handle of the right-hand side door furthest from the attempted assassin.

Acknowledging an awareness of Kerr's tardiness, the driver broke out into a vicious, almost inhuman laughter. Hugh shot him a steely look of pure hatred and howled in fury.

"Bastard! You bastard!" In a frenzy of activity, the lawyer shook a fist at the gunman, then scooped Ellen up in his arms. "You've hurt her! My God, there's blood all over her face! Ellen!" Tears rolled down his cheeks as he pressed his lips to hers. After a hurried, almost frenetic kiss, a shaky hand attempted to wipe her face before he pushed her down toward the floor. Noticeably trembling, he straightened, stared around himself, then jabbed a finger at Bartholomew Bond.

"This is all your fault! You're in on this with him!"

Bond, already pale and horrified, recoiled at the charge.

"For God's sake, Hugh, I had nothing to do with this!"

"Sure you didn't... Bartholomew," he added with bitter sarcasm. "You're involved right up to your neck. You knew damned well Ellen and I didn't plan, much less execute a murder, yet you treated us like common criminals – the lowest of the low. You demanded we turn ourselves in and then interrogated us with the viciousness and cruelty of a man without a soul. What was it, Bartholomew? Jealousy? Because when we're up against one another you're always on the losing side? Or is it my money? You're forced to make do on a meagre civil servant's salary while I live high on the hog? I always knew you resented that, but to go this far – to join sides with that devil out of hell, Carey Price –"

"Oh, so you remember my name now, *Counthelor*?" the driver taunted, drawing a step nearer. "How refreshing. It would have been a pity to kill you without having a full and equitable triumph."

Kerr tore his eyes off Bond and drilled them into his nemesis.

"You? You're nothing," he scoffed in disdain, leaning toward the open door for a better view of a man he had not seen for almost five years. "In truth, I wouldn't have recognized you unless I was staring at a mug shot with your name underneath. To me, you're nothing but a petty embezzler. I've seen hundreds like you in my career. You're indistinguishable from one another."

While Carey Price attempted to digest the dire insult heaped upon him, Kerr turned back to the district attorney.

"Now you, Bond – I'll remember your face until hell freezes over. You're the one who took an oath to uphold justice and yet knowing I was innocent, stood behind that god-damned black glass with your accomplice –"

Bond's Adam's apple bobbed as he swallowed hard.

"Dr. Charles Dunning was not an accomplice! He was sent by the Department to evaluate you. I never called him in –"

"But you stood behind that one-way glass and enjoyed what he did to me, didn't you?"

"He didn't do a damn thing, Hugh. He never spoke a single word to you. And neither did I!"

"You didn't have to; you were satisfied with the way he set out to torture me. And, by God, I was tortured." Satisfied at the D.A.'s gaping mouth, Kerr redirected his ire at Price. "The doctor was your stooge, wasn't he, Price? How much did it cost to buy a psychologist?"

"Oh, not as much as you'd think," the murderer casually admitted, regaining some of his aplomb. I had twenty-five thousand dollars to spend and he hardly made a dent."

"How much did Bond cost?"

Clearly enjoying the repartee between the two men, Price's smile widened.

"He came along on the ride for free."

Hugh hissed and made a mad attempt to open the side door. Finding easy egress impossible, he lunged forward as though to make a leap into the front seat. Price leveled the gun at his head.

"I think not, Mr. Kerr. You've gone as far as you're going to."

As his finger exerted pressure against the trigger of his gun, a shadow behind him metamorphosed into a man. Arms raised in imitation of wings, the figure flew across the alley, landing on Price's exposed back. With a primeveal scream, the avenger wrapped an arm around the assassin's throat and dragged him backward into the open area by the left headlamp. Summoning the strength of a bull elephant, the apparition's biceps tightened around the narrow windpipe and snapped it back. Instantly insensate to the loud crack of bone, Price's eyes popped open, his mouth gaped into an un-circular "O" and the gun slipped from his hand. Just as his knees buckled, Kerr shoved the car into gear and it shot forward, crushing the crumpling victim against the brick wall with deadly force.

Narrowly avoiding being pinned alongside Carey Price, the tall, silent, ghost-like man danced away. Three pair of eyes turned on him.

"Jack!" Ellen cried.

Breathing heavily, the earthly manifestation of Jack Merrick offered her a polite nod.

"Where the devil did you come from?" Bond gasped, hardly recovered from the sudden, bloody conclusion to their potentially murderous confrontation.

"Out the door," Jack explained in a toneless voice. "I caught on as soon as Price turned onto that side street. I figured that couldn't be right. I tried to tip Hugh off when I complained about my hands going numb. I wanted to drop down and disappear from sight, hoping Price would forget about me, as in, 'out of sight, out of mind.' And I guess it worked. Once that maniac fired the gun, Hugh jumped on Ellen, giving him the opportunity to open the door. I slipped out and crawled backward until I got to the end of the alley. After that, it was easy – I just ran around to the other side, praying Hugh would find a way to stall until I saw my chance. He did and I did –"

Catching Jack's eye, Kerr concluded, "and I finished him off by driving the car through him."

Bond looked from one to the other and slowly nodded.

"Of course, it could hardly be considered a crime to kill a man who intended to murder four *innocent* people."

Kerr shrugged, allowing Bond the grace of including himself in the count.

"Considering we're all a little *gun shy* about being charged with crimes we didn't commit, it's just as well to have no doubts about the cause of death."

"Killed by having a car rammed through his guts," Ellen concluded. "One could almost call it an accident."

"And I suppose one will," the district attorney finalized. Slapping his hands together as though to rid them of an unsavory substance, the prosecutor squinted at Ellen's face.

"You weren't cut at all. Jesus, Hugh, you scared the... devil out of me. All those things you said. You really had me going."

Hugh Kerr grinned. Realizing the expression conveyed a total lack of amusement, the two who understood the import could only interpret it one way: relief that, with a little help, Bartholomew Bond had exorcized Satan from his soul. It didn't erase the slate but his unconscious reference to redemption helped pave the way toward healing.

"Let's get the hell out of here."

Any one of the four might have been the speaker.

It was almost dawn when the District Attorney's office issued a statement to the press that renowned defense attorney Hugh Kerr, his secretary Miss Ellen Thorne and investigator Jack Merrick had not only been exonerated from any complicity in the murder of a decapitated stranger, they had actually cooperated in the apprehension of the depraved perpetrator.

Once Bartholomew Bond finished reading the statement on the steps of the police precinct, Hugh addressed the crowd of those loyal and eager enough to have stayed outside the entire night. After receiving the applause and hat-waving of the reporters, he held up his hands for silence.

"First of all, I'd like to thank you boys for the help you gave us in conveying Miss Thorne, Mr. Merrick and I to the station. I'm not sure we could have gotten here without you. Second, I'd appreciate it if you'd all help me petition the mayor to award Mr. Bill Mulcahy a commendation for sacrificing his life in the performance of his duty. While not a police officer, he worked on the side of justice and he deserves that recognition." His voice choked and he paused a moment to recover.

"For myself, I think I'd like to establish a scholarship fund in his name at the Police Academy."

"Here, here," a voice from behind him approved. It did not tax his powers to identify the speaker as Jack Merrick.

"Lastly, I'd like to remind everyone that a man – or a woman – isn't guilty in the eyes of the law until after a legal trial and a conviction by a jury of their peers. There's been a lot written in the papers about a murder case recently solved – I won't mention which one – where those convicted in the newspapers turned out to be the innocent victims of a damned dastardly plot. Jumping to conclusions before the facts were known might very well have ruined their reputations, to say nothing of their freedom and even their lives. I'd ask all of you to keep that in mind the next time something like this happens."

After a moment of silence, a reported raised his hand.

"Mr. Kerr, I can promise you one thing; ten minutes after the early morning edition hits the streets, everyone in the state of California is going to know the truth. By the time you get to the office, your phone will be ringing off the hook with prospective clients vying for your legal services."

Hugh Kerr gave a tired nod of appreciation.

"On one hand, I hope that's true. On the other, I'd hate to think there were that many suspected murderers out there needing my help."

The crowd of reporters cheered and Kerr stepped back, glad to have a moment of reprieve to savor his liberty. Ellen came up and slipped a hand around his arm.

"That's enough, Counselor. Let's go home."

Taking Jack's arm with her other hand, Ellen led her boys down the steps and into a waiting taxi. Flashbulbs lit up the night as they ducked inside the back seat.

"Well, Hugh," Jack yawned. "What's next on the docket? I'm all ready for –"

"Bed," Ellen decided. "That's where we're all going." Casting a suggestive look at Hugh, she added, "Jack to his apartment, you to yours and me to mine. No work today. If we're awake by seven o'clock this evening, we'll all meet at Rossi's On The Strip for a steak and lobster dinner. With champagne."

"Who's paying?" Jack asked, sleepily stretching his arms.

Leaning back, Hugh closed his eyes and smiled.

"The State of California: once I petition to recoup my losses on the convertible and our cross-state excursion."

"To avoid prosecution?" Ellen blithely inquired. "Good luck with that."

"All right, then; from the fund Bond and Wade will put together to repay us for doubting our innocence."

"And better luck with that!" Jack exclaimed, settling in beside his two companions. "And what about *my* expenses? First, there's that new set of clothes I'll need to buy. Next, there's doctor bills; third, time lost from work. Say, do you think I can get workman's comp for that?"

"I'll file a brief right after I submit mine to the State."

"Good luck with that," they agreed in unison.

The taxi stopped in front of Jack's apartment house and he slowly extricated himself from the cab, every muscle in his body aching. Putting a finger to his forehead in salute, he offered one final grin.

"At least I have the satisfaction of knowing you're paying for the taxi, Hugh. See you two this evening."

"Good night, Jack," Ellen called.

While neither she nor Hugh could see through the door of the complex, both heard in their mind's ear Jack whistling to himself as he traipsed up the stairs.

"All's well," Ellen finally observed as the cab drove away, "that ends well."

Hugh held out his arm and Ellen snuggled against him, pressing close to feel the warmth of his body.

"It's getting on toward winter," she decided, eyes closed. "Mother will expect me home for Christmas. She'll expect you, too."

"As Santa Claus or something else?"

The answer was obvious.

"Both."

"We wouldn't want to disappoint her."

"As to that, I think I'll pass on going up to Northern California for the holidays."

She felt his chest heave in silent laugh.

"We still haven't had that conversation, have we?"

Ellen took his hand in hers.

"You know, Hugh, I was thinking."

"Good."

"About what you said to Bartholomew Bond in the car."

He grunted in what could have been mock annoyance.

"I was just trying to keep Price occupied until Jack got around behind him."

"I know. But what you said had a lot of truth in it. I almost believed every word."

"So did I."

"That's what I thought. I'm glad you said it."

"Me, too." With his free hand he tapped her on the nose. She "beeped," and he chuckled at his forgetfulness before growing serious. "Want to come home with me?"

"Yes. But I'm not going to. I'm tired and you're tired and we both have a lot to consider."

"And there's that dinner date we have for tonight."

"We wouldn't want to miss that. Jack loves lobster."

"And champagne and steak," Hugh added. "Want to come home with me *tonight*? I still have that condom in my pocket."

Ellen's eyes opened and she stared into his.

"You know, a girlfriend of mine told me that while condoms are sold in sizes, no man ever buys any but extra-large – and that it really doesn't matter because they're all the exact same size. Is that true?"

This time she elicited a belly laugh from him.

"We'll have to ask Jack."

"I think not."

By the time the taxi pulled up outside Ellen's apartment house, the pair had attached themselves at the lips, arms encircled around one another's. The cab driver gave them an extra minute then politely cleared his throat.

"One of you getting out? Or do you want me to drive around the block a few times?"

It was with great reluctance that their lips parted and the two both sighed in resignation. This time it was Ellen's turn to tap him on the nose.

"Nighty-night. Sleep tight," she whispered.

"Do not let the bedbugs bite," he finished. After remembering to "beep," he started, "Ellen, I..." He left the rest of the thought unfinished although her heart translated his silence.

"I know," she whispered. "Me, too. We'll talk about it." He whispered the words with her as she added, "See you later."

"Want me to walk you inside? To see you get there safely?"

"Better not."

Ellen slipped away and started up the sidewalk. Hugh blew a kiss at her back, then settled into the seat.

"Home, James."

The cab pulled away from the curb. Ellen waited until it had gone several hundred yards, then returned his kiss she did not have to see coming to feel.

Hugh Kerr was deep in sleep when the phone rang. Only vaguely aware of it, he incorporated it into his dream, and it was only when the annoying, persistent sound refused to go away did he identify it. With a stifled curse, his fingers groped for the handset and brought it to his ear. The man at the other end spoke before he had an opportunity to say, "Hello."

"Hugh? Hugh, are you awake?"

"No."

"Hugh, it's Bart Bond. I'm sorry to bother you at home, but I have to ask you one question."

"Can't it wait?" came the groggy interrogative.

"No. Well, yes it can, but *I* can't. I have to ask you something."

"Well, what is it?"

"Did you and Ellen get married?"

Kerr snorted so hard his nose dripped.

"You woke me up to ask me that?"

Bond raced through his pressing question.

"It was something Wade said. About what Ellen said, actually, when he was questioning her. He reminded her that a husband and wife wouldn't testify against one another and then implied that *you* said the two of you had gotten married, and she responded that you were a gentleman and slapped him. Even though she denied it, he thought perhaps you two had…"

Caught between a mad blush and an outright laugh, Hugh sniffed.

"Wade has a dirty mind. And so do you. No, we did not tie the knot or otherwise get ourselves into a bind. All right?"

"All right," Bond tried in his best placating voice. "I just wanted to know in case wedding presents were in order."

"Good night, B. B."

Hugh started to hang up the phone, then ordered in a voice sure to carry over the line, "Turn the light out, will you, Ellen?"

Dropping the receiver on the phone rest, he rearranged his covers and snuggled under them. As a smile curled over his lips, Hugh Kerr knew that if he hadn't evened the score with Bartholomew Bond before, then he had at least won the last round. Even if he had cheated.

And perhaps added a little pressure on one Miss Ellen Thorne.

GSFE

ALSO by S.L. Kotar and J.E. Gessler

From: Ahead of the Press

The Hugh Kerr Mystery Series
A chronological character based historical 1950's courtroom-based murder mystery series

Book I	The Conundrum of the Decapitated Detective
Book II	The Conundrum of the Absconded Attorney
Book III	The Conundrum of the Sins of the Fathers
Book IV	The Conundrum of the Two-Sided Lawyer
Book V	The Conundrum of the Clueless Counselor
Book VI	The Conundrum of the Loveless Marriage
Book VII	The Conundrum of the Executed Defendant
Book VIII	The Conundrum of the Jettisoned Jury
Book IX	The Conundrum of the Perjured Pigeon
Book X	The Conundrum of the Haunting Halloween Party
Book XI	The Conundrum of the Tuneless Tunesmith
Book XII	The Conundrum of the Meddling Motorcar
Book XIII	The Conundrum of the Blundering Bear
Book XIV	The Conundrum of Shooting Fish in a Barrel

To Be Continued!

The ReproBate saga
Another character-based series centered around the 1860's American Civil War

Book I	Beneath the Rose
Book II	skull and cRossBones
Book III	Redefining Bastions
Book IV	thickeR than Blood

To Be Continued!

New Beginnings
1950's medical drama featuring brothers – one genius one … not

Book I	The Believer
Book II	The Heretic
Book III	Arrow Song
Book IV	Peas in a Pod

Catman
A stand-alone novel "*He was every man: He was no man.*"

ONE
A stand-alone novel of a harrowing space travel adventure

Shepherd of the Kingdom
A stand alone horror novel

The KEPI

An iconoclastic publication that specialized in the American Civil War and 19th century life. These two volumes reintroduce the ground breaking research, historically accurate timelines, period photography and an eye to the life and times of this unsettled period of American history.

Volume I and II

Volume III and IV